THE ROAD TO FERO CITY

Thank you: There is every chance that you bought this book based entirely on its fabulous cover, for which my eternal gratitude goes to Tim Shay (TimShay. com) Punctuation was never a strong point so if you happen to find any in the right place then it's probably due to the wonderful Neil Perry, to whom I am also eternally grateful. Any smelling mistooks are now his fault. There are others, too numerous to mention... Burgundy Room, Clutch, Lemmy, Krusher, Metal Hammer... thank you all. And, of course, to my beautiful wife, Masuimi, without whom this could have been written a lot quicker, but might not have been written at all. I love you, wifey. With due respect to MCs worldwide.

ISBN: 0615894046
ISBN 13: 9780615894041

Library of Congress Control Number: 2013918953
Road To Fero City The,
West Hollywood, CA

THE ROAD TO FERO CITY

MORAT

CHAPTER ONE

"Fuckin' weirdos."

Scarecrow scuffed his cigarette out as he watched the cop car speed away towards Camden, still trying to figure out exactly what had just happened, and half expecting to see some dimwitted TV presenter pop out and tell him that he'd been 'framed', 'punk'd', or otherwise humiliated in the name of cheap entertainment. But, no, that couldn't be it: as long shots went, that was Lee Harvey Oswald in the book depository. Few of Scarecrow's friends would be stupid enough to think he'd find that kind of thing remotely amusing, and, though they'd get some vicarious pleasure from the hope that he'd beat said TV presenter senseless with his own microphone, those who knew him well enough to have set this up would also know that jokes where the law were concerned weren't very funny.

All the same he did a double-take, glancing up and down the street. Nope, no cops, no film crews, no Jeremy Beadle's or whatever that fat bird's name was. Just the slow rumble of traffic, and the usual mix of winos and diseased pigeons that frequented this part of Kings Cross on a grey Sunday afternoon.

He'd picked up the unmarked cop car on the Westway flyover, spotting the tell-tale aerials as he passed them at around a hundred and twenty miles per hour, way too late to back off to a sensible speed that might just get him a ticket instead of a ban. He slowed for a moment thinking maybe he could still talk his way out of this, but then remembered the small, but nonetheless conspicuous, baggy of coke in his jacket pocket. Not good. Reckless driving,

1

probably drunk driving since he was nursing a vicious hangover, possession of a Class A drug, and...oh fuck! He still had a set of custom made brass knuckles in his other pocket, a gift for Dum Dum that would now be a gift to some spotty-faced arresting officer looking for promotion. No talking your way out of that one, my son, he thought, winding back up to one twenty with gears to spare.

Scarecrow's bike wasn't just fast: hand built from the wheels up with the ZZR1100 motor more tweaked out than a meth lab, it made the space-shuttle look sluggish and had won him numerous trophies on the drag strip. Shame the nitrous was empty, but still, he could easily outrun these muppets and then lose them completely as soon as he hit traffic on the Euston Road, zipping through gaps that no cop car could possibly follow him through. He changed up a gear with that satisfying Kawasaki clunk and started to put some distance between himself and the rapidly disappearing sirens and flashing blue lights.

The problems started as he was passing Regents Park, trying to decide whether he should throw a left up through the park or take the straight line to Kings Cross. Traffic and traffic lights conspired to allow the cops to gain some ground, and Scarecrow had just remembered a convenient cycle path, big enough to fit a bike through, but a dead end to cars, when his engine started cutting out. He reached down to put the tank on reserve and then, sickeningly, realised that it already was, and that he was quickly running out of both petrol and options. Fuck! Maybe he could make it as far as York Way and then hide around the back of the station somewhere, maybe...but no. The bike popped and choked one last time as he swung a left onto York Way, and then the engine died completely. Nowhere to run and nowhere to hide. Scarecrow had just enough time to dump the coke and the brass knuckles into a nearby rubbish bin before the cops rounded the corner, pulling over in front of his bike, as he swiftly chewed on a stick of minty fresh gum in the hope of disguising any lingering alcohol smell from last night.

That was when things started to get weird. The cops suddenly seemed confused as to why they'd pulled him over, or indeed if they had pulled him over at all.

"What seems to be the problem, officer?" said Scarecrow, figuring he may as well play dumb until they decided what to arrest him for.

"I thought perhaps you could tell us," said the younger of the two cops, late twenties, maybe thirty-something, but certainly not some bum-fluffed kid fresh out of Hendon. "Sounded like you were having some engine problems."

"Ran out of gas," shrugged Scarecrow. No point in lying about that since they'd have to tow his bike anyway if they were going to arrest him.

"Nice bike," said the other cop, leaning down to inspect the exhaust and apparently failing to notice the 'NOT FOR ROAD USE' stamp. "You build it yourself?"

"Mostly," Scarecrow nodded warily.

"Nitrous too!" cooed the first cop. "Man, I'll bet this thing is fast! What's the top speed?"

"Couldn't say, officer," said Scarecrow, getting the distinct feeling that they were just fucking with him until backup arrived.

"Must be at least a hundred and ninety," said the cop. "Faster if you had a fairing."

"It's pretty quick," allowed Scarecrow, unable to disguise a hint of pride. "It'll outrun most things on the road." He glanced at the cop car, mentally adding that it would outrun almost anything if he remembered to fill the fucking tank.

"I'll bet!" repeated the cop, apparently keen on gambling.

Nearly twenty minutes later the cops had still failed to ask Scarecrow for any ID and showed no sign of wanting to arrest him for anything. There was no sign of any backup either. They just kept ooh-ing and ah-ing about how great his bike was, and as much as he was, in normal circumstances, happy to talk bikes all day, they were beginning to piss him off. It was sheer dumb luck that they caught him in the first place. It wasn't just Scarecrow's bike that was fast: sometimes his reactions were so quick on the drag-strip that the timer failed to even register a difference between the lights going green and him taking off from the line. And God help anyone who thought they'd get to throw the first punch in a fight. If Scarecrow was feeling nice then they'd be swinging wildly at the empty space where he'd just been standing, if not then they'd find themselves on the floor, with a number of teeth missing, wondering what the hell had hit them.

But, fantasies about beating up TV presenters notwithstanding, Scarecrow was not a violent man. He would fight if he absolutely had to, but otherwise gave people several chances to right any wrongs before he resorted to amateur dentistry and, even then, he would disarm and restrain his opponent rather than hospitalise them. The fact that he could catch flies in flight, just pluck them out of the air with his fingers, gave him, he always felt, a rather unfair advantage, and, for reasons that he had never quite been able to fathom, he had a strong aversion to bullies. Not that he had ever been bullied as a child, for the simple reason that there was no one to bully him. He and his family - mother, father, and sister – had lived in a remote farmhouse outside Lezayre on the Isle Of Man, a population less than two thousand.

To add to the isolation both siblings were home taught rather than going to school. It was a simple lifestyle, too simple for Scarecrow. They raised chickens, grew vegetables, chopped wood, milked goats, watched paint dry. And all year long Scarecrow yearned for June to come around and with it the TT races that filled the entire island with motorcycles and noise and speed and music and anything but home-grown carrots and goat's tits. Most of all, despite the track claiming over two hundred lives, the races brought life to the island.

During the day Scarecrow would find a secluded spot to watch the races from, somewhere with a bit of cover in case it rained, with a good view of at least one fast corner, and as far away from any humans as possible. Motorcycles were everything, and by the time he was nine he could name every bike by sound, long before it passed his hideaway. He timed the laps of the loudest bikes on a stopwatch, writing them down in a scrap book with a picture of the bike beside it.

It was around this time that Scarecrow met his friend Buggane, a large and crotchety old tramp who seemed to spend most of his time in jail for vandalising the local church. Buggane was hiding in the bushes waiting for some tourists to pass so they didn't see him and Scarecrow was looking for a new hideout. They watched the racing together and Scarecrow shared his sandwiches because he sensed that no one had ever been very nice to Buggane.

"How old are you?" he asked, still young enough to ask questions that age would censor.

"As old as my nose and a little older than my teeth," said Buggane. Beneath a wild grey beard it seemed that his teeth were too long for his mouth, but it was difficult to tell because he seemed to be mostly made of hair. Even his knuckles were hairy.

"Why are you hiding in the bushes?"

"None of your business," grunted Buggane, shuffling around trying to get comfortable. "Bloody church."

It turned out that Buggane was hiding from the police who wanted to question him about a huge boulder that had been thrown through the windows of the local church early that morning.

"I told 'em," he said. "Need a bloody crane to lift that rock. How is it my fault? There's no tyre tracks. Act of God I told 'em. Got any more of them cheese and pickle ones?"

"So why are you hiding then?"

"Ah, well," said Buggane, deciding that a large root was the cause of his discomfort. "The thing is, ya see, is... Well, the thing is, I done it. I done it and I'll do it again! Bloody church."

Buggane grasped the root and pulled it sharply. Most of the bush came out of the ground. They found somewhere else to watch the racing from and spent the rest of the day jotting down meaningless facts in Scarecrow's scrapbook.

Although Scarecrow was vaguely aware, even at that age, somewhere in the back of his mind, that Buggane was not only freakishly strong for his age, but also completely insane, he was nonetheless fascinated with the old man and they became firm friends. As far as Scarecrow could tell, Buggane either lived in a cave or some sort of hut in the mountains. He also seemed to have a sixth sense about when there was going to be a crash and they always found the best places to watch from, but, strangely, he knew to steer them away from anything really bad. He would mutter something about "not thanking the faer-ies" and lead them in the opposite direction, and Scarecrow would later find out that the crash had been fatal. As he grew older Scarecrow insisted they watch less crashes and he started saving for his own bike, a wretched little Honda with no brakes.

Scarecrow was nineteen years old when he first met Aberrant MC. It was the same year that Buggane went to prison. Proper prison. He remembered that Buggane insisted he drive him down to Douglas to meet the late ferry coming in for the first day of the TT races. He thought it strange because Buggane usually refused to go anywhere near his bike, which, by this point, had progressed to a desperately unstable Z650, but he needed little excuse to show off his riding skills. Having grown up on the Isle Of Man he could now complete the race circuit faster than many of the bikes that were actually com-peting in the races, and a local shop was talking about sponsoring him to enter next year. Despite the cold chill to the night air he was thinking about going down to the harbour anyway to catch the first wave arriving on the island and check out the bikes.

It was spitting with rain when they got to the harbour, the thin spray high-lighted in street lights and headlights. Buggane paced around looking nerv-ous, possibly just relieved that the ride was over, while Scarecrow went into train-spotter mode: lots of ZZRs, Fireblades, GSXRs, a nice old Guzzi, an MZ with German plates, which seemed like an awfully long ride for one of those things. Not that Scarecrow had much idea as he'd never left the island, but he'd ridden an MZ and didn't envy the rider. As the ferry emptied Buggane paced around more anxiously, straining to look down the gangplank.

"I can't see 'em," he grumbled. "They said this boat, I know they said this boat."

"Who?" said Scarecrow, still none the wiser since Buggane hadn't actually told him why they were meeting the ferry.

"Aberrant," said Buggane bluntly, as if it was obvious to everyone why they were here. "Good boys, they are. Always looked after me they 'ave. Good boys."

It was then that Aberrant MC came rumbling up the gangplank and Scarecrow would never forget it. He remembered Mad John, the wild gleam in his blue eyes as he headed the pack, then Mental, who looked more like a pirate or a wizard than a biker, then Numb Tongue, a wall of a man, over seven feet tall, with the devil's own eyes and a face full of scars. Scarecrow could remember all of them. Joker, Flashback, Loud-As, with his ear all stitched back on after a fight, Smiler, grinning from ear to ear, which later turned out to be a squint because he couldn't see very well. And still they came, like a dark cloud sweeping into the bay, all chrome and black leather. It seemed like there was a spotlight on their arrival, like somehow the harbour lights had got brighter, and people scurried to get out of their way. Scarecrow was suitably impressed.

As the crowd parted the club headed straight for Buggane, who was still frantically waving in case they hadn't seen him. Mad John got off his bike and embraced Buggane like a long-lost brother, exchanging words that were muted in the noise of the bikes.

"And you must be the one I've heard so much about," said Mad John, turning to Scarecrow. "Good things," he added with a grin. "Although, I'm not sure the goat thing was entirely legal."

Scarecrow had no idea what Mad John was talking about, but instantly warmed to his sense of humour. He was nervous, or at least apprehensive, and knew enough not to disrespect any member of an outlaw club, but they seemed on very good terms with Buggane who was currently walking down the line of bikes, greeting each rider with a warm hug.

"You know how it is," said Scarecrow. "It gets lonely up here in the winter months."

"So long as you leave Flossy alone, she's mine" smiled Mad John, before turning back to the club. "Gentlemen," he said quietly. And for a moment it was as if the harbour fell strangely silent. "If I might have your attention..."

Scarecrow stuck with the club like a magnet for the entire two weeks they were on the island, riding at the back of the pack wherever they went, absorbing their menacing presence, but, nonetheless, trying not to grin like an idiot the whole time. He loved the mixture of fear and curiosity they provoked in the general public and, despite parting crowds like something out of the Bible, they always had people to party with and, more often than not, a girl on each arm. It struck him as a little odd that they were staying in a remote country inn on the outskirts of town, but they seemed to know the staff, who treated the club like royalty.

In those two weeks Scarecrow had got to know all the club members fairly well. He'd also been introduced to cocaine, ecstasy, and acid. Most of the club were open and friendly, but a few of them scared him. Numb Tongue and Loud-As felt unpredictable and dangerous, like they might smash him in the head with a beer glass at any moment, even though they never showed any sign of wanting to do so. And it wasn't difficult to guess where Mental got his name. One night in a bar it looked like there might be trouble with a huge pack of mods and Scarecrow, quietly tripping his nuts off, voiced his concern.

"Put these on," said Mental, handing him a pair of sunglasses. "What you can't see can't hurt you. Put 'em on."

The weird thing was it had worked.

The sadness that Scarecrow felt when the TT races were over was almost unbearable. It was bad enough in normal circumstances, but this time he felt like some great adventure had come to an end and he was losing his new friends along with having to return to every day life. It didn't help that, just two months later, Buggane was arrested for blowing the roof off the local church. Scarecrow went to visit him a few times, but couldn't seem to get much sense out of him.

"Not the first time," he kept muttering. "St. Trinian's was the first. Put 'em up, knock 'em down. Bloody churches!"

It was the same at every visit and Scarecrow was beginning to worry that Buggane was losing his mind. He knew for a fact that St. Trinian's Church had been a derelict ruin since something like the fourteenth century, so why Buggane was claiming to have done it was anyone's guess. He wrote to Mad John, who, much to his delight, had kept in touch since the races, but John just kept telling him not to worry. 'Buggane has been a dear friend to myself and the club for many, many years' he had written. 'He's a lot stronger than you think.' It had been a small comfort, but more than anything Scarecrow was desperately lonely. Buggane was sentenced to twenty years.

The following year Aberrant MC came back for the TT races and it was Scarecrow who met them from the ferry, swelling with pride as they made their usual dramatic entrance and then headed straight for him. They partied, though not as hard as previously since Scarecrow was actually competing in the races this year, and with Aberrant as his pit crew Scarecrow won his class outright and was presented with a huge trophy. The next day he and Mad John went to visit Buggane, who wept with joy when he saw them both.

"Good boys, I always said," Buggane smiled. "You stick with these boys, Scarecrow. Good boys they are."

When Aberrant MC went back to London, Scarecrow took Buggane at his word and went with them, staying first at their clubhouse before finding a small flat in Mile End. He found work as a motorcycle mechanic and repaid the club's kindness by working on their bikes for free. Together they built a drag bike and Scarecrow won so many trophies that Mad John, apparently quite the carpenter, built him a cabinet to put them all in.

It was the last time he saw Mad John, who seemingly disappeared without trace, but, by then, Scarecrow was like part of the furniture at the clubhouse. He drank with them, went on runs with them, and, on more than one occasion, fought beside them. He was flattered but not surprised, when - two years ago at the Bulldog Bash - they had approached him before his final run of the day.

"We thought you might want to represent while you were out there," said Joker, handing him a sleeveless leather vest with three patches on it. Scarecrow put the trophy for that run in the clubhouse alongside assorted awards to other club members, usually won for drinking or fighting.

"I don't mean to be rude, officer," Scarecrow ventured finally, realising that his mind had drifted, "but I'm running kind of late."

"Oh my goodness! Of course! Of course! You mustn't let us detain you," said the cop, completely missing the irony. "I'm afraid it's quite a walk to the nearest petrol station from here and I doubt you'll want to leave this beauty unattended around here. I'll tell you what; we've got a spare gallon in the back of the car if this beast'll run on regular unleaded. We can give you that to get you on your way."

And with that, the cops filled Scarecrow's tank, bade him good-day, and left him standing by the side of the road, not a little confused and with the vague feeling that he'd somehow been tricked. What the fuck was all that about? Good cop, good cop? He glanced up and down the street again, but the cops had definitely gone, so he fished the coke and the knuckles out of the bin and started his bike just as his mobile went off.

CHAPTER TWO

As outlaw motorcycle clubs went, Aberrant MC were far from the biggest or the most notorious, but Vincent was okay with that. Admittedly he'd been a bit pissed off last year when a biker magazine listed every known outlaw biker club in the world and they weren't even on it, but, still, this was his club and he'd fight to the death for them. They were his friends, his brothers, his family. Besides, he wasn't entirely sure that any other bike club would take him.

Aside from being built like a coat hanger, Vincent had terrible luck with motorbikes. Every couple of months some idiot would pull out in front of him, wrecking yet another bike that the insurance from his last accident had only just paid for. The insurance companies got so suspicious that they tracked down footage from a couple of surveillance cameras after his last two accidents, which showed Vincent to be entirely in the right. Both cars had just ploughed into him like they hadn't seen him. They hadn't even slowed down. Middle of the afternoon, bright sunny day. "Sorry mate, I didn't see you".

Vincent picked himself up and ran over to his bike, the back wheel still spinning as it lay in the road, about twenty five yards away at the end of a line of scratched concrete and broken glass. He hit the kill switch and angrily heaved the bike upright to inspect the damage. The front brake lever was snapped, the back one was bent, the mirror and headlight were smashed, but otherwise it didn't seem like anything major, no bent frames or square wheels to deal with.

"Fuck's sake," he sighed. "Not again."

"Are you all right, mister?"

Vincent looked up to see a small boy perched on a nearby wall with his finger up his nose almost to the knuckle.

"I seen everything," said the boy, removing his finger and examining something unsavoury on the end of it like he was considering eating it.

"I don't suppose you got the license number?"

"The what?"

"Never mind." Vincent wheeled his bike to the curb to inspect it for further damage.

"It was a red car what done it," said the boy, deciding against an early lunch and wiping his finger on his jeans.

"Yeah, I noticed that much, kid," sighed Vincent, pulling his long, blonde-ish, ginger hair away from his face. Little details like the colour of the vehicle that had U-turned in front of you were difficult to miss when you'd just flown over the hood and landed in a crumpled heap in the middle of the road with gravel rash all over your bum.

Sometimes Vincent thought he wasn't cut out to be a biker. As long as he could remember he'd wanted to join a bike gang; it was in his blood, coursing through his veins, an unstoppable destiny. Thanks to a father he'd never met, he was even named after a motorcycle, the legendary Vincent Black Shadow. And he was trying to grow a beard, though admittedly it was a pitiful bum-fluff. But, he reflected sadly, on days like today - and there were many days like today - he couldn't help wondering if he was somehow cursed. Even Evel Knievel never crashed this much!

As a kid Vincent had lived just a few houses down from the Aberrant MC clubhouse. He loved the smell and the noise of their bikes, the rumble as they roared off in a pack, setting off every car alarm in the street. They'd been kind to him, too, surrogate father figures who'd taught him the basics of motorcycle mechanics and taken him for rides on the back of gleaming Harley Davidsons and mean looking Suzukis and Kawasakis. His mother worked two jobs and was rarely home so he'd hang out at the clubhouse, running small errands, cleaning bikes, and picking up packs of cigarettes from the corner shop. He wanted nothing else in life but to join Aberrant Motorcycle Club and at eleven years old, when his mother had moved them to the countryside, he had been so devastated that he ran away, trekking two days across country in the rain to be back with them, too scared to hitch a ride in case he was caught and taken home.

He'd finally turned up at the clubhouse, soaked to the skin, shivering, skinny and bedraggled, at three o'clock in the morning. Club president Mad John had let him in, showing no surprise and offering no judgement. He'd found Vincent some dry clothes and they had sat and talked until the sun came up. It was the best and worst night of Vincent's young life. Mad John had treated him as an equal, not some stupid little kid, but at the same time he explained to Vincent that he couldn't stay with the club. As a runaway he was a liability, and at eleven years old he was too young to even own a motorcycle let alone join them. Late the next morning Mad John had driven him home. It was the longest ride Vincent had ever been on, a blur of adrenaline and exhilaration, but he cried all the way home, unable to disguise the hollow misery he felt inside.

"Come back when you're twenty-one, kid," Mad John had told him. "900cc or over. You know where to find us."

"I'll be back," said Vincent in his best Arnie Terminator voice, still trying to hold back the tears.

Ten years seemed like forever. Ten more years of being lonely. Ten more years of being ignored. He was surprised that anyone had even noticed he was missing. Day after day he was like a ghost at school, not even shunned, he might just as well have not been there. With Aberrant MC he felt somehow important, or at least valued. They always had time for him, the older guys showing him little magic tricks and telling him stories, while the younger members taught him about music and motorcycle maintenance. And now he was so very far away from them.

Vincent's mother, Tess, had tried to reassure him that he would make new friends at this new school, in this new town, but Vincent knew better. He'd never really had any friends. Ever since he could remember he had never been picked first for anything, always dead last like an afterthought to even up the teams, but after they moved it was even worse, like he wasn't even there. He was sure he'd be quite good at football if anyone would ever pass him the ball.

Eventually Vincent had got so sick of it that he'd stopped going to gym class at all, and when no one seemed to notice he started dropping out of other classes. It got to the point where he barely went to school at all and with nowhere else to go he would aimlessly wander the streets, rapidly discovering that he was an expert shoplifter. As far as he could tell, this was the only benefit of being virtually invisible, because while Vincent's CD collection grew exponentially, his list of friends did not. He didn't even want to be liked particularly, just noticed occasionally. Maybe that was why he liked Aberrant MC so much, not just because they always had time for him, but because they stood out. When Aberrant came down the street as a pack they'd set off every car alarm within a few blocks, like some mad fanfare. People would move out of their way as they thundered down the streets, a small army of dangerous, dangerous men on roaring beasts of black and chrome. More than anything Vincent wanted to be a part of that.

Six years after driving Vincent home on that miserable day Mad John disappeared without a trace, but good to his word Vincent showed up at the clubhouse on his twenty-first birthday on a Z1300 Kawasaki, not wanting to take any chances in case they had raised the cc limit. He still vividly remembered the fear and excitement he'd felt as he knocked on the door, with no idea what he was going to say other than "Mad John sent me."

The club's treasurer, Mental, a wild looking man with flaming red hair and a beard down to his waist, answered the door looking angry and hungover. He glared at Vincent for a moment that seemed to drag on for days and then simply grunted at him: "You're early. Go and get me some smokes and a couple of packs of Rizlas."

When Vincent got back, the entire club was waiting for him. They handed him a leather vest with three patches on it, his 'cut'. On the back was the club's bottom rocker, NFA, meaning No Fixed Abode, a throwback to the early days when most of the club drifted from place to place, living in squats. On the front it said 'Vincent' 'Prospect'. Nine months later he still had no idea how they knew to expect him, and he swore to himself that he wouldn't ask until he got his full colours.

The kid on the wall gave his finger one last wipe and clambered down to inspect Vincent's bike.

"Can I have a go on it, mister?" he said.

"I thought you said you saw everything." Despite himself, Vincent couldn't help smiling. Is this kid retarded or something?

"I did," challenged the kid. "It was a lady in a red car. She looked at you and I thought she seen you, but then she just hit you and you fell off."

"You saw that and you still want a go?"

"I'd be careful," offered the boy.

Vincent laughed as he realised that the kid actually wanted to ride the bike himself: his newly acquired CBX 1000 chop, a six cylinder, roaring, snorting, and-now-fucking-scratched, monster that he could only lift because, having finally got the hint, he had some custom made crash bars put on it.

"I think you might have to start off on something a bit smaller," Vincent said kindly. "How old are you?"

"Seven and a half," the kid challenged again, like anyone who had a problem with that might get a kick in the knee.

"Yeah, you've got a bit of a wait then, kid" said Vincent, putting his gloves back on. "But it'll give you time to save up for a bike."

"Will you take me for a ride?"

Vincent sighed. He wasn't having a particularly good day so far what with one thing an another. His elbow was bleeding and sticking to his jacket.

"Today's not a good day," he said frankly, a less grumpy part of his mind seeing himself as a kid.

"Another time then!" the kid said boldly. "I seen you around here a lot on lots of bikes. People never see you, but I do. It's brilliant when there's all of you! It sounds like dragons!"

"Maybe some other time then, kid," said Vincent, knowing all too well that he couldn't refuse.

And so, satisfied after one last glance that there was more damage done to his pride than to his bike, Vincent started his engine just as his mobile went off.

CHAPTER THREE

Dum Dum kicked his bike over. The kick-starter snapped back and bit into the back of his leg, tearing a hole in his jeans. He swore and punched his petrol tank, putting a large dent in it, which made him even more angry. It started to rain, big, long, heavy spatters that, having found the back of his neck, would rapidly turn torrential.

"Fucking piece of..." He tried the electric starter again, already knowing it wasn't going to work. It made a single click and then a horrible whirring noise.

"Oh you fucking...come on...you cunting fucking arse...bastard!" Dum Dum launched himself at the kick-start again and his bike puttered and then backfired like a shotgun going off. Several passers by ducked and thought about giving Dum Dum nasty looks until they saw the size of him, all six foot eight, three hundred and fifty pounds of him, ranting and swearing madly at a bike that looked and sounded like a two-wheeled Satan.

"Start you fucking bastard!" he bellowed at it, Basil Fawlty furious, now kicking uselessly at the bike and managing to bend the gear level. "Oh you fucking...arrrgh! Not now you cunt!"

Dum Dum had poured a small fortune into his '76 Shovelhead and it had never run right. He was beginning to wonder why he even bothered putting petrol in it since it never seemed to use a whole tank before it broke down again, and he would never normally consider riding it if he actually had to be somewhere, but he'd loaned his other bike to The General.

Dum Dum slowly counted to ten, let out a sigh, and launched at the starter. Nothing. He counted a further ten and tried again. The bike coughed a couple of times, threatening to start as he toyed with the throttle. It backfired again and died, and Dum Dum had to catch himself before putting another dent in the tank. He was running horribly late.

He should have been at the clubhouse early today, cleaning up whatever crap needed doing from last night, restocking the bar, making sure the board-room was in order...the usual shit that he'd been doing since he started pros-pecting for Aberrant Motorcycle Club four years ago. Not that he minded; he was good at menial tasks and even enjoyed them sometimes in a strangely vacant way. And it was easier these days with four prospects instead of just him. Besides, it wasn't news that prospects had to do all the shitty jobs, it was just part of what you went through to get your colours, and, though no one had said so, Dum Dum had the feeling he would be getting his very soon. There was no set time that you had to prospect for the club, but Dum Dum felt that his time was near. Maybe even today...if he could ever get there! Fucking bike.

Spark plugs. Dum Dum remembered that spark plugs were somehow important and spent ten minutes looking for them before taking them out by hand. He examined them, not entirely sure what he was looking for, and gave both plugs a good wipe on his t-shirt just in case. Then he screwed them back in, careful not to over-tighten and strip the thread. He checked the kill-switch again. It had a sticker on it that said 'TURN THIS OFF'. It was off.

Dum Dum scratched his head. Spark plugs, kill-switch, petrol...he knew about petrol, that was an easy one, just make sure it doesn't run out. And don't drink any again. He found and checked the fuel lines, pretty much exhausting his knowledge of motorcycle mechanics, and took a deep breath.

"Right..."

He kicked down on the starter. This time the engine puttered, backfired, and then suddenly caught. Dum Dum held the throttle just so while he put his helmet on with his other hand and fastened the chin-strap. He managed to get his left glove on and then swapped hands, holding the throttle with his gloved hand while he tried to pull the other glove on with his teeth. Finally, awkwardly, he swung a leg over the bike, swapped hands again on the throttle, then checked and adjusted his mirror which, thanks to ceaseless vibration, was pointing at the rapidly darkening sky. He gunned the throttle, kicked back the side stand, pulled in the clutch, clunked into first gear, checked for traffic... and then his bike cut out again.

It was unfortunate timing, then, that a van load of skinheads chose that exact moment to pull up alongside Dum Dum and gleefully inform him that they thought he was a "greasy wanker", before completely misjudging the traffic lights and promptly getting stuck. To say that what followed was a fight would be to suggest that the skinheads had a chance of winning, though for a few moments a couple of them made that their second very big mistake of the day. The skinheads were still cowering inside with Dum Dum doing horrible things to their van when it finally lurched away, trying to escape in the wrong gear as the driver panicked. The passenger side of the van was totally caved in and both the back doors were hanging off, one with a large hole where Dum Dum had punched clean through it. He was very good at punching things. Not that he got an awful lot of practice as one punch was generally more than sufficient, but, still, it was a natural talent and one that he was proud of.

Dum Dum wasn't the sharpest knife in the drawer. He had trouble counting to twenty without taking his socks off and before prospecting for Aberrant relied solely on his size to get him through life, reasoning that anyone stupid enough to try and rip him off must be even more stupid than him and therefore too stupid to pull it off. It was a philosophy that worked well for the most part, though he had paid a visit to the shop in Surrey that sold him his Harley when, a week after buying it, the clutch had fallen apart. In hindsight perhaps he should have got them to fix the problem before he destroyed the shop, especially since his bike had broken down again on the way home, but at least they wouldn't be ripping anyone else off for a while, it being rather difficult for the shop owner to sell anything at all with his jaw wired onto his face. Dum Dum knew he wasn't the brains of any operation, but if anything needed punching, lifting, bending, or breaking, then he was the man for the job. He was probably overqualified. It had kept him safe while he was pushed from place to place as a kid, always a new orphanage, a new school, and the hell of being the new kid, all countered by occasional bouts of his crazy mother trying to kidnap him.

From foster care Dum Dum progressed quickly to borstal and then to prison, where he had spent most of his life on and off until he met Aberrant MC. He'd been working as a bouncer, doing the rock shows so he'd get to see his favourite bands for free, when Numb Tongue, Mental, and Chaos came down to see a show. Later they invited him back to the clubhouse where they'd stayed up all night doing coke and playing poker. Dum Dum lost all his money, but since it was their coke he didn't really mind. When he left the next morning the sun was too bright, his pockets were empty, and his nose was bleeding, but he didn't have a care in the world. Here, at last, he had found a family.

"I wanna join this club," he told Mental as he left.

"You haven't got a bike."

"I'll get one."

"You haven't got a bike license!"

"Have you?"

"Yeah, well, fair point I suppose," said Mental. "But really, you haven't got a bike and you said you'd never even ridden one."

Early that evening Dum Dum came back to the clubhouse on a 900cc BMW and pounded on the door. A kid called Scarecrow answered the door, his hands covered in motor oil.

"Mental said if I got a bike I could join the club," he told Scarecrow, rather stretching the truth, and standing aside to reveal what looked suspiciously like a police bike that had been hurriedly painted matte black.

Scarecrow went back inside and fetched Mental, who, as usual, looked hungover and none too pleased to be awake. They went outside to find Dum Dum standing expectantly beside his new ride.

"You said get a bike," beamed Dum Dum.

"Yes, I did didn't I," groaned Mental, inspecting a series of dents and scratches all down the left side of the bike. "Did you have some problems with it?"

"I fell off it twice on the way here," admitted Dum Dum, looking more annoyed than embarrassed. There was a chunk of skin hanging off his elbow where he had landed badly the second time he fell off and the palms of both his hands were raw with roadrash.

"Dum Dum," said Mental, completing his inspection. "Where did you get this bike?"

"Um," said Dum Dum, suddenly looking painfully guilty.

"I ask this, Dum Dum, because I can't help noticing that bits of the paint are still wet and, if you look at it in this light, you can still see the word 'police' on the side."

"Um," said Dum Dum again, shuffling uncomfortably.

"This is a police bike isn't it, Dum Dum?" said Mental. "This is a police bike that you have stolen, then painted, very badly I might add, and then brought here to our fucking clubhouse!"

"Um."

"You brought a stolen police bike to our clubhouse!" repeated Mental, shaking his head.

"Um, sorry," said Dum Dum. "You said get a bike and..."

"Dum Dum," said Mental.

"Yes, Mental?"

"Get your *own* bike."

"Right, yes, stupid of me really," muttered Dum Dum, glumly getting back on the still wet police bike.

Scarecrow and Mental turned to go back inside. "They don't call him Dum Dum for nothing do they?" said Mental. "But you've gotta love his style."

The next day Dum Dum took all his savings to the nearest Harley dealer and bought his regrettable Shovelhead. Then he saved up for a proper bike that didn't break down all the time. Which he should have been riding today...

There was a low boom of thunder as Dum Dum trudged back to his bike. It was instantly followed by a flash of lightning that lit up the whole sky and then a heavy, dirty, rain began to fall.

"Oh that's just fucking perfect," muttered Dum Dum. "Thank you God."

Slowly he repeated all the checks, fuel on, kill-switch off, bike in neutral, and kicked miserably at the starter again. His foot slipped on the now wet metal and this time the starter took a chunk out of his shin.

"You vicious fucking..." Dum Dum cursed, instinctively bringing his knee up and catching it painfully on the handlebars. It was a full two minutes before he stopped swearing long enough to notice that he had accidentally kneed the electric starter button and that, amid the noise of the rain and the traffic, his bike was actually running.

"Fucking thing's got a mind of its own," he said, clambering cautiously aboard.

Dum Dum's mobile failed to go off because he had no signal.

CHAPTER FOUR

In the depths of the Aberrant MC clubhouse, The General was not a happy man. He stomped around the basement angrily looking for things to tidy up, while not actually tidying anything at all. Not that he could tell what was junk down here anyway. Before he disappeared, the club's legendary ex-president, Mad John, had apparently used the place as a study of sorts and, aside from an ancient oak desk containing an even older looking typewriter and a few old black and white photos, the place was littered with weird contraptions and things in jars that looked like they should be bubbling. The walls and most of the desk were covered in gibberish symbols, runes and numbers and strange words that appeared to be written backwards. The place gave The General the creeps.

Finally satisfied that there was nothing else to do he sat down heavily at the desk and lit a cigarette. He probably wasn't even supposed to be in here, but having cleaned the clubhouse boardroom and bar, *on his own*, he was fucked if he was going to start on the rest until the other prospects showed up. Fucking lazy bastards. The General had had a desperately long night and was in no mood for this. He'd been stuck here all night with the whole clubhouse in uproar and then that nasty bastard had showed up at about five o'clock in the morning and questioned him for hours on end. And still he had somehow managed to get lumbered with all of the cleaning. It just wasn't fair! Where the hell were they? Surely they must know that something big was going down, especially since their mobiles would have been ringing off the hook all morning. Mad John was back, with eyes blazing fire, and he was very angry indeed.

The first thing that struck The General was that he had expected Mad John to be taller. He'd heard all these wild tales about the man, how he never stopped for red lights and knew the Bible word for word, how he was psychic and had no lifeline on his hands. There were crazier tales, too, about how Mad John never had to refuel his bike, it just kept on running. The club would say weird things sometimes, but The General put most of it down to the amount of drugs they did. All The General knew was that Mad John had disappeared five or six years ago apparently leaving a trail of baffled cops in his wake.

The story was that he had robbed several banks before he vanished, which was true. But instead of going in with guns blazing and a getaway car, Mad John had opened numerous accounts at different banks using fake IDs, built up excellent credit over many years, and then taken out massive loans on the premise of starting a new company. He took every bank for about £75,000.

Even though he'd seen photographs The General had expected a giant of a man, someone who made Numb Tongue look like a midget, but instead Mad John was about five-ten, dirty blond hair, deeply tanned, perhaps even half-caste, with kind of a Jesus meets Charles Manson look about him. He'd shown up in the middle of the night and stormed into the clubhouse, demanding that The General tell him everything about last night. They sat in the boardroom and The General told Mad John what he knew, omitting the part where he'd hidden from the police: Mental and Flashback were in jail on some serious charges after wrecking a bar and then taking on the dozen or so cops who had turned up to stop them.

"What time was this?"

"About midnight, maybe earlier," said The General.

"Was it midnight?"

"I guess..." said The General.

"It's important, try to remember," insisted Mad John.

"Yeah, it was midnight."

"Amateurs," said Mad John mysteriously. "Well, that's good at least."

Mad John wanted to know every detail, how they'd both come down to see a band at the club that The General was working at, then gone backstage to do a few lines with the band when they were done. What they didn't know, and apparently failed to notice, possibly because they were both tripping their tits off, was that in their absence the venue had chucked everyone out and reopened its doors as a gay club.

Mental and Flashback headed back to the bar where some very friendly men bought them a lot of drinks, and Mental got chatting to a tall lady with a suspiciously deep voice. Having not taken any acid The General could see that the lady was in fact a deeply unconvincing transvestite who looked like a builder in a dress, but decided it was funnier not to say anything. Ten minutes later all hell broke loose and Mental was jumping up and down on the bloke's head screaming about false advertising! It was at this point that The General had ducked away under the pretence of doing some work. Chairs and tables were broken, much of the bar was covered in blood, and Mental and Flashback weren't leaving.

They were not inconspicuous people. Mental was not particularly tall, five feet nine inches in his thickest socks, but his flaming wild red hair, that stuck out at all angles like a bushfire, and a beard that did much the same in the opposite direction, ensured that he stood out in a club largely populated with muscular, clean shaven men in tight shorts. Flashback, too, had a habit of completely failing to blend in with a crowd, but being clad from head to foot in custom made black leather, including a leather kilt, only served to make him very popular here.

He was by no means an obnoxious drunk, quite the reverse, one of those rogue sots, somewhere between Richard Harris and Al Jourgensen with a hint of Ollie Reed. He could stand toe-to-toe with anyone and drink them under the table, and did a passable and surprisingly un-annoying Mickey Rourke in Barfly, yelling "Drinks for all my friends!" before buying drinks for anyone within earshot. Which was usually the entire bar as Flashback was also rather loud. There was a dash of pimp about Flashback. His silver jewellery shone in the club light, one silver tooth glinting when he laughed, rapping his silver tipped cane on the bar as if applauding.

Mental's outburst notwithstanding, they had already made their presence in the room felt, and, since the bouncers knew better than to try and throw them out, they carried on sitting at the bar knocking back shots. The police turned up about five minutes later and once again the bar erupted as Mental and Flashback vigorously resisted arrest.

"Where were you when this happened, Ian?" said Mad John, insisting on using The General's real name.

"I was down on the stage loading some gear," said The General. He didn't like all these questions, it felt like Mad John could see right through him. And he certainly didn't like being called Ian.

"Where was Dum Dum?"

"Dum Dum was off for the night."

And so it went on. Mad John asked about everything, repeating questions and doubling back at every turn. How did the cops behave? Did they put up a fight? What did they look like?

"I didn't see the cops," repeated The General. "Someone came and told me they were arresting Mental and Flashback, but by the time I got up to the bar they were gone."

"Who?"

"What?"

"Who came and told you they were getting arrested, Ian?"

"Er," said The General. Fucker could see right through him.

After a couple of hours of this Mad John dismissed him, telling him to get on with cleaning the clubhouse while he used The General's phone to call the other prospects. About half of the club, or at least those that weren't in custody, were already at the clubhouse and the mood was dark and restless.

The General was relieved to have a moment of peace down here among the inner workings of Mad John's mind. Well, briefly. There was a Bible on the desk and he picked it up to find handwritten notes on every page, corrections, additions, and insane ramblings on page after page.

John 6: 5-15 "Nonsense, it was next to the sea! Where doth they think all the fish came from?"

Luke 14:1-6 "Remove contaminated cooking oils. AVOID MUSTARD!"

Matthew 17:24-27 "Sleight of hand. A child could do it."

Matthew 17:14-21 "Tourettes syndrome/Epilepsy."

He shuddered and put the book straight back down. Creepy fucking place. There was a weird feeling of age in the room, like it had been here for centuries, and The General realised that his brain had slowed to a crawl, like he was having to think through treacle. Absently he tried the desk drawer which slid smoothly open, doubtless something of Mad John's own making. There was a photograph inside in a battered silver frame. It looked like something from World War One, maybe, judging by the old biplanes and the age of the picture, an old runway somewhere with a couple of guys in air force uniform posing with their planes. The one on the left looked the spitting image of Mad John except he had short hair and a handlebar moustache. Probably his dad, thought The General, or maybe his granddad. He put the picture back.

"Find anything useful, Ian?" said Mad John directly behind him, startling The General so much that he leapt out of his seat.

"Oh, no, no, I was tidying up and..." he trailed off, inadvertently glancing down at the still open drawer.

"You were, were you?" said Mad John, with a stare that burned right through him. "I'd be very careful if I were you, Ian. Very careful indeed. The others are here. Go and help them out in the workshop."

The General resisted the urge to answer back and clumped heavily up the stairs to the workshop. Mad John frightened him. Well, maybe not frightened, but certainly unnerved him, and he wasn't about to start arguing with a founder and former president of the club, especially not one that they all seemed slightly in awe of. The General could see how all those exaggerated tales about the man got started. There was something about him, not just the way he looked at you, but this strange feeling of power, like there was a personal exclusion zone around him and if you crossed it without permission he'd turn you into a frog or something. He'd tried to get a glimpse of Mad John's palms to see if there really was no lifeline, but all he saw were nasty scars on the backs of both hands, burn marks possibly, that looked like they had healed many years ago.

When he got to the workshop The General found Vincent, Scarecrow, and Dum Dum not very hard at work, smoking cigarettes, and catching up on what they knew about the events of last night. There was never anything to tidy up in the workshop since Scarecrow virtually lived in it, keeping the place in immaculate condition, always putting tools back on the right racks, always emptying the ashtrays and mopping up even the slightest oil leak. Naturally they wanted to know The General's version of what happened so he retold the story, resisting the temptation to embellish it and make himself a hero.

"Man, the one night I'm off work and this shit goes down," grumbled Dum Dum.

"Yeah, I know," said The General. "I was right there, but by the time I got upstairs it was all over, there was just a bunch of broken glass and stuff."

The General liked Dum Dum. He always knew where he stood with Dum Dum because, occasional bike theft notwithstanding, he was as honest as he was stupid. All you had to do was follow the basic rules - well, one basic rule really. Don't annoy Dum Dum or he'll break things. Not that much actually seemed to annoy him, but you certainly didn't want to be around if something did. That was how they'd met in the first place: The General was working as a roady for a band one night and Dum Dum was working security in the photo pit. The venue had this weird system - apparently passed down by some guy called Neville who'd died a few years back - where they'd hold up a finger for each crowd surfer that was headed their way, left or right hand depending on which side the surfer was on. Dum Dum wasn't very good at following the signals, but he was very good at catching crowd surfers without dropping them, and The General had watched him from the side of the stage as he lumbered around the photo pit catching two kids at a time sometimes. It looked like some of them were aiming for him like he was a human bouncy castle and it soon became obvious that a lot of the kids knew him and gave him high five's as they went over.

About halfway through the band's set there was a fight in the mosh pit and the singer took it upon himself to go in and sort it out. The General dutifully followed him and threw his not inconsiderable weight around a bit, and it all seemed to die down. Then suddenly the violence flared again and The General realised that the singer was already back on stage, and he was on his own. He puffed up and made himself look big while managing to back away at the same time. Thanks to a little help from steroids he was a big lad, just over six feet, barrel-chested, with arms bigger than most people's thighs, and most of the time all he had to do was look mean. If that didn't work he always had back up, venue security and such. On this night, however, his chest-inflating, mean-face routine didn't work: three guys squared up to him and showed no sign of backing down.

The General puffed up a little bigger and backed a little further away, starting to panic. They weren't particularly tough looking guys, but, still, there were three of them, maybe four, and, beneath all the bluster and steroids and an occasional lucky punch, he really wasn't very good at fighting. He wasn't sure he could puff himself up any bigger without passing out and he had backed so far away that the crowd behind him was starting to push back. And then, just as The General was beginning to think he was going to have to run away, he spotted Dum Dum looming through the crowd towards them. He was behind the three guys so they hadn't seen him yet and were momentarily confused when The General smiled at them and took a step forward.

When The General told that story these days, depending on who was around to hear it, there could be anything up to fifteen guys and he had beaten most of them into submission before any help had arrived. The truth was that Dum Dum had literally picked two of them up and bashed their heads together, and the other one, in his efforts to get away from Dum Dum, had run straight into The General, knocking the pair of them down with The General landing on top. It was hardly much of a fight, let alone the Western movie bar brawl that it had become. And he hadn't even been called The General back then, it was a nickname he acquired later from the club when they found out he'd been kicked out of the marines. He'd added the 'The' himself because it looked cool.

After the show Ian - the soon to be The General - and Dum Dum had got to talking about bands, and Dum Dum was immediately impressed by the depth of The General's musical knowledge. Any band Dum Dum could mention, The General had either worked for them or knew them personally, and had their number dialled into his phone. When the bar closed they headed down Charing Cross Road to the Crowbar, a noisy rock dive that was over-spilling with people. They squeezed their way to the bar and ordered drinks, Dum Dum shovelling enough money into the jukebox that it would still be playing his selections next Christmas, and they shouted over the music about music for a while before Dum Dum went outside to take a call.

"There's some people I want you to meet," said Dum Dum, when he got back to the bar. "They're on their way now, be about five minutes."

It was only then that Ian noticed the two patches on the front of Dum Dum's jacket, 'Dum Dum' and 'Prospect', and knew that inevitably there would be a third patch on the back.

Fuck.

The General was desperately wary of outlaw biker clubs and tried to steer well away from them. A long time ago he'd tried to bluff his way into the Hells Angels, thinking his inflate and snarl routine would work, but no one was remotely impressed and, having got it into his head that they were going to kill him, The General had moved to Cornwall to be as far away from them as possible. A few years later he ran into one of the Angels at a service station on the motorway and the Angel showed no sign of being even slightly interested in him. The General figured he must have just been paranoid and eventually moved back to London, but, still, he kept himself away from any patch clubs, no matter who they were. And now here he was stuck in a very small bar with this gigantic prospect, waiting for God knows what to show up! How could he have been so stupid and missed the patches?

"I'd love to, mate," lied The General, looking at an imaginary watch, "but I'm meeting this bird in half an hour and I've got to get going."

"They'll only be five minutes," insisted Dum Dum, keen to show off his new friend who knew all his favourite bands.

"No really, mate. I'd love to, really, but I can't. You know what girls are like..."

The General downed his drink and started edging towards the door, making excuses all the way out to the street to where his old nail of an XS650 was parked in the motorcycle bay opposite. Dum Dum followed him outside, saying he wanted a smoke and to, perhaps politely, check out The General's far from impressive bike.

"Good solid motor, them things," said Dum Dum encouragingly, as The General tried to get it started with increasing urgency. "They make good little chops, they do."

"Yes, lovely, lovely." The General panted, pumping at the kick starter like he was trying to inflate an airbed.

Dum Dum was still giving unhelpful advice about not flooding the carbs when suddenly all the car alarms on the street went off at once. There was the sound of hell on 'run what ya brung' day and Aberrant MC rounded the corner, low, loud, and radiating evil. Hell, this wasn't even the whole club! The General later learned that there were thirteen full members in all, but just six of them - seven with Dum Dum - was enough to be massively intimidating. Tonight, aside from Dum Dum, there was Loud-As, Chaos, Mental, Andy One-Leg, Joker, and Numb Tongue. Numb Tongue terrified The General on sight, to the point that he stuttered like something out of a Monty Python sketch when they parked their bikes and came over to see what was the problem.

"He's flooded the carbs," announced Dum Dum, who'd managed to learn little to nothing about motorcycles despite the best efforts of the entire club. They tried. They'd *really* tried. And Dum Dum really tried too, but it was hopeless, he couldn't tell a brake pad from a sanitary pad. Not that he would ever let on to anybody outside the club, which is why, ten minutes later, he was still offering increasingly dreadful tips to The General on how to get his bike started.

By now the General was almost frantic to get away, but, with sweat running down his face and his jacket starting to stick to him, he simply had to stop for a rest. He collapsed over the bike, panting and out of breath, then suddenly Numb Tongue loomed over him, his face a maze of scars over scars.

"Kill-switch," he said, with a voice so low and deep that it bothered earthworms.

"W..what?" said The General, almost paralysed with fear.

"Your kill-switch is on," repeated Dum Dum, radiating wisdom as if it was him who had spotted the problem.

The General felt about three inches tall. Still panting and sweating he flicked the switch to 'off' and let out something that may have been a sigh or a whimper.

"Can't go and see your bird looking like that," said Dum Dum. "Come on, come and 'ave a drink."

The General felt he had no choice. Dum Dum had saved not only his reputation but possibly his life, earlier that evening. He owed it to Dum Dum to at least have another drink with him. Or at least actually buy him a drink since Dum Dum had paid for all the drinks so far. But more than that, The General was just desperate that none of his actions be considered in any way, shape, or form, disrespectful to the club. And so he had gone back into the bar for a drink. Just one, mind.

When he woke up the next morning or afternoon The General was on an unfamiliar sofa, his eyes gummed together and a taste in his mouth like something had died in there. He wiped away some eye bogies and tried to get a fix on where he was. It wasn't difficult. Filling the entire wall opposite him was a huge wooden carving bearing the words 'Aberrant MC' and the club's weird logo, that seemed to be all sorts of things depending on how you looked at it, a skull, a fire, a mathematical equation.... Reminiscent of the often copied Reflections Of Death painting, either drawn up by an idiot or a genius, whatever the fuck it was.

The General let out a groan. Oh God no! How the hell had he ended up here? He didn't even remember leaving the bar! He closed his eyes, trying to recall the previous night, but it was a complete blank. He remembered that his bike wouldn't start and he'd gone back into the bar, bought Dum Dum a drink and been introduced to a couple of the club members. Then what? Nothing. His head was pounding and he could hear someone moving around, music in some distant room.

When, eventually, The General plucked up enough courage to stop pretending to be asleep, he found Dum Dum trudging around the clubhouse cleaning up what looked like one hell of a party. Every surface was littered with empty bottles and cans and there was a large amount of very small lingerie liberally scattered around under the stripper pole at the end of the bar. Two of the girls who presumably owned some of the microscopic underwear were asleep on the pool table, underneath a huge Union Jack flag.

"Couple of the boys nicked that at Le Mans a few years back," grinned Dum Dum, thinking that The General was gawping at the flag and not the naked girls spooning beneath it. "Middle of the night they went down to where all the flagpoles are and nicked it. Trouble is, some English bloke actually won the race and when they come to do all the prizes and shit, all the national anthems, there was no British flag to put up. They had to put up this little tiny flag about the size of a sock, it was fucking hilarious! You want some coffee? You look like you're gonna throw up."

More than anything The General wanted coffee. He was too hungover to even be scared of where he was any more and, although he remembered little to nothing of last night, all the evidence suggested that this wasn't such a bad place after all. These boys certainly knew how to party. He sat and drank coffee with Dum Dum, who appeared none the worse for wear, and gradually the clubhouse came back to life, first Chaos, hungover and wanting a cigarette, then one of the girls from the pool table, wearing just a g-string and wanting a Bloody Mary. By the time The General was on his third coffee a few more people had emerged from different rooms seeking various hangover cures or, in some cases, a means to keep drinking and avoid the hangover completely. Inevitably the music got cranked back up a notch and somebody offered The General a line. He finally left the clubhouse three days later and then had to come back and ask them where he'd parked his bike, which was still outside the Crowbar.

From then on The General spent most of his weekends at the clubhouse and, ever the music junkie, Dum Dum latched on to him as his new best friend. Not that The General minded. He liked being protected and having Dum Dum around was like having your own pet giant. He got on well with most of the other guys, too. Numb Tongue still terrified him, but since he rarely spoke more than a few words it was easy to avoid him. The other two prospects, Scarecrow and Vincent, were both kind of annoying for reasons The General couldn't quite pin down other than they seemed to get laid more than him, but, with Dum Dum as his pet, they posed no real threat. If anything they got pushed to the sidelines a little every now and again, The General finding that he could occasionally get away with ordering them about as if he were a full patch member.

The irony was that he had never even wanted to join the club. One cold and rainy afternoon, six months ago, he had woken up on that couch again to find he was wearing prospect patches. He had no recollection of being given them and was too scared of the consequences to ever tell the club that he didn't want them.

"So what did you think of Mad John?" said Dum Dum, breaking a silence that had fallen over the workshop as the four prospects tried to listen for signs of what was going on upstairs in the boardroom. There was nothing, no more shouting, no footsteps, no sound. It was as if the rest of the clubhouse was empty, a Marie Celeste, the spooky qualities not helped by the fact that a dark and heavy rain now lashed the windows, and a vicious wind rattled the workshop door like an angry dog trying to get in. The shouting had been much easier to deal with.

"I don't think he likes me much," said The General, his voice coming out cracked and quieter than he expected.

"Don't be daft," said Dum Dum. "He don't even know you. I'm sure if all this weren't going on then...well, y'know."

"No, really," said The General. "He didn't even say hello, nothing, just started yelling at me about last night and asking all these questions. I'd never even met him before!"

"I'm sure he just wants to figure out what happened and how we can get them out of jail," said Vincent. "They've got to get lawyers and all that shit, find out if there was any witnesses..."

"Any witnesses?" sputtered The General. "It was the main bar of one of the biggest clubs in London. On fucking gay night! I mean, the whole club's wearing Speedos and blowing whistles, and there's Mental and Flashback tripping their nuts off and wrecking the bar in the middle of it all. Of course there's no witnesses, no one could have possibly noticed them."

"Yeah, but you know what I mean," said Vincent. He was getting sick of the way The General put him down all the time and he knew that, no matter how close they were, Dum Dum wouldn't get in the way of a fair fight. The trouble was he was pretty sure he wouldn't win a fair fight against The General and couldn't bear to think of the crap he'd have to put up with if he lost. He wanted to say something about how prospects were supposed to be first into a fight, to prove their worth to the club, not conveniently as far away from the action as possible, but he wasn't sure if anyone else had started noticing a pattern. It seemed like the slightest whiff of trouble and The General was nowhere to be seen unless the odds were heavily stacked in his favour.

"The tranny bloke prob'ly won't press charges," said Dum Dum, court-rooms and jails being his speciality subject. "Prob'ly happily married, gonna tell his wife he got mugged or something. It's the cops you've gotta watch out for. Some of 'em like a good ruck, but if you win too much they'll stitch you right up in court, 'tempted murder and all sorts."

"John'll know what to do," said Scarecrow loyally.

"He didn't look like he knew what he was doing last night!" scoffed The General. "All these stupid questions about what time it was and what the cops looked like, and he didn't even ask which station they got taken to!"

"That's because he already knew which station they were taken to," said Mad John, suddenly directly behind The General, making him jump for the second time in so many hours. How the fuck did he do that? It was like he'd been in the room all along.

"Ian, go and bring my bike in and then join us in the boardroom," said Mad John, again with the blazing blue eyes, softening as he turned to the others. "And if the rest of you gentlemen would be so kind..."

CHAPTER FIVE

It had stopped raining, but drops like water bombs still fell from nearby trees and the wind fired soggy leaves at The General as if using him for target practice. By his reckoning it couldn't have been later than about three in the afternoon, yet it was dark already, winter trying to muscle in on spring one last time. Poxy fucking weather. It hadn't stopped raining for weeks.

Shining in the rain-light, Mad John's old Harley sat on its own under a lamp post that gave it a curious glow. The General paused when he got to the bike and had a look around. Everything around him was soaked, car wind-screens with leaves and sweet wrappers stuck to them, and the gutter was a small running stream, and yet Mad John's bike wasn't even wet. Not a drop of rain. More than that there wasn't a speck of dirt on the whole bike, it was showroom clean, with only the tyres showing any sign of wear, and indicating that the bike had been ridden to its very limits. The speedo said it had done over 96,000 miles and this model, a Harley Knucklehead, was considered virtually antique, but it looked brand new. The General flicked the bike off its side-stand and it felt curiously light. It had one of those old screw top petrol caps and The General unscrewed it and peeked inside the tank. It was empty, like it had never been opened before. Not the slightest smell of fuel.

The General didn't want to be in Aberrant MC any more. He'd never wanted to be in Aberrant MC in the first place, he'd just sort of got swept up with it and, until now, they had been the only club who didn't see through his tough guy act. But now he knew for sure that he wanted out. It was fun for a while and he'd miss the girls, the free drugs, and throwing his weight around knowing that Dum Dum had his back. But now that this Mad John character was back... Well, there was something weird about him, something portentous in his arrival. Missing for five years and then he just turns up out of the blue on the very night that Mental and Flashback get arrested. And why the big fuss anyway? The club was formed way back in 1984, and none of them were exactly inconspicuous to the law, so surely a few of them had been arrested before. Certainly Dum Dum had done time.

The General grumbled his way over to the lock-up compound where all the other bikes were parked. Even his old XS650, broken and forgotten and rusting. He didn't even have a bike that ran anymore, he'd just sort of permanently borrowed Dum Dum's XS1100, and he had a feeling Dum Dum would be wanting it back soon. Maybe that was his way out of the club. Maybe if Dum Dum took his bike back then The General's non-running XS wouldn't meet the club's requirements and, regrettably, he'd have to leave. He paused for a second and looked around. It felt, not as if someone was watching him, but as if someone was listening to his thoughts. But there was no one around, just the warm glow from houses up and down the street, normal families watching the Sunday movie. Or whatever it was that normal families did.

As The General climbed the stairs to the clubhouse boardroom all he could think about was how to get out of prospecting for Aberrant MC whilst retaining the ability to walk, reproduce, and eat food without the aid of a straw. With some clubs you could just walk away, no hard feelings. Others wanted blood.

What if he went to the cops? He knew enough about the club to get most of them sent down for a several years, but then what? Witness relocation? He'd have to leave the country, but these fuckers travelled far and wide. Chaos had just got back from riding all the way across the Sahara, and down to the Ivory Coast. Andy One-leg and Loud-As were just back from Berlin, and others were planning a run through France to Spain. Where would you hide from a reach like that? Even Cornwall had been a stupid idea. If the Hells Angels had wanted to get The General then they would have, but he simply wasn't important enough, not worth the bother. Hopefully Aberrant MC would feel the same way, although he'd only been a hang-around with the Angels, never even making prospect.

The General paused outside the boardroom door, and took a deep breath. He wasn't sure if he should knock or go straight in, but he felt increasingly like running away, maybe leave a little note with his prospect patches and hope they forgot all about him. In the top corner of the hallway The General spotted a gigantic spider, a huge, hairy brown thing, some distant relative of the Tarantula that you only seemed to find in old English houses. He could swear it was watching him.

"I have *got* to get out of this place," he shuddered to himself.

"What's that?" Suddenly Numb Tongue was right behind him, a cross between Lurch and Lenny McLean that Frankenstein had thrown together in his lunch hour. Those two words were probably the first thing he'd said all month.

"Oh, I was just thinking I've got to clean this place up," The General lied quickly. "There's a big spider up in the corner."

Numb Tongue glanced at the spider and gave a look that suggested he might already have been aware of it. Most of the time it was impossible to know what he thinking. He shovelled endless amounts of coke up his nose, to the point where if it hadn't already been broken several times then it would probably have collapsed anyway, yet he rarely spoke, treating words like a miser treats money, as if each syllable came out of his mouth via his wallet. Most of the time he looked angry, but if you dared to glance for long enough you'd see a sadness in his eyes, like he'd suffered some awful, unthinkable loss, and all of the rest of it, the club, the coke, the bikes, all of it was just auto-pilot. Something to do because he wasn't dead yet.

The General had never seen Numb Tongue fight and he was pretty sure he never wanted to. It wasn't just the scars, the razor lines over bottle scars over stab wounds, that made Numb Tongue's face look like a map of the London Underground. It wasn't even the tattoos across his knuckles that said simply, 'who's next?', though the combined effect seemed to intimidate everyone, with the curious exception of little old ladies. It was more that Numb Tongue was empty inside, an angry and somehow inconsolable shell. As tactfully as possible Scarecrow had once asked him why he wore a battered silver wedding ring when he clearly wasn't married and seemed to have little time for women other than the little old ladies who were so resolutely unafraid of him. There was no outburst or any flicker of emotion. Numb Tongue just grunted and gave Scarecrow a look. It was the look that said, in plain and certain terms, matter of fact: 'I'll let you off this time because you didn't know any better, but if you ever ask that question again, even so much as *think* that question again, then I will make the rest of your life very short, and very, very painful'. And just for a flicker The General had seen it in his mind, the horror as Numb Tongue's steel capped boots relentlessly smashed teeth and bone and skull to pulp.

There was talk of how Numb Tongue could be a dominant force in the UFC light heavyweight division, except that he refused point blank to ever take his leather jacket off even on the hottest day, let alone consider wearing shorts. Instead, he ran a mixed martial arts gym where people learned to fight in their everyday clothes, a glorified 'fight club' that stayed barely within the law. There were rumours of fights to the death and big time mobster money, but The General had been sure never to ask any questions. He knew that Numb Tongue went to Thailand every six months or so, either to train or to fight, and that he'd trained with Shaolin monks in China.

The General also knew what had happened to a rival bike club who were proving troublesome to Aberrant, their colours nailed upside down to the boardroom wall, like so many hunted heads. Numb Tongue had apparently gone to their clubhouse one night, dismantling it and the rival club, on his own, before bringing Smiler back with him and insisting that he be allowed to prospect for Aberrant as he was the only one to put up a decent fight. The General doubted it had been a long conversation.

"In?" rumbled Numb Tongue, with careless verbosity.

"What? Oh, yes..." said The General, who so desperately wanted out.

A heavy cloud of weed and tobacco smoke hung low across the long boardroom table making it difficult for The General to spot a vacant seat, but Dum Dum caught his attention from the far end of the room, waving cheerfully, and pointing to the empty seat beside him. The General had always been nervous and uncomfortable in the boardroom. It wasn't just the stolen and bloody colours of the rival club nailed to the wall, more the sense that this was somehow a secret room, steeped in history, and that if bad things happened here then no one would ever find out about them. It was the kind of room that felt like it should have trapdoors and hidden rooms, though quite where a trapdoor would go from a third floor room, other than the bar below, was anyone's guess.

The mood of the club seemed to have drastically improved though. Smiler was handing out cold beers, while Joker and Loud-As were in hysterics at some private joke. The General thought that maybe he'd been getting paranoid again like he had with the Hells Angels. He'd run into a few of them since moving back to London and they still showed no indication that they wanted to kill him. He'd failed their vetting process and wasn't the right man for their club, but apparently that was the end of it, there was no bounty on his head.

It was the drugs, that was all. This lot did so many drugs that it was bound to make you wig out every now and again. Paranoia, that was all.

"Fucking spiders watching me, for God's sake," thought The General. "I've got to slow down on the acid and E."

He clinked beers with Dum Dum and took a long swig. It had been a long night and things were bound to be a bit tense with two of the club facing jail time. Vincent was right; they needed to get a lawyer on the case, rally round, maybe lean on some of the witnesses. Paranoia, that was all.

"The big fuss, Ian," said Mad John, suddenly so close to The General's ear that he could feel his breath, hissing 'fuss' like a snake, "is that no full patch member has ever been arrested while wearing their colours. There is an... arrangement. Therefore we have a problem. And we do *not* lean on witnesses. Clear?"

"Yes," whispered The General. The colour had drained from his face and his hands were shaking so much that he spilled beer down the front of his jeans.

"See, I said you'd get on," Dum Dum nudged him keenly in the ribs, apparently failing to notice the The General's terror. He knew! Mad John knew what he'd been thinking! How could he possibly have known? And what fucking arrangement? Were they paying the cops off? Bang goes his plans of running to the law!

"You wanna be a bit more careful with your beer though, mate," grinned Dum Dum, oblivious. "Looks like you've pissed your trousers." For once Dum Dum was right.

"Gentlemen, if I might have your attention..."

And suddenly Mad John was at the other end of the room, at the head of the table, like he'd been there all along. He spoke quietly, but his voice cut through the hubbub and there was instant silence except for the tap, tap, tap, of Numb Tongue chopping out a line of coke on the table. He looked up and gestured 'sorry', putting the razor down.

"Thank you, Numb," said Mad John and Numb Tongue nodded.

Completely out of the blue Mad John was back, acting like he'd never been away, an illusion that wasn't helped by the rest of the club treating it as totally normal. Even Mad John's colours had changed, and once again he wore the 'president' patch, still frayed on one edge like it had always been there. And almost miraculously there had been a shuffling of patches sometime before the meeting, and now, aside from Mad John being president again, presumably with Flashback as vice president in his jail cell, Chaos was once again road captain, Joker becoming secretary, and so on. Only Numb Tongue remained in his post of sergeant at arms. When Mad John spoke they listened.

"Now, gentlemen, it seems we have a few inconveniences to deal with. Mr General here.." Mad John motioned to The General who was still shaking like the Pope, oblivious to all but fear. "...has told me as much as I'm sure he can about the unfortunate events of last night, and we can't even think about bailing them out until tomorrow morning when the courts open. Loud-As, you and Chaos go and see Lockstock, take Dum Dum with you. Joker, I'll need to talk to your good lady wife if I might. Numb, I'll be needing you with me tomorrow. The rest of you, ears to the ground, I want to know anything you can find out, badge numbers, shoe size, I don't care, anything that might be relevant. Prepare yourselves gentlemen, it seems we may be at war."

A heavy silence fell over the room, stern faces taking in what they had just heard. Several of them weren't the kind of faces you would ever want to be at war with unless you were, for instance, the entire United States Of America. They were the kind of faces that looked rather pleased at the idea of being at war, like it would make a nice change from all the endless partying. The silence was broken by the tap, tap, tapping of Numb Tongue, smiling quietly to himself as he resumed chopping out a line that would keep most normal humans awake for the rest of the month.

"Um," said Dum Dum cautiously. "Mr John, Mad.. um,"

"Yes Dum Dum? And just John will do."

"Um, who are we at war with?"

"Good question!" beamed Mad John. "And one that I notice no one else thought to ask. Shows initiative. Not entirely sure yet, but not to worry. I'm sure we'll find out and, rest assured, you'll be among the first to know."

"Fair enough," shrugged Dum Dum.

"Good man! That's the spirit! That sort of attitude will get you far. Meeting adjourned." And with that Mad John rapped on the table with an ornate gavel tipped with a small silver skull. "Now then, Numb, I notice you're being rather shy with the marching powder. If you'd be so kind, it has been a long night... Tight git."

The General was still in a state of shock as his tried to process what had just happened. Mad John could apparently read his mind, the club was "at war" with some unknown enemy, and Numb Tongue had been called a "tight git" without anyone having their arms pulled off and inserted into any small orifices.

"War eh?" Dum Dum nudged him keenly in the ribs again. "It's exciting isn't it?"

The last thing that The General would ever describe war as was exciting. Having been forced into the Marines straight out of school by his parents, The General had been as surprised as everyone else when he'd sailed through basic training. Unfortunately the first time he'd been sent to a war zone all that training had gone out of the window, and the first time he'd been shot at he'd dropped his rifle and run away, leaving his fellow Marines to fend for themselves. He was court-martialled and given a dishonourable discharge, made worse by the fact that the gunshots had turned out to be some kids letting off firecrackers.

"Fancy a game of pool?"

"No, Dum Dum, not really. I really think I need to get some sleep. I feel a bit sick."

The gathering wound itself down and it seemed that there was nothing much else to do beyond having a few beers and watching UFC reruns. Scarecrow, Vincent, and Joker adjourned to the workshop, while Mad John, Chaos, and Numb Tongue headed for Mad John's study. Before Mad John left he tossed Dum Dum his bike keys.

"Take my bike tomorrow, Dum Dum," he said. "Your Harley sounds awful. I'll get Scarecrow to look at it."

"Thanks Mad, I mean, thanks John," Dum Dum's face lit up.

"No worries. If I need to pop out I'll take your XS."

"See, I said he was all right," grinned Dum Dum, as he and The General left the boardroom. "Fuckin' hell! '37 Knucklehead and he's letting me ride it!"

A worried look crossed Dum Dum's face as he considered his riding abilities or lack thereof. He still fell of quite a lot. "I'll go careful on it," he added.

The General could only nod stupidly. Without Dum Dum's spare bike he was effectively a pedestrian, trapped at the clubhouse unless he fancied a long walk and an even longer train ride home. Full patch members did not give rides to prospects, so Mad John had deliberately set him up to be dependent on the club, forcing him to stay nearby. It occurred to The General that maybe he was safer here anyway. If the club was at war with some unknown enemy then he didn't want to be going out anywhere on his own and, while the clubhouse was an obvious target, at least here there was safety in numbers.

As The General left the boardroom he glanced up at the corner of the hallway, but the spider was gone, leaving a large web in its stead. The General took a closer look and instantly wished that he hadn't. Perfectly symmetrical, the web was littered with the same kind of strange symbols that The General had seen all over Mad John's study. It was a message. When he had finished shaking, The General went straight to bed in one of the clubhouses' many spare rooms and some hours later he finally got to a fitful sleep, full of night-sweats, and strange and terrifying dreams. The spider watched him from the corner of the room.

CHAPTER SIX

The next week was a difficult time for the four Aberrant prospects, not least because they had little idea what was going on or what they were supposed to be looking out for. Only Dum Dum had any real insight, which meant, as usual, that he had none whatsoever. The day after the club meeting - all fifteen minutes of it to inform them that they were at war - he had gone with Loud-As and Chaos to a desolate looking industrial estate in Hackney and been told to wait outside and keep watch. Ten minutes later Chaos came out and told him not to keep watch anymore because he was drawing attention. But he still had to stay outside.

Dum Dum had spent the next half an hour trying, and completely failing, to look like he wasn't on guard, and then the three of them had left and gone for a late breakfast. As far as Dum Dum could tell, this Lockstock bloke that they'd been to see was in fact two blokes, twin brothers, called Lock and Stock, with pretensions of being East London gangsters. Their dad was a big fat bloke called Barrel, except you weren't to call him that because he was a big fat bloke. It was hardly useful information, though it did rather suggest that the club were arming themselves, and Dum Dum said he had the curious feeling that he was being watched all day.

"Well," he told the other prospects later that evening, "not like watched, but more like someone knew what I was thinking."

Again, hardly a well of useful information beyond when you'll be having another bacon sandwich and which bands are coming through town next, thought The General unkindly. Dum Dum wasn't exactly one of life's great thinkers and having been cooped up in the clubhouse all day, as he was every day that he wasn't at work, The General was in no mood for him. The trouble was that someone had known what The General was thinking, too. He was sure of it. And it hadn't been bacon sandwiches and Motörhead. Although he found no evidence, he felt watched the whole time, and would have been somewhat relieved to know that Dum Dum felt the same, if not for the fact that it confirmed his suspicions.

Two days later the prospects were instructed not to use or even carry their mobile phones, and Dum Dum was told to turn off the GPS on his bike, which caused him to spend most of the rest of the week completely lost. Having spent almost an entire day riding around in increasingly angry circles he eventually complained and was told that GPS and phone signals can be traced so he should buy a map and take a stab at learning to read. Thinner skins would have taken offence, but instead Dum Dum took lessons and with help from Scarecrow managed to work out rough navigation by following bus routes.

But almost three weeks later there was still no real news about Mental and Flashback, other than the fact that they had been refused bail and were on remand in Pentonville. And the four prospects heard nothing from their president other than the music from his study, the dulled thump of some stoner rock tune played over and over again.

"Mad John's thinking music," Vincent told Scarecrow as the four of them breakfasted in a particularly greasy spoon, trying to judge the timing of their meals with the weather to avoid getting soaked in one of the frequent downpours. Great grey clouds like battleships hung in the sky and there was a bitter chill to the air.

"Well, he's doing a lot of thinking," said Scarecrow, wiping condensation from the window and peering out to check on their bikes. "You think he's all right?"

"Dunno," shrugged Vincent. "I remember he used to do that a lot when I was a kid. It was just before me and my mum moved away, he used to play the same song over and over...well, not the same song, it was Hawkwind or something back then. I only ever saw him once after that."

"Where do you think he was? Jail?"

"Dunno," said Vincent. "He's still got a tan and you don't get them in Parkhurst. And you'd have thought the rest of the club would've known about it. No one's ever mentioned visiting him, but then, they all act like he's never been away."

"I asked him the other day," said Scarecrow, turning his attention back to his egg and chips. "He said he'd been to see a man about three dogs."

Scarecrow still worked for the same bike shop under the railway arches in Bethnal Green that he'd worked at since he first moved to London. It was one of those rare shops that did good, honest work, and, if anything, under-charged their customers. It was the kind of place bikers would stop off at just to hang out, especially on days when the weather was their enemy. Scarecrow was there rain or shine working long hours, but had almost pulled a sickie one particularly miserable morning.

It was early, still dark, and having crashed at the clubhouse, he padded downstairs in thick socks and long johns in search of coffee. Though it was muted Scarecrow could hear the now familiar riff from Mad John's study, his thinking music. Pulling on a t-shirt he padded further downstairs and knocked on the door, unsure how loud to knock above the music or even if he should disturb the club president at all at a time like this. There was a lull in the music and he knocked louder, perhaps hearing voices on the other side of the door, or at least Mad John's voice.

Yes, it was definitely Mad John: "I'm going to need you to keep an eye on the clubhouse for me for a while..."

Scarecrow could only hear one side of the conversation, but it sounded important. No one came in or out of the clubhouse without Mad John knowing about it.

"What? No, of course they don't have to ask permission, I just want to know everyone who comes in or out of the clubhouse..."

"I don't know how long we'll be away..."

"Well, I hope not that long, but only time will tell."

"Yes, the whole club."

Scarecrow realised that he was eavesdropping and knocked on the door again, firmly this time.

"Come in, Scarecrow." It was an old trick, though Scarecrow had no idea how he did it.

Mad John was alone in his study, a single lamp lighting his desk, which was piled high with ancient looking books bound in faded brown leather. It took a moment for Scarecrow's eyes to adjust to the gloom and it seemed, in that moment, that things were shuffling into the shadows, a vague sense of movement as if something was trying not to be seen.

Mad John's study had always fascinated Scarecrow, and he was quietly pleased that it still looked exactly the same as it had when Mad John disappeared. It was like stepping back in time a hundred or more years, Mad John's nearest concession to the modern age being the lamp and the old record player, to which he had grudgingly added a CD player. There was no telephone in here either, so, unless Satan was skating to work and Mad John had got a mobile phone, it was likely that he'd been talking to himself. It was nice to know that nothing had changed. Scarecrow had missed his old friend pacing around the clubhouse talking to random corners of the ceiling, though this was the first time he could ever remember him behaving as if they answered back. Still as mad as a bag of weasels then. There was a clue in the name.

"Well, look at you," beamed Mad John. He hugged Scarecrow, grabbing his shoulders and looking him up and down like a proud father. "Put on a bit of weight," he grinned.

"Hopefully some of it's muscle. I've been training a bit with Numb Tongue."

"Yes, I heard. Very fast hands I'm told, though I'd expect nothing less, of course," Mad John trailed off, looking Scarecrow in the eyes. "I can't say how pleased I am that you're prospecting for us," he said. "I'm only sorry I wasn't here to welcome you. I'm afraid I had some rather important business to attend to and it took rather longer than I expected."

"Five years."

"Yes, so I'm told," Mad John grinned, a stickler for time when it came to hours and minutes, but with no concept at all of days, months, or even years sometimes. "Like I said, it took a bit longer..."

Even though Scarecrow was the prospect Mad John made them both coffee, and they caught up as much as real friends can or need to after many years apart. Mad John was overjoyed to hear that Buggane had escaped from prison a couple of years back, and even more pleased that the club had been to visit him again at the TT races, where Scarecrow had won yet another trophy.

"Buggane's fine," Scarecrow assured him, before smiling. "He's been a dear friend to myself and the club for many, many years, and he's stronger than you think."

"You too, I think," said Mad John, his wild eyes shining that strange blue that never seemed to match his dark complexion.

Five years wasn't so long in a lifetime but Scarecrow could swear Mad John hadn't aged at all. Not that it was possible to pin his age down more accurately than between thirty-five and fifty-five, but, thinking about it, he had always looked like that, slightly weather worn, but more by sun than rain, with a tan that never entirely faded.

"And speaking of time," Mad John said suddenly, as if they had been, "you're going to be late for work if you don't get a shift on, young man."

"I told him I was thinking of pulling a sickie," Scarecrow told Vincent later, mopping up egg yolk with his toast, "and he goes on about needing me at work, ears to the ground and stuff. I still don't know what the fuck we're supposed to be listening for."

"Kyuss," said Dum Dum, with his mouth full.

"What?"

"It's Odyssey by Kyuss."

"What is?"

"Mad John's thinking music."

"Well, whatever it is, it's getting on my nerves," muttered the General, slurping at bad coffee. He hated this place, hated the way dust and cold blew in from the street every time someone opened the door, the menu with its pictures of food that looked nothing like what eventually turned up, lukewarm, on your table, the old men wheezing and coughing. Most of all he hated the old men, with their yellow teeth and yellow fingers and greasy dandruff hair. He hated the way that death and fear seeped from them like the smell of sweat and stale alcohol and stolen Old Spice that lingers beneath half a century of tobacco smoke. He hated the way they'd all lower their voices just a fraction when Aberrant came into the café, like they'd interrupted some wheezing, cancerous, conspiracy. There was one of them looking at him now, some wizened old fuck with egg yolk all down the lapel of his worn out suit.

"What the fuck are you looking at?" grunted The General.

The old man regarded him for a moment, slowly chewing on the end of a leaking Biro. The General was surprised to see no fear in him. They were all scared around here, a lifetime of struggle and debt and doffing their caps to nasty East London gangsters who would cut them as soon as look at them. And yet, pissed by lunchtime, they'd still sit here and croak on about the good old days, "cor blimey guv'nor, I was at Ronnie and Reggie's funerals..."

But not this one. This one just stared at The General, a look of genuine evil in his over-sized eyes. He considered his response, while regarding The

General in much the same way as a child who's about to pull the wings off a fly. The man seemed to radiate nastiness, real creepy, like he tortured people for shits and giggles. It was The General who looked away first.

"Nothing," said Creepy. "Nothing at all."

Creepy returned to his crossword puzzle. "Long eventful journey...seven letters," he said aloud. "O, something, something S..."

CHAPTER SEVEN

On the morning of Joker's birthday Scarecrow was holed up in the clubhouse workshop, trying to solve an electrical problem on a project bike he was building based around a Triumph Rocket 3. Unfortunately Dum Dum was trying to help which meant the job was taking twice as long as it should, but he didn't mind the company too much since Dum Dum was playing DJ on his I-pod, and always had a knack for playing the right tune at the right time, if not finding the right tool.

The mood was relaxed and productive, weed smoke hanging in the air in slow moving circles. Whatever war the club was supposed to be involved in had shown absolutely no signs of materialising, and spring was around the corner at last. Even The General had got over his gibbering paranoia that death, rather than spring, was around every corner, and had bravely ventured out of the clubhouse on his own for the first time in a month, albeit to meet half the club at the greasy spoon before heading to a swap meet for the afternoon.

Aside from the incarceration of two of their members, life for Aberrant MC and its prospects had returned to as near as could, for them at least, be considered normal. At Scarecrow's request Dum Dum had just put on some Crystal Method and was rolling another joint, when Mad John surprised them by sticking his head around the door.

"Sounds like I might have some competition," he grinned at Dum Dum.

"Hardly," said Dum Dum. "I heard you were a wicked DJ back in the day."

"I was?" said Mad John, looking slightly put out. "This was years ago I'm sure of it and I rather thought I was quite good."

"Itsh yush a hurn of phase, Yohn," said Scarecrow, still holding a small flashlight in his teeth and fiddling with the wiring somewhere under the bike. He took the torch out out of his mouth. "It's a turn of phrase: back in the day. It means happening years ago, at the origin of something, that kind of thing. And wicked means good."

"Does it *really*?" said Mad John, his head tipped lightly to one side as if considering and remembering the phrase. It was an odd habit, but one that Scarecrow was familiar with. "New to me, but in that case, yes, Dum Dum, I was quite a wicked DJ back in the day, though I say so myself. So interesting the way words change their meaning...a wicked DJ back in the day." Mad John smiled to himself. "Anyway, I need a couple of things taking care of. Scarecrow, I need you to call these people for me and employ them both immediately."

"Private detectives?" Scarecrow glanced down at the papers Mad John had given him. Maybe there was a witness that Mental and Flashback needed finding or something. Maybe there was some dirt on the tranny that Metal had battered, something that would make him drop the charges. At this point it seemed like a long shot since both of them were facing an ever increasing array of charges, the prosecution pressing for attempted murder.

"Brilliant idea isn't it?" Mad John beamed. "I'll want them both to start today, of course."

"Wait a minute," said Scarecrow, taking a closer look at the papers. "You want me to hire these two private detectives to watch each other? How's that going to help Mental and Flashback?"

"Help Mental and Flashback? What are you talking about? It won't help them at all. Well, it'll make them laugh I suppose. It's Joker's birthday present, you know how he likes practical jokes! I rather thought we could have side bets on how long it takes them to go crazy."

Scarecrow had to admit that it was a perfect gift to the man who was already plotting for April Fools Day years in advance, having pranked the entire club on numerous occasions. Well, the entire club except for Numb Tongue, whose sense of humour had yet to be pinned down to the point where anyone would be tempted to play games with it. Joker was the first name that came to mind when Scarecrow had his weird run in with the cops a month or so back, but he'd dismissed it just as quickly due to the man's pathological hatred of anything with a uniform and a badge. Detectives, as far as Joker was concerned, were borderline authority figures, so driving a couple of them nuts by having them running around endlessly spying on each other would amuse him no end. Joker and mischief went hand in hand.

"Dum Dum, I need you to..." Mad John trailed off.

Giving Dum Dum a task any more complicated than tying his own bootlaces could be a risky business, and this one involved going somewhere without getting lost, which Dum Dum proved to be consistently useless at. He still had to follow behind the 73 bus just to find his way to work.

"Second thoughts, where's Ian and Vincent?"

"Um, Gen'ral's at the swap meet," said Dum Dum, "and Vincent's, um, dunno, might be over at Numb Tongue's gym."

"Right," said Mad John. "Scarecrow, when you're done calling those detectives go and find Vincent. Tell him I need him to keep Joker distracted for the day. I don't care how he does it, but Joker's not to come near the clubhouse until at least nine o'clock. Dum Dum, if you'd be so kind as to come with me, I have some very heavy things that need lifting and then there's some balloons to blow up."

"I like balloons," beamed Dum Dum, and they left the workshop.

Scarecrow made the calls to the unfortunate detectives whose lives were about to take a turn for the ridiculous. It was good to know that the club still had a sense of humour. These had been a strange few weeks, with an underlying tension that was never really spoken of aloud. Aberrant were at war, but life went on as usual, with no visible threat from anywhere and no visible enemy. It got tiring being jumpy the whole time when you didn't know what you were supposed to be jumping at.

As far as Scarecrow could tell they had no problems with any other clubs, the last one being solved by Numb Tongue and then nailed to the clubhouse wall some years ago. And maybe there were a few more cops around than usual, but that was hardly news to an outlaw club. It came with the territory and you watched your backs, something that Aberrant had apparently been doing with great success until now. It felt like the club were blessed sometimes. At any given point in the day at least half of them could be breaking a dozen or more laws, from speeding and possession of class A's, all the way to Mad John robbing banks, and yet no one ever seemed to get more than a parking ticket.

London's ever increasing traffic made the ride over to Numb Tongue's gym more of chore than a pleasure. Even with Scarecrow's talent for splitting lanes there simply weren't enough gaps to go anywhere, and he spent most of his time sitting behind buses that belched black fumes at him. And the pot holes were getting worse, too, great gouges and grooves and caverns in the road. Now that he came to think about it, Scarecrow couldn't actually remember the last time he'd really enjoyed riding a bike since his brief chase with the cops. Just rain and bad traffic every day, rush hour every hour. Jesus, what happened to this club run he'd overheard Mad John talking about?

"Better be a bloody good one, not some half-arsed biker rally in a muddy field near Watford with rubbish bands and lumpy beer," Scarecrow muttered under his breath, as a young mother decided to use her child's push chair to test his brakes. South of France maybe, at least somewhere you could put a few miles on the clock on decent roads, somewhere you needed a passport. As Scarecrow daydreamed of long open roads, a couple more grimy buses conspired to make him into sandwich meat, before grinding to a halt and neatly trapping him in a large red corridor of poison, until his eyes watered. Fucking rat race.

Numb Tongue's gym completely failed to lighten his mood. He liked the place at night when the glow above the door looked welcoming, a beacon for all the lost kids on nearby council estates, who now had to take it in turns watching training because there were so many of them. They'd sit there around the edges of the gym, silently watching as these gigantic bikers knocked the crap out of each other and tied each other in knots, and then they'd sit outside recounting all the moves to their friends until it was their turn again. On some nights it got to where Numb Tongue would have one of the prospects work out rotations for the little fuckers, but Numb Tongue seemed to enjoy having them around. And if he ever heard that one of them was being bullied, he'd quietly take them aside and show them how to break the bullies' kneecap in four places.

By night the entrance to the gym was a doorway to sanctuary, and somehow the name above the door, The Flame Of The Woods, made sense, even though the nearest woods were in a dogshit infested park several miles away.

By day The Flame, or FTW as it was more commonly known, looked like a prison. Not Pentonville where you could blast past late at night to let them know you were out there at three in the morning - something they'd all been doing regularly to keep up Mental and Flashback's spirits. FTW was like some Eastern Bloc prison, the only building standing in a weed ravaged wasteland that had yet to be spotted by developers.

It was no wonder that the local kids had only noticed the place in the last few years. On greyer days it was difficult to see where the sky ended and the building began unless you noticed the glimmer of razor-wire, and the wall alongside the duel carriageway blocked most of the view from the council estate. That's how the kids got there, playing chicken with the traffic and speeding headlights across four lanes, and then scrambling up the wall at the other side. Sooner or later one of them was going to get themselves spread all over the road, but it was difficult to find the place any other way unless you had transport and knew the back-streets of East London intimately. Even then you'd never even notice the place until you rounded the last corner in a dead end street, to what looked like the arse end of a building site or disused car park.

There were half a dozen or so bikes lined up outside and Scarecrow pulled in alongside them and killed his engine. He could tell who was here by the bikes: Numb Tongue's Harley, obviously, Loud's GSXR, Apple's Fireblade, Smiler, Andy One-leg, Chaos, and, yes, Vincent's CBX. At the end of the line there was a mean looking Guzzi that Scarecrow had seen parked pretty much everywhere in London over the last few years, one of those enigmatic machines that he could never associate with a rider even though they clearly put decent miles on the thing. He'd become attached to the bike in a way, even if it was merely a flicker every time he passed it, somehow knowing that it was ridden by a kindred spirit, flying way low under the radar. It was ticking quietly to itself as it cooled so whoever owned it hadn't been here long.

Scarecrow had never been to any other gym, but he was pretty sure they didn't all look like FTW, a cross between the inside of some Berlin dive bar and a state of the art facility, all black and chrome with dulled red lighting so the punchbags looked like real bodies hanging from the beams above. The place even had a full sized octagon with enough room for a couple of hundred spectators on ground level and another fifty or so on the balcony that circled it.

The room had been nicknamed The Point, as in The Point Of No Return. On fight nights it was open only to invited guests, and long black cars parked outside, though never too close to the bikes. Some of the best underground fighters in the country had been through here at some point, even Lenny McLean back in the day, and the local mobsters would pay good money to see them fight, despite an uneasy relationship with Aberrant that dated back many years.

Maybe twenty years ago they'd offered Numb Tongue a substantial amount of money to take a dive against some local nutter who fancied making a reputation for himself. He was also the son of one of the biggest gangsters in North London. Scarecrow had never heard the story first hand from old Flapjaw himself, but the upshot was that Numb Tongue took their money and then completely dismantled the gangster's son, dislocating everything that would come out of a socket and breaking anything that wouldn't, in just under a minute.

By all accounts the next few weeks were like a Guy Ritchie movie, and there was still a black stain up the side of the building from where the gangsters had tried to torch the place. Scarecrow wondered for a moment if that was where the gym had got its name, but that still didn't explain what woods had to do with anything. Either way that war was long resolved and the gangsters knew never to offer one of the club a dive again.

Not that Numb Tongue fought much these days, but there was always some mouthy little shit ready to take on one of Aberrant's Fight Crew, occasionally even a real mixed martial artist looking to step up their game. The latter were treated with the utmost respect. The former generally went home with their teeth in a bag.

Scarecrow followed the shouting of "Elbow! Elbow! Elbow!" down the long corridor past Numb Tongue's office. He caught a glimpse of Numb in conversation with someone, or at least listening to someone, since he considered anything more than "yes" or "no" to be excessively verbose. He turned left at the weights room, and down another long corridor as the shouts grew louder. There was a sudden thump followed by a collected "ooh!" suggesting that one of the elbows had landed.

Inside the cage Loud-As and Smiler had been doing some sparring, just a gentle knockabout, when things had got a little out of hand. After the pair had been separated a referee was called in and they'd been allowed to fight it out. Smiler's nose was now very horribly broken. Again.

Scarecrow failed to see the attraction. He liked watching the fights, but he had no real desire to hit anyone and certainly wasn't going to risk his good looks to prove a point. The one and only time he'd stepped into the cage he had simply dodged every blow from his opponent until the poor sod got tired and gave up without landing a signal punch. Numb Tongue and some of the club sat and watched the whole thing, and for a minute Scarecrow thought he'd be stripped of his prospect patch. Instead Numb Tongue clapped his big hands together, grinning from ear to ear. He even shouted "Yes!" when Scarecrow was absolutely nowhere near a spinning back fist that should have landed. There was no higher praise and it was one of the few times he ever remembered Numb looking really happy, but it was safe to say that Scarecrow wouldn't be getting his Fight Crew patch any time soon.

"Ow! For fug's sage!" grumbled Smiler.

"Sit still you big baby," Andy One-Leg said, twisting the remains of Smiler's nose back and forth in an attempt to get it to point in the right direction. "It's fucked, mate, "he said finally. "I don't know why you keep fighting him. You never win and he's broken your nose four times!"

"Yeah, bud one day," smiled Smiler.

"Yeah, yeah, one day you'll knock him out." Andy patted Smiler on the shoulder. "One day, mate," he said, and lurched out of the cage, looking as always like his prosthetic leg, attached at the left knee, was slightly too long.

Scarecrow spotted Vincent over in the far corner with Chaos and Apples. Evidently Apples had been foolish enough to bet on Smiler and was parting with a large wad of bills from a fancy silver money clip hidden somewhere inside his hideous white racing leathers.

"What?" he'd protested when he'd first shown up in them a couple of weeks ago, complete with the Aberrant colours on the back. "These are fuckin' pukka, these are, man! The birds fuckin' love 'em."

"Looks like it!" said Joker. "Looks like they've shit all over it."

"Bollocks mate! You wouldn't know style if it bi'chew on the 'arris! It was only last year you was still wearin' fackin' Lionel's."

Apples had extravagant, if rather poor, taste in pretty much everything: women, clothes, motorcycles, aftershave, you name it, Apples threw money at it with generally disastrous results. Suits that would make a pimp blush, aftershave that acted as an insect repellent, a motorbike that looked like Jackson Pollock had thrown up on it, and all of it stupidly expensive. And with those stupidly expensive tastes came stupidly expensive and, often, expensively stupid women.

Apples was a romantic at heart but had somehow got it into his head that since money attracts women, the more he threw it around the sooner it would attract the one he'd waited all his life for. You had to give him points for persistence, but so far all he had succeeded in doing was making a great many strippers very wealthy.

On club runs his white leathers made him stand out like a capped tooth in a rotten mouth. Add to that a Cockney accent so thick that it bordered on a speech impediment and you could be pretty sure that the aforementioned strippers were usually just completely baffled by the poor man. Sure he was loud, but he was also kind, and generous to a fault, fiercely loyal, wealthy, good looking even, now that he was losing the paunch. And yet he'd sit there chatting away and throwing out bills like a broken cash machine, and they'd go, "Sorry love, I don't know what you're on about. Do you want another lapdance?"

"How much did you lose?" Scarecrow smiled as he approached them.

"Fuckin' monkey!"

Scarecrow had no idea what a monkey was. Well, obviously he knew about the ones in trees and that they probably had something to do with Oasis, but as a monetary term he hadn't the faintest. A pony's twenty quid? Is that right? So a monkey... No idea. Five hundred? It looked like at least a couple of hundred.

Apples spoke no other language than Cockney rhyming slang and if people didn't understand him he just said it louder. That's even where he'd got his nickname, 'apples and pears' being Cockney rhyming slang for 'stairs', the one term in this gibberish that anyone with a postcode not beginning in E would actually understand. And even that was nonsense! What the hell did fruit have to do with stairs?

Scarecrow understood that the language had developed in the East End as a means of staying one step ahead of the cops, but given that they now had surveillance cameras and computers, and not just some flatfoot running around going "'ello, 'ello, 'ello, what's all this then?" the whole thing seemed fairly redundant.

"I can't believe you bet on Smiler," said Scarecrow. "No offence, Smiler."

"Dud taged," said Smiler, still dabbing at his nose with a towel that looked like it came from a murder scene.

"I ditn't fackin' bet on 'im!" said Apples incredulously. "What are you, fuckin' radio rental? I bet he'd get knocked out in the first. No offence, Smiler."

"Dud taged," said Smiler, who was pleased to have made it to the second round.

"What brings you 'ere anyway, me old China?" said Apples. "Need some more dancin' lessons?"

If fighting were dancing then Scarecrow was indeed a ballerina, while Smiler was still doing the pogo. It didn't help that Scarecrow was quite ridiculously good looking to the extent that random strangers, usually the jealous boyfriend of some girl who'd been eyeing him from across a bar, would occasionally attempt to do something about it. Sometimes with a bottle.

On such occasions, Smiler - had he gleaned such unwanted attention - would be all head-butts and windmilling fists and chair legs. And, more than once, attempting to fit someone's head in a postbox. Scarecrow would simply not be in the way of anything the jealous boyfriend threw at him, and the boyfriend would either get embarrassed and go away or the bouncers would show up and throw him out. Scarecrow could do this without spilling his drink. Aside from the odd fight night he only ventured into FTW to train on quiet nights with Numb Tongue, the old master often learning more than his student.

No one was really sure why Smiler kept insisting on fighting Loud-As. The two of them were best friends, proper best friends for ten years or more, and yet Smiler had this weird bee in his bonnet about beating Loud-As in a fight that somehow dated back to some macho crap on the night they first met.

It was a fight Smiler could never win. Aside from being about a foot taller than Smiler and built like the proverbial brick shithouse, Loud-As looked like he was a completely different species. Where Smiler was, he admitted himself, pasty-faced, and a little doughy around the edges, Loud-As had the kind of tan that was ingrained from doing hard manual labour outdoors year after year, his skin now almost leather so his long-faded tattoos looked like stains in mahogany. His close-shaved head may as well have been a crash helmet. And that ear didn't make him look any less formidable, bitten off in a pub car park and then apparently sewn back on by someone with no previous experience of handling a needle and thread.

But still, every year or so, Smiler got it into his head that the few hours of training he'd done when he wasn't drinking would somehow equip him to tackle this lunatic. And, every year or so, he would be proved unpleasantly and irrefutably wrong. His nose was now almost completely flat.

"Actually," said Scarecrow, "I'm on a mission from His Madness. He wants Vincent to keep Joker distracted for the day so he doesn't go to the clubhouse and fuck up his own birthday party."

"I don't know where he is!" protested Vincent. "Ever since we had to stop using mobiles, I never know where the fuck anyone is!"

"I fig he's ad hobe," said Smiler.

"Yeah, he's at home," nodded Loud-As. "I was round there this morning. His missus said she'd keep him there as long as she could, so he'll be about ready to be rescued."

"Is she that bad?" said Vincent, not wanting to traipse all the way across town to get involved in a domestic argument.

"What Lilith?" said Loud-As. "She's a diamond, she is. Salt of the earth. But that was a couple of hours ago, and I doubt very much that he'll want to spent the rest of his birthday fixing broken drawer handles and oiling anything that dares to squeak."

"Good point," said Vincent, grabbing his helmet and jacket and patting himself down for bike keys.

"Ain't you ever met Lilly, then?" said Apples, with a suspicious looking glint in his eye.

"Don't think so," shrugged Vincent, instantly feeling that there was something he wasn't being told. "I've been round his place a bunch of times, but she wasn't in."

"Oh she was in all right," grinned Apples. "She don't ever go out!"

"Well, I never met her. Maybe she was asleep."

"She don't ever sleep either!" Apples gave him a wink.

Figures, thought Vincent. Joker was one of the few club members who still bothered with speed, and if you were around him for too long you'd eventually end up doing a line and then staying up for days on end tinkering with an engine or making a table. It would make sense if his wife never slept.

All too often Vincent had sworn off speed after long, long nights, always night even though the days had definitely passed. And sure, they'd have a new table, some fantastically ornate work with dragons and skulls carved all over the place. But the price of the spiritual hangover, that filthy tainted feeling that clings to your skin after too much speed, was way more than just buying a fucking table. And Joker had to be fifty...wasn't today his 50th? No one seemed to have mentioned a number, but all that speed at his age couldn't be good for his heart.

Still, whoopee cushions notwithstanding, he liked visiting Joker's place because he usually came away with a cool gift. Joker seemed to lose interest in almost everything he made shortly after he'd finished making it and Vincent had come away with everything from swords to swinging arms, all of it built to last a lifetime, and each piece entirely individual. Vincent's current bike was sporting a chain guard and exhaust system courtesy of a bored and speeding Joker.

Vincent and Scarecrow headed out of the gym, the unexpected sunshine momentarily blinding them both as they stepped outside. The mean old Guzzi was gone, but even though Scarecrow was a little disappointed not to have finally met the owner, he felt better for knowing that his intuitions about the rider were probably right. Any friend of Numb Tongue's was a friend of his, club member or not.

"Which way are you going? he asked Vincent.

"Dunno," shrugged Vincent. "Round the wossname and over the flyover, try not to hit any of Numb's fan club on the way."

"I nearly hit one of 'em the other day," Scarecrow shook his head. "Little fucker legged it right out in front of me. Loud-As says it'll cull the weak!"

"Yeah, that's why he was giving them rides home on his bike the other night. He's a fucking softy really."

"I'll tell him you said that."

"Ah now," grinned Vincent. "No need to be hasty."

"I'll ride some of it with you if you like," said Scarecrow. "I'm going back to the clubhouse, but I'm not in any hurry. I'm not gonna get the Triumph finished today, and Dum Dum was last seen on balloon duty. Don't ask," he added when Vincent gave a quizzical look.

"Fair enough," said Vincent. "I've got to get a skip on though if his missus is keeping him busy with chores. She's probably gnawed his ears off enough by now. I overheard Andy saying she's a proper witch!"

"I don't think that's what he meant," said Scarecrow, putting his gloves on. "He meant it literally!"

CHAPTER EIGHT

Joker's house always raised a wry smile from Vincent. Tucked away in quiet residential streets, all speed humps and window gardens and Neighbourhood Watch. It would have done The Munsters proud. Window box, picket fence, window box, window box, black walls and gargoyles! The parking situation was equally telling, with lines of those shoebox cars and then Lilith's gleaming vintage hearse with Joker's ZRX 1200 chop parked alongside, both blacker than midnight and oozing stylish menace. Surprisingly the neighbours loved them.

"You looking for J, my darlin'?" said an old lady, poking her head up over the hedge as Vincent got off his bike.

It was funny how the old dears never called him Joker, like it was disrespectful or he would get offended. Or maybe just because old people habitually ignore what you might like to be called and use an embarrassingly endearing name of their own.

"It's J's birthday you know," continued the old lady. "I told him, I said, if I was forty years younger..."

"Then I'd still be a cradle snatcher," said Joker, opening the front door. "Heard your bike," he nodded at Vincent. "Come to help with the spring cleaning or are you just here to keep me away from the clubhouse so I don't spoil the surprise party?"

"I don't look good in a maid's outfit."

"What, with those pretty little legs! I caught Dum Dum wrapping my birthday present the other day, in case you were wondering. Bless him, he couldn't think of a lie quick enough and then he got all flustered and let on about the party. Don't tell him I told you."

With the old lady still flirting outrageously over the privets, Joker and Vincent headed inside to the living room, where Joker had clearly not been doing any spring cleaning at all. On Any Sunday was on the big screen TV, with Malcolm about to tackle the widowmaker, and beside the comfy chair was a cold beer, a joint, and a bacon sandwich.

"Well, it *is* my birthday," shrugged Joker. "Pull up a seat and I'll get Lilly to make you a sarnie."

Somehow the image of Lilith preparing bacon sandwiches - or indeed Joker instructing her to do so - didn't sit well with Vincent's mental image of her. Her recent visit to the clubhouse, at Mad John's request, had been treated with a mixture of curiosity and, for want of a better word, reverence, like they were getting a visit from the Queen.

She'd shown up in the dead of night in that shiny, shiny hearse, apparently the same one used in Marc Bolan's funeral, and was ushered swiftly to Mad John's study. Her car stayed outside for many hours and then she was ushered away again, a ghost of the wee hours. Vincent had caught only a glimpse of her as she left, but had to admit that she had some style, film noir almost, a long way from the Hot Topic goth he'd half expected.

Her skin had literally seemed to glow white in the moonlight and there was such grace that she appeared to glide to her car rather than walk, her long black dress reaching just the tips of equally long black heels. System Of A Down's 'Old School Hollywood' popped into Vincent's head, his mind perhaps registering that she looked as if she were from a different age, while a crueller part of his mind wondered what the hell she saw in Joker with his beer belly, semi-mullet, and rats ass beard. Joker actually looked a lot meaner than he really was, that sense of humour keeping him in check most of the time, but still it was hard to imagine a man who liked drinking real ale from metal tankards being married to Lauren Bacall. Vincent sat down carefully, checking first for whoopee cushions.

"You'll be Vincent," said a voice like honey over ice.

Lilith was standing in the kitchen doorway wearing worn blue jeans and a wrinkled Harley t-shirt, a million miles from the brief glimpse Vincent had caught of her in the moonlight, though a backlight from the kitchen gave the impression that her snow white skin still glowed. Her complexion was flaw-less, long black hair hanging just so. Nice tits, too, thought the part of Vincent's mind that he occasionally wished would fuck off. Lilith's eyes batted down as if reading his thoughts and then back up to meet his eyes.

"I've not met you before," she said, offering her hand. Vincent wasn't quiet sure if he was supposed to kiss it or shake it.

"Vincent," he said pointlessly.

"A pleasure meeting you," Lilith said, after holding his hand for a few more seconds than he felt comfortable with. Her touch was like silk, but there was no hint of flirting. It was more like she was sizing him up, scrutinising him.

"Yes," she said, finally releasing his hand and giving the merest hint of a nod. "Welcome."

"You want ketchup?" shouted Joker from the kitchen.

"Ah, that'll be the birthday boy burning your sandwich," Lilith smiled, radiating so much love to her husband that Vincent felt genuine shame for the part of his mind that had mentioned her tits. He was frequently in the company of tits so there was no need to be looking at some that were spoken for.

If anything, Vincent, the only child to a single mother who was never around, craved their relationship, that lock-tight love. It may have been a bit strange that Lilith never went out, but she and Joker had been together forever, even when he was a kid fetching cigarettes from the corner shop.

He remembered her turning up at the clubhouse in the old Hearse one hot Saturday afternoon, the chrome gleaming like mirrors in the sunlight. She looked the same as he remembered, barely a day older. Lucky git. But then, Joker knew he was a lucky git, and no matter how long or how far he strayed from her, he was always faithful. Joker wore his love for Lilith like he wore his colours, and would not hesitate to die for either.

"I'll go and give him a hand," said Lilith. "I got him the new UFC game if you need to keep him busy until the party. Just don't play as that Coatcheck bloke. Joker can't stand him."

Vincent took a seat again. Steve McQueen was blasting around the desert on the big screen and like most of the club Vincent had seen it so many times that he knew the commentary word for word. He noticed that Joker had been busy since his last visit: next to the TV there was the start of what looked like it was going to be a mechanical fish, possibly with potential as a very large bottle opener. Beside that, inevitably, was a new table made from mannequin arms and the back wheel off an old T100 Triumph.

It occurred to Vincent that he'd never actually been here in the daytime. Well, okay, technically he'd been here many times during the day, but this was the first time he'd arrived in daylight and not seen the place through a haze of teeth grinding, and the stench of whiskey to take the edge off it.

Aside from the TV and Joker's wild creations, the most dominant feature of the room was the bookshelf, almost an entire wall of books that Vincent liked to feel revealed almost too much about their owners. Harley Davidson-A History, The Greatest Pranks Of The 20th Century, and the usual suspects like Fear And Loathing and The Lord Of The Rings probably belonged to Joker, while The Satanic Witch, The Goddess Within and The Bombshell Manual Of Style were more likely to be Lilly's. Enochian Sex Magic, too. Lucky bugger. Vincent had no idea what enochian meant and did his best not to think about how magic the sex must be.

Not that he believed in all that nonsense, moon in your anus and all that bollocks, but whatever floats your boat. At least it explained why Andy had called her a witch. He'd been referring to all that earth mother, moonchild, mumbo jumbo, and thinking that lighting a candle that smells of moth balls will change destiny. Herb medicine and waving burning sticks about. Vincent's mother had been into all that crap, too. Still was, as far as he knew or cared.

Joker emerged from the kitchen with a couple of cold beers in one hand, a plate in the other bearing the kind of bacon sandwich that Scooby would be honoured to call a snack.

"Here you go mate," he said. "Let me know if you fancy a line when you're done."

"You're watching On Any Sunday on speed?"

"Yeah, yeah, man," grinned Joker. "Three times. Let me know if you fancy one."

"Not really, mate, to be honest," said Vincent, his internal organs momentarily relaxing until his brain reminded them that it was only a matter of time. "Oh fuck it, go on then. It is your birthday. I heard you've got the new UFC game, too!"

"You're on!" said Joker. "But no playing as Koscheck. I can't stand him!"

When Lilith walked into the room, although floated would be more accurate, she was again wearing a long black dress, a single diamond pendant sparkling against that white, white skin.

"You gentlemen might want to start your engines," she said, that honeyed ice slowly melting. "It's eleven thirty."

"What?" said Joker. "What the fuck? Oh shit! Why didn't you tell me? Never mind, you're telling me now."

Joker was well accustomed to losing days, even weeks, on speed, so a few hours between friends was not entirely unexpected, but, still, they were supposed to be at the clubhouse over an hour ago. The pair hurriedly got their shit together, crash helmets, jackets and keys, and Joker chopped out one for the road. On the way out of the house he popped his head into the bedroom, Vincent catching a glimpse of the old lady from earlier.

"See you later babes," said Joker.

"What no kiss?"

Joker disappeared into the room for a moment.

"Have fun," Lillith called after them as they left. "I'll see you when you get back."

"Is Lilith not coming?" asked Vincent, as they clumped downstairs and out to their bikes.

"No mate," said Joker, his face momentarily unable to hide a deep disappointment. "She doesn't ever go out."

CHAPTER NINE

"Zulus!" panicked The General, hammering desperately on the clubhouse door. "Thousands of them!"

He paced wildly on the doorstep, the Zulus watching his every move. He hammered on the door again, sweat running down his face. Dum Dum opened it and stuck his head out to see The General on his knees, with his hands on his head, pleading not to be shot.

"Zulus, Dum Dum," he said, sheer terror in his eyes. "Don't shoot! Please don't shoot!"

Dum Dum stepped outside and looked up and down a street that appeared to be completely empty. By the bus stop two black men were looking over to see what all the noise was about.

"Please don't let them kill me," whined The General from the doorstep.

Dum Dum looked over at the black men and shrugged.

"Sorry," he called, pulling The General to his feet. The General was now sweating profusely, eyes wide open, and tears streaming down his face.

"Listen to me," said Dum Dum. "Listen. You're just havin' a bad trip. There's no Zulus, it's just two blokes waiting for the bus."

"But..." stammered The General, confused and desperate.

"There's no Zulus," repeated Dum Dum. "Just take a few breaths and chill out for a minute. I'm surprised they didn't call the cops."

"Cops?" bleated The General, instantly panicking again.

"No, no, there's no cops. Now pull yourself together, you don't want the club seeing you like this. What did you take?"

"Stone gave me some acid," The General managed, tears still streaming down his face. "Fuckin' Zulus."

"There's no Zulus," said Dum Dum, his long scraggly hair flaring like an oil rig before writhing in a nest of snakes, his face contorting and pulsing like there was something under his skin trying to find a way out. "You should have known how strong Stone's acid is, man. He's got some fucking sixties recipe passed on by Ken Kesey or something. Take another deep breath, mate. You want a cigarette?"

The General nodded and wiped his face with the sleeve of his jacket, and Dum Dum handed him a smoke. He clicked the lighter and a naked blue girl danced into flaming orange and was gone. Dum Dum clicked the lighter again and distant suns collided, spawning new stars through a halo of fireworks. The General just stared at the lighter.

"They work better if you light them," said Dum Dum, lighting The General's cigarette for him and handing it back.

"No Zulus," The General assured himself.

"No. No Zulus. No one's out to get you."

"Mad John is," said The General, glumly puffing on his cigarette.

"No he ain't," said Dum Dum. Even Dum Dum had to admit that he'd noticed an animosity on the part of Mad John towards The General, but for once he was smart enough to keep it quiet while his friend was tripping his nuts off. "It's just a difficult time, what with everything and that..."

"He is," said The General. "He watches me all the time, everything I do! He's even got the spiders watching me! That big one in the hallway sends him messages in the webs, all these fucking secret codes everywhere, and his bike..."

"How much acid did you take, Gen'ral?" said Dum Dum gently.

"His bike knows what you're thinking when you ride it," babbled The General. "I swear to God, it was reading my mind when I touched it and it's got no petrol in it. Doesn't even smell of petrol. He's talking to the spiders, Dum Dum."

"How much did you take?" repeated Dum Dum.

"Two tabs," said The General.

"Two. And you think Mad John's talking to spiders? What the fuck did you take two for?"

The General's face searched for answers. He'd done it because Chaos had taken four and he didn't want to look like a lightweight, but his mind recoiled from that answer because it lead to a whole world of insecurities.

"Stone said it wasn't that strong," he said finally.

Stone was the club's drug genius, apparently dormant until the Acid House explosion in the eighties when he decided to "show them what real acid was about". The result was less psychedelic fun and more some crazed psychological experiment. Those who survived always came away different, though often they had a greater appreciation for life, quit meaningless jobs, and generally fucked off to live somewhere sunny or dug in to help the community. Stone's drugs weren't simply about recreational tripping, and by doing more than half a tab of his acid you were taking a vast step into the unknown. A mind like The General's could be turned into soup by two hits.

"It's probably a bit stronger than you're used to," said Dum Dum charitably. There was dust on his face, deep, deep lines melting until they met resistance from a beard of long sharpened stakes, like the horse charge in Braveheart. He blinked tiny black arrows, his eye cameras taking a constant flow of pictures.

"It's gonna take a while to wear off, but you'll be all right," he said. "You're just seeing things is all it is. Mad John don't talk to spiders and there ain't any Zulus."

Just two rather embarrassed black men who'd given up on the bus and were trying to shuffle past on the other side of the road without drawing The General's attention. Dum Dum nodded sorry at them again.

"I don't think I can do the party," said The General heavily. "I'm tripping balls here, mate."

"Well you can't sit out here all night. We're on duty and I'm on the bar in about half an hour."

"You can't leave me here!" pleaded The General.

"I won't leave you here, but you'll have to come inside. Just stay by me and if anyone tells you to do anything I'll try and help you out. Joker ain't even here yet and then we'll have Vincent to help out too. You're my brother, man, we'll get through it."

"No Zulus."

"No," smiled Dum Dum. "No Zulus. And if you see any big scary spiders watching you then let me know and I'll make 'em a drink."

It was difficult not to feel protected when you were around Dum Dum. Though he and Numb Tongue were entirely different builds - the latter nearly a foot taller but built like a baseball bat, while it would be fair to say that Dum Dum carried a fair amount of blubber - there was never any real sense of threat from Dum Dum. He'd bash someone occasionally if no obvious alternative suggested itself, but there was never any particular malice about it. Numb Tongue always seemed like he was trying his hardest not to attack the entire human race on principle.

The club came in all shapes and sizes, from the twin towers, eye to eye with skyscrapers, right down to Apples' five feet nine inches, and when they lined up for club photos it looked like the diagram of the evolution of man. Except there were rather more Neanderthals. But it wasn't just Dum Dum's bulk that made The General feel safe. Maybe it was that they were both prospects, in it together, especially since Dum Dum had introduced him to the club. The General's mind wasn't open to analysis at the moment.

"Thanks, man." He sighed and took another breath. "I am off my fucking nut!"

"No kidding," said Dum Dum.

Two. Two hits of Stone's acid! What people failed to understand is that Stone's acid wasn't compatible with normal human beings. The likes of Chaos, Flashback, and Mental could take vast amounts of it because they'd been doing it for so many years that their minds were completely fried anyway. But it wasn't without consequence, and Chaos had never been the same since he ate a whole sheet of the stuff for a bet. The night had ended with him giving away most of his furniture, including a heater that he'd unbolted from the wall and presented to Loud-As with the immortal words "I've always wanted you to have this."

"Thanks, that'll keep me warm," said Loud-As, who, having also indulged in Stone's pharmaceutical experiments, then carried it around with him from bar to bar all night.

Despite being six feet eight inches tall and weighing over three hundred pounds, Dum Dum had quickly learned that Stone's drugs were in no way dependent on size. Just a little dab of that shit would do unless you wanted to be scared of the Toilet Monster for the next twelve hours.

"Spiders," mumbled The General, wiping dribble from his chin.

It was going to be a long night.

Dum Dum lifted The General to his feet and ushered him indoors, propping him up at the bar while he went behind to begin his shift.

"What's up with him then?" growled Loud-As.

He was in one of his moods, sitting at one end of the bar, drinking heavily and becoming increasingly belligerent. Despite himself he wasn't quite stupid enough to start on Dum Dum, but he spotted The General, now clinging to the other end of the bar in much the same way as he was clinging on to his sanity, and The General became the focus of his unpleasantness.

"What's the matter with that cunt?" repeated Loud-As, this time pointing his bottle at The General.

"Oh he's all right, just ate something dodgy" said Dum Dum, neatly removing the near empty bottle from Loud's hand and putting a fresh one on the bar. A full beer was less likely to be used as a weapon.

An hour later Dum Dum's night still wasn't getting any better. He'd done his best to disguise the fact that The General had been reduced to a gibbering imbecile, he'd tended the bar as fast as possible and attempted to delegate more menial tasks, but unfortunately that didn't narrow it down to much. He'd asked The General to go and get another case of Buds from downstairs and found him twenty minutes later clinging to the top step like he was halfway up a mountain. He couldn't even open a beer without instructions. And to top it all Loud-As was still inflicting his little tantrum on everyone.

Today's particular grievance could be anything from the fact that he was going bald to Honda having built a production bike that somehow met his disapproval, but he was damn sure he was going to make it everyone else's problem. Usually Vincent got the worst of it, but he was doing far too good a job of distracting Joker from his own birthday party, which left The General as all too easy pickings. Thankfully the sound of ten unmuffled cylinders and a few stray car alarms signalled the arrival of tonight's guest of honour and his increasingly unfortunate escort.

"Little prick's finally decided to bring Joker to his party then," spat Loud-As, clumping away to grudgingly join the party.

I'm going to have words with him about his attitude when I get my colours, thought Dum Dum, opening another bottle of cold water for The General.

"Spiders," mumbled The General gratefully. He was due to replace Scarecrow on the front door in a while. Fuck knows what he'd do if anyone called Spider turned up, but it was probably better that he was away from everyone else. There would be another rush on the bar as soon as Joker got upstairs, so maybe Dum Dum could do some juggling and stick Vincent behind the bar while he got The General down Everest to the door. The General let out a strange moan.

"I told you!" he hissed at Dum Dum. "I told you!"

Oh for fuck's sake! Now what?

"Told me what, Gen'ral?" said Dum Dum calmly.

"The music," whispered The General. "Listen, listen... I told you he's out to get me."

Dum Dum listened for a moment. He'd actually been trying to listen for a while because Mad John was doing a quick spot of DJing, "a bit of practice to warm the old bones," as he'd put it, and it was difficult not to be impressed. He mixed literally everything, punk, techno, soul, metal, gabba, weird movie samples...

"Ministry," said Dum Dum finally. "You Know What You Are. Sex Pistols, Liar, a bit of Tricky..." Dum Dum trailed off. He didn't recognise the loop sample, but it sounded very much like, "I can see right through you, Mister Smith", very subtle but nonetheless present. The beat was hypnotic, coming from every angle... "You know what you are. You're a liar!" There was no missing it if you were listening.

"How do you feel about doing the door for a while?" said Dum Dum gently. It must be a coincidence. It had to be. But coincidence or not it was stirring The General's brain soup and he wasn't even close to peaking on two tabs of Stone's acid.

The funny thing was that Dum Dum, never one to grasp an idea in a hurry, was starting to notice the odd truth in The General's paranoia. The only real time he'd spent with Mad John had been today when they'd goofed about with balloons and carried many crates of booze up from the cellar, and Dum Dum was pretty sure the president liked him. The fact that he'd said, "I like you, Dum Dum" had been a clue. But there was something else...

Mad John had asked him a few questions: Where he was from? Why did he want to join the club? Could he burp the entire alphabet? And, now that he came to think about it, some of the questions had seemed a bit strange. Like, what would he do if he lived to be three hundred years old? Did he believe in magic? What would he eat if he had to live in the wild? Having spent a lot of time in jail Dum Dum was used to those sort of conversations. Idle banter.

But it wasn't the questions that bothered him, it was the feeling that Mad John already knew most of the answers and was just double-checking. And then there was the day he'd ridden Mad John's bike and, until The General said something about it, he'd never have admitted it, but it really did feel like it was reading his mind. No, it was different to that, it was weighing his character, his pros and cons. It knew him. When he had gone to refuel it, the tank had been empty.

"Now you've got me at it," Dum Dum muttered to himself. Talking spiders and mind-reading motorbikes, for crying out loud! He poured himself a large shot of whiskey and then remembered that he wasn't supposed to be drinking tonight. Anything The General had taken was obviously with the club's permission since they had given it to him in the first place, but the prospects were expected to be on duty, so drugs and alcohol were off limits unless they were told otherwise. He'd heard of a contact high, but surely Stone's acid wasn't that strong! Next it'll be elves and pixies running around on the bar!

"Go and find Scarecrow or Vincent," he told The General, as the bar began to fill up again. "Tell them I need them here for a minute."

"Spiders." The General nodded and shuffled away.

CHAPTER TEN

It was starting to get light much earlier, maybe six, six thirty in the morning, and Scarecrow tried to ignore the amount of it that was coming in through the window. He'd carelessly failed to check if the blind was drawn before passing out fully dressed in a guest room at the clubhouse around ten o'clock the night before. Sunday. The party had started on Friday, and what with the return of Mad John, and Joker's birthday, and everything, it had been a lively one even by Aberrant MC standards.

Dum Dum and The General were downstairs in the bar, cleaning away empty bottles and full ashtrays. Vincent was behind the bar, his only customers being Chaos and Stone, each quietly sipping on old rum that had bits floating in it. Chaos had recently brought this and a large quantity of cocaine back from his travels in Africa, the cocaine being rather better than the rum. His short cropped blond hair was now so bleached by the sun that he glowed in the dark, an effect not helped by the deep tan, or by sitting too close to the UV light on the bar that sporadically flashed the words 'live nu es'. It was positively startling when he smiled, which was possibly why Stone was wearing sunglasses.

It was also not at all what Scarecrow wanted to see first thing on a Monday morning when he had to be at work in a few hours.

"Make us a cup of tea," said Stone.

Scarecrow nodded. Slowly. On reflection, he really didn't feel very well at all.

"You want tea, Chaos?"

"Coffee. That Irish stuff with the whiskey in it." Even Chaos was winding down, though that was probably due to a lack of drinking partners than a need for sobriety or sleep. As if to prove the point he pulled a large knife from his boot and dipped it ruthlessly into a bag of white powder.

"You want some?" he waved the bag at Stone.

"Not for me," said Stone. "I've got to get the missus home." He motioned over his shoulder at a pair of feet sticking out from under a blanket on a heavy leather sofa. "She spent eight hours talking The General down."

Stone seemed to find it vaguely amusing that The General now had the mental capacity of a root vegetable and still occasionally mumbled about spiders under his breath. The clubhouse had been swept four times.

"Sure you don't need a livener for the road?" said Chaos generously, but as careless as ever with the pointy end of the knife.

"Nah, I'm all right," said Stone. "There won't be much traffic out if I don't leave it too long. Dum Dum, take a break, you've been on for hours. Go and help Scarecrow with the tea or something. Get him to make General a cup too. He looks like he needs one. Vincent, you want one?"

"Coffee, two sugars please, Stone."

"Coffee for Vincent. Two sugars."

Dum Dum trundled towards the kitchen. After four years of prospecting for the club he already knew exactly how everyone liked their tea and coffee. And every other possible kind of beverage for that matter. He'd found out some time ago that other clubs didn't expect anyone to prospect for nearly so long, just six months for some of the smaller clubs, but he figured he'd made his choice and he'd stick with it. He'd done longer in prison and that was far less fun, and most of the time he was treated like a full patch member anyway.

Still, he couldn't help feeling a hint of disappointment that last night's party hadn't seen him finally get his full patch. Scarecrow too. He'd been prospecting for two years and hanging around the club since he was a kid, and here they were making the fucking tea.

Instead of any patch ceremony Mad John had announced that they had a week to prepare for a mandatory club run. Only Mental and Flashback were exempt, on account of being in prison, a fact that some of the club already seemed to have forgotten.

"You're going to be putting some miles on the clock, so I want all bikes in running order," Mad John had said pointedly at Dum Dum and a couple of the full patch members. "If you break down where we're going then you'll be in trouble, so check your fluids and cables and then get Scarecrow to double check them for you. Chaos has drawn up his usual list of essentials, doubtless available in German and signed in triplicate, so check with him for anything you might need and then ignore most of it because it won't all fit on a bike."

"But remember," Mad John paused, suddenly serious. "We are at war, so coming, I believe the phrase is 'tooled up', might be a wise idea. Numb Tongue's your man for that, unless you've forgotten to give Dum Dum his brass knuckles and they're still in your pocket and you intend to keep them, Scarecrow."

Scarecrow patted his pockets down and passed his belated gift over to Dum Dum. It was difficult to miss a set of brass-knuckles the size of a frying pan, particularly since they'd had to be custom made to fit on Dum Dum's hand, but somehow he'd completely forgotten they were in his jacket. And somehow Mad John had known about them.

"I'm sure you can thank him later," said Mad John, hurriedly curtailing a speech from Dum Dum who tended to get over emotional about gifts. "In the meantime I want you all here 10am sharp on Saturday, ready to go. No excuses. And make no mistake, gentlemen, this is no ordinary run. You will come back changed. That's assuming you come back at all, which I'm told is quite unlikely. Or do I mean likely?" Mad John paused for a moment with his head cocked to one side as if listening to something. "It's possible that you won't all come back, is what I mean."

Mad John paused for a further moment for this to sink in, but it didn't have to sink very far. With the exception of Numb Tongue, who hadn't been paying attention and was quietly chopping lines of cocaine on the bar, all of the members of Aberrant MC looked like they knew exactly what he was talking about and were just waiting for him to finish talking about it so they could get back to drinking and taking drugs. A sniffing noise suggested that Numb Tongue hadn't even waited that long.

"Um," said Dum Dum.

"Yes?" smiled Mad John. "Questions, questions with you isn't it, young man?"

"Um, where are we going?" said Dum Dum.

"But good questions, as ever, I see," beamed Mad John. "Pertinent, concise, and to the point! Wales!"

"Pardon?"

"Wales," repeated Mad John. "M4 west, funny accents and rather too much of a fondness for sheep..."

"Wales?"

"Yes, yes, Wales, or thereabouts. I'm sure even you will be able to find it, Dum Dum. It's a country, among other things. Got their own flag and everything. Big red dragon on it," Mad John added hopefully.

"Wales. Fair enough," shrugged Dum Dum. He'd heard of Wales for fuck's sake. It was hard to miss, slapped on the side of England like that, especially since he had served four years in prison there, in his youth, for a rather inept security van robbery. But unless the club were going to attempt an equally badly planned robbery, then Dum Dum really couldn't see how a run to Wales was going to be remotely life-changing.

"Good man, good man." Mad John was still beaming at him like some eccentric old professor who'd had a breakthrough with a slow, but much-loved student. "And don't forget: tooled up!"

Dum Dum absently polished his brass knuckles on his t-shirt as Scarecrow spooned tea, coffee, and sugar into assorted cracked mugs.

"Wales, eh?"

Scarecrow poured hot water into the cups.

"I did four years in Cardiff nick," Dum Dum persisted. "What do you think we're going to Wales for?"

Scarecrow shrugged. His head was starting to pound and he really didn't feel like talking.

"You think there's a club in Wales we've got to bash up or something?" said Dum Dum, still polishing brass knuckles you could anchor a small ship with.

Scarecrow grunted. There was a fly buzzing around the kitchen and even that was starting to sound too loud.

"Nice roads in Wales though," said Dum Dum, apparently happy to continue a one-sided conversation. "I remember when I got nicked they took me along all these winding country roads, all trees and valleys and that. Lovely it was."

Scarecrow stirred the teas and coffees. Quietly.

"Took 'em fucking ages to find me, as well," continued Dum Dum to himself. "I was on Crimewatch."

Scarecrow put the teaspoon in the sink and took a deep breath. He really was starting to feel unwell. Note to self: do not under any circumstances drink anything that Chaos has brought back from anywhere, ever.

"Mind you, I was on some programme about the stupidest criminals, too," smiled Dum Dum, swatting at the increasingly annoying fly. "It was all the cameras everywhere and the blue paint. It was quite funny actually, when I saw it on telly."

"Blue paint?" managed Scarecrow.

"Yeah, it exploded in the money bags and covered everything."

Suddenly, in not so much as a heartbeat, Scarecrow caught the fly in mid flight as it zipped around the kitchen. He held his hand close to his mouth and hissed into it.

"Listen you little fucker, I have a horrible fucking hangover and I have to be at work in two hours, where I have to tell them that I need an unspecified amount of time off to go on a run to fucking Wales. And the only good thing ever to come out of Wales was Tom fucking Jones, so if you don't want your wings pulled off I strongly suggest you fuck off!" Scarecrow released the fly which headed straight for the window.

"Manic Street Preachers," said Dum Dum.

"What?"

"Manic Street Preachers come from Wales and they're quite good. And Dub War, I like them."

"Shut up, Dum Dum."

There was a moment of silence, maybe just a hint of early morning bird-song drifting on the breeze. Just a moment.

"Scarecrow?" said Dum Dum, utterly spoiling that moment.

"What, Dum Dum?"

"Do you think spiders can talk?"

"What?"

"Do you think spiders can talk?"

"Is this conversation actually going anywhere, Dum Dum? I really do have the most blinding hangover."

"Well." Dum Dum suddenly looked uncomfortable. He shuffled on his feet and leaned against the fridge.

"Well..." He tried again, unsure of himself.

Aberrant MC was family and Dum Dum had never had a family before. He would never speak ill of any one of them, and if anyone else did then he was likely to bend them into balloon animals. But, still, he needed to say something to somebody.

"Mad John..." he started, and trailed off again.

Mad John seemed to know what everyone was thinking, and Dum Dum was unsure that his recent thoughts didn't constitute treachery or even heresy. He leaned away from the fridge and there was a big Dum Dum-shaped dent in it. He was pretty sure that didn't happen to normal people. But then, Scarecrow had just caught a fly in mid air and told it to fuck off.

"Do you think Aberrant's weird?" he managed finally.

"Weird how?" said Scarecrow, taking a much needed sip of coffee.

"You know what I mean," insisted Dum Dum. "Come on. You've been around them longer than I have. Haven't you ever noticed anything, well, weird? I mean, well, you know what I mean.... Do you think Aberrant's a bit strange, like?"

"Dum Dum," said Scarecrow.

"Yes, Scarecrow?" said Dum Dum.

"I think it's an absolute certainty that Aberrant is strange. Strange doesn't even come close to describing some of the shit I've seen from these people, but I wouldn't want to be anywhere else on earth. Mad John talks to walls, you know."

"Spiders," said Dum Dum.

"Spiders?"

"Yeah, spiders," said Dum Dum, more comfortable now that he knew he wasn't alone in his concerns. "He talks to spiders. And I think they watch this place for him, like security cameras or something."

"I'm just hungover enough to think that might be possible," said Scarecrow, picking up mugs of tea and coffee to take back into the bar. "Spiders," he shook his head. "In that case, Dum Dum, I think we have absolutely no idea how weird this club is, but I get the feeling we're about to find out."

CHAPTER ELEVEN

The General had considered every possible excuse not to go on the run. He'd even thought about breaking his own wrist, but given that Andy One-Leg had, well, one leg and he was still going, The General reasoned that he might just end up going on the run with a broken wrist, so quickly abandoned that option.

His head itched.

Joker had informed the four prospects that it would be a 'Mohawk Run', which meant haircuts all round, and the four had dutifully shaved their heads, only to discover, this morning, that there was no such thing as a 'Mohawk Run' and they'd all got haircuts for nothing.

What really pissed The General off was that he was the only one that didn't look good with a mohawk. Dum Dum just looked more intimidating, the close cropped Chuck Liddell stripe revealing several dents in his skull, apparently the result of an argument with a hammer. Vincent looked about fifteen years old, his limp mohawk hanging to one side like a cute little Shetland pony. And Scarecrow, flash twat that he was, had gone the whole hog, his long flowing locks now shaved into a foot long, bright blue plumage that only served to accentuate his already annoyingly good looks. The General meanwhile, sported what could generously be described as a badly sculpted birds nest. His hair, a naturally uncontrollable frizzy bushweed, now resembled a hedge that someone had attempted to fashion into a Roman helmet.

He scratched his head again and lit another cigarette.

Many of the club had stayed at the clubhouse the night before the run, but a few stragglers were still showing up, Joker and Loud-As arriving together, with a club member The General didn't recognise, followed by Stone with supplies strapped to every available surface of his bike.

The General hadn't really known what to bring, but relied on his military training to pack the essentials for survival. Mad John's speech had worried him though, all that stuff about coming "tooled up." He didn't like the sound of that at all. And what did it mean anyway? He was too scared of Numb Tongue to go and ask him, but he'd heard about some of the Scandinavian clubs firing rocket launchers at each other for fuck's sake! Were they supposed to bring their own tank?

In the end he'd settled on an old German army knife with a six inch blade, which he had tucked into his boot, and an even older 9mm Luger pistol, both of which he'd bought in Berlin when he was trying to look cool in front of one of the bands he was working for. He knew that the pistol worked, at least, having fired it just once at a stationary target, but he only had six bullets, now wrapped in plastic with the pistol and hidden under his bike seat. Well, technically, it was Dum Dum's bike seat since The General would be riding his XS1100 again.

Beyond maiming himself, the bike had been his last out, his last chance at not having to ride several hundred miles with over a dozen heavily armed and very conspicuous lunatics. Unfortunately Dum Dum's Harley seemed to be running just fine for the first time since he bought it, which meant The General could use his spare XS. Which now had a loaded gun under the seat. Under Dum Dum's seat. Fuck.

The General had horrible visions of the club being pulled over on the M4, cops first, and then armed response units when Mr Plod found the Luger and hastily called for back up. You'd have to be brave or foolish beyond redemption to pull this lot over, but there was always the chance of some twat trying to make a name for himself, pulling them over on some traffic violation and then getting quickly out of his depth. Christ knows what they'd find on the rest of the club, but it would not be good.

Thanks to the no mobile phone rule The General hadn't had the chance to talk to the other prospects all week. For that matter he'd barely had a chance to recover from Stone's acid and still found himself sitting at traffic lights waiting for the blue one, but, more to the point, he'd liked to have got a clearer idea of what they thought was going on. He'd actually missed Mad John's speech himself, due to the aforementioned acid, spending that time instead sitting in the back yard, quietly making guinea pig noises. All he knew was what Dum Dum had told him while they were clearing up the clubhouse last week, and his mind hadn't been ready for it yet, what with the broom handle leaving acid trailbacks every time he swept, and the fucking spiders everywhere.

His mind still recoiled. He'd swept the clubhouse all day, only finally relenting when Loud-As came back, early in the evening, and resumed throwing his temper about. All he knew was "Wales" and "tooled up".

"Mandatory, John said," Dum Dum had told him. "That means you have to go, like, club rules and that. Haven't had a mandatory run in years, Smiler said. I thought all clubs had mandatory runs at least once a year, but s'not practical with Aberrant, Smiler said. Too many of the club travelling at different times, like. I think mandatory means it's serious."

Dum Dum, thought The General, had probably needed assistance looking up the word mandatory in a dictionary, but he got the message nonetheless. Obviously Mental and Flashback's incarceration gave them a good excuse, the only possible excuse, but everyone else was here, *everyone*. All laughing and joking, smoking, slapping each others backs, making last minute adjustments, ready to roll. Already drawing attention.

Fifteen bikes didn't really sound like that much until you saw them all together, but just half of Aberrant's full strength looked like a small army. Today they were a tsunami of steel and tattoos and noise and leather, that you'd hope to all the gods was on your side. The problem was that The General wasn't so sure they were on his side and it *terrified* him.

A small crowd of onlookers had gathered around the clubhouse, the old ladies outside the florists stopping their chatter to wave over at Numb Tongue. He motioned back, silently of course, as if tipping his hat to them. The General looked at his watch again, which still said 9.47. He barely knew some of these mentalists and he was supposed to be leaving with them in thirteen - 9.48 - twelve minutes, to go fuck knows where. The General was sweating and dabbed at his forehead with his t-shirt. Mad John was clearly insane and hated him to boot. Numb Tongue gave him nightmares. Stone was a walking pharmacy. Chaos... ditto....

Oh Christ! He hadn't thought about that, the amount of drugs that were probably, almost definitely, secreted throughout their assorted bikes, bags, and orifices. Chaos came back from the Ivory Coast with the entire frame of his bike packed with pure cocaine for fu..

"Mornin' Gen'ral." Dum Dum jovially slapped him on the shoulder, breaking his train of thought and, he suspected, a couple of bones. His knees momentarily buckled.

"All ready to go, yeah?" beamed Dum Dum.

"Ready as I'll ever be," said the General honestly. Don Logan prowled his head. Sexy Beast. No, no, no, no, no! No, he wasn't bloody ready! And that was another mental case! Any one of these men could be another Don Logan, suddenly flipping out and inflicting horrific, unreasoning, violence!

Well, okay, not *all* of them: Stone wouldn't start a fight if you paid him, he'd just turn your brain into hummus, and Joker wasn't really the violent type, but still, there were far too many loose cannons and a great number of cannonballs.

"You know Billy, right?" Dum Dum was saying.

"Billy?"

"Billy," grinned Dum Dum, before realising that he was completely obscuring Billy. He stepped to one side. "Billy."

Billy Toothless. The General had only met Billy once, a month or so after he'd woken up wearing the prospect patch. A couple of the club had dropped in at Billy's workshop, an old barn in the middle of Hertfordshire, and spent the afternoon tinkering on various bikes, and blasting the hulk of a broken-down truck with a shotgun.

Billy's workshop had a curious, overwhelming, and lingeringly disgusting smell to it - damp dog, old sofa, body odour and mouthwash, - but Billy had seemed nice enough. They hadn't really spoken much: Billy made driving aids for the disabled, converting cars and bikes, and he was behind schedule, so he just gave them free access to his welding gear and got back to work. Beyond that, The General knew nothing about him, much less why he was called Billy Toothless, since his teeth, though an interesting shade of brown, were all present and correct.

"Yeah, I know Billy," The General was all smiles. "We met up at your workshop, couple of months back."

Billy smiled back at him through a mouth like a festival porta-potty, and shook his hand rather too vigorously, leaving behind an oily smear. Now that The General got a proper look at him, Billy was a grubby little individual with vaguely rodenty, weasly features that were accentuated by his shaved head and scraggly goatee. He didn't look much more than thirty, but he had the mannerisms of an old man, these accentuated by the fact that he was smoking a tar-stained wooden pipe.

The most striking thing, however, was the smell. What The General had thought, on a brisk, windy day in Hertfordshire, was a fairly noxious odour, was in fact a mere appetiser for what was standing before him, in closer proximity than he'd have cared for by about ten miles, on a warm spring morning. The General's eyes began to water. Clearly the smell in Billy's barn, the very essence of it, had originated here with Billy.

"Arr mayabin," said Billy cheerfully. "Don' afern get vizters, not roun' moi way. 'Ard to fine, see?"

The General could see the question mark at the end of the sentence, but had absolutely no idea what Billy had just said. None of it, not a single word. It could have been anything: "I'm desperate for a bath and this mouthwash really isn't cutting it?" thought The General. Or how about, "I'm a horrible, stinky, little hobgoblin who eats rats and boiled cabbage for breakfast and shouldn't be let out in public?" The General continued smiling vacantly. "Yes, I'm sure it is," he managed finally, hoping he was agreeing with something rather than to something.

But here was another fine example, another clearly abnormal, and possibly dangerous individual, that he was expected to travel to God knows where with, for God knows how long. And for all The General could understand him, he may as well have been saying, "Yes, I remember you and if you bother me in the slightest, I'll drive you out into the woods and shoot you in the testicles with a crossbow."

"Yer closeren y' hink wi' the secun wan, boy," said Billy, matter of fact, "An' yuv ne'r bin so righ' wi' the larse one, 'cept Oi wunt was'e me bows onya. An', fer your inf'mation Oi loikes moufwarsh."

"Looks like we're off!" interrupted Dum Dum, an overgrown child unable to hide his excitement at going to a theme park. Disneyland this is not, thought The General.

Mad John was standing on the seat of his bike, one hand held up for silence that came instantly, like they'd all spotted him at the same time. Even the onlookers, which had become quite a crowd by now, fell silent as if waiting for his word, like they were coming on the run with them.

"Gentlemen," Mad John spoke quietly, barely raising his voice, but his voice carried like the world had turned its volume down a notch and was listening in. "If I might have your attention. The time of our departure is upon us. If you've forgotten anything then it's best that it remains forgotten because you won't be seeing it again for some time. And probably could have lived without it in the first place."

"It is, as I'm sure you're only too aware, far too early in the morning for speeches," he continued with a deep breath. And with that he climbed down off his bike and started fastening his crash helmet. The General had been waiting for the "but", the "too early in the morning for speeches, but..." But apparently that was it. They were leaving.

The General fruitlessly searched his mind for last minute excuses, some way that he wouldn't have to ride with Aberrant MC, but there was nothing. He would have to ride with them. Reluctantly he strapped his helmet on. It was already starting to give him a rash from the stupid bloody mohawk. He dug his bike keys out of his pocket and put them in the ignition, before pulling his gloves on.

But what if...?

The bikes were started on Mad John's signal, something he'd picked up from the first Mad Max movie, and the street was an instant thunder of booming motorcycles and car alarms, like a bomb had gone off in an underground car park.

What if.... thought The General. Let's just say that in all this noise... Well, it would be very easy for a bike that had, say, run out of petrol, to fall behind and get lost, especially since no one but Mad John seemed to know their destination. True, they'd probably send someone back to look for him, but they'd be expecting to look for someone who had broken down, not someone who was heading for home in the opposite direction as fast as possible.

What could they say? They had no mobiles so he wouldn't have been able to call any of them, and it wasn't his fault if no one said where they were going. And Dum Dum would probably volunteer to come looking for him, which was even better because then he'd get lost as well.

Sweet.

Of course, he might have to wait for some windy country roads to lose them properly, but it was better than spending however long with them, wherever the fuck they were going. Could be weeks, Dum Dum had said. Fuck that. The General would be home by last call.

Suddenly the bikes fell silent again and the world hushed its tongue. Even the car alarms stopped. Mad John stood on his bike seat.

"One last thing, gentlemen," he said. "We'll be riding diamond formation today. Numb Tongue will be taking the rear, Loud-As and Smiler left and right. We wouldn't want to lose anyone, would we?" Mad John winked at The General and started his engine.

CHAPTER TWELVE

Ever since he was a small child running errands for the club Vincent had dreamed of this day. In his months prospecting for Aberrant MC he had ridden with only a few of the club at a time, four on one night, maybe six the next, but never a pack this strong, fifteen of them in all, bellowing through Central London before roaring through sleepy Twickenham, down towards the M3 motorway. Every nerve in his body was alive with adrenaline, fear and excitement running neck and neck as the bikes thundered onwards, twice as fast as everything else on the road.

With no reading material about Aberrant MC, Vincent had spent his teen years consuming every book he could find about every other outlaw motorcycle club, everything from seventies pulp fiction to biographies to the undercover cops telling all. He made a point of stealing the cop books and had developed an instant dislike for the authors, misguided wannabes at best, out and out scumbags at worst, all trying to bring down a lifestyle they were too chickenshit to join. But in every book there was always a vivid portrayal of the club run, "the burst of dirty thunder" Hunter S Thompson had called it. And Vincent had thought about little else ever since he'd been old enough to read, quietly afraid that when the time came he wouldn't be able to keep up, wheel to wheel through the traffic at eighty miles per hour.

Thankfully, people tended to keep out of the way of such a pack and the diamond formation had been pretty easy to figure out, being exactly as it sounded - diamond shaped, with the prospects at the back in a V and Numb

Tongue as the final rider, the lower point of the diamond. It took up all the road and only really worked on motorways, but Mad John seemed to be avoiding those in favour of country roads, clattering through villages at what must be top speed for that old Knucklehead, so, really, it was just a matter of trying to keep up.

Behind Mad John rode Joker and Chaos, and then behind them was Apples, Stone, and Andy One-Leg. With only Numb Tongue behind him Vincent rode alongside Scarecrow, behind Dum Dum and The General. On the outer points of this supposed diamond rode Smiler and Loud-As, with Billy Toothless and this new mystery rider, presumably the much talked about Zig Zag McClintock, somewhere in the middle.

Although Vincent had heard of Zig Zag, and, now that he thought about it, had heard his name mentioned back in the days when he was running back and forth to the corner shop in short trousers, he'd never actually met the man and knew very little about him. His arrival this morning hadn't filled in many gaps either, other than the fact that he was very short and stocky, five-five at most, rode a very low Z1000 lowrider, and never took his crash helmet off.

Vincent searched his mind for a face to put with the name, but nothing came to him, just the name and, strangely, the same black Simpson crash helmet. Maybe he'd joined the club after Vincent's mother had moved them away. Must have, thought Vincent. He would have remembered if he'd been taller than one of the club members. It would have given his scrawny, coat hanger, frame some hope back when he was all bumfluff and blackheads. Not that he wasn't still bumfluff and blackheads. And yet, here he was, booming along in the midst of that "burst of dirty thunder".

Vincent's face was starting to hurt from smiling so much when, suddenly, his mind was brought back to focus, the smile wiped from his face by The General weaving erratically in front of him, frantically checking his mirrors as if something behind him was on fire. Vincent checked his own mirrors to see what was going on, but all he could see was Numb Tongue looking even more surly and annoyed than usual, waving his hand about and mouthing something above the engine noise. Up ahead Dum Dum had now started to weave and, for lack of a mirror that showed him anything other than his own stomach, strain to look over his shoulder. At him. Vincent looked down and checked his bike for smoke, then looked down behind him in case something was loose.

Suddenly Numb Tongue pulled up alongside him, motioning with his hand again, waving it under his own scar strewn chin.

"Cut it out!" he yelled above the noise.

Now that Vincent got another look at him, Numb Tongue actually looked more amused than annoyed.

"Cut what out?" Vincent yelled back.

"Disappearing!"

Numb Tongue pulled back again leaving Vincent completely baffled, while up ahead The General and Dum Dum were still giving him curious backward glances. And all this while roaring along at eighty plus through traffic.

Thankfully the tales about Mad John never stopping for red lights had yet to be put to the test as, astonishingly, the club hadn't hit a single red light right the way across London. But on the roads John had chosen, such a pace was still furious in places. And, now that he thought about it, Vincent wasn't entirely comfortable with the amount of speed cameras they'd blasted past at nearly three times the speed limit.

The route wasn't exactly a winner either, heading as it did, down the A303 towards Stonehenge, little more than spitting distance from the small and aptly named Strangeways, where his estranged and definitely strange mother still lived. What happened to the M4 straight to Wales?

It was hardly surprising however. Vincent knew that Stonehenge held some deep significance to Mad John, something to do with the Battle Of The Beanfield back in 1985, when Wiltshire police had brutally broken up some hippy gathering. Mad John had told him all about it that night he'd run away from home to the clubhouse, how the cops had gone hog wild battering women and children, and how the ITN reports about the police brutality suddenly disappeared.

Many of the Aberrant crew had been there that day, ostensibly heading for the Stonehenge festival, but more as a show of solidarity against a massive police presence, many of whom had removed their ID numbers. When the trouble started Aberrant had been able to break through police lines on their bikes a couple of times and rescue people, but still they were unable to help when families and homes were attacked by the police.

"Would've been a lot worse too, if it hadn't been for Lord Cardigan," Mad John had told Vincent. "And such is the way of the press that they said he was crazy! It took years for them to get any sort of justice and even that was an utter disgrace, £24,000 between twenty-one of them. Disgraceful."

Mad John, it transpired, had become something of a legend that night, not only being one of the few people, if not the only person, to get through the four mile exclusion zone around Stonehenge, but actually making it to the stones themselves. Even so there was a bitterness in his eyes when he spoke that Vincent had never seen before, an anger still burning.

"It took everything I had not to..." Mad John trailed off, his eyes cast down. "Well, let's just say, it's probably lucky that Numb Tongue wasn't there. I was tempted to put the word out on our good friends at the Wiltshire constabulary, every single one of them, but that way lies folly...and orphans. And then where does it end? No, I'm afraid, their children will just have to live with that shame. At least no one was killed that day."

There were no cops around today when Aberrant arrived at the heavily fenced off Stonehenge, just coaches full of tourists and, as Mad John had put it, "stupid petty little people in uniform who are trying to fleece us for our own heritage." These days you had to pay to visit Stonehenge.

The bikes pulled into the parking area, all eyes and not a few tourist cameras upon them. A scruffy looking man wearing jeans and a leather jacket - bearded with long unkempt hair hanging down over the collar - approached Mad John and was greeted with a warm hug. It looked, for a moment, as if Mad John slipped something into the man's pocket, but it was difficult to see from were Vincent now stood. Clearly the pair had urgent business to attend to and the rest of the club seemed happy to wait, a few of them lighting smokes while others made minor adjustments to their bikes. Zig Zag, Vincent noticed, was the only one not to take his crash helmet off.

"So," said Dum Dum casually. "You gonna tell us how you did that?"

"Did what?" said Vincent. The General was still giving him odd looks and somewhat keeping his distance.

"Your little disappearing act," said Dum Dum. "I've got to admit it was pretty fucking cool, but you could of give us some notice. I nearly fuckin' fell off me bike. Again."

"What are you on about?" protested Vincent. "I haven't been anywhere, I've been with you lot all day."

"Well, you *were,*" said Dum Dum. "And then you weren't. One minute you was right behind me and the next minute you'd just vanished! Fucking invisible, mate!"

Vincent searched the faces around him for answers.

"It's true," said The General, edging slightly closer now that Dum Dum had broached the subject. "I swear to God I looked around and you'd gone, and there's Numb Tongue waving his arms about." The General glanced quickly at Numb Tongue, afraid even to speak his name in case it was in any way taken out of context and got him in trouble.

Vincent said nothing. What was there to say? Obviously they'd been dabbling rather too heavily with Stone's acid if they were seeing people disappear, but all the same it was disconcerting that they were both saying the same thing. Thankfully, before the conversation could get any more ridiculous, Mad John called Vincent over to meet his scruffy new companion.

"Vincent, this is my good friend Dennis," said Mad John. "He'd like a quick word."

Vincent knew of old that when an outlaw biker introduced someone as their 'good friend' it meant just that, not some casual acquaintance, but someone who was trusted by the person who was introducing them and, by association, the entire club.

"Remember when you asked if I thought Aberrant was weird," said Scarecrow, as Vincent walked away.

"Yeah," said Dum Dum.

"Well, I think it's just got a lot weirder!"

CHAPTER THIRTEEN

It was late in the afternoon when Aberrant MC finally rolled away from Stonehenge, the sky turning grey and threatening rain. Mad John and Vincent had taken off with some bloke leaving the club waiting around with little to do until Loud-As and Chaos had decided on some impromptu drag racing, which eventually attracted some police attention.

It had been an uncomfortable afternoon, to say the least, and The General was grateful for the small mercy of being on the move again, though nonetheless fearful of what lay ahead. The club weren't even halfway to Wales yet and already they were on the police radar, even if the squad car had just cruised past a couple of times without stopping. That was very little comfort when you had a gun under your seat.

The General's discomfort had not been eased, either, by the nagging feeling that he was going completely insane, like maybe Stone's acid had done some permanent damage to his already frayed mind. If it hadn't been for Dum Dum The General was fairly sure he'd have been carted off by men in white coats. But, idiot though he was, Dum Dum was nothing if not honest and swore blind that he, too, had seen Vincent vanish, though he still insisted it must be some kind of trick. Yeah, right. Let's see Criss Angel pull that one off!

Thankfully Vincent hadn't done any more vanishing acts since they got back on the road, but then The General wasn't checking his mirrors much, riding with gritted teeth as the club bellowed along narrow and twisty country roads. Mad John was still keeping a furious pace on his old Knucklehead, nothing less than eighty miles per hour, and on unfamiliar roads littered with blind bends it was all The General could do to keep up. Dum Dum was struggling, too, his Shovelhead frequently clipping bushes as he tried to stay on the road, a look of deep concentration on his face.

Mile after mile went past and darkness fell. Still the club rode on. The General knew they were in Wales now, recognising some of the street signs a while back, but he had no real idea where, particularly since Mad John seemed to be taking the most obscure route possible. They passed very few towns, let alone cities, just the occasional village, if you could even call them such, a post office, a pub, and a few houses. The General was starting to worry again about running out of petrol. They hadn't passed any signs of life for what seemed like hours, not even a remote farmhouse, and his tank was already on reserve.

The worst thing was that, on top of Vincent's vanishing act, it looked like the stories about Mad John might very well be true. His Madness, as many of the club referred to him, had needed reminding about filling the bikes with petrol before they set off, and when they'd pulled into the petrol station The General had watched his every move. It wasn't just Mad John who hadn't filled his tank, at least four of the fuckers never went near the pumps, Numb Tongue, Chaos, Stone, that little dwarf or whatever he was who hadn't taken his crash helmet off all day... None of them filled up, they just stocked up on cigarettes.

And still more miles passed with nothing but dark, dark, forests and mean forbidding mountains, the Brecon Beacons or some such if The General's geography was any good. It was cold and his arms ached, his arse long dead. Mad John had at least been honest about putting some miles on the bikes, though they'd have been there, wherever that was, hours ago if it hadn't been for the long wait at Stonehenge and the ludicrously scenic route. Wherever they were going it was not on the beaten path.

Finally The General caught a glimpse of light between the trees, still some distance ahead and quite a long way up in the winding mountain roads. He caught Dum Dum's attention and pointed at his near empty tank, running on vapours. Dum Dum nodded and shrugged, which caused him to lose concentration and swerve wildly to avoid a thick stone wall.

Thankfully the pace slackened at last, though, as always, it was too fast for safety on steep and narrowing roads. The General had resigned himself to either crashing, freezing to death, or running out of petrol in the middle of nowhere when, at last, he caught another glimpse of the light, closer this time, although it was difficult to judge distance on these dark and treacherous roads. Whatever and wherever this place was, it was clearly where Aberrant MC where heading. There was nothing else but forest and mountains for miles.

Despite the cold and his relief that the long ride was seemingly over, The General was singularly unimpressed by the club's destination, particularly since there was no sign of a petrol station. The Dragon's Head was one of those ancient white stone taverns with a thick thatched roof, the kind of place some old git will put a plaque on just because fifteen generations of their inbred family have spent their lives getting pissed there on lumpy beer. A couple of months from now it might be a tourist attraction, but it was way too early in the season now, just a couple of cars and an old black Moto Guzzi in the gravel car park. Unless they were here for a spot of rambling it seemed that the club had ridden all the way here for a couple of pints and a home cooked meal. If the place was even serving food. Indeed, if the place was even open. It had to be nearly midnight.

"I'm fuckin' starving," moaned Dum Dum, echoing his thoughts as they climbed from their bikes and stomped some life back into their legs. "I 'ope they've got some good pub grub in this place."

"Prospects!" announced Mad John, instantly dashing their hopes. "If I might have your attention. Scarecrow and Ian, you're on guard duty. Vincent and Dum Dum, at ease."

"I'll take guard," said Numb Tongue quickly, his voice a quite rumble.

"You sure, Numb?" said Mad John.

Numb Tongue nodded. He'd already used at least six words today. The General had never been so pleased to hear him speak. The thought of sitting out here for hours on end after a ride like that, guarding the bikes from nothing but the odd stray fox, was more than he could bear. A light mist hung in the night air, already wetting their bikes. If Mr Chatterbox wanted to sit out here getting slowly soaked to the skin then more fool him.

"Man, thanks Numb Tongue," said Scarecrow keenly, as The General muttered his gratitude. "I could have ridden that road forever, but I must admit I'm getting fuckin' hungry. You want me to bring you something out?"

Numb Tongue's expression changed just a fraction to indicate that, no, he didn't want anything bringing out.

"You all right for smokes?"

Numb Tongue nodded again. And with that Aberrant MC went inside The Dragon's Head.

Appearances had been deceptive from the outside and the tavern, with its high, wooden beamed ceiling, was surprisingly busy, its customers the kind of strange mixture of young and old that you only get in remote places where there is nothing else to do. The chatter was loud and music thumped from a back room at the other end of the bar.

"Now this will do nicely," grinned Dum Dum.

Even The General relaxed a little. There was no obvious threat here, no cops for miles beyond the village bobby - who was probably one of the drunken customers - and no sign of any rival clubs. Aberrant MC were not here for trouble. A couple of the club took up seats beside the roaring fireplace, while the rest headed for the bar. The prospects did likewise.

"Fuckin' have you seen some of the birds in here?" said The General, nudging Dum Dum.

"They've got roast beef and dumplings," said Dum Dum, his eyes still on the menu above the bar.

"I'll bet they have," grinned The General. "Fuckin' dibs on the blonde one!"

"And I'm sure she'd appreciate that no end," said Scarecrow sarcastically.

"Now then ladies, I'm sure they're out of your league anyway," said Joker, joining them at the bar.

He had a point. While The General, in his usual uncouth fashion, might be slavering like Dum Dum in a pie factory, Scarecrow wasn't entirely sure he had ever seen such beauty as he saw at the other end of the bar. Pink hair, long, but tied at the back, a perfect fringe above dark smoky eyes. Was that a tiny star on each cheek? Something light blue to go with the bows in her hair and her light blue gloves. Their eyes met, blue eyes of course, and Scarecrow smiled at her, but she looked away. Figures. He wasn't looking his best all covered in a couple of hundred miles of road dirt, his mohawk all flattened to one side by his crash helmet. Even on a good day she was, as Joker had mentioned, completely out of his league.

"Bitter?" said Dum Dum.

"Not really," sighed Scarecrow, with one last look at her before she drifted away from the bar with a gaggle of friends who, if not for her, would be considered angels sent from heaven.

"No, I mean do you want a pint of bitter?"

"Oh," said Scarecrow, back in the real world. "Are we?"

"Yeah, drinking's fine," said Dum Dum. "We're off for the night. Numb Tongue said he'll do guard all night."

"Really? Well, in that case a Jack and coke would be splendid, thank you Dum Dum."

The club spread out through the tavern, some of them clearly friendly with the locals, Mad John and Stone deep in conversation with the land-lord. The prospects ordered food and found themselves a table by a window that looked out onto the car park. Numb Tongue was out there alone, his back to the window, his breath and cigarette smoke visible through the thin mist.

"Nice of him to take guard," said Dum Dum, as Scarecrow peered through the window where he'd wiped the condensation clear with the sleeve of his jacket.

"I think there's something wrong," Scarecrow frowned.

"What because he was nice?" said The General.

"No. It's like he's worried or... I don't know," Scarecrow trailed off. "I've know him a long time and he looked...sad, lost or something."

"Worse than usual you mean?" said Vincent, grateful not to be talking about vanishing acts again. In light of what he had learned this afternoon, it was absolutely the last thing he wanted to discuss with his fellow prospects.

"Well, yeah, I know what you mean," allowed Scarecrow. "But this was like... fuck, I don't know. I'll take him some food out in a bit."

The prospects ate in silence, their hunger overtaking the need to speak, and when they were done -Dum Dum consuming two full roast dinners-Scarecrow went back to the bar and ordered a couple of huge sandwiches.

"Be back in a bit," he said, as the others headed for the back bar. "I'm just gonna take these out to Numb, make sure he's all right."

It was cold outside, a bitterness to the air that said summer was a while away yet. Numb Tongue was still alone in the car park, but from the look of him he may as well have been alone in the universe. As Scarecrow got closer he saw that it looked as if Numb Tongue had been crying, though it was more likely the damp air. Last time Numb Tongue cried was when he was born and the doctor slapped him on the arse, thought Scarecrow. And there's a fifty fifty chance that he hit the doctor back!

"You all right, Numb?" smiled Scarecrow.

Numb Tongue nodded.

"I've brought you some sandwiches, thought you must be hungry. I didn't realise how hungry I was 'til we ordered. Dum Dum got through two roast dinners!"

Scarecrow had long ago learned that the best way to deal with Numb Tongue was simply to talk to him. Admittedly it could take a while, but sometimes, just sometimes, he would open up a fraction and talk back. Aside from a couple of the full patch members Scarecrow knew Numb Tongue better than anybody, or at least had seen a little further behind the wall that the man had built around himself.

There was the obvious faux pas when Scarecrow had asked about his wedding ring, the response making it plain that his wife had died and that Numb Tongue had never got over it. But beyond that, Scarecrow had slowly chipped away at the wall during their long nights of training one-on-one at Numb's gym.

Given Scarecrow's pacifist nature it was an odd relationship, but nonetheless one built on mutual respect, particularly since the student often taught the master. Numb Tongue made no secret of the fact that he found it amusing that a pacifist was so fascinated with, and so very good at, mixed martial arts. He also understood that that was the whole point: being so good meant Scarecrow never had to hit anyone.

Over time Scarecrow had learned the subtleties of Numb Tongue's hard and scarred face. He suspected that deep down, some place long buried, was a kind and gentle man who appreciated the fact that Scarecrow wouldn't harm a fly, and wanted somehow to be that man again. In his own weird way he, too, fought so that he wouldn't ever have to fight, releasing his inner hatred in the cage rather than inflicting it upon the innocent. Unlike Loud-As, who could be an asshole and start fights for no reason, Numb Tongue would count under his breath, one-one thousand, two-one thousand, three-one thousand, and try to maintain his temper.

Despite appearances Numb Tongue wouldn't harm a fly either. Unless that fly provoked him and then he would completely destroy it. His approach was the same with people, but thankfully very few people were ever stupid enough to provoke him.

"Wicked ride down here, man," said Scarecrow. "Fuck knows where we are, but I love all these twistys. Reminds me of the Isle Of Man."

"Hm."

"I think Dum Dum was having a bit of trouble though. He's got all bits of hedge sticking out of his jacket. Fucked his hand up a bit, too, when he scraped a wall. It's just a graze, but it's pretty bruised up."

Numb Tongue dug in his pocket and pulled out a wrap, digging into it with a vicious switch-blade. He snorted coke from the blade and gestured to Scarecrow.

"Yeah, don't mind if I do, thanks Numb," said Scarecrow.

Scarecrow chopped out a line on the back of his hand and passed the wrap back.

"Needed that, thanks Numb. Looks like quite a decent place. I think Andy said there was a band playing, but you know what he's like with bands. Anything that happened before acid house didn't happen and anything after is rubbish."

Numb Tongue nodded, a hint of wry amusement. Andy One-Leg had dismal taste in music and, given his one leg, wasn't any better at dancing.

"Remember the dance tent at the Bulldog?" said Scarecrow, the same vision crossing his mind. "All fucking gurning on X and jumping up and down so much he snapped his wooden leg. I was fucking crying laughing! I don't know why he doesn't get a better one."

In fact the entire club knew why Andy didn't get a better prosthetic leg. Because having a crappy wooden one was funnier. Andy had a warped sense of humour like that, frequently falling asleep with his wooden leg in the campfire, much to the horror of passers-by. Or worse still, he would suddenly wake up screaming and stabbing violently at his leg with a knife. That tended to make people jump when they didn't know it was a wooden leg. Andy thought that was very funny.

"Remember that time it came off when he was doing a bungee jump?"

Numb Tongue let out something that may have been a faint chuckle. He was warming up.

"Fuckin', I have never seen so many people running out the way of a flying leg! And then he gets down and goes "what happened to everyone?" And Apples goes "they legged it!" Fuckin', my face was hurting from laughing so much."

That was definitely a smile. Numb Tongue rubbed at his face as if trying to get rid of it. He took a deep, deep breath, and exhaled, his breath hanging in the cold air. Scarecrow studied his face as they sat in silence for a while.

"You need a break or anything? We're s'posed to be on duty tonight anyway, and I'm still lit up like a Christmas tree from that ride and a line. I won't be falling asleep out here if you need a break."

Numb Tongue shook his head, the merest movement. He glanced at the tavern and quickly away. Scarecrow knew to watch. Numb Tongue wasn't particularly happy to be out here with his thoughts, but there was no way he was stepping foot inside the tavern. Whatever the reason, and there was no point in asking, it was probably for the best. Numb Tongue had no desire to maim anyone tonight, at least not here, so it was safer if he stayed outside. Scarecrow knew not to push it.

The pair sat for a while longer in silence, Scarecrow suddenly aware of the all enveloping darkness, real country dark, and not a little relieved that Numb had taken guard duty. Aside from the tavern there was nothing but black mountains and black forest, no distant lights from even the closest village. They really were in the middle of fucking nowhere.

Scarecrow had clocked up nearly five hundred miles today and knew for a fact that London to Swansea was two hundred tops if you went down the M4. If they'd gone in a straight line south they could have been halfway through France by now, down near Lyon. Not that Scarecrow was complaining, any road being a good road, particularly the kind of roads that gave other people nightmares.

"Well, if you're sure, mate. Let me know if there's anything you need. I can probably get a coffee sent out or a fuckin' shot of rum might be better in this cold."

The slightest flicker in Numb Tongue's face said, "No, thank you, I want to be alone". No you don't, thought Scarecrow. You want to be in there, in the warm with everyone else, having a few beers, but something about that place won't let you, hurts you too much. Numb Tongue was absently shining his wedding ring on the hem of his t-shirt. It seemed to glow in the darkness. So that was it.

"Go," said Numb Tongue finally, kindly...sadly. "Have fun."

"I don't mind staying," offered Scarecrow. But no, Numb Tongue wasn't going to allow him to miss out on the party.

"Hm," he said, offering another line on the end of that nasty blade.

"Yeah, wouldn't mind," grinned Scarecrow.

Just then the front door of the tavern opened, the noise of distant music somehow intrusive of the night. Vincent came out and looked their way.

"Scarecrow!" he called across the car park. "Band's on in ten minutes and that bird at the bar has been asking about you!"

Scarecrow's heart skipped a beat but he waved his friend away. "Be right there." He turned to Numb Tongue. "Sure you're okay?"

Numb Tongue nodded. His wall was back in place and it had no windows.

"Well, if you change your mind..." Scarecrow meant it even though all he could think about was the girl at the bar. Surely it couldn't be the same one that was asking about him, that gorgeous little pink haired pixie whose eyes seemed to sparkle like sunshine on a river.

Numb Tongue shook his head, go, and Scarecrow turned to walk away.

He caught himself, guilty that he was leaving Numb Tongue to the night and his memories, and he briefly turned back, but Numb Tongue, with a subtle twitch of the eyebrow, said, "That's okay, I'll be okay. Just dealing with some unhealed wounds".

"Go," he said, barely more than a whisper.

Scarecrow hesitated, giving the big man one last out, but no, not tonight. Not here.

As he was walking away Numb Tongue called his name, stopping him in his tracks. They looked at each other for a moment, such sorrow in Numb Tongue's eyes.

"You're a good kid," he said, his throat dry, not used to such lengthy conversation. "Be careful. You could lose your life in that place."

CHAPTER FOURTEEN

When Scarecrow got back inside The Dragon's Head the place was packed and he caught himself doing a double-take. What the fuck? He'd just been outside and not so much as a push-bike had arrived, much less the couple of coaches it would have taken to get this lot here. Oddly dressed bunch, too, they looked, for want of a better word, like how he imagined wood folk looked. Must be a fancy dress party.

Scarecrow peered out of the window in case he'd somehow missed something, but besides Numb Tongue and the bikes it was deserted. The only weird thing was he'd spotted that black Guzzi out there, the same one that he saw all over London and outside FTW, another mysterious guest to go along with the little fella, Zig Zag, who still hadn't taken his crash helmet off. Otherwise it was all quiet, no cars, no coach parties. Outside Numb Tongue blew into his hands for warmth, his back still to the tavern.

"Oh there you are! I've been looking everywhere!"

Scarecrow's heart rose and sank in an instant. It wasn't her, just one of her friends, a fifteen on a scale of one-to-ten, but not her.

"Your friends said you were out here," said the girl. "I'm Snow."

"Nice name," said Scarecrow disinterestedly. He peered out of the window again, part of him wanting to go back out there and join Numb Tongue in his misery. Any other day, any other lifetime, he'd have been delighted to have a girl this beautiful apparently looking for him, her flawless porcelain skin framed by hair as black as the night outside. But that was before he'd seen *her*, and now, quite frankly, he just wasn't fucking interested.

"He's a good man," said Snow, looking towards Numb Tongue. "I hope one day he will forgive himself, though there is nothing to forgive. He loved her like no other."

"You know Numb Tongue?" said Scarecrow, surprised.

"Oh for many years. We were good friends."

"Were?"

Snow smiled an upside down smile. "I'd like to think we still are, but it's been a very long time since we spoke. He won't come in here since..."

"His wife."

"You knew Sunshine?" said Snow, her turn to be surprised. Snow must have been just a child when she met Numb Tongue's wife.

"No, I never met her," said Scarecrow. "Before my time, but it doesn't take a rocket scientist to join the dots. He's just sitting out there polishing his wedding ring and looking all lost."

Snow sighed. "He should let her pass. Even she wouldn't have wanted this for him. There are many others who would love him, perhaps even make him whole again."

You, for instance, thought Scarecrow. After a few years of trying to get conversation out of Numb Tongue he could read faces in an instant. The expression on Snow's face begged the question why she was looking for him and not out there talking to Numb Tongue.

"Sorry," he said, catching himself. "I'm Scarecrow." He offered his hand. "Why were you looking for me?"

"Oh yes, my friend Rain..."

"Rain?" interrupted Scarecrow, his heart skipping a beat again, while his mind began to wonder why they were all named after weather conditions.

"Yes, Rain," said Snow. "She was by the bar earlier... pink hair. She asked me to give you this."

Snow handed over a carefully folded napkin. "She said she'd be watching the band."

Scarecrow looked at the napkin, suddenly unable to make his fingers function. It was from her! It was from her! It was from...

"I think," said Snow patiently, "that if you open it, there's a message."

Scarecrow unfolded the napkin and stared at what was written inside. He read it again in case he'd missed anything, but it was pretty concise. Written in pink lipstick were the words 'I LOVE YOU'.

Scarecrow read it again.

"Are you sure this is for me?" he said finally.

"Are any of your friends called Scarecrow?"

"No, but..."

"Then it's for you."

Scarecrow found the other prospects in the back bar - which turned out to be converted stables - along with most of the full patch members, to whom they were passing a seemingly endless chain of beers. Much to Scarecrow's delight, Rain and a couple of her friends were at the other end of the bar. He pushed through the crowd to join them.

"Gonna fuckin' miss 'em at this rate," muttered Dum Dum, waving cash at the bartender in the hopes of getting served quicker, even though they hadn't been charged for anything at all yet. The landlord insisted that drinks were on the house for Aberrant MC.

"Dum Dum, you can see the stage from here," said Vincent, failing to catch the attention of the barman as he passed by once more. Fourth time he's looked straight at me, thought Vincent, with a wry smile.

Given what he'd learned today, it was no surprise that Joker always made a habit of sending him to the bar despite the fact that it took him twice as long to get served. Typical Joker sense of humour. Vincent half-heartedly fluttered a twenty at the barman, who ignored him again. At least now, he knew why.

"In layman's terms?" Mad John's friend Dennis had said this afternoon, in his quaint little countryside cottage. "You've got a magic ring that can make you invisible."

That had come as a bit of a shock. It would really. But then the more Vincent thought about it, the more plausible it was. His entire life he'd felt like no one could see him and would even talk about him as if he wasn't there. If nothing else this explained all the times he'd been knocked off his bike, why he'd been such an expert shoplifter in his youth, and, even more tellingly, why Joker thought it was so funny to send him to the bar.

"Pretty much," nodded Mad John. "Except some of the crashes might just have been cunts who don't look where they're going."

It hadn't been what Vincent expected when Mad John had called him over to meet this Dennis bloke. They'd ridden half an hour or so following Dennis in his beaten up Morris Minor to a small cottage somewhere near Amesbury. And Dennis had put the kettle on, and fed his pet bird, a large black crow. Which was the last time he'd done anything remotely normal. He had spent the rest of the afternoon muttering to himself as he examined the ring on the middle finger of Vincent's right hand.

"Fascinating," he breathed, peering at the ring through a giant eye glass. "And you can't take it off, of course?"

Vincent tried to take the ring off but it wouldn't budge. If anything it felt tighter and was starting to cut the circulation off.

"No, no, Droogie," said Dennis. "You'll just hurt yourself. The only way that's coming off is with the finger. My only worry, well, not my only worry if I'm quite honest, but a rather large concern, is which finger it's on. I'm afraid it's considered very bad luck on that finger. Tell me, do you remember the first time you were aware of having it?"

Vincent had to admit that he'd never even thought about it. He'd had the ring for as long as he could remember and it only now occurred to him as odd that it must have somehow grown with him. Admittedly he had small hands, not exactly being built like an outdoor khazi himself, but surely his hands weren't the same size as they'd been when he was thirteen or even younger.

"I can't remember ever not wearing it," he said. "It sounds stupid now, but it's like it's part of me."

"Hmm, probably more so than you think, Droogie," said Dennis, twisting the ring around on Vincent's finger to get a better look at the markings. "Well, it's definitely the real deal. The question is where does it come from and what exactly does it do?"

"You mean besides make me invisible?"

"Precisely, Droogie! Would you like some tea?"

Vincent felt he needed something rather stronger than tea. Crack, for instance. Clearly that was what these two were on.

"This is a wind up, right?" He looked searchingly at Mad John, but Mad John shook his head.

"In some ways I wish it was. And I might add that I am a fool for not spotting it before, but in my defence it seems to have less effect on club members, we can often see you when others cannot. It was Joker who noticed, a few months ago when Dum Dum was trying to find you and you were standing in the same room. It seems only ineffective on full patch members, and folks with a great knowledge of magic, but then, we are rather more experienced in these matters."

"Which is why Joker always sends me to the bar, cos he knows no one can see me."

"Yes, I'm afraid Joker's little bar games may have drawn rather more attention than is helpful at the moment," Mad John sighed. "These rings, Vincent, they are extremely old, extremely powerful, and in the wrong hands, even in the right hands, extremely dangerous. Not least because the bounty on them is astronomical. Clearly no one knows about this one or, I regret to say, you would have lost both the ring and finger when you were a child."

"But you're saying someone might know about it now because of Joker fucking about?"

"I'm afraid it's a possibility," conceded Mad John.

"I'm guessing you'd like that tea now, Droogie?" said Dennis.

"Um, coffee if you've got it. And what's a Droogie?"

"Another one that doesn't know his Clockwork Orange," tutted Dennis, heading for the kitchen. "A fine man, Burgess. Did I ever tell you, John, that I once met him outside..."

"You did mention it once or twice," said Mad John kindly. "I think Vincent could probably do with that coffee."

"Of course, I do beg your pardon. It must be rather a shock."

Rather a shock didn't really cover it as far as Vincent was concerned. He had so many unanswered questions that he had no idea where to even start. The whole idea was preposterous, a fiction, and yet...

"How come Dennis can see me then?" Vincent said finally.

"Ah, straight to the tricky questions, I see," Mad John smiled. His eyes were kind, concerned, but with that flicker of light that told you everything would be all right. It was easy to see why he was club president, people would follow him anywhere. He looked at Vincent and held eye contact.

"In that case," he said, "I'll just come out and say it. Any questions you may have afterwards, and I'm sure there will be many, will be answered in due course. Preferably after I know the answers. Dennis is a wizard."

"A wizard?"

"Yes, spells, robes, wizard, that kind of thing."

"A *wizard*?"

"Yes, we've established that much. I was rather hoping we could move along faster than this since we still have many miles to ride today."

"You mean like Harry Potter, Lord Of The Rings, wizard?" persisted Vincent incredulously.

"I'd rather prefer the latter," said Dennis, re-emerging from the kitchen with a tray full of steaming mugs. "If you don't mind. Sugar?"

The afternoon had been as surreal as it was informative. There were, Vincent was told, several thousand such rings dotted around the world, mostly in the hands of the very rich and the very powerful, which tends to amount to much the same thing. For obvious reasons the rings were priceless and, since they never came to auction anyway, the very rich, very powerful people tended to send very violent, very nasty people looking for them.

"Last I heard," said Dennis, "the bounty on a much less powerful ring than this one seems to be, was around the eighteen million pound mark. People will do really rather unpleasant things for eighteen millions pounds. From what I can tell, this one is worth at least twice that, probably more since that bounty was some time ago, sixteenth century, a dealer in France, I believe."

"So if it was worth eighteen million then," said Mad John. "That means today it's worth..."

"A fuckload!" exclaimed Vincent. "Fucking hell! That's... Wait a minute... Sixteenth century? And you said *you* heard this? How old *are* you?"

"Well, let's see," mused Dennis. "I'd have been in my early thirties back then. What year did you say it is again? Two thousand and something, you say?"

"Dennis, we do have rather more pressing matters and not nearly as much time as I'd like," Mad John interrupted.

"Indeed. My apologies. These markings on the third rubbing, do you think they could be some kind of early Sanskrit?"

Dennis, the wizard, had taken several rubbings from the ring and found the markings to be different every time, and each time equally unfathomable. Around them lay a stack of leather-bound books, their covers worn through by endless reading, and each one had been found to be equally unhelpful. The wizard lit, as Vincent had always imagined they did, a big wooden pipe, and blew the obligatory smoke ring.

"I'm afraid I'm going to need time to study these," said the wizard. "How much time, I'm afraid I really can't say. Would it be intrusive to ask where you and your Droogies are heading?"

"Dragon's Head tonight," said Mad John. "Then on to Fero City by way of Vernon Wells."

"Fero City?" the wizard raised an eyebrow. "No good ever comes of that place. I've warned you of that before, but I suppose you know what is best for your own club. There for a bit of the old ultra-violence no doubt. I do hope none of your good men are partaking?"

"Numb's fighting again," said Mad John, his expression suggesting that he wasn't entirely happy about it either.

"I feared as much," Dennis sighed a deep sigh. "Four prospects? You are expanding I hope, not preparing?"

"It will be either a celebration or a wake," Mad John conceded. "These orange markings," he changed the subject and pointed to one of the old books. "Do they mean anything? They seem to have been added after the fact."

"Yes, unfortunately it means that one of my little terrors has been in the library again with his crayons!" The wizard took the book from Mad John and examined the pages with an exasperated look. "Little bugger. I do keep telling Jill to keep them out of there, some of these books are priceless."

"My best advice at the moment," continued the wizard with the wife and two kids, "would be that young Vincent, here, keeps the ring hidden as best he can, perhaps a glove. But as you mentioned, I doubt this ring is widely known or you'd have had trouble by now."

"Any help you can give will be received with much gratitude," said Mad John. "If all goes to plan we should be in Vernon Wells for the new moon. You can send word to me there."

"Rest assured, Droogie, if there is a debt of gratitude then it is I who shall always owe you. Now gentlemen, if you don't mind, it seems I have much work to do."

That was only this afternoon, but already it seemed like days ago. Vincent waved the twenty at the barman again and the barman leaned across him and served the person behind him.

"Apologies," said the man behind him. "It seems the barman didn't see you."

No, thought Vincent. But you did.

CHAPTER FIFTEEN

By three o'clock in the morning The General was well on his way to being very drunk indeed. All in all it hadn't been a bad night so far, free drinks, a decent band, no hassles from anyone, and lots of hot girls everywhere. Not that The General was having much luck with them tonight, unlike Scarecrow who'd been halfway down the pink-haired bird's neck all night, but their presence also helped to keep Loud-As under control since he was too preoccupied with trying to get laid to start any trouble. Even Vincent looked like he might get some tonight, little prick.

The General scratched at the rash on his head, stumbling a little as he misjudged the distance to the wall he was about to lean on. Maybe he needed some air. Then again, maybe not. He'd been outside earlier and, by virtue of him being the only person out there, had been forced to smoke with Numb Tongue. It had not been a pleasant experience.

The air had been good, real fresh, country air, cold enough to be refreshing if you weren't out there for too long and a welcome respite from the noise and heat inside. Sitting with Numb Tongue, however, had been more terrifying than refreshing. Minutes had passed as days until the silence became overbearing. The General had tried to make conversation, but Numb Tongue just sat there staring at the ground like he despised the very earth. The General tried not to look at him, just smoke and get back inside, but something, some car crash mentality, kept compelling him to glance at the big man, each glance becoming longer, more daring, as they went uncaught.

The General had never really looked at Numb Tongue, not properly looked at him. First rule, never make eye contact with someone who might eat the contents of your head through your eye-sockets with a spoon. Not many people made eye contact with Numb Tongue. The General watched as he snurfed coke up his nose from a razor sharp blade that glinted horribly in the pale moonlight. He imagined this was how it felt being up close with a tiger in the wild. Any second it could attack and maul him beyond recognition, but still The General looked.

Numb Tongue might have been a handsome man once upon a time, but now his face was so scarred that it looked like he'd shaved with a weedwhacker, leaving only a long black goatee beard behind. It was difficult knowing where to start. Aside from the dents and scars on his close-shaved head there was a deep scar through Numb Tongue's crooked nose, accompanied by what looked like teeth marks. That was probably the only thing most people would see, as they hurriedly looked away. But look closer.

Along with the obligatory Chelsea Smile, there was a vertical scar through Numb Tongue's lower lip and another two, thicker, maybe serrated, that ran parallel through both lips, disappearing into his goatee. Both cheeks were a mess, a school desk, carved and gouged, his forehead a kitchen chopping board. Numb Tongue's left eye looked as if the skin had once been torn all the way to his ear, which was missing part of the lower lobe. But it was the right eye that topped them all on the nutter scale as far as The General was concerned. Not only was there a vicious scar from forehead to cheek, but his actual eyeball was scarred, a white line running through a deep grey iris and splitting his pupil in two. The General smoked his cigarette as quickly as possible and hurried back inside.

So, no, maybe he didn't need any air. Maybe a line was a better idea.

But who to ask? The General wasn't carrying and the club's main supply was out in the car park shovelling it up his tooth-marked nose with a switchblade. Chaos always had some, but he overcharged the prospects for it, only handing out freebies to full patch members. The only free line you ever got out of him was the first one, which he insisted you did in front of him to prove you weren't a cop.

Dum Dum was probably holding too, but he was down the front having started a one man mosh pit. The rest of the crowd had gradually got their heads around the fact that this human dump truck meant no harm and had joined in. Now Dum Dum was all sweat and beer, pressed up against the barrier, singing along to every song. He'd nearly wet himself when the band dedicated a song to Mad John and Aberrant MC. Vincent was nowhere to be seen, probably off with one of those birds, although the one he was talking to earlier now appeared to be talking to herself.

Maybe if The General had a line he'd sober up enough to try his luck. The place showed no signs of closing and the night, it seemed, was still young. He spotted Stone on the far side of the bar, but dismissed the notion immediately. Never, under any circumstances, go anywhere near Stone's drugs.

"Might I say, sir, that you've got one hell of a righteous motorcycle club."

The General turned and was about to say "Yeah, and what the fuck's it got to do with you?" when he thought better of it. Besides being dressed all in black - jeans, polished boots, long leather coat - there was something about the man next to him that said he was not to be messed with. A cop maybe? No, not a cop, perhaps ex-services, but certainly not to be messed with. Mid-forties with a kind of Nick Cave dourness, he looked like he could handle himself, and The General had no intention of testing Aberrant's 'one in-all in' policy just now, particularly with Dum Dum being on the far side of the venue. It takes only seconds to disfigure someone.

"Thanks," said The General, deciding on nonchalance as a best avenue.

He swayed a little, puffing himself up to big-guy mode. This man wasn't a threat, he *admired* them. And, fuck it, if he was a cop, then he was a long way from any back up, and anything The General could be arrested for was safely stashed on Dum Dum's bike. Let him take the blame. Half the Welsh constabulary could burst in right now and they wouldn't find anything. Well, they'd find all kinds of things on the rest of them, exactly the kinds of things they were looking for, but the point is they wouldn't find anything on him, The General. He could really do with a line though, he was starting to slur, sweating at the temples, his mouth showing the first watery signs that all was not entirely well. That'll be the Jager bombs.

The General was about to tell the man how important he was in the club, pretty much top man, indispensable, when he realised that he was having trouble with speech.

"Might I ask if we are in discreet company?" said the man.

"Huh?" The General was having some difficulty focusing.

"Are we, ah, cool?" persisted the man.

"Wha'? Yeah, yeah, cool. No prolbem. Problem, I mean..." The General trailed off, taking a big gulp of air. "Ver' hot. Ban's ver' good," he tried to focus in the direction of the stage.

"No, I mean," said the man, surreptitiously waving a small wrap under his coat. "Do you party?"

"Wha'? Oh yeah! Fuckin' lifesaver, man!" said The General, perking up somewhat. He dabbed his finger into the wrap and poked about for a decent amount. It was hardly subtle, but, fuck it, the place was dark and no one was looking. "Oh man, that tastes fucking disgusting."

"Only water I'm afraid," said the man, handing him an open bottle. "I thought it best to have at least a few glasses before tackling those roads again."

"Fucking tell me about it! It was pitch black when we came up here and there's all these fucking huge drops off the edge of the cliff." The General had stopped enjoying the ride long before they got to Wales and had spend the rest of it clinging on for dear life. Through vast quantities of alcohol, he'd successfully managed to forget about it until now and was not relishing the return journey.

"If you don't mind me saying, it takes a brave man to do that on a motor-cycle. I'm not sure I'd have the courage."

The General didn't mind him saying at all. "I couldn't get another little dab of that, could I?"

"Be my guest," the man smiled. "I would consider it an honour. My name is Elron, Elron Stoob, at your service."

"Do you mind if I ask?" said Elron, as The General dug around in the wrap with his bike key. "Your friends said you'd come all the way from London. Do you have a base there?"

The General had talked to Elron for rather too long, he thought later. That was the thing with coke, you'd hang around some arsehole all night just because he was holding, jabbering away and changing the world, while you were actually missing the band and any remote chance you may have had of getting laid. The place was winding down now and he'd spotted a comfy looking sofa by the fireplace in the front bar.

Despite the coke he still felt drowsy and blurred around the edges. He remembered going outside for some air and another cigarette. He'd gone with Elron this time, shying away from the car park where Numb Tongue prowled. They'd done another line and Elron had asked a lot of questions. A *lot* of questions. People always wanted to know about outlaw bikers and The General had been happy to brag, but careful enough not to say anything incriminating. What did it matter if this Elron bloke knew that they had a clubhouse? It was hardly a secret.

The log in the fireplace crackled and settled lower into glowing embers and The General sank a little lower into the sofa. He was having trouble remembering what this Elron bloke even looked like. The morning sun began to poke intrusive fingers through the curtains. Elron was long gone anyway, nothing to worry about, just a random who happened to have a lot of drugs and was happy to share. The General couldn't even remember the bloke leaving. It was long after the band had finished playing, he knew that much because Dum Dum, straight out of the pit, had given him a big sweaty hug and then gone off to find Vincent. Elron had seemed very interested in Vincent after that.

"Last time I saw him," The General slurred, "he was talking to that bird at the bar. I think she's a bit mental though, talks to herself."

"But you haven't seen your friend for some time?" said Elron, staring at the space where Vincent had been standing. "That *is* interesting."

"'S nothing," said The General, misjudging the wall again. "You should've seen what he did this afternoon..."

CHAPTER SIXTEEN

Dum Dum pulled his bike into the side of the road and turned off the engine. He considered turning around and going back the way he had come, but wasn't entirely sure if that would take him further away from the rest of the club. He took his crash helmet off and sat on a low stone wall.

"Hmm," said Dum Dum, one of the rare people who actually said this aloud when he was thinking. "Where the bloody hell did they get to? Whole bloody club's gone this time."

Though he had no idea how it was done, Dum Dum had been, and indeed, still was, enormously impressed by Vincent's disappearing act. Ever since he was a child he had loved riddles, puzzles, and tricks, although he was hopeless at solving them himself. But unless this was some new trick, perhaps an initiation of some kind, it was rather more worrying. Not least because Dum Dum had absolutely no idea where he was.

They'd done about fifty miles since setting off from The Dragon's Head this morning and, again, Mad John had set a pace that required Dum Dum's full concentration. His left hand had swollen overnight after clipping that wall and, having thoroughly poked at it, he now suspected that it was broken. In hindsight perhaps he'd been concentrating so hard on staying on the road that he hadn't paid enough attention to where they were actually going. He had been following over a dozen very conspicuous motorcycles and had thought there was little chance of losing them. But, nonetheless, here he was, clueless and lost. What to do?

"Wouldn't hurt just for a minute, I suppose," he muttered to himself, digging his GPS out of his luggage. "At least find out where I am."

It hadn't helped that, having got lost, Dum Dum had then driven randomly back and forth up and down several winding country lanes in the hope of spotting something familiar from which to get his bearings. It all looked the same, trees and rocks and stuff, and now he had no idea which direction he should be heading.

"If I can just find where we came to that bloody roundabout...."

The screen on Dum Dum's GPS lit up and informed him that it was searching for a signal. He felt bad enough even bringing it with him and truly awful disobeying a direct club order by turning the thing on, but Loud-As had said it was okay to bring them, that Mad John was just being paranoid. And since Loud-As was a full patch member, they had obviously changed the rule about mobile phones and GPS devices and forgotten to tell the prospects. That said, he hadn't actually been given permission to use them.

But it was that or ride around in circles until he stumbled across some signs of civilisation, the tavern being the only building he'd seen all morning. It was a weird place to put a pub, out in the middle of nowhere, but perhaps that was why it had survived. When drunk driving finally became frowned upon in the late eighties, early nineties, most of these country places had been forced to either adapt, devolving into Happy Eaters, or close down entirely, there being little point in a pub that you drove to if you couldn't drive back home again.

The Dragon's Head was so far away from anywhere else that the cops probably just couldn't be bothered. If you managed to tackle those roads, particularly at night, then you were obviously sober enough to drive, and if not the only thing you were likely to hit was a tree. Or indeed a wall.

Dum Dum's hand was throbbing. His GPS found a signal and then promptly lost it again. His bike ticked gently to itself as it cooled, a small puddle of oil forming beneath it where it was leaking. The last thing Dum Dum needed, with his limited mechanical knowledge, was for the bike to break down. At least they'd filled up with petrol before leaving, but that wasn't much use beyond starting a fire if the bike wasn't running. It was certainly no good for drinking. Horrid, foul tasting stuff.

By midday the club had assembled in The Dragon's Head car park, many of them rather the worse for hangovers, a couple of them still drunk. Dum Dum didn't really suffer from hangovers. It took a lot to get him drunk in the first place, the average drinking partner long passed out before Dum Dum was even tipsy, and even within Aberrant there were only a few who could match him drink for drink. Those who tried usually deeply regretted it the next day, and often for many days to come.

Smiler was green around the edges, his eyes reduced to sunken slits in dark grey sockets, a light sweat gathering on his forehead. He never seemed to learn, always up for a drinking or fighting challenge no matter what the odds, and now he had a ferocious hangover to accompany his broken nose. There was a vague smell of vomit and a strong smell of stale alcohol about him.

"I swear to God I am never drinking again."

"Until next time, right?"

"No, really," Smiler croaked. "I think I'm dying. Just kill me now and get it over with."

"Tempting," muttered Loud-As. He was probably joking, but had been particularly unpleasant of late so it was difficult to be sure. And he had not been entirely unsuccessful with the ladies last night, but unfortunately the lady in question was only slightly smaller than Dum Dum and only marginally prettier.

It was a common occurrence. Even those who liked a bit of rough didn't want anything quite as rough as Loud-As. But while the larger ladies kept him occupied when he was too drunk to do anything other than swear and break things, they tended to leave a lingering self-loathing and bitterness about him. "Any hole's a goal, right?" "It's like riding a moped, lots of fun so long as your mates don't see you." But deep down Loud-As resented anyone who could maintain any sort of relationship. Hell, it wasn't even deep down, just bubbling beneath the surface waiting to call you a "poof" if you expressed any emotional attachment whatsoever to a member of the opposite sex.

Dum Dum didn't really understand how that made anyone a poof, but then women in general were something of a mystery to him and, because they were small, he tended to treat them as children, especially since they both seemed to like chocolate. Besides, when Dum Dum thought about women, which was not particularly often, he liked to think of them big, the bigger the better, so he really couldn't see why Loud-As got so upset about it. At least the big ones wouldn't break if you rolled over on them.

"Good afternoon, gentlemen," said Mad John, rousing Dum Dum from fond memories of a very large lady called Brenda who once worked as a bouncer in one of Manchester's more boisterous establishments. Mad John was standing on the seat of his Knucklehead, and the world turned it down a notch. "If I might have your attention."

There were nods and a few coughs, the sound of Smiler quietly throwing up in the bushes. The general consensus was that it was indeed afternoon, but there was some debate over whether this was good or not. They tried their best to give him their attention.

"I trust you all had a thoroughly enjoyable evening and that you're all packed up and ready to go."

There was some grunting and shuffling of feet. Smiler threw up in the bushes again.

"A couple of points before we go," Mad John smiled unperturbed. "Numb Tongue tells me we had visitors last night, three of them sniffing around in the shadows. They'll have trouble keeping up with us, but I want everyone to keep their eyes peeled all the same, and be careful who you talk to, loose lips, etcetera. We're not sure who they are yet, but that rather suggests that we should find out, don't you think? Rhetorical question, Dum Dum. Any questions? Yes Dum Dum?"

"I haven't got any petrol left," said Dum Dum.

"More of a statement than a question, but you'll find a pump round the back of the stables."

Dum Dum couldn't think of any questions that actually ended with a question mark. If the club was being followed then, as Mad John had already pointed out, whoever was following them would have trouble keeping up at all, let alone keeping up with them unnoticed. Mad John would have said if he thought they were cops and Dum Dum prided himself that, after so many years in and out of jail, he could smell cops a mile away.

There had been no cops around last night, just good party people in the back bar where the band had played, and local farmers or whatever they were in the front bar. Dum Dum had had the time of his life, not only getting to hang out with pretty much the entire club, as close as he'd ever been to a family reunion, but also getting to know a few of those brothers far better.

To top it all he'd got to see his favourite band and they'd dedicated a song to the club! Well, okay, they'd dedicated a song called Immortal to Mad John, but Dum Dum had swelled with pride by association, singing extra loud to that one: "Who's the man who stole fire for the people? Who causes trembling in the bones of evil? Who carved a mountain into a cathedral?" It had been a brilliant night.

"Oh, and one last thing," said Mad John genially.

"Yeah, we know!" laughed Andy One-Leg. "Anyone who needs a good crap in a nice clean toilet had better knock one out now!"

"Precisely," Mad John grinned. "And don't be stealing all their toilet paper just because you forgot to pack any. These are good people."

Some of the good people had even showed up to wave them farewell, the landlord supplying a bottle or two for the journey and generally fussing over them like a worried father sending his kids off on a school trip.

That had been...well, although he owned a watch, it was a digital thing and Dum Dum hadn't quite mastered telling the time, but it had been at least a few hours ago. The club could be miles away by now. He was sure they'd come back and look for him, but still wasn't entirely sure how he'd managed to lose them in the first place.

They'd been booming along more of those tight and twisty, tree lined roads, some of them dark as night where the intertwined branches blocked out the sun, others like being inside a strobe light as the sunshine broke through. The road snaked this way and that, up and down, following the contours of endless mountains, the temperature rising and falling with the altitude. They passed no other vehicles and Dum Dum was pretty sure no one had followed them. At last they had come to a steep declivity, the road curving down into a narrow valley. Which is where it had all gone awry.

Mad John halted their convoy at the bottom of the valley at the weirdest looking roundabout Dum Dum had ever seen, entirely enclosed by overhanging trees like you were riding into tunnels. It was a magical sight, one of natures little wonders, and all lit up like a disco ball every time there was a gentle breeze. There was no telling how many roads led away from it.

Mad John had told them to follow him very carefully. "Numb's on point, but I want everyone keeping an eye out. We don't want anybody getting lost."

Famous last words. How hard could it be to follow everyone around a roundabout? Except that Mad John seemed intent on going at it like it was a wall of death, fast enough to build up centrifugal forge, and had then missed the turning a couple of times and gone back around again and again. Finally the pack veered off down one of the narrows roads that lead away from the roundabout and Dum Dum had followed only to find himself completely alone on a country lane.

Dum Dum's GPS lit up again, searching, searching, searching...

"Ah, now, here we are."

Snake Pass. It was a suitably pointy and vicious trail that traced a path through the middle of nowhere. Dum Dum scrolled along the display and found what he thought he was looking for, The Circle Of Seven, a roundabout with, Dum Dum counted them twice, eight exits. He checked again. Yes, that must be the place he lost them, about three miles east of here. Best place to start looking.

Dum Dum fastened his crash helmet and pulled his gloves on, inching the left glove over a hand that was slowly turning purple. He sensed, for a moment, that he was being watched, but the only sign of life was a large black bird, a crow or a rook or something, lazily picking at what had perhaps once been a rabbit. It had to be the unluckiest rabbit in the world to end up as road kill on this road. It might have died of old age waiting for a car to jump in front of.

The bird stopped picking and looked at Dum Dum.

"Aaaarrk."

"Aaaarrk yourself," muttered Dum Dum. "Give you a tenner if you can tell me where Aberrant's got to."

"Aaarrk," said the bird that Dum Dum had decided was definitely a crow.

"Yeah, that's what I thought," said Dum Dum, launching himself at his kick-start. "Back to that roundabout and hope for the best."

Dum Dum's bike coughed into life on the third kick, the bird lumbering slowly out of his way as he headed back the way he'd come, completely failing to notice three big black dogs watching him intently from behind the opposite wall.

"If we hurry we may still catch them."

As one the dogs set off at a trot.

"Aaaarrk," cursed the crow and followed them.

CHAPTER SEVENTEEN

It was the easiest club rule to abide by and yet the easiest to forget. And The General had broken it. Retribution had been harsh, unforgiving, and seemingly permanent. He peered into the mirror on his bike and his face was a mess of black and blue.

He spat on the hem of his t-shirt and rubbed furiously at the badly drawn penis that adorned his cheek, but, like the 'TWAT' across his forehead and the 'I LOVE COCK' moustache, it refused to budge. The worst thing was that he had only just noticed it! All morning he, The General, prospect for Aberrant MC, had been riding around with 'TWAT' written all over his face. And then they had finally pulled over because Dum Dum got lost and he'd caught a glimpse of himself in the mirror. Joker the fucking speedfreak prankster had been at work, writing obscenities all over his face and, inevitably, removing his left eyebrow. And all because The General had fallen asleep with his boots on.

The rule was simple. If you took your boots off before passing out, no matter where you passed out, then you were off limits to practical jokes, having intended to rest. It was something to do with dying with your boots on. Someone might even get you a blanket. Boots on meant you were fair game, and very little was off limits. So much so that Loud-As and Smiler had taken to occasionally removing their boots before they started drinking, just to avoid any problems.

The General knew the rule and had partaken in the pranks. Joker, usually the wide awake instigator, had filled crash helmets with tyre weld, glued boots together, put sheep in tents, moved tents to different fields... One time Loud-As had passed out in his tent with his boots still on and Joker and friends had moved him and the tent three miles away to the front garden of an old people's home. And now The General had forgotten and paid the price.

But that was the least of his problems.

"He's a fucking liability!"

The General could hear bits and pieces of a many-sided conversation, all the full patch members, except Numb Tongue who had gone to look for Dum Dum, off to one side in a semicircle. What he was hearing wasn't good. That had been Apples' voice and he caught Mad John's next.

"He may have already said too much, but if we just cut him loose then there's no doubt they'll catch him. They won't be so friendly in their methods next time."

"Cut him loose?" ranted Apples. "I'll fackin' cut 'im up! Give 'im a fackin' Mars across his boat!"

Oh God, please someone talk some sense into him. The General had picked up a fair amount of Apples' cockney gibberish, adopting a phrase or two himself once in a while, and he knew what had been said: Mars, meaning Mars bar, rhyming with scar. Boat, boat-race, face. Not content with drawing all over it, they were now going to cut his face. With a sense of futility he rubbed at the penis again. He didn't want to die with a penis drawn on his face. He didn't want to die at all.

"Serve him fackin' right if they did catch him!" Apples was still fuming.

Mad John spoke again. "*If* it was them, and it seems more than likely, then, as I said, gentlemen, they are toying with us and they want us to know about it. Either they're very brave or very foolish."

"Or they know fuckin' something we don't. More n' likely something Sergeant Stupid told 'em last night."

The General spat on his shirt again and rubbed hopelessly at the penis. So, Sergeant Stupid now was it? All he'd done was party, just like everyone else, and, for the most part, with everyone else. How was he supposed to know that this Elron bloke, who he now barely remembered, would drug him and relieve him of his thankfully slightly limited knowledge of Aberrant MC and their movements.

Thank God he didn't know where they were going, but still he felt...Well, Sergeant Stupid probably summed it up. Not to mention Captain Crapping-Himself and Lieutenant Legging-It-The-First-Chance-He-Got. They wouldn't even have known about Elron if he hadn't shown the fucker's business card to Chaos. And it wasn't a particularly clever anagram, taking Mad John, with an exasperated sigh, mere seconds to point it out.

"Born To Lose. You useless oaf!"

Well, how the hell was he supposed to know to look out for stupid anagrams in people's names? And worse still was the fact that he couldn't answer any of the club's questions. He couldn't remember what this Elron Stoob bloke looked like, had no idea what he'd told him, and only knew his name because the fucker had given him a card with it on there. Except it didn't say Elron Stoob anymore. It said, quite clearly, Born To Lose.

"Cheap trick," Mad John growled as it changed in his hands. "Only reveals itself once it is solved."

Oh rub it in why don't you? The General spat on his shirt again and tried once more to remove the COCK from his face while he awaited his fate.

"We're not common murderers." Mad John's voice again, from over in the impromptu club meeting.

"If we leave him here it'll be the same thing," said Andy One-Leg.

"Fuckin' won't be our hands." Would somebody please shut Apples up. The General had been under the impression that the two of them got along okay, and now the Cockney twat was suggesting they abandon him to whatever it was that was worse than actually being with them. Obviously this saved him the bother of running away, but there was no doubt they'd want the prospect patch back and The General had seen what happened to those who got on the wrong side of the club. His plan had involved more of the running-away-when-they're-not-looking, than being-dumped-off-in-the-middle-of-nowhere-to-await-slow-death. This also begged the most terrible question: Who or what was following them? What could be worse than Apples kind offer of a Mars bar across his boat?

Something bad enough to rattle their cages, that was for sure. Mad John looked worried and he was the club president for fuck's sake. He kept looking over at Vincent like he expected him to disappear again, like he was checking on him the whole time, and he'd been overly concerned about losing Dum Dum. Chances were that Dum Dum's bike had broken down again and all they had to do was go back and get the fat oaf, maybe show him how to turn the reserve tap on, and yet Mad John had been all "make haste" and "time is of the essence", furrows in his forehead. This was Dum Dum they were talking about! Six foot eight, three hundred-plus pounds, with a fucking dent in his head! And Mad John had sent Numb Tongue to find him! Whoever was following them The General was in no hurry to make to their acquaintance. Again. So much for running away.

The meeting was finally broken up by the sudden sound of two booming Harleys, one that popped and farted as it boomed, indicating that Numb Tongue had found Dum Dum safe and well. Curiously there had been no warning of their arrival, no distant rumble of engines, they just roared around the corner as if someone had turned the volume on. The General had noticed the same thing when Numb Tongue set off, his bike, usually audible for miles, had fallen silent the moment he rounded the bend out of sight.

That was another thing; these roads were starting to give him the creeps, the sound vanishing behind him like a door closing, the lack of any road signs whatsoever, the things in the woods.... He'd caught glimpses of them as the trees flashed past, bears maybe, but he couldn't be sure. Big fuckers, not something you'd want to stand around arguing with, that was for sure. Maybe that was why Mad John had told them to come tooled up, why he had a gun under his seat, but it seemed almost unfeasible. Whatever they were here for it wasn't to hunt grizzlies.

The General made sure no one was watching and retrieved the Luger, tucking it into his jacket pocket. He'd give them tooled up.

"Gentlemen." Mad John was on his seat again, their meeting over now that Dum Dum and Numb Tongue had returned. The world bent an ear in his direction. The General didn't like that much, either, how everyone seemed vaguely hypnotised when Mad John spoke, like he was a fucking messiah or something, every word a gift of wisdom. He was a wanted bank robber for Christ's sake, let's not get carried away. The club gathered around him with The General lurking at the back.

"As you may have gathered, there is a distinct possibility that we're being followed, but still we have speed on our side," said Mad John. "Might I suggest that we put some distance between us and them, at least until we find a better place to make camp. I'm sure some of you have noticed we've had a bit of company now and again, so let's not make the night any harder than necessary."

He's going to say "We must make haste", again, thought The General.

"Let us make haste."

Twat.

The club started their bikes, shattering the countryside quite in an instant, and then suddenly there was a huge bang from their midst that sent more than a couple of them ducking for cover. There were no gunshots, however. Dum Dum's Harley had very noisily blown its engine.

The club dismounted, Scarecrow among the first to go and help, but it was fairly obvious that the bike wasn't going anywhere without some major surgery, its vital fluids in a big pool of black beneath it.

"Gonna take at least a couple of hours to fix it," said Scarecrow, poking around under the bike. "And that's if we don't need too many parts. I can make a couple of gaskets out of cardboard, that should do the trick, but I'll have to strip it down first to find out what else is going on."

"Sorry," said Dum Dum.

"We need to move from here," said Mad John bluntly. "It'll be dark soon and this road is an ambush waiting to happen. Chaos?"

"I reckon we can fix it, but you're right, we shouldn't hang around here too long. We've got rope so we could tow it, but..."

"Yes, yes," said Mad John urgently, looking about him as if expecting to be overhead. "Tow it. Even now it grows dark too early."

As he spoke the night did indeed seem to close in, the shadows growing long and portentous. The road was narrow like all those they had travelled this morning, but though it was a little wider where they were parked it was fully enclosed by forest on one side, and a drop of two hundred or so feet on the other. They would be able to guard either side of the road, but the forest sloped down towards the road offering a clear and well hidden line of attack. If anyone or anything was in the forest then they wouldn't need to do much more than lob rocks at Aberrant to do some significant damage. What was more worrying to The General was that anyone or any*thing* would think that was a good idea in the first place.

A rope was tied to Dum Dum's stricken Harley and the club moved on, making slow progress, but at least moving ahead of the darkness, west towards the lowering sun. The roads were finally starting to widen, the forests finally beginning to thin, and thankfully the steep drop to their right had gone, the river that was at the bottom now running parallel to the road. The club had probably done fifteen miles when their left hand side opened up to lush green fields and the most astonishing view down into a distant valley. They drove through a gap in the low wall and parked in the middle of the field.

"Bikes in a circle, gentlemen," said Mad John. "Lights facing out, with enough room for tents in the middle. Scarecrow and Vincent take first watch."

"Wouldn't I..." began Scarecrow.

"Yes, yes, good point," said Mad John, as if Scarecrow had actually finished his sentence.

"You'd be better off working on the bike. Chaos, you, Loud, and Billy give him a hand. We need it running as soon as possible, and running well enough that it won't break down in the middle of nowhere. Vincent, you and Dum Dum take first watch, but that doesn't mean the rest of you can start partying, we must be well rested and well prepared."

The General could have sworn that he heard growling noises from the helmeted head of Zig Zag, who, he just noticed, was standing beside him at about elbow height.

"That's a very powerful spell to perform without Flashback, and I fear that it would take longer than fixing the bike," Mad John replied to the growling. "And even if it were possible, the creature would be very slow and, given it's temperament, would very probably, I'm afraid, bite its owner."

There was definitely a growled response from beneath Zig Zag's crash helmet, some guttural snarling sound, like there was a caged creature behind the visor. The General backed away a pace or two. He'd thought, when he'd bothered to think about it, that maybe the little Zig Zag fella modelled himself on the Stig from Top Gear with all the anonymity and none of the height. Frankly he'd had too much other shit to worry about to even think about it, but he was thinking about it now.

"Personally I think that might be a little too soon," said Mad John calmly.

There was more growling, this time with the merest hint of something that might have once been English, like a tiger trying to form a sentence.

"He's got a point," Stone chipped in casually, apparently conversant in animal noises, too. "They're gonna find out sooner or later. If nothing else it'll give them an idea of what they should be scared of. No offence, Zig Zag."

There was a grunt, perhaps a shrug from under the black, dark-vizored helmet.

"Fair enough," Mad John shrugged. "There's no going back now anyway."

At which point Zig Zag McClintock took his crash helmet off and The General fainted.

CHAPTER EIGHTEEN

There was a rustling sound, something moving in a long circle around the bikes, just out of range of their headlights, the hint of a shadow against the blackness. Every other bike had its lights on, covering a wide path in every direction. Something was moving just out of their range, across the field in the darkness. Dum Dum shone his torch about but could see nothing.

"You think there's anything else out there we should be looking out for?" he said.

Vincent smiled. "Mate, after what I've seen recently, I'd say we could be looking for pink elephants and giant squid with machine guns."

"You mean?" Dum Dum nudged Vincent in the ribs, almost knocking him over. He nodded to where Zig Zag McClintock was sleeping beside the camp-fire.

"Among other things," said Vincent.

Zig Zag had, it must be said, come as quite a shock, and, if not for at least a little preparation, Vincent was sure he'd have reacted in much the same way as The General. Like The General, he'd also had too much to consider to really give the little man much thought, and had also started to think of him as The Stig, or mini-Stig. This was definitely not The Stig. If you revealed this face on the Top Gear end of season special it would cause panic in the streets. Or people, being people, would think it was the Halloween rerun and that it was all make up. But it definitely wasn't make up.

Zig Zag McClintock wasn't actually human. This was the reason he kept his crash helmet on all the time. Upon realising there was no make up the public tended to react badly and either attacked him on sight or ran screaming to the authorities. Which, frankly, was a pain in the arse. He was, it later transpired, part dwarf and part orc, a very rare breed indeed given that the two races utterly despise each other. Technically he was a dworc, but strongly preffered orc.

He was also, it had to be said, not exactly blessed with the most attractive traits of each species, with the leather facial features of the latter, the height disadvantages of the former, and, due to the aforementioned prejudices between orcs and dwarfs, a vast scar down the centre of his head. Unfortunate genetics and pointy leather ears aside, Zig Zag's appearance had not been enhanced by the... well, scar, wasn't a strong enough word. It didn't really cover what had happened to Zig Zag's face when it had, many, many years ago, been split in two with an axe and then bound back together with dockyard rope.

Having removed his helmet, he had growled something else at Mad John, revealing a surplus of vicious teeth, and then set about building the camp-fire that he was now sleeping beside. Mad John had hurriedly explained the basics to three of the four prospects, The General still out cold beside the bikes, and then left them to get on with it.

"If we get through this night then there will be plenty of time for questions," he said, bustling off to confer with Numb Tongue. "Now get on with it. It could be a *long* night."

Not a little perplexed the prospects had got on with it, the general consensus being that if Zig Zag was on their side then they definitely didn't want to meet the opposition. And in their own way they had all taken it rather calmly, Scarecrow hurrying off to work on the bike, Dum Dum simply shrugging the way Dum Dum shrugs. Vincent stood for a moment with his mouth open.

"Orcs," he said finally. "Right. Wizards and shapeshifters and invisibility rings, and now orcs! I knew I should have played more Warcraft."

Now he and Dum Dum were patrolling the perimeter of their camp, Vincent nervously flicking his torch towards the slightest noise, while Dum Dum, being Dum Dum, appeared more curious than afraid.

"Shapeshifters, John said," said Dum Dum. "Means they can change their shape."

"Yes, Dum Dum, I heard."

"They can't change into much though, John said. Dogs or people, he said."

"Yes, Dum Dum," said Vincent. "I heard. I think I met one of them last night in the bar."

"Was he a dog or...? No, I suppose not," pondered Dum Dum.

There was the crackle of a broken branch away across the field and both their torches scanned the area, seeing something and nothing, a flash of eyes maybe, a moving shadow. There was definitely something out there, lurking, waiting, observing, always just out of range.

Another curse arose from the small team still working to fix Dum Dum's bike, forced to make many of the parts from scratch. Somehow, along with the kitchen sink, Chaos had managed to pack some welding gear and an angle grinder, but they had run into constant problems, like the bike itself was refusing to be mended.

"Bloody thing's cursed," muttered Dum Dum, as he and Vincent continued their patrol. "It's never run right. Even Scarecrow can't get it to run right and he knows everything about bikes."

"I know it might sound stupid, but you should probably tell Mad John about that."

"What?"

"That you think it's cursed."

"What? You think it might be?"

"At this point," said Vincent, "nothing would surprise me."

The night wore on and the pair continued to shine their torches at shadows, the wind, sometimes nothing at all. They talked about wizards and rings, and shapeshifters and orcs. The rest of the club slept except for those still working on Dum Dum's bike, though Chaos had got fucked off with it a couple of hours ago and gone to sleep, leaving Scarecrow, Loud-As, and Billy Toothless to it. Perhaps unsurprisingly, given the day they'd all had, Scarecrow seemed distracted and kept making mistakes, the job dragging on into the small hours. There was a sense that whatever had been out there lurking in the darkness had probably turned in for the night, too. Vincent let out a yawn.

"Did you hear that?" said Dum Dum.

"What?"

"Probably nothing." Dum Dum lazily shone his torch. "I think they've gone for the night. Could be a rabbit."

"Yeah, and it could be fucking Smeagol for all we know!"

Dum Dum let out a chuckle.

"No, it's not funny, mate! This fucking ring, half the time no one can see me! It takes fucking forever to get served! And no one knows how it works so I can't tell if people can see me or not, which might come in handy once in a while if I fancy nipping off to the ladies shower room."

"Or not getting knocked off your bike," Dum Dum chuckled again, tension flowing from both of them.

"Oh, don't get me fucking started on that!" Vincent laughed ruefully. "I'm fucking driving along half the time going 'Hello? Are You fucking blind?' Most of the time I don't even know if people are talking to me or not!"

"Smeeeagol," giggled Dum Dum, dissolving into fits of laughter, his shoulders shaking like tree trunks. It felt good to let off some steam.

"No, mate, really," grinned Vincent. "Who else do you know with a chat up line of 'can you actually see me or are you just going to step on my foot again?' At least that girl from last night could see me, but then that's probably because she claimed to be a faerie, which, hindsight being twenty/twenty and all that, was probably true. I'll have to remember to ask Scarecrow. He was getting all loved up with that one with the pink hair. I'm standing by the bar with them and he goes to her, "You look like a pixie with that hair." I swear to God, he's got this big dopey grin on his face, and she suddenly went all serious and goes, "Faerie, silly, not pixie." All of them, there was about five of them, all saying they were faeries!"

"There were very small," observed Dum Dum, his laughter settling down.

"Dum Dum, everyone's very small compared to you. I always thought faeries were supposed to be about three inches tall, not five-seven with a cleavage that makes your eyes hurt. They were fucking gorgeous! Not that I had any luck, but Scarecrow's right loved up! You see him this morning with that big soppy grin on his boat? Fair play though, she..."

"Shh," whispered Dum Dum.

Vincent fell quite, listening.

"What?" he whispered back.

"I heard something. Shh, listen."

They listened and heard nothing at first, then...

"We should wake Mad John and the rest," said Vincent.

Dum Dum shook his head. "No, they'll be really pissed off if it's nothing. Let me go and check it out first."

"Dum Dum, no. What if it's..." Vincent left it unspoken. It could be fucking anything out there.

"Don't worry," smiled Dum Dum. "If it's anything bigger than me *then* we can wake everyone up."

He headed off towards the noise leaving Vincent with a sudden sense of overwhelming vulnerability, finally aware of how far out of his depth he was, how ill equipped he was to deal with even prospecting for a motorcycle club, let alone one that went up against demon shapeshifters or whatever the hell they were.

He'd seen it in that fuckers' eyes last night in the bar, the one guy who had looked straight at him when he couldn't get served. The stare had been so direct, so violating, that it was like being raped through his eye sockets. It sapped him of his will, making him almost dizzy until the man broke eye contact. And he had only looked at him! How the fuck were you supposed to fight that? Fucking Ju Jitsu?

The night closed in on him, the darkness suddenly seeming closer as if the shadows were sneaking nearer. Behind Vincent, some ten feet or so away, Scarecrow, Loud-As, and Billy, still toiled to fix Dum Dum's bike, but they seemed a long way away and there was an awful lot of black night out there in front of him. What if the noise had been a distraction?

"Dum Dum," Vincent hissed at the darkness.

Dum Dum crept across the field to where the noise had come from, his vast brass knuckles firmly in place. Whatever was out there was going to seriously regret it. He caught a glimmer of light, a flicker of something metallic in the torchlight, and crept quietly forward.

"Gotcha!"

The General was so startled that he dropped Dum Dum's spare bike and inadvertently soiled himself.

"Fuckin' hell Gen'ral, what are you doing out here?" exclaimed Dum Dum.

The General looked about him frantically, sweat running down his face, his bike - well, Dum Dum's bike - firmly stuck in a muddy patch in the field.

"I, I, I..." he began hopelessly.

"Mate, are you fuckin' mad?"

"I, I,..."

"You can't come out here and take them on all by yourself!" said Dum Dum, regardless of the fact that that's exactly what he'd been intending to do himself. "I know you were in the marines and stuff, but."

The General looked at Dum Dum, utterly perplexed, frightened and cornered.

"Listen," said Dum Dum kindly. "I know you fucked up a bit and that, but there's no good going off being a hero just to make it better. I'm sure Zig Zag ain't that bothered really," he added hopefully. "It ain't his fault and I'm sure he's a really nice bloke once you get to know him."

"Yes, yes!" said The General hurriedly, his face lighting on an idea, relief spreading across it like a wave. "That's exactly what I was doing! I thought I heard a noise so I came to find out what it was and I, I, I..." The General floundered. There was no possible reason, if this were even remotely true, for him to be pushing Dum Dum's spare bike across a field.

"Mate," said Dum Dum, and hugged The General almost dislocating his collar bone. "You don't have to tell me. I knocked Numb Tongue's Harley over a few years ago. Just started prospecting and I knocked his bike over, big scratch all down the side. I thought that was it, they'd kick me out."

Dum Dum left the rest unspoken, a bonding moment as The General struggled for air.

"Very brave, but not very clever," said Dum Dum, finally releasing his grip.

Yes, you are, aren't you, thought The General.

Dum Dum pulled the bike out of the mud and turned it around to face the Aberrant camp once more. Fear returned to The General's face. Not that anything else could be expected, but they were heading straight back to where he was trying to sneak away from. Out of the frying pan and into the mental asylum. Who the hell were these people? And what in the name of living fuck had been under that crash helmet? It had been talking! If you could call that horrible noise talking! And John, Mad John let's not forget, had been talking back, something about powerful spells and creatures that bit people, all of it completely terrifying.

The General had woken, unnoticed between the bikes, and waited for a time to sneak away, listening for sounds in the night and the optimum time to flee. It had taken an age to cover even a small distance. Gently he'd clicked up the side stand, gently he'd pushed the bike, the mud growing thicker and deeper the further he got from the camp, until finally he was stuck. He had just been about to dump the bike where it was and run when Dum Dum had showed up waving a torch about in those big clumsy hands. And now the big cretin was going to take him straight back to where he'd come from and proclaim him a hero. Only an idiot, only Dum Dum, would fall for that.

"Dum Dum, I...you won't..."

"Don't worry," said Dum Dum, as they headed back to the camp. "I won't tell no one. I know you was only trying to make things right, but you don't want to get in no more trouble. I won't tell no one."

"You promise?"

"Cross my heart."

It was depressing to see how little ground The General had covered during his escape, a hundred yards, maybe two hundred at most, but it was an eternity in either direction. On the way out each hushed footfall was another agonising step into the unknown, the possibility of freedom driving him on as he pushed the heavy bike through muddied fields. On the way back there was no such offer of freedom, just the Munsters of motorcycling, whose prospect patch he was still, reluctantly, wearing. At least if he had run into 'them', whoever they fuck 'they' were that had the club so rattled, he'd maybe have been able to bargain with them, tell them what little else he could in return for his release. But now...

"Dum Dum," Vincent hissed into the dark again. It seemed an age since he'd been left alone, jumping at every imagined noise, but he was sure the last sound hadn't been imagined. Something was out there. It was close and getting closer.

"What's up?" said Loud-As, suddenly emerging from the night, shaking one leg as if trying to remove something from his boot.

"Loud-As? What the...? I nearly had a heart attack!"

"I went off for a piss and I could hear you hissing and making a racket." said Loud-As, still zipping his fly, apparently having not shaken quite enough. "What's up?"

"Dum Dum heard a noise and went off to investigate. He's been gone for a while." Vincent tried not to appear panicked.

"He's a big lad," shrugged Loud-As. "I'm sure he can look after himself. Got any fags?"

"Um," said Vincent, patting his pockets down. "You're not worried he might run into a shapeshifter or something? John told us to be alert."

"John's just paranoid," dismissed Loud-As. "Gets himself banged up for being a hippy and thinks the world's out to get him. Come on, cough up, I know you've got a pack of smokes somewhere." Loud-As sat himself down and started scratching irritably at his back.

"I didn't know John had been to jail," said Vincent, handing over a cigarette.

He felt a sudden feeling of, not betrayal, it wasn't unusual for patch club members to do time, but of being slightly let down. Mad John, like most of the older club members, had been a father to him and he'd always imagined him as this Robin Hood character. Perhaps not exactly giving to the poor, though he'd always shown a generous charitable streak, but certainly stealing from the rich and getting away with it. Now it seemed that perhaps Mad John had simply been in jail for the five years he was missing, a lesser man for getting caught. Even when the possibility had been mentioned among the prospects Vincent preferred to think that their president had been sunning it up in the south of Spain with the proceeds, rather than getting his deep tan on some outdoor work party.

"John?" said Loud-As. "Who said anything about him going to jail?"

"You said he got banged up."

"Yeah, but I didn't say anything about him going to jail." Loud-As lit his cigarette and continued poking at his back, trying to reach that unreachable spot.

"You shouldn't scratch that, you'll take the colour out," said Vincent, calmer now that he wasn't a lone guard against unseen and unknown terrors, though not particularly pleased to see Loud-As.

"I am fucking aware of that, thank you," grumbled Loud-As, still poking. He had recently had a tattoo finished, his entire back now covered with the Aberrant MC colours, and it should have healed by now. But instead it seemed to be causing Loud-As more and more discomfort. Doubtless this explained why he had been so unbearable of late, but, given that he was built like a brick wall, it didn't explain why he was making such a fuss about an itchy tattoo. He'd once walked around on a broken ankle for two weeks and not noticed until it went blue, so a bit of new ink shouldn't be a problem. He hadn't even had it all done in one sitting.

"I think it might be infected."

"You want me to have a look at it?" said Vincent.

"No," Loud-As scowled ungratefully. He'd been only too keen to show it off when he'd got it done and was just being contrary for the sake of it.

"How's the bike coming along?" Vincent tried another line of conversation.

He always found Loud-As the most difficult club member to get along with. It wasn't that he was unpleasant the whole time, but that he was totally unpredictable and you never knew when he was going to turn into an utter cunt, one minute likeable and funny, the next minute starting fights for no reason and generally behaving like a three year old. Already Vincent had learned to keep away from him as much as possible when he was like that, but it was impossible to avoid him every time.

Thankfully, talking about motorbikes had the effect of defusing him somewhat and it was an easy subject with which to distract him, particularly with Dum Dum's bike nearly ready to roll again. Predictably Loud-As went into lengthy detail about the repairs that were now near completion.

"Not that there's any point going anywhere tonight," he said, still rubbing at his back. "We'll have someone off if people ain't awake and paying attention. We're better off leaving when the sun comes up."

Already there was a hint of warmth to the sky, the earliest signs of dawn, and Loud-As noticed Vincent stifle a yawn.

"You been on all night?" he said, the merest whiff of concern.

Vincent nodded. "Me and Dum Dum."

It had been odd to Vincent that so many of the club had opted for an early night when they were apparently in some sort of danger, but many, Smiler being the most vocal, had complained that their hangovers weren't gone. And since Mad John had insisted on no partying and no music, they didn't see a lot of point in staying up. By about two am it had been just him and Dum Dum on watch.

"Speak of the devil," said Loud-As, as Dum Dum and The General emerged from the shadows. "You find anything?"

"No, it was just Gen'ral," said Dum Dum, neatly avoiding a lie, but still doing the Dum Dum shuffle, from one foot to the other, that was always a give-away that something else was going on.

"Good," said Loud-As. "I'm off to get some kip. You and Vincent are off duty. General, you're on watch and don't fall asleep."

And with that Loud-As grumpily headed for his tent, still poking furiously at his back.

"Well, I've gotta get some sleep, too," yawned Vincent. He was too tired to care what was going on any more. Dum Dum was still shuffling about like a small kid, well, a fucking huge kid to be more precise, bursting to tell something while desperately biting his tongue. Vincent didn't care. The sun was coming up, slowly bathing the field in its glow, and who knew what lay ahead of the club tomorrow, well, today... Fuck it, time for sleep. Dum Dum and The General bade him goodnight, good morning, whatever.

"Long night," observed Dum Dum. "Don't worry, I'll stay up with you. Not that's there's much to watch for. Whatever was out there fucked off hours ago."

Dum Dum could feel it in his bones. There had been something out there, three somethings, sneaking around in the shadows, like hyenas checking out potential prey. But they were gone now. Dum Dum felt it, knew it as instinctively as any wild animal when a predator is near. The General knew it, too, since whatever was out there would have heard his clumsy escape bid and come to investigate as Dum Dum had.

"Seriously, mate, you don't have to," said The General, suddenly all smiles and generosity. "You've been on all night and I..." He stumbled over his words. He had fainted and then tried to run away. "Seriously, I'll be fine. Like you said, there's nothing out there anyway."

"Well, if you're sure," said Dum Dum. It had been a very long night and his hand still throbbed to remind him that it was broken.

"Yes, yes, of course, mate," beamed The General. "Seriously. Go and get some sleep."

"Well, all right then, if you're sure." Dum Dum wasn't sure. He would never leave a club member or a fellow prospect to fend for himself, but, then again, it seemed like the worst they'd be fending off was sleep, and he wasn't in any position to fight that.

"Absolutely!" smiled The General, patting him on the back, ushering him towards his oversized tent.

"Yeah, all right," said Dum Dum reluctantly. "But you've got to promise you won't go running off and being a hero."

Dum Dum," said The General earnestly, "I promise you I won't be a hero."

CHAPTER NINETEEN

When Aberrant MC rose from their slumber The General was gone. A brief search of the camp revealed that Dum Dum's spare bike was also gone. Loud-As - being The General's sponsor, and therefore responsible for his actions - was furious, stomping around the camp, kicking at the remains of last night's camp-fire, and unnecessarily spraying embers and ash all over the place, but there was surprisingly little reaction from the rest of the club. Billy Toothless sniffed around as if following a scent, which was exactly what he was doing.

"Wen' 'atway, 'boutn' ah 'go," he announced to those who could understand him.

"Solves that problem," shrugged Chaos, echoing the general consensus on The General.

Dum Dum, however, was crestfallen, unable to accept the facts at face value - despite one of the facts being that his bike had been stolen - and unable to accept that he had thwarted an escape attempt rather than some heroic bid. He trusted The General, as he trusted all the club members and prospects. Betrayal was completely unthinkable.

"But he couldn't have..."

"Dum Dum, he's gone," said Stone gently.

Reluctantly, Dum Dum had told them the story of how he'd found The General halfway across the field, and how The General had been out to tackle the bad guys single handedly to make up for his earlier mistakes. The club had laughed, which didn't make Dum Dum feel any better about breaking his promise.

"But what if *they* sneaked in here and got him?" he persisted.

"If they could get him then they could have got us all," Mad John pointed out. "And, believe me, they have other targets in mind." He glanced at Vincent.

"But..."

It couldn't be true.

The General was his friend. And Loud-As may have been his sponsor, but it was Dum Dum who had introduced him to the club. It was Dum Dum's fault.

"No one's blaming you but yourself," said Mad John. "You and Vincent did a fine job last night. I'm afraid our former companion may have chosen his own fate. Now, we really should press on, we've wasted enough time already."

The country quiet died in an instant as the club started their bikes and pressed on. Dum Dum's bike popped, farted, and backfired every now and again but otherwise appeared to be running reasonably well, and the roads, though narrow, were increasingly flanked with open fields and meadows. The sun did it's best to lighten Dum Dum's mood, and, despite himself, he started to enjoy the ride. There were no nasty walls or tricky corners to jump out at him, just the occasional long swooping bend on an otherwise arrow straight road.

And, perhaps refreshed by a good night's sleep, the majority of the full patch members were in remarkably good spirits too. Maybe it was contagious: Scarecrow had an ear to ear grin on his face and hadn't stopped smiling since they'd left The Dragon's Head. And given that Mad John had announced, before they set off again, that crash helmets were now "optional" it was also plain to see that Zig Zag McClintock was smiling. He had so many more teeth than everybody else.

Thankfully, riding a bike made it difficult to stare, but it was difficult not to. The only orcs Vincent had ever seen were in The Lords Of The Rings, and, other than being considerably shorter, Zig Zag, it had to be said, looked very much like them. He was unmistakably an orc. Vincent smiled to himself. An orc! A real live fucking orc! On a motorbike! This was turning out to be one hell of a motorcycle club!

Not that he'd ever had any doubts about that. Well, apart from the name. Aberrant MC. Vincent remembered looking it up in the dictionary when he was a kid. Somehow Aberrant had never had quite the same ring about it

THE ROAD TO FERO CITY

as Hells Angels, Satan's Slaves, or Road Rats, not quite the same menacing authority. So he'd looked it up. 'Aberrant', it said, 'not normal or acceptable'. Today he couldn't have been more proud, his stomach tying itself into knots of excitement.

Last night in the darkness, with the grass whispering in the wind and the shadows playing tricks, and something out there lurking, all this had been overwhelming, frightening even. Today it felt as if Aberrant MC were in their element and completely invincible. They could be heard for miles, that 'burst of dirty thunder', daring anyone to cross it. Three shapeshifting dogs against this lot? No chance! thought Vincent. We've got a fucking orc on our side! And Numb Tongue. Only a gibbering lunatic would take on Numb Tongue and he wouldn't be a gibbering idiot for very long. Loud-As was no slouch either, and, come to think of it, he looked a bit, well, orc-ish. Maybe there was some orc blood in him too.

It didn't take a genius to work out why they were being followed, but at least now Vincent had a better idea of what they were up against and, booming along in a pack of powerful motorcycles, it didn't seem quite so scary. Admittedly Vincent wasn't very scary either, the runt of the Aberrant litter, and better at the fighting games on X-Box than he was at actual fighting, but surely he'd picked up a thing or two at Numb Tongue's gym. And if he could just figure out how the ring worked then maybe it could be of some use, if only to pick the bad guys' pockets. Except they could see him even when it was working, so maybe he'd have to build up to that.

Vincent had a lot of time to think as they rode, the bikes' meditative effects kicking in after only a few miles. And while he did consider, for a moment, the fact that there might be other clubs out there with bigger fucking orcs, and that a rear naked choke was unlikely to bother a shapeshifter who could give you a headache just by looking at you, the overwhelming feeling was one of pure joy. This was it: this was the bike run he had always dreamed of! Well, okay, he hadn't thought to include orcs and faeries and such, but for all their oddities, and, yes, aberrations was right, they were, nonetheless, one cool bunch of motherfuckers. Sure, there were some shapeshifters chasing them, but they'd have to catch them first, and if they wanted his ring then they'd have to fight for it!

And then they found Dum Dum's spare bike, abandoned and destroyed, and Vincent's spirits fell once more, like a brick thrown from a tower block window. It wasn't simply that the bike had been crashed - Vincent had enough experience with that kind of thing to know exactly how unpleasant that could be - but that the bike had been twisted and mangled in a way that was barely possible, even in the worst crash. One of Vincent's old bikes - and there had been many - had been run over by a truck and it hadn't looked half as bad as this. The petrol tank was torn with what looked like claw marks and there were teeth marks in the tyres. Vincent knew they were teeth marks because there was still a tooth stuck in the rubber. It was about the same size as his hand.

And then there was the blood. On everything. Bits of hair and skin, and bone fragments. The General's crash helmet lay beside the ruined bike, blood spattered and smashed. If there had been a head in it at the time then there was no sign of it now.

Billy Toothless sniffed around the horrific scene for a scent and found a piece of The General's jacket in a hedge, it, too, covered in blood.

"Holy fackin' shit!" exclaimed Apples, pretty much summing it up for all of them.

Billy sniffed around some more. It was a wonder he could smell anything at all over his own stench, but he found two separate trails leading in opposite directions across opposite fields. In fairness, Stevie Wonder could have found one of the trails as there was a large amount of blood leading to a gaping hole in the hedge.

"Warg," said Billy finally. "Big'un too, Oi reckun."

"Warg?" said Mad John. "This far out? You're sure?"

"Oh-arh," nodded Billy.

It seemed unlikely, but from what Billy could tell them The General had been attacked by a warg, some monstrous wolf hybrid, and not only put up quite a fight, but managed to scare the beast off before getting away on foot. The General was bleeding and afraid, but he was alive. Or at least he was when he left this place. The beast, too, was long gone.

"Maybe he's got some balls after all," said Loud-As, possibly eager to redeem his charge, if only a little. "He's fucking lucky they're not being worn as earrings if he went up against a warg."

"When you say warg," said Vincent. "You mean?"

"Almost exactly as you'd imagine, but probably considerably bigger," said Mad John quickly. "We're many miles from their usual territory though, particularly at this time of year. No warg lives within two hundred miles of here."

"Well, this one does," said Stone. "And if what Billy says is right, it's a big one, twenty-five hundred pounds or so, and very pissed off, with a very bad toothache."

"And The General fought this thing off on his own?" said Vincent. It did seem just a tiny bit unlikely given that he had fainted when he saw Zig Zag.

"So it would appear," said Mad John, apparently unconvinced.

Dum Dum immediately wanted to go looking for The General, but he didn't argue when told otherwise. The General was on his own, in a mire of his own making, his chances of survival slim at best. The club salvaged what they could from the wrecked bike, but there wasn't much of any use that wasn't too heavy to carry. Even the handlebars were snapped in half, the end of the right side, where the throttle and front brake lever should have been, now completely missing, its cables bitten in two.

"We should move on," said Mad John finally. "It may be injured, but a warg that size could cover a lot of ground and they're not known for their sense of humour."

"We won't get far without petrol," said Vincent. "I'm running on fumes."

"Me too," said Dum Dum. "Put it on reserve about ten miles ago."

"Already?" Mad John sighed. "Chaos, sort them out would you, there's a good chap."

Chaos distributed fuel to those who needed it from a seemingly endless supply of containers strapped to his bike, prepared, as always for anything. Even his name, though partly due to hell-raising, was a reference to him being so organised. This was, after all, a man who had crossed the Sahara single-handed on a hopped-up dirt bike and thought nothing of blasting from London to Berlin "for the weekend". For a while someone had tried to stick the nickname Branson on him due to his travels, but Richard Branson wasn't in the habit, when he ran low on readies, of cutting the anchors on billion dollar yachts and then offering to rescue the stricken boats for an astronomical fee. When he wasn't smuggling drugs or, indeed, taking drugs, Chaos did this sort of thing quite a lot.

"We'll stop for provisions at Bertha's," said Mad John once they were ready to move on. "But please do try to use less fuel."

Typically Mad John set a pace that showed no regard for fuel consumption. So that rumour was true, thought Vincent, he really doesn't ever put petrol in his bike. Maybe it comes in handy being friendly with a wizard, or maybe, just maybe...

The club covered fifty or sixty miles, through beautiful open countryside on a road with no turns, until, at last, the road widened and eventually they encountered a crossroads with just one building, a sign outside its razor-wired fences announcing that it was Bertha's Big Back Yard.

Compound would have been a better description. Or fortress. The razor fence fizzed and crackled, a pointless sign warning that it was electrified. Behind it in her wooden rocking chair, armed with a pump action shotgun, sat Bertha, in a dress so large and brightly coloured you could hold a rave in it. She bustled to her feet when she heard the bikes, propped the gun against her rocking chair, and hurried to turn off the electric fences, before opening the gates in a series of awkward curtseys.

Aberrant pulled into Bertha's junk-strewn, and, indeed, big, back yard, and parked their bikes. Bertha bustled to close the gates and turn the power back on, a fizz like a gigantic wasp on steroids making it clear when it was fully charged.

"Forgive me, your 'ighness, John, sir, I had no idea you was coming." Bertha bobbed and curtsied her way across the yard to Mad John. "The place is such a mess. I'm afraid it's been rather busy here of late what with one thing and another." Bertha fussed at her hair, a tumbleweed of grey, and patted down her best dress, which had clearly been thrown on in a hurry and was not used to being worn. Bertha was a solid lady, almost as round as she was tall, and a former black belt of the January sales, her chest like a barrage balloon wrapped in gingham.

"Now, now, Bertha," said Mad John, as she continued to bob up and down obsequiously. "I've told you before there's no need for such graces. The pleasure is all mine and your welcome, if I might say so, is as charming as ever. We'd like to purchase provisions, if we may, and perhaps sample some of the delicious soup you've no doubt got simmering."

"You know your money's no good here, your 'ighness, John, sir," smiled Bertha, still bobbing like a dinghy in choppy waters. "And as it happens I do have something in the pot that'll fill a few hungry bellies. Good thing it's a big pot though, your 'ighness, John, sir," she added, looking over the rest of the club with a particular eye on Dum Dum.

"Just John will do, thank you miss Bertha," said Mad John kindly. "Now let's do the introductions..."

The rest of the club, it seemed, already knew Bertha, and she treated them with the same doffing respect as she treated Mad John, while they behaved like she was a favourite granny. Mad John introduced the three prospects, each of which Bertha was "delighted and honoured to meet", and then they headed inside to the smell of fine home cooking. And in a kitchen full of knick-knacks and pictures of small kittens Bertha provided all fourteen of them with a feast of bread and soup and wine and cake, ferrying endless plates to whatever the club could find to sit on, while all the time apologising that there wasn't more.

"Bertha," said Joker, slapping at his belly, "if there was any more I think we'd have to carry Dum Dum out of here in your truck."

"Very gracious of you to say so, mister Joker, sir," smiled Bertha. "How's your good lady Lilith, if you don't mind me asking, sir?"

"She's very well and sends her love," said Joker. "I've got a little gift from her to you out on the bike, just a couple of little spells she's been working on."

"You're both too kind, I'm sure," bobbed Bertha. "I'm afraid things have been a bit hectic of late so I haven't had the time to keep up as much as I'd like."

"Yeah, I'm surprised you didn't know we were coming," said Joker, concern in his voice. "I thought you were the eyes and ears around these parts. Is everything okay?"

"Well, to be honest, Joker, sir," said Bertha. "Business has been a bit slow of late. It's them bloody wargs, pardon my language, running around scaring the customers and whatnot, *eating* the customers sometimes, they are. They come sniffing around here at night trying to get at the ponies. One of them took a big zap off the fence the other night, scorched all its fur and burnt its nose, it did. Ran off yelping something horrid."

"You mean there's more of them?" said Mad John. "We came across tracks earlier today, but I had no idea there were more."

"Oh yes, John, sir. Breeding they are, sir. Bloody nuisance they are, pardon my language. There's some good eating on them, I'll grant you, but it doesn't seem right, what with them eating the customers."

The club knew better than to ask Bertha if she needed their protection. For over forty years she had been living out here, alone in the middle of nowhere, at the only crossroads for miles around, and she had lived through far worse than wargs.

"I've got a couple of nice warg skin coats if any of you gents would like one," she added brightly.

"I think I know someone who'd die for a warg skin coat right now." Mad John grinned, nodding at Vincent, whose jaw had yet to realise that it had dropped some time ago and was making him look rather stupid.

"No one's got to do any dying," said Bertha firmly. "And I won't have any of you thinking about paying either, thank you very much."

This is real, thought Vincent, staring out of Bertha's kitchen window at Bertha's Big Back Yard. The place was a salvage yard essentially, littered with broken cars, bicycles, and junk. But among the things that gave it away as something very different, aside from a fence you could power small countries on, was the skeleton climbing frame made from what looked like it had once been a whale. Vincent hoped it was a whale. Nothing that big should have been wandering dry land since dinosaurs were fashionable. Even that would have been, if not in the least bit normal, then perhaps no more than a curiosity if it weren't for all the skulls that decorated it, the majority of which clearly weren't human. Vincent could tell they weren't human because humans don't often have horns or more than a dozen rows of teeth.

"First time through the Circle is it, my dear?" said Bertha. "It does take a bit of getting used to."

"Circle? What circle?" said Vincent, his thoughts broken.

"The Circle Of Seven," said Bertha, failing to disguise an incredulous look. "Oh now, don't tell me they never told you? No wonder you've had that look on your face since you got here. It's not my place to interfere your 'ighness," she added, turning to Mad John, "but I really do think you should have told the boy."

"No one told you, Bertha, and you did all right," smiled Mad John.

"Ah well, that's different," Bertha blushed a deep beetroot colour that clashed with her dress. "I got dropped in the deep end and didn't have much choice about it."

"Nonetheless you thrived," said Mad John. "In my defence there seems to have been so little time to fully explain to them, but you're right, forewarned is forearmed. We lost Dum Dum for a while at the Circle, which could have been very unfortunate if there are wargs on the prowl. And if I'd been forewarned of the wargs then I would never have put just the two of them on guard."

"Quite right, John, sir," nodded Bertha. "And I wouldn't presume to tell you your business, but I think you'd all be safer staying here tonight and leaving in the morning, if it's all the same to you. It's not safe out there at night, even for strong lads like Aberrant. So you'll have plenty of time to fill in some of those blank expressions."

"Dum Dum always looks like that!" hooted Joker.

"Well, that's as it may be, mister Joker, sir," said Bertha, "but they won't last five minutes out here if they don't know their arses from their elbows, pardon my French, sir. Now I'll go and put the kettle on, shall I? And you can tell them all about it. Anybody want some more cake?"

And so, armed with cakes and pastries, Mad John sat the three prospects down on some old car seats that now served as sofas on the front porch. The electric fence fizzled and buzzed in the warm air like a gigantic bug killer, which is exactly what it was.

"Soooo," said Mad John, with a wry grin. "What do you want to know?"

"How about *everything*?" ventured Vincent.

"I'm afraid even Bertha's hospitality might be stretched if I told you everything. And I will be needing to speak to you all individually. But how about we start off with the easy stuff?"

"What like The Circle Of Seven, which actually has eight exits, if you know how many times to go 'round the roundabout, and is really a magic gateway to another world? That sort of thing?"

All eyes turned to Scarecrow as he casually helped himself to another generous slice of cake.

"What?" he grinned. "It's true isn't it? I figured if you weren't telling us then we were probably supposed to work it out for ourselves."

All eyes turned to Mad John who let out a hearty laugh, slapping his thigh with his hand.

"I've said this before," he said, "but I really am most honoured to have you prospecting for the club, Scarecrow, all of you," Mad John looked each of them in the eyes. "Yes, Scarecrow, in essence it's no more than a locked door, but the Circle Of Seven is, as you say, a magic gateway to another world. Perhaps we should move on to some tougher questions?"

CHAPTER TWENTY

"Is Harry Potter real?"

"No, Dum Dum," sighed Mad John.

They had been on the porch for some hours now and, having got the gist of what was going on, Dum Dum had some questions of his own. *Lots* of questions.

"What about Dr Who?"

"No, Dum Dum."

"But faeries are real, right?"

"Yes, Dum Dum."

"What about Batman?"

"No, Dum Dum."

Dum Dum had listed every creature he could think of, mythical, fantastical, and occasionally imaginary, and had now moved on to movies on the reasonable assumption that if orcs, elves, and faeries were real then so were Superman and Father Christmas. Reindeer were real, after all.

"What about Hellboy?"

"No, Dum Dum."

And so it went on.

"X-Men?"

"No."

"Casper The Friendly Ghost?"

"Now you're just being silly."

Dum Dum smiled. He'd been slyly taking the piss for a while now, having caught an encouraging look from Joker, and Joker had been miming behind Mad John's back since Dum Dum ran out of ideas. He was now almost beside himself trying not to laugh and give himself away.

"Bigfoot?"

"Actually yes," said Mad John. "And I know you're there, Joker. I rather thought that last impression was supposed to be King Kong, but your Wonderwoman really was very funny."

"How the...?"

"I can see your reflection in Vincent's glass. There will be a fee for the revelation of further tricks."

"How much?"

"Hmm? Back with us are we, Scarecrow?" said Mad John. "Your mind seems to be somewhere else this evening. What would you like to know?"

"All right then," said Scarecrow, sitting forward in his seat, an intent look on his face. "How do you always know when I'm outside your study, sometimes before I've even knocked?"

"Ah, that'll be Boris," Mad John said expansively, as if that explained everything.

"Boris?"

"Yes, Boris the spider. He's a Brown Extrovert, very rare. Rather like the Brown Recluse except bigger, and, obviously, not quite so shy. He let's me know when people are coming to visit."

"Didn't I say!" Dum Dum nearly exploded with excitement, his seat creaking in terror as he bounced rather too vigorously. "Didn't I say it was spiders! I said the other day, I reckon John talks to spiders..." he trailed off, suddenly recalling where he'd first heard those once paranoid babblings about talking spiders.

Somewhere out there, beyond the crackle of the fence, The General would be spending his first night alone in a strange new world full of strange new creatures, many of which considered him a light breakfast snack. Loud-As said they'd bring him back if they found him. He and Bertha and Numb Tongue had headed off in Bertha's battered pick-up truck to retrieve the remains of Dum Dum's spare bike, to be added to all the other useful and useless junk in Bertha's Big Back Yard. But realistically the chances of The General being with them when they returned were somewhere between fuck all and none. They weren't even looking for him, just picking up the bike and heading straight back, and The General had been out there for hours, unlikely to return to where he had been attacked and even less likely to be actively looking for Aberrant. Aside from the one road leading here there was nothing else out there for miles in that direction but wargs and shapeshifters and approaching darkness. Bertha had taken her shotgun.

The sun was setting by the time the trio returned with the remains of Dum Dum's XS strapped to the back of the truck. Dum Dum hurried out from the kitchen, where he and the other prospects had been on dish-washing duty, but Bertha and company had seen no one else on the road and no signs of The General. On the plus side there were no signs of any wargs either, but, since they were capable of greater speeds than Bertha's truck and didn't have to stick to the road, they could be anywhere by now. The General was probably lucky if he was still alive, but only probably. As soon as night fell he was a dead man.

And yet there was always hope. Bertha had survived against all the odds, and now thrived against all the odds, and she had been armed with little more than an umbrella and a pair of sensible hiking boots when she spent her first night in the wilderness. That was over forty years ago.

As Mad John told it, Bertha had been on a weekend hiking trip, intent on getting some nice clean air to clear her head after being fired from a job that she hadn't really liked very much. She had wanted some alone time and got rather more than she bargained for. It had been twelve months before she saw another living soul.

Apparently, she had reached The Circle Of Seven in her VW camper van and somehow contrived to go around the roundabout the right amount of times to go through the eighth exit. Lost and confused she had run out of petrol at the crossroads where her infamous Back Yard now stood, and - having cried until it got boring and pointless, and then walked about aimlessly until that, too, got boring and pointless - she eventually had no choice but to fend for herself. It was Chaos who came across her first, on another of his long solo runs, and, after cautious introductions, it being a year since she had seen anyone, the pair shared some of Bertha's rabbit and mushroom soup and Chaos explained to her about The Circle Of Seven.

"Well, if it's all the same to you I think I'll stay here," said Bertha finally. "If what you're saying's right, and I've got no reason to doubt you, then I can go back any time I like. But, to be quite honest, I don't think I want to. I came out here for a bit of peace and quiet, and, granted, I never expected so much of it, but, do you know what? I think I prefer this, when all is said and done. They can stick their jobs and their bills where the sun don't shine, pardon me for saying."

And so Bertha had stayed. Chaos had given her fuel and directions on navigating the Circle in case she changed her mind, her VW starting first time, but when he came by that way again three months later she was still there. Bertha had given Chaos soup and asked that if he ever pass this way again he bring her some books on "how to do stuff" and "some Marmite, if it's not too much trouble."

Forty years later Bertha's Big Back Yard was almost as legendary as her soup and Bertha herself had become much respected in many fields, including witchcraft and salvage, her ramshackle house as much a haven to weary travellers as it was a pit stop. Over the years it had gradually turned into a hotel of sorts, too, with weird guest rooms built at odd angles from the main building, which itself had started out as Bertha's camper van. Nowadays if Bertha didn't have the supplies you needed then you probably didn't need them. She even had Marmite.

And, since people now had somewhere to stop on their long journey, the place inevitably became a hive for any passing news or gossip, so what Bertha didn't know about other people's business probably wasn't worth knowing. If a bird farted fifty miles away Bertha was usually the first to know about it and it was very unusual for her to be caught off guard as she was today, even if Aberrant arrived a lot quicker than her other visitors and outran her many furry and winged lookouts. Today her Back Yard seemed unusually cluttered with birds and feral cats, all on some uneasy truce, all grateful to Bertha in the harsh winters.

"None of mine really wants to go out much, what with the wargs and everything, and I can't say I blame them." Bertha had settled into her favourite chair, the old, and now very battered and much repaired front seat from that fabled VW. She was on her third bottle of a home-made red wine that took varnish off tables, without showing the slightest signs of being even remotely drunk. Smiler had consumed just one bottle and was now unconscious on the porch, a trail of dribble hanging from his open mouth. He still had his boots on.

"Would you be needing a permanent marker, mister Joker, sir?" winked Bertha, as Smiler slumped a little further into his seat.

"I've got a selection, thanks, Bertha," grinned Joker. "Don't suppose you've got any superglue?"

"I've got just the thing," said Bertha, and bustled off to the kitchen.

She came back five minutes later with a tin of Evostick and her shotgun.

"I don't like to bother you gents," she said, "but it looks like we've got company."

They headed outside to Bertha's Big Back Yard.

Vincent had never seen a warg before. Well, you wouldn't have, would you? They don't have them in zoos. He'd seen bison and this thing was about the same size, but it most certainly wasn't a fucking bison. Snarling and slavering it paced back and forth outside Bertha's fence, all teeth and drool and rage, black eyes glaring with malevolence. Its disposition hadn't been helped at all by the broken handlebars stuck in the side of its head, brake cables and wiring trailing like mutant dreadlocks.

The beast stopped and let out a roar that would carry for miles, thrashing its head to dislodge the handlebars. The fence crackled a warning as it got too close and the warg roared back, defiantly clawing at the ground. It was not a happy camper.

"We could stick it in Smiler's tent, I suppose," suggested Joker.

"Don't you be so cruel," chided Bertha. "Poor thing doesn't deserve that!"

"Well, it's that or we glue his boots on, Bertha," laughed Joker. "And you did supply the glue."

"I don't mean him," said Bertha, starting to betray the wicked sense of humour that lay beyond the third bottle. "Daft bugger deserves it trying to drink a whole bottle of Bertha's Peculiar. I've got a potion that will make his hair grow in a most amusing fashion if you'd like to try it. No, I mean the warg. Poor bugger's in a lot of pain, pardon my French. Look, it's got tooth marks all down one side."

The warg let out a fearsome bellow, shaking the ground with rage, all steam and slobber and teeth and claws at the front end of about a ton of angry steak. It looked like a London black cab possessed by Satan.

"What the fuck would bite that thing?" exclaimed Vincent, then glanced at Bertha and added, "pardon my French."

CHAPTER TWENTY-ONE

The General had run as far as he could run. Then he walked as far as he could walk. Nowhere was far enough away from that thing. Everything hurt, his face scratched by cruel branches, his palms bloodied from falling again and again, his body bruised and battered. And still he struggled on, but each time he fell it was harder to get back to his feet. Exhausted and crying The General staggered on until he could go no further. He fell to the ground, barely able to sob, all hope gone, alone and lost and scared beyond his wits end. And then he heard growling. It was coming.

With the help of breaking daylight, The General's second escape bid had been rather more successful than his first. Not wanting to risk lingering too long in case someone woke up, he had waited just half an hour after being put on guard duty before sneaking back over to Dum Dum's spare bike. The tracks from his abortive first attempt were still in the grass, leading off in completely the wrong direction for a hasty getaway, directly across the field, away from the road. In daylight he made no such mistake the second time. Again he pushed the bike, this time through the gap in the wall and back out on to the road, and, though tempted to start the bike immediately and race away, he took the time to move a few boulders into that gap, adding valuable seconds should the club take chase. Even then, The General pushed the bike further for fear of its engine waking anyone, the sudden noise sending birds scurrying into the sky.

He had no idea where he was going, just away. And, since they hadn't passed a petrol station or anything else on the way here, there was no point in going back the way they had come. So, The General went the same way the club were going, hoping against hope to stay ahead of them or that the road took him somewhere, anywhere, that wasn't here.

He'd been doing about seventy miles per hour, flying hell for leather and accelerating, when he hit the beast full on as it darted into his path. There was no time to slow down or even swerve to avoid it, but time itself slowed, as it does in such a crash, allowing The General a lifetime to take in the full horror of what was happening. He hit the beast, whatever the hell it was, square in the head, his handlebars snapping clean off as he was thrown from the bike, his fall miraculously broken by the hedge. Stunned for a moment, The General struggled to scramble loose from vicious, thorny branches that grabbed and scratched at him, his clothing tangled and torn. The beast, meanwhile, went completely fucking nuts.

The General had come face to face with it on that godforsaken stretch of road and he now knew pure terror. It had destroyed Dum Dum's bike in mere seconds, tearing at it with tooth and claw before slamming it repeatedly into the tarmac, sparks and fuel flying but failing to ignite. And then, as The General freed himself from the grasp of the bushes and, inevitably, unavoidably, dropped down into the road, the beast had turned its attention to him. Steam came from its nose as it roared, advancing slowly on him, slavering and ferocious, wounded and angry. Thankfully The General's trousers were now well accustomed to the sensation of being soiled.

It had been pure dumb luck that he got away. In sheer desperation he had thrown his crash helmet at the beast as it bore down on him, and, by some miracle, it hit the handlebars that were protruding from the beast's head. The beast let out a howl of pain that made the ground shake, thrashing its head back and forth and spraying blood about the road. The General ran like he had never run before.

And now the beast had found him and there was nowhere to go and nowhere to hide. The General scrabbled away backwards on his hands and feet until he backed into a tree, his momentum finally gone. Nothing left but desperation. And a gun. He remembered it in a flash, frantically grabbing the weapon from his jacket before opening fire with only yards to spare. There was a click and, once again, it was not the best time to be The General's trousers. In hindsight he should probably have loaded the gun first.

The General closed his eyes as the beast pounced, its final roar seeming to come in surround sound, a wall of noise that most death metal bands could only dream of. And yet the attack never came. There was a noise like someone smashing meat trucks together, and when The General - still pinned by terror to the tree - opened his eyes, his underwear regrettably suffered the consequences for the third time in so many hours. Bloodied, torn, and utterly pissed off, the beast was backing away. That was the good news.

Unfortunately the reason it was backing away was that between it and The General were the three biggest, most evil looking dogs he had ever seen. Not that he was particularly a dog man, beyond them being either small and kickable or big and threatening, but these things were like something you'd see if Rob Zombie remade The Omen. There was a tense stand-off, but the beast was wounded and no match for three gigantic hellhounds with teeth like ivory razors. Slowly it backed away, thoroughly aggrieved and undeniably dangerous, the dogs still snarling and snapping to ward it off.

Fumbling desperately and dropping the clip twice, The General loaded his Luger and, with hands shaking beyond his control, aimed at the dogs as they turned to face him, their coats as black as coal, their eyes a fiery silver. However, their manner had changed now that the beast had departed. The dogs looked at him as if pondering some question they wanted to ask, and the gun grew heavy in his hands. Tears and snot and blood and dirt smeared his face, his eyesight a blur from sobbing. Still waving the pistol from one dog to the next, The General hastily wiped his eyes. Before him stood two dogs and a man dressed in black.

"A little ungrateful, don't you think?" said the man.

"You!" spluttered The General. "I know you, you bastard!"

"The gun, if you wouldn't mind," said the man.

"You drugged me!" accused The General. "You drugged me and those bastards..." He trailed off, the gun gradually lowering itself in his weakening arms. "I..." he tried, completely out of his depth. "You, you were a dog!" The gun came up again.

"Indeed," said Elron calmly. "And perhaps it has escaped your attention that my companions and I just saved your life at considerable risk to our own. The gun, if you wouldn't mind. I assure you I mean you no harm."

The gun lowered again and The General let out a broken sigh, suddenly acutely aware that he was, not to put too fine a point on it, sitting in his own slowly drying feculence. He was also still alive. The tension ebbed.

"Thank you," said Elron. He offered his hand and helped The General - who was still shaking like Ozzy Osbourne on a bad day – to his feet. He wasn't having the best day himself, and had no reason to expect it to get any better, particularly since he was talking to someone who had very recently been an extremely large dog.

"You drugged me," he said sullenly, all the fight gone.

"And you have my deepest apologies," said Elron smoothly, "though it was no more than a mild truth serum and you will suffer no ill effects. I'm afraid it was.... necessary."

"Necessary," repeated The General. His mind was a whirlwind of madness, nothing making sense. Part of him hoped that this was all due to Stone's acid, like maybe he was still tripping balls at the clubhouse and all these weird and ferocious creatures were just some bizarre hallucination. The reality was too much to deal with.

Elron put a hand on his shoulder. "I understand that this is all rather overwhelming," he said. "You were wise to escape when you did, but you were also very lucky we found you when we did. A moment later and you would not have been so fortunate. Might I suggest that we move to somewhere a little safer? Perhaps with a shower," he added, as a dark stain inched its way down The General's Levis.

There was really no choice. The General was exhausted, both physically and emotionally, running on no more than some atavistic instinct. He had no idea where he was, no transport, a wild beast and an entire motorcycle club hunting him down, and, to top it all, his underpants were filled with a particularly noxious bum hummus.

Still, there was a flicker of caution. Only a few minutes ago this bloke had been a gigantic hellhound, and now here he was looking not a little like Nick Cave, all dour expression and receding hairline, the other two equally massive dogs sitting patiently by his side like they were shooting an album cover. He looked like the sort of person who would say 'sardonic' a lot in conversation and know what it meant. But what other choice was there?

"I know how your trick works," The General said, a defiant child lingering in his voice.

"Trick?" said Elron.

"That trick with the card where your name changes. It wasn't even your real name. Mad John said it was a cheap trick."

"Did he now?" said Elron, with an expression that suggested he'd just stepped in something unsavoury. "Forgive me my sardonic humour. It was a cheap shot, not aimed at you but at those we are tracking. You might say I am a detective, of sorts, so I'm afraid my deception was also necessary. Allow me to introduce myself..." He flourished another business card, black with silver lettering on expensive paper.

The General examined the card suspiciously, turning it over in his hands. He stared at the name on the card, willing it to change, willing some message to make itself clear, but there was nothing. Peter Escani, seemed like a normal enough name, Italian maybe. He looked at the name again. Escape In...no, that didn't work, the letters didn't move. Pets Can...no, that's silly. The letters still refused to budge.

"I assure you," said Peter, formerly Elron. "If we meant to cause you harm then we could have done so by now, not least by leaving you to the warg. You are quite safe for the time being, but we should leave this place immediately. Even a wounded warg is not known to give up so easily. There is no telling when it might return."

That pretty much settled it for The General. He looked at the name again, Peter Escani. Sin Arse... no. And what did it matter if there was a hidden message? Ooh, scary joke shop business card versus recently fictitious monster with half a motorbike stuck in its head and teeth that could take an arm off with one bite? He put the card in his pocket.

"A shower you say?"

"Indeed," said Peter. "Let's find you somewhere to rest."

CHAPTER TWENTY-TWO

"They'll find out sooner or later," said Scarecrow. "We can't keep it a secret forever."

"And what if they do?"

It was a fair question, but Scarecrow was pretty sure he wasn't going to like the answer, especially when Numb Tongue found out.

"For all I know, they might throw me out," he said glumly.

Rain took his hands in hers. "I've already told you I won't get between you and the club."

"It's not that," said Scarecrow. "Well, partly I suppose. Numb Tongue..." he trailed off.

And yet somehow he knew it was right. The moment he met her at The Dragon's Head, he knew that she was *the one*, the fabled 'one' that rational people spend their entire lives searching for, often at the expense of their entire lives. They were crazy about each other, blindly, joyously, foolishly, and gloriously in love, talking and fucking, and talking and fucking long into the night. Already planning marriage, there was no question of them ever being parted again.

"The funny thing is," said Scarecrow, as they lay in bed recovering from several more acts of gross indecency, "my friend, Buggane, used to tell me when I was a kid that I should always thank the faeries on certain bits of road, and I always did just in case he was right."

"What *the* Buggane?" exclaimed Rain.

"You know him?" said Scarecrow, surprised.

"Doesn't *everyone*?" said Rain. "Well, of course, I don't know him personally, but everyone knows who he is. He's legendary!"

Scarecrow had learned a lot of things that night and had many more confirmed, not least that his dear friend Buggane was in fact a very famous - or at least infamous – ogre, who had lived on the Isle Of Man for several hundred years. He was something of a folk hero to those who knew his name, his legend beginning with the demolition of St Trinians Church in the fourteenth century. Somehow this hadn't come as much of surprise, and, instead, little pieces of the jigsaw began to slot together. He'd always known that Buggane was an extraordinary character.

"He does have a bit of a problem with churches," laughed Scarecrow. "He's always ranting on about hallowed ground."

"I don't blame him," said Rain. "Bastards have been harassing him for years, trying to get him to move. There's no such thing as hallowed ground, it's a curse, a curse on the ground to keep people out."

Scarecrow lay and listened, gently stroking Rain's wings as she lay beside him talking of ogres and faeries and witches and hobgoblins. Apparently Billy Toothless was a hobgoblin, which explained the smell. Clearly faeries were very real, too, as Scarecrow had spent some considerable time examining one in extremely intimate detail. Many of the other things Scarecrow had learned that night were in the pop-up Karma Sutra, and those that weren't almost certainly deserved books of their own.

"That's very sensitive," said Rain.

"Sorry," said Scarecrow.

"I didn't say it was bad."

The problem with all this falling madly in love stuff is that it had happened on the very first day of a mandatory club run, on which no one had brought wives or girlfriends, and on which they obviously weren't welcome. Doubtless Mad John and the rest of the guys would be pleased for him, but it was out of the question that Rain join them on the run, which meant that he wouldn't see her again until who knew when. This was also unthinkable.

The solution had been as simple as it was hopelessly romantic, stupid, and, probably dangerous. Since faeries could alternate, at will, between human size and the more traditional creature that rarely lived at the bottom of anyone's garden anymore, Rain simply shrank down and stowed away amongst Scarecrow's luggage. Admittedly it wasn't the best plan, but it was the only plan the lovers had to avoid being parted. Scarecrow jettisoned some of his own luggage and padded out one side of his saddlebags with a couple of Rain's human sized outfits, clothing apparently not given to changing size when faeries did. Thus, when Aberrant MC left The Dragon's Head that day, Scarecrow was carrying rather less in the way of essential supplies and rather more in the way of questionably skimpy underwear.

Not that the lovers had seen much of each other since they left the tavern, a few stolen hours in Scarecrow's tent after he'd spent the night working on Dum Dum's bike, the repairs dragging on as he made foolish mistakes, unable to concentrate. Now, at Bertha's Big Back Yard, he had finally snuck away while the others were distracted by a large and angry warg. Even then they had precious little time and he had to keep telling Rain to keep her voice down, her hearing having suffered on the ride while she was hidden in panniers that were far too close to the exhaust. The pair hid around the back of a broken-down truck, Rain still naked, shivering slightly, having adopted human size. Scarecrow draped his jacket around her.

"Even Numb Tongue will find out sooner or later," said Rain. "We can't just hide forever. What did you find out?"

"That's the problem," said Scarecrow. "We're going to see Numb Tongue fight. This whole run is to some tournament in the middle of fucking nowhere, where, get this, he's fighting in a death match. It's fucking nuts!"

"He's still trying to get himself killed, "sighed Rain. "I'd have thought maybe after all this time..." There was a hint of annoyance in her voice, like this was a subject that came up with irritating frequency and her patience had run thin.

"His wife, you mean?" said Scarecrow.

Rain nodded. "Ever since she died he's been doing everything he can to join her. It's heartbreaking to see him now, so broken inside when it could have been so different."

Numb Tongue had never told Scarecrow his story, and probably never would, but now, with the remaining pieces of the jigsaw added to what he had learned over the years, it all made sense, a tragic love story with all the obligatory unpleasant twists of fate.

Numb Tongue had met Sunshine in The Dragon's Head many, many years ago and fallen inexorably in love. They had married immediately, trying for a child that never came until the day Sunshine was murdered and the news was broken to Numb Tongue that he had lost both his wife and his unborn son.

Though he dealt a heavy justice he was never the same again, an increasingly battle scarred shell, willing a death that never came, while treating every kid in the neighbourhood as a surrogate for his lost boy. Only Aberrant MC kept him together and, even then, barely. Unfortunately, according to Rain, he also held a bitter resentment towards faeries, Sunshine having been a faerie, and reactions to such a loss not always being entirely rational. He would not be first in line to bless their union.

A gunshot rang out into the night, and moments later the buzz from the electric fence fell ominously silent, the constant hum more noticable by its absence.

"I'd better go and find out what's going on," said Scarecrow. "If they notice I'm gone then they'll send someone looking for me. I'll come back as soon as I can."

The lovers embraced, another stolen moment among far too few, Rain still shivering and half deaf.

"I love you," she said.

Scarecrow laughed. "Shh, keep your voice down! I love you, too."

"Sorry, was I shouting?"

The gunshot turned out to have been Bertha blasting a sizeable hole in the warg and killing it stone dead. The fence had been shut off while she and a handful of club members retrieved the body with the aid of a bright pink forklift truck.

"Hurry now dears, there may be more of them," she instructed, deftly reversing the forklift back into the yard as the gates were closed and the fence turned back on.

"Poor thing's probably better off," she said, climbing down from the forklift to examine the dead warg. It had clearly seen better days, even for a warg, who tended not to be particularly cheerful in the first place. Head-butting a speeding motorbike before fighting three hellhounds hadn't helped to lighten this one's mood. Now it was so many jackets and boots, steak for those who could ignore the fact that it might have eaten a few people, the broken handlebars a stark reminder that it might even have eaten The General.

Scarecrow pitched in with moving the beast to a refrigerated storage unit in another part of the labyrinth that was Bertha's Big Back Yard, but there wasn't much to do that couldn't be done between Dum Dum and Bertha with the forklift truck. The rest of the club were either standing around watching or had gone back to drinking. Many of them were managing both at the same time, Loud-As having already removed his boots in order to avoid the fate that shortly awaited Smiler. Among them was Numb Tongue, silent as ever, his guard as close as it ever gets to being down, the vaguest possibility that he was enjoying himself. For a moment he looked almost at peace with himself, but then he caught Scarecrow's glance, caught him staring, and his expression changed, the wall back up, shutters boarded firmly in place.

A hand rested on Scarecrow's shoulder, Mad John suddenly appearing at his side, concern written on his face.

"I'm told you have grown very close."

"We, uh, yes, you could say that," said Scarecrow, caught off guard. How could Mad John possibly know about Rain already? And yet the tricky fucker seemed to know everything, always one step ahead of everyone else.

"Maybe you could talk to him then," said Mad John, "talk some sense in to him. This fight is suicide and he knows it. He may as well put a gun to his head."

A slither of guilt stabbed at Scarecrow. All he cared about, all he'd been thinking about, was how Numb Tongue was going to take his relationship with Rain, and yet there was a very real possibility that if the fight didn't go his way then he wouldn't be around long enough for them to find out. And miserable cunt though he was, he was also, as far as Scarecrow was concerned, a top contender for best man at his wedding, assuming he got over the whole faerie thing. At least the speech would be short.

"I've told no one but Numb Tongue himself, and I'll thank you to keep it quiet," continued Mad John. "But death is among us and we await only the rooster. It is written in the cards."

Scarecrow looked at him blankly. "Can you do the last bit again in English? You think Numb's gonna lose the fight?"

"Let's just say I think it's highly likely. You may recall I had a meeting with Lilith? Death has been foreseen. I've tried telling him, but..."

Joker's wife, Lilith, made no secret of being a witch, but Scarecrow had always thought she was just being a goth or something. In light of recent events he was given to take her rather more seriously. Clearly Mad John took her seriously enough to be worried and, mad though he undoubtedly was, he was no fool.

"What makes you think he'll listen to me?"

"I don't, but what else can we do? I've tried talking to him myself. You train with him more than most, you're closer to him than most. He respects you more than most. I think you understand each other."

Better than you think, thought Scarecrow. Only two days in love, the notion of losing Rain was beyond comprehension, the end of life itself. Numb Tongue had been married forever and lost everything. There were worse things than death.

"If he fights he will die," said Mad John. "And we will have to watch him die. I'm just asking that you talk to him."

It was easier said than done, you didn't just go up to Numb Tongue and start a conversation, you had to kind of sidle up to it. On numerous occasions Scarecrow had trained with him for hours before a single word was spoken, and that was when old mister Chatterbox was at his most relaxed. Besides, ever since the club left The Dragon's Head, Scarecrow got the impression that Numb Tongue was being a little off with him, news perhaps having reached him about Scarecrow's new girlfriend. Christ knows what he'd do if he found out she was actually here, but Scarecrow didn't want to find out.

It was some hours later when Scarecrow finally chose his moment. Numb Tongue was sitting alone on the front porch, his feet propped on a large plant pot as he took in the night stars. As was customary they sat in silence for a while. You had to start off slowly, with something innocuous. Chilly out tonight. Don't the stars look so much brighter out here in the countryside? That kind of stuff. Most people who weren't too intimidated to talk to him in the first place usually gave up long before they got a response.

"Do you know where we're going?" said Numb Tongue, a quiet rumble, his eyes still on the night sky.

Scarecrow stared at him for a second, his mouth unavoidably open. Numb Tongue had never instigated a conversation before. Ever.

"What, for the fight, you mean?" he said, hoping it wasn't some sort of metaphysical question.

Numb Tongue nodded.

"Place called Fero, John said."

Numb Tongue nodded again. "Fero City. It's an orc city. Not a nice place."

Scarecrow waited for more, unsure how to proceed without risking an end to a conversation that was, so far, aiming in the right direction. A prompt might be clumsy, but too long a pause and the moment might pass. The empty seconds ticked.

"It's where the word comes from, you know?" said Numb Tongue, apparently more to himself than to Scarecrow. "Ferocity. Ferocious. Even fierce, I believe, is derived from it. Rough fucking place, it is, like Beirut on a bad day except without the law and order."

There was another agonising pause, a conversational aeon, Numb Tongue seemingly lost in thought.

"Mad John thinks you'll die if you fight," said Scarecrow, suddenly blurting it out. "He asked me to talk you out of it."

There was silence. Tumbleweed and crickets. Or at least assorted junk and the constant hum of the electric fence. Eventually Numb Tongue took a long breath, laced with a sigh.

"When I met Sunshine," he said slowly, painfully, "it all seemed so perfect. The two of us living together forever, so much time together..."

There was another silence, but Scarecrow made no attempt to fill it, opting to let Numb Tongue talk in his own time and try to figure out what he was talking about as he was going along. Numb Tongue still looked at the night sky.

"Faeries are immortal, you see," he said finally. He let out a sad, bitter laugh. "But then, so was I. I'd been to Athens with Mad John, years before, and swam around the rock. There's a rock in the harbour that's said to bring eternal life if you swim around it three times at the full moon. I nearly drowned. But then..."

Then Sunshine had died. No one was immortal when they'd been beheaded.

Numb Tongue's retaliation was swift and brutal, but dead was still dead. And he was still alive. Without her. Forever. Dead inside.

Maybe that was the key, or at least the door or something, thought Scarecrow. If Numb Tongue really was dead inside then it wouldn't still hurt. Would it? Scarecrow could only try to imagine, but he could no more imagine life without Rain than he could imagine life without air. Of course it would still fucking hurt!

"I've been shot forty-seven times, stabbed, strangled, and, on more than one occasion, blown up," said Numb Tongue, not a man one should ever play poker with. "And none of it even came close to how much it hurt when I lost her. It's not like a normal marriage, being married to a faerie. It becomes an obsession, almost a curse. You don't have a choice. You want nothing else, and then when it's gone..."

Somewhere over the other side of the yard, Rain was hidden in Scarecrow's saddlebags. Even now he could think of little else. Her smile, her eyes, her hands, her stomach, her sex, her everything, already worried about the bit

MORAT

where you have to say your real name at the wedding. Losing her was a horror beyond his comprehension, a blasphemy.

"Where is she, Scarecrow?"

"Wha..? I... Who?" managed Scarecrow, again caught completely off guard.

"I know she's here, Scarecrow," said Numb Tongue. "I'm not stupid."

"I don't know what you mean," Scarecrow stammered.

"I believe that's the first time you've ever lied to me," said Numb Tongue sternly. Suddenly there was a flicker of violence about him, nothing you could pinpoint, but nonetheless a sense that a man taking part in a death match has very little to lose and is not someone you should lie to twice. "I know she's here, Scarecrow, and do you know how I know?"

Scarecrow shook his head, speechless.

"I'll tell you, shall I?"

Scarecrow nodded.

"Because, dopey bollocks, you've been sat out here for the past hour and a bit with her lipstick all over your chin."

"Oh," said Scarecrow.

CHAPTER TWENTY-THREE

It took rather longer than it should have to leave Bertha's Big Back Yard the next day, due mostly to her handing out last minute gifts and supplies to the club members, before hugging them each in turn and telling them how lovely it was to either meet them or see them again. Twice. She seemed to have taken quite a shine to Dum Dum, who was now the proud owner of a wargskin jacket, as was Vincent.

"Now then, Bertha, we really must be on our way," said Mad John at last. "The pleasure has been all ours, but we have many miles to cover and many bridges to cross."

"Ooh, that reminds me, your 'ighness, John, sir," said Bertha, back to bowing and curtsying and bobbing up and down like an overgrown chicken. "I hear tell there's a bridge troll set himself up on the road to Eyeball Bay, asking far too much and doing far too little, if you know what I mean. Big bugger, I'm told, pardon my French. Might be nice if someone had a word with him if they happened to be passing that way, your 'ighness, sir."

"Consider him spoken to," said Mad John smoothly.

"And don't you worry about them three that's following you," grinned Bertha. "I've dealt with worse than those puppies in my time. I'll have them chasing their own tales in circles."

"I don't doubt it," laughed Mad John. "Now we really must be on our way."

Among the many things Vincent had chosen not to ask Mad John last night was why Bertha kept calling him 'your highness' and now, as they hit the long road to who knew where, he regretted the missed opportunity. Last night was the perfect time. He could have just asked, no matter how crazy he sounded, but instead he kept quiet, and now his mind was a tornado of mixed emotions and what ifs. What if the notes he'd stumbled across in Mad John's study all those years ago were more than the insane ramblings they had seemed to be? Somehow that was even more scary than the wandering wargs, and shapeshifters, and all the rest of it.

Admittedly, meeting Bertha had done a great deal to allay Vincent's fears, simply because she was Bertha, a big, fat, old lady, who wasn't scared of anyone or anything. But then she'd also had forty years to get her head around all this and wasn't remotely perturbed by such things as wargs and shapeshifters. And she might be an old lady but she also had a shotgun and an electric fence that could power Blackpool illuminations. Vincent didn't have any weapons.

He'd been to visit Numb Tongue before they set off to find out exactly what 'tooled up' meant and had basically been told, in as few words as possible, that if he didn't know how to use a weapon, which he didn't, then he shouldn't carry one as it was likely to be taken off him and used against him. It was a fair point, but it hadn't done much to boost his confidence. And that was when he thought, rather naively, that the club would be going to some place inhabited by humans, maybe just going to give a rival club a bit of a slap, not to a battle to the death in some far off orc city, known for, and indeed notorious for, its ferocity. It sounded like exactly the sort of place where being 'tooled up' would be an extremely wise idea. He had told Mad John as much last night.

"And could you shoot or stab or maim without hesitation?" said Mad John. "Could you gouge out an eye? Bite off an ear? Shatter a jaw?"

Vincent liked to think he'd have a good go if it came down to it, but the theory was rather different than the practice. In theory he knew everything there was to know about so-called self-defence having taken an advanced class from none other than Numb Tongue himself. It had been on the night of Vincent's eleventh birthday, just before they'd moved away. It wasn't late, maybe seven-thirty, eight o'clock, and Numb Tongue pulled his bike over near Chelsea Bridge so they could both get a burger from the burger van. While they were ordering their food a group of seven or eight blokes started throwing their weight around, picking on a small Asian man who had been singing Elvis songs quite poorly. They then, rather unwisely, started making snide remarks about Gary Glitter that were clearly aimed at the age difference between Vincent and Numb Tongue, alleging, in no uncertain terms, that Numb Tongue was a "kiddy toucher".

Numb Tongue had seemed to ignore them at first, even when one of them insulted his colours, an unforgivable act in the biker world. He paid for their burgers and coffee, fiddling with little packets of sugar and plastic stirring sticks, while all the time the insults continued. Quite why anyone would be foolish enough to pick on Numb Tongue was completely baffling, but there was always some muppet, or in this case muppets, looking to make a name for themselves. Elvis had sensibly left the building.

"Excuse me," said Numb Tongue politely, as if reaching for something. And then he'd gone off like a nail-bomb in a crowded bar. The man who put the bang in gang.

Ironically, given where they were now going, one thing Vincent learned that night was that ferocity counted for a great deal, particularly if you were outnumbered. It wasn't just about being quicker or getting the first punch in, it was about putting your opponent down as rapidly as possible and making sure he stayed down. Not surprisingly, Numb Tongue was horrifically adept at this and took just seconds to utterly dismantle the whole lot of them. Everything became a weapon, scalding hot coffee, a glass ketchup bottle, elbows, knees, fists, feet, even the plastic stiry sticks, one of which later had to be surgically removed from one of Numb Tongue's hapless opponents. Victims would have been a better word.

That was the theory. In practice being invisible for much of the time ensured that Vincent had never been in so much as a school yard punch up, and had no idea if he could fight or not, but deep down suspected not. The fact that he suspected not was also a problem, neither doubt or hesitation being an ally. Vincent had always known that by joining an outlaw motorcycle club he would inevitably have to fight someone sooner or later, but he had always hoped it would be later rather than sooner. He hadn't thought to hope that his opponent would be human. In every biker book he'd ever read there were lurid tales of wild and drunken bar brawls, but not one of them had ever mentioned wargs or orcs.

"We have several members capable of doing such things," Mad John continued. "They're really very good at it. You might even say they specialise. Stone, on the other hand, has rarely raised his voice, let alone a fist. Does that surprise you?"

Actually no, when Vincent thought about it, it didn't surprise him at all. It was no secret that the wrong dose of anything Stone had concocted was far worse than any beating anyone could ever inflict. Broken bones would heal, but a mind that Stone had shattered would need to be carefully pieced back together by a team of psychiatrists over the course of many years. When Vincent thought of him he was always reminded of Danny the drug dealer, from Withnail and I: "If I medicine you, you'll know you've been spoken to." He even had the same frizzy hair. Except that if Stone 'medicined' you, at least with intent, then you'd have to be spoon fed for the rest of your life. Don't fuck with Buck, cos Buck will fuck you up.

Mad John had instead asked about Vincent's strengths, what he was good at, but the only thing that came to mind, which didn't seem like an option if he was serious about joining the club, was not bloody being there when it all kicked off in case he got the crap kicked out of him.

"Exactly!" beamed Mad John, all smiles. "And you're very good at not being there, even when you are there. I'm afraid there's no word yet from Dennis about your ring, but I'd suggest you practice with it. Get Dum Dum to let you know when you disappear. Or you could even get Zig Zag to let you know when he can see you!"

"Wait, Zig Zag can't see me at all?"

"Apparently not," said Mad John, his face alight with amusement. "That's why he hasn't said hello yet, he didn't know you were here. He only said something because there was an extra bike every time we parked up. I really must introduce you."

And so they had got sidetracked from the million other questions Vincent wanted to ask, but was too afraid, and instead he'd got to meet a real live orc, which, along with Bertha giving him the wargskin jacket, was the coolest thing that had ever happened in the history of ever. True, it would have gone slightly better if Zig Zag had been able to see him and hadn't talked to a space near his left ear, but, since Vincent couldn't understand a word he said, it didn't really matter. Vincent was a bit disappointed that the orc didn't sound like an East London cab driver, but as it was he struggled to pick anything out from what sounded like words being tortured. If GWAR ever needed a new frontman they need look no further.

"He says he's heard a lot about you and if you get out of line he'll cut your nuts off," Mad John translated when they were introduced, and then when Zig Zag protested, "Okay, I'm sorry. He said, 'it's good to meet you even if he can't see you, and he's heard about your prowess for thieving so if you touch any of his stuff he'll cut your lips off and make you eat them'."

Zig Zag seemed satisfied with this translation and gave a broad and carnivorous grin, before strangling some more words.

"He says he's had a word with Joker as well, and if Joker encourages you to fuck with him because he can't see you then he'll cut Joker's lips off, too."

Zig Zag growled.

"And make you eat them," Mad John translated.

It was only later that Vincent found out Zig Zag was "probably" joking, but somehow the threat was already muted. Zig Zag would have to find him first. And if being invisible gave Vincent the upper hand, it also gave him the opportunity to stare without feeling self-conscious. It's an orc for fuck's sake! Who wouldn't stare?

It wasn't hard to see why Zig Zag wore the club's 'fight crew' patch. He was small in the same way that bullets are small, and both would make an equally nasty hole if you pointed them at someone you didn't like. He just looked *dangerous*, everything about him a warning, like a bug that you instinctively know is either poisonous or will bite you. Or both. Then again, it was very difficult to poison, bite, or eat someone you couldn't see, and already Vincent understood what Mad John had been getting at and how he could be an asset to the club. The problem was, he had no idea how the ring worked, and it hadn't come with an instruction booklet. Some people could see him and some couldn't, and he generally didn't find out who until they stood on his foot or knocked him off his motorbike.

Vincent practised as they rode along, willing himself invisible, but, so far as he could tell, nothing was happening. He'd have to practise later with Dum Dum or pluck up the courage to ask Zig Zag who, apparently, wasn't entirely pleased about it.

"He says not to run him over or he'll pull your fingernails out," Smiler translated at one point.

"And make me eat them?" said Vincent cheekily.

"What?"

"Nothing," Vincent smiled. "Tell him I have more trouble with people running me over."

"You can tell him yourself," said Smiler. "He speaks English. He's just got a bit of an accent. And yes, I know I've got cigarette butts glued to my eyebrows, thank you."

As ever, Joker had not been kind to Smiler for passing out with his boots on. Smiler had yet to notice that along with having cigarette butts glued to his eyebrows, his ear and nostril hair was growing at an extraordinary rate thanks to one of Bertha's potions. He now also had a tattoo on his leg that said Bertha's Big Back Yard, alongside a very crude rendering of a warg with an obscenely large penis. He wasn't going to be happy about that either, when he found out. And his vow of getting Joker back was impossible to keep because the bastard hardly ever went to sleep and *never* forgot to take his boots off.

From Bertha's Yard there had been four possible directions to take, and the club took a right, turning south. This road was much the same as the last, hedges and trees, then wide open meadows, always mountain ranges lurking in the distance. Once in a while there was another road, usually no more than a dirt path, leading off to places unseen, but there were no houses or farms, just more miles and miles of nothing. Vincent's mind wandered everywhere and nowhere, last seen wondering *everything,* but with an undercurrent of fear for what lay ahead.

Suddenly Dum Dum was shouting and waving his arm around, frantically trying to get Vincent's attention. He looked incredibly excited and swerved wildly, collecting part of a hedge before righting his bike.

"That's it! That's it!" he yelled, barely audible over the noise of their engines.

"What?" yelled Vincent.

"You just went invisible!"

CHAPTER TWENTY-FOUR

It was late in the afternoon when Aberrant MC made their one and only pit stop of the day, the shadows growing long and a chill coming back to the air. The club had ridden for mile after mile, the scenery never less than spectacular, when they came to another crossroads and what essentially looked like a heavily fortified outside toilet, an ugly concrete slab littered with graffiti and burn marks. There was just one window, heavily barred, more of a slot at eye level than a window, the shutter on the inside firmly closed. Aberrant pulled into the gravel parking area and killed their engines. Silence descended in an instant.

"Gentlemen," said Mad John quietly. "Those of you who have been here before will remember that this is no ordinary convenience store. Let me do the talking first and see if they'll sell us anything, but remember, one customer at a time and don't do anything that looks like you might be pulling a weapon unless you mean to trade it. They are not of the opinion that the customer is always right."

Mad John put his hands above his head and walked slowly towards the slot in the wall, besides which, almost hidden in the graffiti and dirt, could now be seen a small hatch with a handle on it, like you'd see outside a bank. Mad John trod carefully forwards.

"Man, you're gonna love this place, it's hilarious," grinned Stone, whose idea of hilarious, given the massive amounts of LSD he ingested, was abstract to say the least. "There's a couple of these places and this is the easier one to deal with. Basically it's a shop, right? But there's no price list, no way of knowing what they're selling, they don't take money, and there's only a fifty/fifty chance they'll sell you anything in the first place. Man, I wish I'd thought of that!"

"So what do they sell?" said Vincent. "And how do you buy anything?"

"Theoretically you can buy or trade anything that fits in the hatch. The whole shop's underground and no one knows how big it is or what's in there. Shit, no one even knows who runs the place, all you ever see is a pair of eyes. Billy said there's too many other scents around here to pick anything up. It's cool, man."

It didn't sound cool to Vincent, it sounded stupid. And it looked dangerous, scorch marks and bullet holes suggesting that customer service wasn't all it should be.

"I don't suppose there's any chance they speak English?" he said, quickly learning to expect the unexpected.

"They don't speak at all!" grinned Stone. "Good luck."

The club watched as Mad John reached the slot, which slid suspiciously open. He said something into the slot and the hatch beside him slammed open. He put something in the hatch and it slammed shut. Moments later the hatch banged open again and Mad John took something out. It was a large bottle of Jack Daniel's.

"You're kidding!" said Vincent.

Not all the club members wanted something from the shop, although a few asked others to get things for them, unwilling or unable to negotiate for themselves. And still not all of the shoppers were successful. After Mad John, Chaos, Stone, and Apples had no problems, but then Loud-As returned empty-handed and angry, the shutter having been slammed in his face. He kicked the wall and a lick of flame shot out of the slot, singeing his beard, a warning that the establishment retained the right to refuse service to anyone. Smiler and Zig Zag got a similar response, but wisely refrained from kicking the wall. The three prospects anxiously awaited their turns, each desperately needing petrol and not entirely averse to the idea of a bottle of Jack.

Vincent was the first of the prospects to approach the inconvenient convenience store, realising, as he did so, that he had little or nothing to trade. He had rather banked on being able to use a credit card. As it was, the slot remained firmly closed and showed no signs of opening for him. Vincent gave the other prospects an expansive shrug. Tentatively he called out: "Hello?"

Suddenly the shutter slammed open and, just as Stone had predicted, all that could be seen was a pair of eyes staring out. Stone had neglected to mention that the eyes had vertical pupils. They looked straight at him, straight through him, but before he could say a word the shutter slammed shut again. Vincent waited in case the hatch opened, but nothing happened and he had no choice but to give up.

"I don't think Tubbs and Edward can see me," he told the other prospects. "Something in there looked straight at me, but I thought if I said something and they couldn't see who was talking then they might get a bit happy with the flame-thrower again."

Now that he thought about it, there was every possibility that those lizard eyes had seen him, but he'd been too startled to speak up, gone blank, and forgotten that these strange shopkeepers were even less chatty than Numb Tongue. He felt he had just failed a test.

"You could always rob the place if they can't see you," offered Dum Dum jokingly.

"Man, I *really* wouldn't advise that," said Stone, with a Cheshire grin. "Believe me, people have tried. About twenty years ago this gang of faeries came up with a plan to rob the place and no one's seen them since. They figured they'd get one of them, human sized, to do the trade and make out she was trading weapons. When the hatch opens she puts all the weapons in the hatch and half a dozen faeries sneak in with them, then the hatch opens on the other side and you've got said faeries leaping out armed to the teeth, ready to rob the place."

"So what happened?"

"I told you," said Stone. "No one ever saw them again. The weapons came back into circulation again though, and I heard rumours of a trade in faerie wings."

"You mean...?" said Scarecrow, horrified.

"Yeah, man," nodded Stone. "These are bad motherfuckers. One time this guy put a bomb in the hatch to try and blow them up. Nothing happens and he thinks maybe it didn't go off, so he goes back to his car, puts the key in the ignition, and the fucker blows up! Boom! Bits of him all the way from here to Mordor."

"You couldn't have told me this before I went over there?" said Vincent.

"Man, I didn't think you were going to try and rob the place," shrugged Stone. "I've never had any problems with these guys, but I suppose it depends on what you expect. I love the place, man. You have to get them to understand what you want or it's like a giant lucky dip, *anything* could come through the hatch."

"So what did you get ?"

"Cheese and pickle sandwich, bottle of ginger beer, and some double A batteries," said Stone. "I was trying for chewing gum and a shaving razor."

Stone seemed to think this was very funny indeed, but then Stone also seemed to be in no immediate need of fuel for his bike. The prospects were all running on empty and way beyond. It shouldn't be possible for bikes to do this many miles on one tank of fuel and yet none of them wanted to mention it.

It wasn't long before Scarecrow, too, returned empty handed, having fared only slightly better than Vincent. The shutter slid open, the eyes peered out...

"I need petrol," said Scarecrow quickly, his hands still above his head, holding the few items he had scraped together to trade after getting rid of much of his luggage to make way for Rain's knickers. "Fuel," he nodded towards the bikes.

The eyes never left him and never blinked. For an instant, the thought rather surprised Scarecrow's mind by crossing it, that he was probably quick enough to pull one of those eyes out, just pluck it right out of the fucker's head. But as fast the thought crossed his mind, so the shutter slammed shut again. The hatch beside it remaining steadfastly closed.

They watched across the gravel car park, now, as Dum Dum approached the building.

"Tenner says he comes back with nothing," said Joker, one of the club members notable for not having attempted a purchase himself.

"Twenty says he gets something, but it ain't what he wanted," added Loud-As.

There was some hurried betting, the odds being in favour of Dum Dum returning empty-handed and possibly on fire. All eyes were upon him, including those behind the shutter, and as they watched Dum Dum slowly reached out his hand towards the open slot.

"Fuck's he doing?" muttered Loud-As. "He'll get his hand bitten off."

Dum Dum removed his hand and the shutter closed. The hatch opened and he placed something inside, various club members exchanging money having already won or lost bets. Others watched on. The hatch opened again and Dum Dum lifted out what looked exactly like a fuel canister.

"Well I'll be..." grinned Stone. He handed Mad John a large wad of cash.

Dum Dum was about to walk away when the hatch opened yet again. He reached inside and pulled out another fuel canister. And then, as the club watched on with open mouths, Dum Dum continued to pull fuel from the hatch for the next five minutes.

"Fucking hell, what did you trade with them?" said Joker incredulously, when he returned.

Dum Dum shrugged. "Just my watch. I didn't know what else to put in there. If that didn't work I was gonna put my hip flask or something in there. They must like watches I suppose."

"Like them?" exclaimed Joker. "How the fuck are you going to carry it all? There's got to be enough here to fill all the bikes and have some left over."

"Could trade it back again," suggested Dum Dum.

"Seriously?"

"Well, we don't need it," said Dum Dum. "Might be able to get some sandwiches or something."

Thus when all the bikes had been filled to the brim, even those which rarely needed petrol and whose owners where just trying not to hurt Dum Dum's feelings, he prepared himself for a second visit. Again, the club watched on fascinated, this time more so as Dum Dum tipped a small amount of whiskey from his hip flask onto his fingers.

"It worked last time," he explained. "Figured if I poured some petrol on my hand and let him smell it then it wouldn't matter if he didn't speak English."

"Actually, I said that they don't speak, not that they don't speak English," Stone pointed out. "But all the same, man, if I had a hat I'd take it off to you. That's genius."

"Did you want a hat? I'll see what I can do," said Dum Dum, before heading back to the hatch.

It wasn't the best hat by any stretch of the imagination, battered and dusty and slightly crumpled, but it was definitely a hat. A top hat in fact, once black and expensive, but now very much in its twilight years.

"I will treasure it," Stone smiled, putting the hat on and then doffing it promptly at Dum Dum, as promised.

"Best I could do," said Dum Dum almost apologetically.

"Are you kidding?" said Stone, putting the hat back on. He looked vaguely like Slash. "I love it! I still can't believe you traded this for their own petrol though."

"You don't do as long as I have in jail without knowing how to trade," Dum Dum quietly glowed with pride. "Their sense of smell must be a bit off though, they gave me Jim Beam instead of Jack."

"But that doesn't make any sense," said Loud-As, not a little put out by having been unable to trade anything at all and having lost his eyebrows in the process. "You give them a watch that you couldn't even tell the time with, they give you more gas than you can carry, so you trade it back for a hat and a bottle of whiskey. It doesn't make any fucking sense."

"I'll tell you what doesn't make any sense," said Dum Dum. "They gave me my watch back, too!"

CHAPTER TWENTY-FIVE

Water dripped from the ceiling, a steady metronomic plop, plop, plop, that tightened the internal springs of the mind like winding a clock too much until it broke.

Plop. Plop. Plop.

The General wept.

Hours passed.

Plop. Plop. Plop.

The General had no idea how long he had been here, tied naked to this desperately uncomfortable wooden chair, in this dank and miserable cellar, cold and afraid, alone and bleeding.

Plop. Plop. Plop.

He struggled to shift from one buttock to the other, but whatever they'd tied him to the chair with was like some Japanese bondage shit. Even his incessant shivering was restricted by the restraints.

Plop. Plop. Plop.

If it was designed to drive him crazy then it had long since worked.

Plop. Plop. Plop.

Every time The General drifted back from the all too brief respite of unconsciousness, there it was...

Plop. Plop. Plop.

It probably shouldn't have surprised The General that this Peter Escani, or whoever the fuck he was, had drugged him and left him tied him up in a freezing cold cellar. He was, after all, having that kind of day to begin with. The worst thing was that Escani had not only turned out to be a bad guy, but also an insufferable twat who seemed to think he was some kind of Bond villain. "I expect you to die, mister Bond, but first I'm going too tell you my dastardly plan to show you what a genius I am." Unconsciousness had definitely been a blessing at that point.

Escani's sidekicks hadn't turned out to be much better. There was a creepy little bald bloke with bug eyes, and this other blond twat, with chiselled male model looks, who seemed to think he was the scary one of the three and stood around trying to look suitably intimidating. As if there was any point! The General couldn't have been more intimidated!

But it wasn't Escani's blond bum boy that frightened him, all posing and posturing, it was the creepy bald bloke who, if The General had had any crap left in him, scared it out of him in no uncertain terms. Worse still, The General recognised him from the greasy spoon café, that evil old man with his crossword puzzle. No more than five feet tall, there was just this aura of spiteful nastiness and malevolence about him, of knowing full well that you were going to tell him everything you knew and he was going to cut under your fingernails with a razor anyway, just to see what face you pulled, whose name you cried out. The General had cried every name he could think of, including a few biblical names that he didn't even believe in.

"Please!" he begged. "I'll tell you whatever you want to know!"

"But that's the trouble, isn't it," sneered Creepy, his German accent not helping things at all. "You don't actually know anything. And now that we have your clothes we don't really need you for anything."

They had tortured him anyway.

Plop. Plop. Plop.

Who knew when they'd be back? Maybe they weren't coming back. Maybe they'd left him here to die.

Plop. Plop. Plop.

All they needed, Escani boasted, was The General's clothes, his jacket with his prospect patch to be precise, and they could apparently track the club anywhere. The General didn't care how it worked, some GPS voodoo shit, "one of the oldest magics" Escani said, probably spelling magic with a K. Whatever, the three Stooges had been gone for a long time, twelve hours or more, maybe a whole day.

Plop. Plop. Plop.

And some stupid fucking Nirvana song was stuck in his head: "Something, something, something, and the drippings from the ceiling, it's okay to eat fish cos they don't have any feelings."

Plop. Plop. Plop.

Hours passed. The General wasn't a religious man, but he prayed.

He awoke in the still empty room with a startled panic that instantly made way for pain.

Plop. Plop. Splash. Plop.

The splash was new, a slower pulse, but made more annoying by the fact that it landed on back of The General's neck, cold as ice.

Plop. Plop. Splash. Plop.

He pulled himself more upright and it landed on the top of his head.

Plop. Plop. Thunk. Plop.

They weren't coming back. Why would they? Not before he'd either starved to death, or frozen to death, or gone stark raving mad from the constant dripping. His head slumped.

Plop. Plop. Splash. Plop.

It could take them days, weeks, to catch Aberrant, even if their black magic tracking device actually worked. And frankly, that was the least of their worries. What if they did find Aberrant? What then? There were still only three of them against that whole mob of lunatics, Numb Tongue and Dum Dum and Smiler and that horrible little Stig creature and... they didn't stand a chance. The General had told them as much.

"I rather think you might be underestimating us," gloated Escani, failing to add "mister Bond."

Oh fuck off and stroke your cat. And take Oddjob with you.

Apparently Nick Cave, Creepy, and Bum Boy had been tracking Mad John for months, though The General suspected from their tone that it may have been years. A large bounty had been placed on Mad John's head by persons unknown, or at least unknown to The General, and however much it was worth, it was enough to keep these three on his tail. Reading between the lines of Escani's arrogance, they had only recently gleaned some insider information letting them know that the entire club was in The Dragon's Head. They honed in on The General as the weakest link and flattery and drugs did the rest. They hadn't even known about Vincent's ring until The General blabbed about it, but now considered it a bonus just as soon as they could get it off his finger. Creepy had brought some wire cutters and was looking forward to that bit.

Either way it didn't matter. They weren't coming back and he'd starve to death, or they were coming back and they'd cut his fingers off.

Plop. Plop. Splash. Plop.

He was probably better off with the first choice. You have selected starvation.

Plop. Plop. Splash. Plop.

How long could the human body survive without food or water?

Plop. Plop. Splash. Plop.

Oh wait, he had water. He raised his head and cried out.

"Heeeeelp!"

The sound fell dead against thick stone walls.

Plop. Plop. Thunk. Plop.

"Somebody please, help me!"

There was nothing. His head fell.

Plop. Plop. Splash. Plop.

There on the floor, beneath his foot, was a business card. Black, with silver lettering, expensive paper, a name on the front. Peter Escani.

Plop. Plop. Splash. Plop.

The General sobbed, the tears flowing down his bruised and graffiti strewn face, until they, too, became another steady drip, drip, drip.

Plop. Plop. Splash. Plop.

He was going to die here, cold and alone.

Plop. Plop. Splash. Plop.

The letters on the business card rearranged themselves before his red and tearful eyes. Rest In Peace, they read.

Plop. Plop. Splash. Plop.

CHAPTER TWENTY-SIX

From the inconvenience store Aberrant had made another change in direction, east this time, driving for three or four miles on roads that rose steeply and rapidly became treacherously twisty. Vincent was not alone in being thankful when Mad John slowed and pulled off the road onto a dirt path that was at least straight if no less bumpy, their bikes bouncing around over potholes and rocks.

It was hard going in the dark, the sun having dipped over the horizon, and tempers were fraying a little by the time they finally pulled over. Even Scarecrow with his feline reflexes had hit a few potholes and kept looking anxiously down at his panniers, clearly worried that something important might be broken in there. Those who knew what to look for may have noticed an exchange of glances between him and Numb Tongue.

Engines ticked as they cooled down, and the dust settled.

"Gentlemen, or rough approximations thereof," said Mad John. He stood, once again, on the seat of his still gleaming Knucklehead, not a speck of road dirt or dust to be seen. "If I might have your attention... Doubtless you'll be pleased to hear that we'll be making camp here for the night. We leave at dawn so if nobody has any objections I'd suggest a fifty/fifty. I'm sure we could all do with some rest."

There were no objections, not least from Vincent, who was on his first proper run with the club and had no idea what Mad John was talking about. It turned out to be nothing sinister, though. The club would be there for ten hours, so half of them would be on watch for the first five hours, the other half for the following five. It was only when Mad John instructed them to park the bikes into a semicircle, lights facing out, that Vincent noticed they were on the edge of some sort of cliff, the drop over the other side hidden by the darkness of night.

"Ah yes," said Mad John casually. "Forgot to mention that. Careful where you tread, it's about five hundred feet to the bottom. Used to be known as Suicide Falls."

"Used to be?"

"It's a bit more dangerous around here these days. People tend to get eaten long before they get here. I'd imagine it makes them think twice about suicide though, if not for very long."

The club set up camp, pitching tents and building a small fire to ward off the bitterly cold night. Vincent was still grateful for his wargskin jacket even though it was about three sizes too big and rapidly earning him the nickname 'Turtle'. The fire had to be kept low in case it was spotted, a lighthouse on the cliff, but Suicide Falls was the prefect vantage point, overlooking every road, including the only one that led to it. If anyone, or any*thing*, was coming their way then they had a pretty good chance of spotting it.

The club settled in for the night, whiskey and joints passed around to blunt the bitter air. Not all of them had come quite as prepared as they might, Turtle's jacket quickly becoming a thing of envy.

"The thing is," said Chaos, blissfully unaware of the chattering teeth around him, and now clad in what appeared to be appropriate clothing for Arctic conditions, "all this is desert out here, so it's nice and warm during the day, but then it's freezing cold at night."

"Yeah, thanks for that," muttered Loud-As, whose idea of coming prepared meant an outside chance of him bringing a tent or a sleeping bag. "I had noticed it was a bit Pearl Harbour."

Scarecrow joined the group, having spent some time poking about in his saddle bags. There was an imperceptible glance from Numb Tongue. Scarecrow gave the merest nod back: yes Rain is fine. Actually she wasn't fine, she was fucking fantastic! And add funny to fucking fantastic. There he was worried sick that she'd be getting battered to pieces in his panniers, and there she was fast asleep in a hammock made out of her knickers. She woke with a smile that lit up his world.

"What?"

"You've made a hammock out of your knickers!"

"Well, why do you think they call them faerie hammocks?"

Numb Tongue had been pretty cool about it in the end, though that was a long way from persuading him to be best man. He'd said his piece, and quite a considerable piece it was, too, for old mister Flapjaw, but then that was the end of it. So long as it didn't interfere with club business he wouldn't tell them about Rain stowing away until after the fight, if indeed he survived the fight. But he could only bend club rules so far. Numb Tongue was doing his best, but there was an undercurrent of 'keep her the fuck away from me', so even the slightest glance of concern was a step in the right direction.

"Wait a minute," said Dum Dum, out of the blue, the subject having been changed some time ago. "I've never heard of any desert in Wales. How can there be a desert in Wales?"

"We're not in Wales, Dum Dum."

"Oh," said Dum Dum.

He considered this for a moment. Wargs were probably not native to Wales and he had a feeling it would have been on the news or something if one had been spotted walking around Newport.

"Would someone mind telling me where the fuck we are then? I mean, it's not like there's any signposts."

"Funny you should ask," smiled Mad John, as if it was. "Might I have a word with you Dum Dum?"

The pair sat on the cliff's edge, their feet dangling over nothingness. Way, way off in the south there was a hint of what might have been lights, and to the west there was a vague orange glow that could be a distant city. To the north and the east there was nothing but darkness. Mad John lit a joint. He seemed lost in thought for a moment, staring out at the night, the glow from the end of the joint lighting his face when he inhaled. He offered it to Dum Dum, exhaling so his entire head was lost in a cloud of smoke.

"Perhaps you don't recognise it because you were too young," said the smoke cloud. "But you've been here before."

Dum Dum considered this. He had no memory of ever being here before, and yet somehow it felt right, like part of him knew the place and belonged here. In the city he was lost the whole time, utterly fucked without GPS and still having to follow buses to find his way anywhere. Out here it felt different, instinctive, like all you needed was the sun and the stars.

"Don't know," he shrugged.

"You'd have been very young, a child," said Mad John. The smoke still lingered around his head giving the curious impression of a halo-like glow.

Dum Dum considered this, too. "Is this a test?" he said.

"Of sorts, I suppose," Mad John allowed, with a smile, "but in the terms you mean, no Dum Dum, this is not a test, though it may well be a challenge. What can you tell me about your parents?"

Dum Dum shuffled uncomfortably. He knew nothing of his father, and what little he knew of his mother wasn't good, a paranoid schizophrenic, in and out of nut houses for the majority of his childhood. He'd been taken away from her at birth and she'd made sporadic attempts at gaining custody and one or two at kidnapping, but had managed to fuck it up every time. The last time he saw her was when she came to visit him in borstal, still nuttier than a complimentary airline snack. She died two months later. As far as he was concerned, Aberrant MC was his family now. Still, this was the president asking so Dum Dum told him what he could.

"You know," said Mad John, apparently drifting from the subject. "When you first started hanging with the club we had to take certain precautions to make sure that you had our best interests at heart."

"Make sure I wasn't a cop, you mean?"

"As I heard it you did arrive at the clubhouse on a police bike, albeit a stolen one."

"Yeah, sorry about that," said Dum Dum.

"Don't be! I haven't laughed so much in years. You're good people, Dum Dum. We just had to make sure you're our kind of good people."

"The cop thing, you mean?"

As evidenced by an endless series of tell-all books, it was no secret that many of the major outlaw clubs had been infiltrated by undercover cops at some point. These idiots would put years of effort and enormous amounts of taxpayers' money into bringing down entire clubs, usually managing no more than a handful of arrests, and, even though Aberrant flew relatively low under the radar, you could never be too careful. Just because Dum Dum told the club that before meeting them he'd spent most of his life in jail didn't mean it was true. All clubs did background checks, the bacon test.

Mad John took a long drag on the joint, a glow, and then a cloud of smoke.

"The cop thing, yes. But more than that," said the cloud of smoke. "When you came here before, it was for a funeral. Your father's funeral. Your mother kidnapped you from the foster home to bring you here."

Mad John let this sink in. It had a long way to sink.

"You mean my mum wasn't mental?" Dum Dum said finally.

"No more than the rest of us. I'm afraid her only problem was wanting to live in both worlds and that's not possible, not now, and certainly not then. I'm sure you'd be horrified to know how many perfectly sane people are locked up...or perhaps not given the time you have spent incarcerated. Unfortunately, it seems your mother had a habit of telling the wrong people and they had a habit of locking her up for it. Your father knew nothing about it. He was a good...um, a good sort."

"Can I see him? His grave," said Dum Dum.

"Of course you can. He's buried about twenty miles from here, just outside a place called Eyeball Bay." Mad John passed the joint back. "Tell me Dum Dum, do you believe in coincidence?"

"Dunno," shrugged Dum Dum. He was more of a cause and effect person. You stole something, you got caught, you went to jail.

"You see," said Mad John. "It turns out that I knew your father, many years ago. He worked near here and he was very much respected for his work."

Dum Dum thought about this. "That's good," he said.

And Mad John told him more.

Dum Dum had, as Dum Dum does, taken the rest of the news in his stride. Admittedly, some of it had to be explained twice, but thankfully they fell short of having to draw diagrams. First of all Dum Dum was his real name. He was named after his great grandfather, Dum Dum, who in turn was named after *his* uncle Dum Dum. It was, Mad John explained, a very traditional name, a fine and upstanding name...for a troll.

"Your father was a bridge troll," said Mad John. "His job was to maintain the bridge to Eyeball Bay, for which he would collect a small toll."

"A small troll?"

"No a toll, Dum Dum, a fee for looking after the bridge."

"So my dad was a bridge toll?"

"No, your father was a bridge *troll*."

It had taken some time.

CHAPTER TWENTY-SEVEN

It was difficult to miss the bridge. The club set out early in the morning, back down the hill for a few miles before rejoining their original path south, as the glow of dawn gradually warmed the sky. The bridge was maybe fifteen or sixteen miles down the road, wood and stone, crumbling and rotted, a shadow of its former glory. Not that it would ever have been that glorious, but once upon a time it had been a good solid bridge, if nothing fancy. It was a bridge you could cross with confidence. Today the rumble of their bikes caused part of the bridge to drop into the stony river, crashing on the rocks a few hundred feet below.

The club parked their bikes and Dum Dum strode forwards, a determined look on his face. Mad John had told him all about this new bridge troll, how the bridge was becoming dangerous and the tolls ever more outrageous. How his father's life work was literally falling onto the rocks below. He hadn't been exaggerating. The bridge was not far from collapse.

The new bridge troll was waiting. He stood up as Dum Dum approached, entirely blocking the entrance to the bridge. He was nine feet tall, at least, and carried a spiked wooden club.

"Twenty quid says the troll ends up paying us to cross the bridge," said Joker, who was fast catching on to Dum Dum's negotiating skills.

There was a hurried taking of bets, though more cautious than last time, a few of the club having been badly stung when they underestimated their prospect. The bridge troll loomed over Dum Dum. Make that ten or eleven feet tall, he made Dum Dum look small.

"I told him just to have a quiet word," Mad John informed them. "Find out what he's charging as a toll and why he's not been maintaining the bridge. This was once an important trade route and bridge trolls were well respected. It's a tough job, especially in the winter. A little diplomacy first I thought, and since he's half troll and his father once...."

"FUCKING HOW MUCH?"

"Hmm," said Mad John. "Perhaps I didn't stress quiet enough."

Dum Dum stomped back over to the waiting club.

"What happened to a quiet word?" said Mad John. "I distinctly heard three very loud words."

"Sorry John, but he wants a bike. If all of us want to cross the bridge, we have to give him a bike."

"I see," Mad John looked less than impressed. "That does seem rather excessive."

"Daylight robbery is what it is," fumed Dum Dum. "Did you see the state of that bridge?"

"Did you try a riddle?"

"I don't need to go at the moment. Will it help?"

"No, a riddle. A puzzle. It's tradition that if someone can't afford the toll fee then they give the bridge troll a riddle to solve, and if he can't solve it then you cross the bridge for free."

"A riddle," said Dum Dum. "Right." And he stomped back over to the bridge troll.

Words were spoken and Dum Dum came back.

"Well?"

"I told him a riddle," said Dum Dum. "I said, "The next thing I tell you is the truth, the last thing I told you was a lie."

"Perfectly good riddle," said Mad John happily. "And what did he say?"

"He said he didn't care about riddles and he wanted a bike."

"Did he now?" Mad John frowned. "Then perhaps this calls for some louder words."

The bridge troll watched them with little more than curiosity, idly swinging the wooden club. There was no doubt that they could take him out, but he could do an awful lot of damage with that club before he went down. Though unused to threatening anything more than the odd fishermen or stray traveller these days, it was nonetheless a weapon for cracking skulls, and on the end of those tree trunk arms it had a pretty wide range. The troll didn't look particularly fast, and certainly not clever, but he could pull an arm off without much trouble and he wasn't taking his eyes off them. Which was curious because Vincent was standing right in front of him waving his arms about.

"Not gonna need words," muttered Dum Dum, and headed back towards the troll.

There was some hurried betting among the club members.

"So let me get this straight," they heard Dum Dum say. "We have to give you a bike if we want to risk crossing this bridge and you don't accept riddles?"

The troll's forehead creased as he formed a sentence.

"Yeah," he said.

It wasn't much of a sentence.

"Well, bollocks to that!" said Dum Dum, just as a rock hit the troll in the back of the head.

The troll spun around with surprising agility, narrowly missing Vincent with the skull smasher. Then there was a sound like a frying pan hitting a brick wall.

"Ow! Ow! Ow! That was the broken hand!" yelped Dum Dum, folding to the ground. The brief moment the troll had been distracted was all he needed to slip on his brass-knuckles and take an almighty swing at him, launching himself off the ground and hitting him clean behind the ear.

The troll's brow creased further.

"Huh?" he said, looking down at Dum Dum, who was crumpled in the dirt cradling his hand in agony. The troll raised the heavy wooden skull smasher above his head. As one the club charged forward, but it was too late, there was no time to reach the troll before he swung at Dum Dum. Then, slowly, the troll pitched forward, landing flat on his face. Although there was something of a delayed reaction, Dum Dum had knocked the troll clean out.

When the troll awoke, he was tied to a tree and Dum Dum was poking him with a big stick. Dum Dum's hand had been bound and liberally dowsed with strange smelling ointments from Stone's first aid kit, but he still wasn't in the best of moods.

"My friend Dum Dum here would like a few quiet words with you," said Mad John, nose to nose with the troll. "I trust you will listen to what he has to say. He's the nearest thing you have to a friend right now."

The bridge troll grasped the situation fairly quickly, at least for a bridge troll, and sensibly chose to negotiate.

"Cunt says he'll do what we want," said Dum Dum finally. He still wasn't entirely sure how he felt about being half troll, particularly since the only example he'd met so far was, not to put too fine a point on it, thicker than concrete and a bit of a wanker. "I told him if he didn't fix the bridge by the time we came back then I'd cut his bollocks off."

There was a growling noise from Zig Zag.

"I really don't think it's necessary for him to eat them," said Mad John. "Besides, I don't think he'll be any further trouble. In troll society Dum Dum would now be considered the dominant troll, so he'll do what he's told."

They untied the bridge troll with some caution, but as Mad John predicted he showed no signs of causing them any further problems and, much to Dum Dum's annoyance, followed him around and did exactly as he was told. They set to work repairing the bridge so it was safe enough to wheel the bikes across.

"Remember," said Dum Dum. "I wanted this all fixed up better than new when we get back. Got that Cunt?"

The big troll nodded obediently. "Yes, Dum Dum."

"I think he's got the message," whispered Mad John. "There's no need to keep calling him that."

"But that's his name," said Dum Dum. "He comes from a long line of Cunts."

"Does he indeed?" said Mad John, a wry smile on his face. "How unfortunate. You reminded him to lower his tolls somewhat and observe the riddle rule?"

"Yes, John."

"Good," said Mad John, with a satisfied air. "Now we should be on our way. One thing though, Dum Dum, that riddle of yours really was rather ingenious: 'The next thing I tell you is the truth, the last thing I told you was a lie'. Really very clever. What's the answer?"

"Dunno," said Dum Dum. "I saw it on Doctor Who."

CHAPTER TWENTY-EIGHT

Eyeball Bay was a small fishing community, full of quaint old houses, and a pub with a thatched roof, but, still, the sound of approaching bikes drew a curious crowd that rapidly became a welcoming committee. Apparently a few of the club were already known and liked around here, and news that the bridge troll had been "spoken to" came as a great relief after a tough winter. The bridge troll may not have been the only reason for a decline in trade, but he certainly hadn't helped. Indeed, when Dum Dum was introduced, not only as the son of the much respected former bridge troll, but also the hero who knocked the current one out, some of the more enthusiastic crowd members attempted, briefly, to raise him aloft in their arms. Failing to get him off the ground they sufficed with vigorous pats on the back. A hearty late breakfast and rather too many drinks, since it was still only ten am, were on the house.

"The ferry leaves at one," Mad John told them, "so I want everyone back here for twelve sharp."

Most of the club elected to stay in the pub, but, since they were off duty, Scarecrow and Vincent decided to go for a wander around the harbour. Mad John had taken Dum Dum to pay his respects at his father's grave, which seemed like rather a personal moment to intrude upon unless they were specifically asked, and watching the club get drunk wasn't exactly a novelty. Eyeball Bay was something new.

Most of the town was set back a little from the harbour itself, and many of the buildings near the water were boarded up and abandoned, a once fine hotel with its windows smashed and its front wall pock marked as if something had been throwing rocks at it from the sea. Scarecrow and Vincent shared the same thought as they stared out at the deep, dark waters beyond the harbour.

"You don't reckon?" said Vincent.

"Mate, we met a bridge troll today."

"Fair point. It's just that John said something about a ferry, and if there's something in the water big enough to throw rocks at a hotel, then I'm not really that keen on being in the water with it."

"Yeah, I know what you mean," Scarecrow nodded. "I've met quite a few things in the last couple of days that I wouldn't want to get too close to again."

"And a few that you would."

Scarecrow gave Vincent a curious look. "Yeah," he smiled cautiously. "Bertha was pretty cool, and even that fucking weird shop was kind of fun."

"And your faerie friend," Vincent pried further.

Scarecrow stared out to sea, the wind blowing his limp blue Mohawk away from his face. The colour was starting to fade and the sides were growing out. There hadn't really been time to fix it. "Yeah," he shrugged non-committally, no big thing.

"Where is she, Scarecrow?"

"What do you mean?"

"I mean," said Vincent, "that if you're gonna shag someone with bells on then you probably shouldn't do it in a tent near anyone else. She fucking jangles, mate, and vice versa, but, either way, I didn't get a lot of sleep. Don't worry, I didn't tell anyone, but I don't know if anyone else heard you. It wouldn't surprise me though, it sounded like someone fighting a wind chime."

"Fuck," said Scarecrow, failing to stifle a giggle.

"Where is she now?"

"In my saddlebags."

"In your fucking saddlebags? What the fuck are you thinking?"

Scarecrow told Vincent what he was thinking.

"Bloody hell, Scarecrow," was the best Vincent could manage.

"Numb Tongue took it pretty well," there was hope in Scarecrow's eyes. "But I don't know if he's just blocking everything out until after the fight, y' know? He said he'd give me until then to figure things out."

"And then what?"

"Well, then we want to get married as soon as possible, but obviously it's gonna have to wait until after the run."

"Married?" Vincent couldn't help an incredulous look. "Fucking hell, she must jangle! You only met her a couple of days ago!"

"Oh, don't you start, I got enough earache from Numb Tongue. And that's a sentence I never thought I'd hear! It's not exactly been a normal couple of days. We're getting married and that's the end of it."

"What you and Numb Tongue?"

"Shut up, you twat!"

But Scarecrow was right, it hadn't exactly been a normal couple of days. Only a few hours ago Vincent had played a part in bringing down a bridge troll, and even now he was sweltering in his oversized wargskin jacket. These things were not normal. At least not to Vincent. But then, the people around here seemed perfectly normal, and yet they were also aware of a fucking great big bridge troll living up the road from them, and seemed to consider that normal, too. And it wasn't like they talked all ye olde and didn't know what a car was. It was more like being in Cornwall by the coast, where badly driven caravans were more of a threat than club wielding bridge trolls. Shit, they'd make a fortune in tourism, selling little plastic bridge trolls to fat Americans. Maybe the old hotel was evidence that they once had. It was madness.

"What do you think this orc city's gonna to be like?" said Vincent finally, his thoughts inevitably drawn to the road, and, more worryingly, the boat, ahead.

Scarecrow shook his head. "No idea. Not nice, Numb Tongue said. Up there with Afghanistan on the tourist wish list. And this is coming from Numb Tongue whose idea of fun is...Well..."

A death match. Say it. Your best friend and mentor is fighting in a death match, and, unless you can talk him out of it, he's going to die. It weighed on Scarecrow night and day. Not that it had actually been that many days, but it seemed like a lifetime, the additional distraction of being head over heels in love already warping time like a badly edited movie. All Scarecrow wanted to do was wallow in blissful harmony, or spend all day in bed shagging, which amounted to much the same thing. But at the back of his mind was a loop-tape of Mad John's voice: "If he fights he will die and we will have to watch him die."

"I don't want to watch him die," Scarecrow said aloud.

"Numb Tongue? You think he's going to lose? I've seen him take out seven or eight blokes on his own!"

Keep it to yourself, Mad John said. It has been foretold. Some bastard rooster would crow three times on the morning of the fight and that night

Numb Tongue would die. And they would have to watch him die. Death has been seen in the cards.

"And what if he's not fighting 'a bloke'?" said Scarecrow.

"Oh fuck! I hadn't thought of that!"

Scarecrow had. It wouldn't be unreasonable to assume that being immortal gave you a definitive edge in a fight to the death, but, unfortunately, as both Mad John and Numb Tongue himself had pointed out, it wasn't as simple as that. Andy One-Leg was an immortal, but he still only had one leg, it hadn't just grown back after he lost it. It stayed lost. A head would do much the same thing if you removed it from someone's neck. Indeed, Mad John had given Scarecrow something of a crash course in the rules of so-called immortality, how there were all kinds of variables, but at some point dead is dead, and there are ways of killing everything and everyone. Everyone had their kryptonite.

"Elves for instance," Mad John had told him, "can die either in battle or from a broken heart. Might be a handy thing to know if you were, well, an elf."

Which was when Mad John had broken the news to Scarecrow that he was, well, an elf.

The funny thing was that it hadn't come as a surprise. At all. Admittedly Mad John's equivalent of a father/son talk, or whatever this was, had come a couple of days too late, what with him having met a selection of orcs, wargs, and witches, not to mention being engaged to a faerie. But it was more than that. As they sat up on the cliff top last night and Mad John told him what he was and why he was, it all seemed to fit into place. It wasn't even an accident that he'd been introduced to the club all those years ago, his old friend Buggane contriving to put Scarecrow among people who would understand him and be able to offer some guidance.

Buggane had kept a protective eye on him when he was a kid, but home schooling and such couldn't keep him hidden forever. When Scarecrow had shown not just an interest but a considerable talent for racing and repairing motorcycles, Buggane had called Aberrant MC.

There would, Mad John told him, be a lot of adjustments in his life.

Scarecrow would never be a world champion motorcycle racer. Not because he didn't have the talent, but because people would start to get suspicious when he was world champion for two hundred years. And that was the least of his problems. Only a few years ago it wasn't too difficult to get new identification and reinvent yourself, but now, in the days of surveillance cameras and ID cards, staying hidden was becoming more of a problem. Naturally Scarecrow had asked why he had to stay hidden at all, but the answers were so many and so obvious, not least that he'd probably get dissected in minute detail for his two hundredth birthday. In some ways, Mad John admitted, the club had been a diversion from his motorcycle racing aspirations, club duties keeping him just slightly too busy to turn pro.

"You think they brought us all the way out here to tell us this shit so we wouldn't freak out?" Vincent asked.

"Would we have believed it if they hadn't?"

"Probably not," Vincent conceded.

"Besides," said Scarecrow. "I did freak out a bit. Told him they had no right to fuck about with my racing career like that, and he just says that since I'm immortal it's more like taking a week off than ending my career. Said I can start again any time I like, but he wouldn't advise it. It's weird. I've always kind of suspected something...I dunno...odd, but I never really knew what. It's a lot to take in."

Scarecrow let out a chuckle. "I even accused him," he laughed, "I said Aberrant wasn't a proper bike club because half of them were around before motorbikes were even invented! Apparently he bought his first Harley in 1906 and he was at Hollister in 1947, and it's not his fault if motorbikes hadn't been invented when he was born. That told me."

"I think he's been around a lot fucking longer than that," Vincent ventured, prying for clues that would back up his own theories without forcing him to voice them yet.

"I don't know," shrugged Scarecrow. "I asked him and he said it was rude to ask an immortal."

The pair sat and watched as a small fishing boat sailed gently into the harbour, a trail of hungry gulls in its wake. For a moment it was possible to imagine that they were still in the real world, the world they understood, the world where trolls and orcs and shapeshifters didn't exist. The sun beat down, making the water twinkle and shine, and the little boat bobbed gently about, a picture of calm and serenity.

"So," said Vincent, breaking the spell. "You're elvish, are you?"

"Apparently," said Scarecrow.

"Can you do Jailhouse Rock?"

CHAPTER TWENTY-NINE

It took some time to load all the bikes onto White's Ferry, not least because they had to be loaded one at a time and there was no ramp. Instead they were lowered onto the deck in a sling that looked as if it was more suited to livestock. It didn't help that many of the club were very drunk, having been left unattended in the pub for more than the blink of an eye.

Mr White, possibly named after his impossibly long and improbably white beard, didn't look at all happy about any of it.

"I'm sure you boys would be extended every hospitality if some of you wanted to stay a few days and do this in two trips," he tried. "There'll be another ferry, same time the day after tomorrow."

"Love to! Very good pies!" beamed Mad John. "But I'm afraid we really do have to press on. We'll have more time for such pleasantries when we return. And we'll be able to check up on the unfortunately named bridge troll."

"Ah yes, the troll. We're all very grateful," said Mr White, his face now almost as white as his hair and, indeed, his boat, which had just sunk a little further below the waterline as Dum Dum's Harley was lowered onto the deck. There were still three bikes to go and many of the club members weren't exactly light on their feet either. Luckily there were only a few other passengers, a grey haired old lady with a gigantic handbag, and two fisherman looking types, possibly father and son, all woolly hats and jumpers.

"Thing is," Mr White cringed further, "it's a bit choppy out there today and..."

He gestured out towards the sea which couldn't have been much flatter if it had been ironed, just an occasional swell in the glittering mirror surface.

"Yes, yes, marvellous," Mad John slapped him on the back with a big cheery smile. "Good to know we're in safe hands then."

When White's Ferry finally puttered out of the harbour it sat so low in the water that the prospects were instructed to stand by with buckets in case it needed bailing out. Smiler was already throwing up over the side, though this was probably more to do with alcohol poisoning than seasickness. Despite Mr White's predictions, the water remained studiously flat.

"You see, Mr White, we'll be there in no time," Mad John enthused. "Nothing to worry about."

Mr White looked wholly unconvinced. Anything bigger than a ripple and they would all be bailing fast.

The ferry puttered on, clinging dangerously close to the coastline. Treacherous black rocks poked evil dark fingers from the water, but Mr White clearly knew each one like the back of his hand. He even had names for them which he grimly recited as they went past. "Razorback, Devil's Elbow, Orphans Cause..."

"You notice none of them have names like Happy Ending or Soft Landing," muttered Vincent.

It seemed, at times, as if they were barely squeezing past some of the rocks, only a few inches away from disaster, and the cliff-face that lay beyond was no more inviting, all sheer and jagged and covered in bird crap. Mr White's ferry ran just once a day and only in daylight. Anyone foolish enough to attempt the journey in darkness was usually forced to take swimming lessons, often rapidly followed by drowning lessons. The alternative of being eaten alive was no less unpleasant, but apparently rather more likely if you were to venture into the deeper waters of what was known locally as the Sea Of Destruction. Many were the tales of sunken treasures and many were the fools who went searching for them, never to return.

"They even sent a bathysphere down there at the turn of the century," said Mr White, though the turn of which century was in some question. "When they pulled the cable back up there was nothing on the end of it, whole thing was gone. If you ask me the Kraken got them before the rocks did."

"And when you say Kraken," said Vincent, hoping that he didn't already know the answer, "...you mean?"

Mr White elaborated rather too elaborately, confirming Vincent's worst fears that it might be some gigantic squid-sea-monster-thing with a penchant for throwing rocks at coastal hotels, and indeed for sinking boats such as the one they were on. Thought to be one of the last of its kind the Kraken, or at least this particular Kraken, was about twice the size of the boat they were currently sailing in, and was known to have been responsible for sinking dozens of French galleons in the seventeenth century. Apparently age hadn't mellowed it much, which was exactly why White's Ferry sailed only once a day and only in daylight, clinging as much as possible to the shoreline. The Kraken preferred colder, deeper seas.

There was a swell in the water, only slightly more than a gentle rise and fall, but enough to have Smiler emptying his stomach over the side again. Thanks to Bertha's humorous hair potion he now had to hold his long and flowing nostril hair out of the way to avoid getting chunks in it.

"This isn't funny you know."

"Yes it is," said Joker.

"No it's not."

"Bet you ten quid."

"Shut up, Joker. How long does this shit take to wear off? I'm having trouble breathing with this crap growing out of my nose!" Smiler lurched for the side of the boat again and made the sort of noises usually associated with really bad death metal. The rest of the club were almost in tears with laughter.

"I'll thank you to do that in a bucket, if you don't mind," said Mr White sternly. "We don't want to be leaving any trails to follow."

"Yeah, man, cut it out," insisted Stone. "You're just leaving a trail of bait."

Smiler was handed a bucket, into which he was copiously sick.

"You think it was something he ate?" grinned Joker.

"It looks like everything he ate."

"How come there's always diced carrots?"

There was another swell in the water, pitching the boat a little and sending Smiler off balance. He stumbled to catch his bucket of warm and sloshing vomit, and slipped, sending its contents all down his jeans and onto the deck. He then slipped again in his own frothy unpleasantness, his nostril hair becoming tangled in the handle, and the bucket swinging and cracking hard against his shin. Joker was actually crying with laughter, the rest of the club not far behind.

"Oh man, for fuck's sake, it's everywhere! Someone give me a knife so I can at least cut this fucking bucket off!"

Joker collapsed, tears streaming down his face. Of all his pranks, this ranked among his finest. The cigarette butts glued to Smiler's eyebrows were mere child's-play compared to Bertha's hair potion, and he still had a full bottle stashed in his luggage for later use, although the chances of anyone being stupid enough to pass out with their boots on again were fairly slim.

"That's odd," muttered Dum Dum, more to himself than anyone in particular. "I could've sworn..."

"Come on, man, give me a knife. I can't get this fucking thing off!"

"....that island was over there a minute ago..."

"Come on, gimme a knife. There's puke everywhere."

"What island?"

There was another swell in the water, bigger this time, enough to throw a few of them off balance and have the rest diving for the bikes to stop them tipping. Smiler slid, again, in the recently vacated contents of his stomach, and grasped for a handhold that wasn't there. He didn't even hit the deck before he was dragged once more, face first this time, through his breakfast, in a tug of war that threatened to pull him overboard. The bucket, now empty of its contents, was firmly suctioned to a black and sticky tentacle, the tip of which was winding inexorably around the handle.

"Fucking hell! Fucking hell! Get it off me!"

At once the little ferry was alive with action as the sticky black feelers crept in from every direction. Dum Dum dived for Smiler's feet, grabbing the boots that he was deeply regretting sleeping in, just in time to stop him from being pulled overboard. Smiler clung desperately to his nostril hair, screaming as the creature threatened to pull his face off. Another tentacle began to coil around the bucket, tugging it below the waves, filling the bucket and making it heavier.

There was a huge frothing of water as Dum Dum's mysterious moving island rose from the sea, its vast bulk some twenty yards away and closing, yet more tentacles thrashing wildly. One gigantic eye was looking straight at them. The boat was sinking and those who weren't bailing with anything they could lay their hands on were fighting with much the same to fend off the creature's grasping black reach. Even the little old lady, not much bigger than her bright yellow life-jacket, was armed with a knitting needle which she jabbed with pinpoint precision at the creature's flailing limbs.

The battle was short, and if a single eye could have an expression then the Kraken's would have been one of surprise followed by sudden and extreme pain. Clearly it hadn't expected such a ferocious defence and its hasty withdrawal wasn't quite quick enough to stop it leaving several tentacles behind. The one attached to Smiler's bucket was about three feet long and still writhing, apparently unaware that it had been left to fend for it self. Chaos was standing in the middle of the deck, black blood dripping from an axe that he clenched in both hands.

But there was no time for reflection. The boat was still sinking and Mr White, now grey enough in the face to warrant a name change, seemed to have completely lost the plot.

"All is lost! Abandon all hope! The Kraken rises!"

The boat pitched again, riding a wave that resulted in a nasty scraping noise from the rocks below. Anyone who could lay their hands on a bucket was bailing fast, but already the deck was ankle deep. Out to sea a dark shape beneath the water was moving parallel to the boat and gathering speed, its wash forcing the boat further onto the rocks. The Kraken turned and repeated the manoeuvre and there was a sickening crunch from the hull. The rest of the life-jackets were hastily handed out.

"It's trying to sink us!" panicked Mr White. "We must lose some weight!"

Suddenly he launched himself at the bikes lined up on the deck and began to loosen the straps on Numb Tongue's Harley. Before he could undo the first strap he found himself dangling above the ground, Numb Tongue's hand clasped firmly around his throat.

"But we're sinking!" choked Mr White. "We must lose weight!"

Numb Tongue shook his head. There were many things that could be thrown overboard to lose weight, up to and including Mr White, before Numb Tongue's Harley was going to get wet.

"But we're sinking!" Mr White repeated, struggling for air. "We must!"

The Kraken made another pass, a vast cloud beneath the surface, trailing blood as dark as ink from numerous puncture wounds. If anything, the little old lady in a bright yellow life-jacket had done almost as much damage as Chaos wielding an axe. Having patted her hair back into place, she was currently rummaging in her gigantic handbag, itself a weapon, from which she produced....

"Fucking hell! She's got a hand grenade!"

"I've told you before, Ron White," the old lady puffed up to her full five foot nothing. "Forty years you've been sneaking up and down this coast, wetting your pants every time there's so much as a wave! What that thing needs is a good bloody seeing to!"

"But they're protected," Mr White croaked, his feet still dangling above the deck.

"So I'm told," retorted the old lady. "But who's protecting us? Would one of you lads be kind enough to give this a good lob?" She offered the grenade to the nearest club members.

Meanwhile, with many of the club still furiously bailing, Dum Dum was attempting to squeeze himself into a life-jacket that had no hope of ever fitting, and offering to throw himself over the side.

"He's right," said Dum Dum. "We need to lose weight. I'm not a very good swimmer, but I weigh a lot."

"Well if he's going then I'm going!" Vincent said bravely, despite the fact that they'd probably lose more weight by throwing the old lady overboard.

The Kraken made another run and there was another sickening crunch from beneath the boat, everyone shouting at once, the old lady still waving a live grenade around, bloody water being desperately bailed over the side. And just as quickly there was quiet. Mad John was standing on the seat of his bike, though surfing it may have been a better description as the ferry pitched and rolled.

"Gentlemen," he said softly. It wasn't exactly Robert Shaw, but it did the trick, the world hushing itself. "And lady," he added, with a nod towards the grenade wielding granny. "If I might have your attention for a moment then no one need get wet...or blown up." He smiled at the old lady, who grinned back sheepishly, grenade in one hand, handbag in the other.

"My good friend Chaos," Mad John continued, "has some considerable sailing experience and has, I believe, encountered such creatures before. He is, as you can see, very much alive. I'm sure that if we all follow his instructions and remain calm, then we will all remain very much alive, too."

Mad John nodded to Chaos, deferring to his greater knowledge. Having served under the command of none other than Edward Teach, and sailed the oceans since back when it was thought you'd eventually fall off the edge of the world, Chaos knew a thing or two about what lurked in the deepest, darkest depths.

"Mr White," he began. "Numb Tongue, put Mr White down. Mr White, I need you to sail directly out to sea...."

"But...but...but..." stuttered Mr White, like an outboard motor with the throttle stuck open.

"Yes, Mr White? Is there a problem?"

"You want me to sail out there?" said Mr White, a man not too long away from a massive heart attack.

The Kraken was building up speed for another run.

"Yes, Mr White. Quickly as you can please."

"Are you completely mad? The Kraken will tear us to pieces!"

"Trust me, Mr White...."

"Well I won't do it! It's madness! I'd rather drown!"

"Numb Tongue," said Chaos. "Please explain to Mr White."

"Okay! Okay!" croaked Mr White, his feet once again dangling above the deck, his face now favouring purple.

With a terrified Mr White at the helm, the ferry turned and began to head out to sea. Again a wash crashed against the boat, forcing it against the jagged cliff-face, but thankfully the change in direction saved them from the worst of it. Nevertheless the ferry had sprung another leak. Blood, vomit, and water sloshed ankle deep on the deck.

Scarecrow was sent to the pointy end along with the fight crew, all of them armed to the teeth with knives, hatchets, and razors. The rest of the club and the other passengers were armed with buckets, though Chaos had briefly considered putting the old lady up with the fight crew.

"Right," said Chaos. "Keys, keys, I need everyone's bike keys, quick as possible. Vincent, gimme a hand getting all the bikes started. We need to make as much noise as possible!"

They dashed around the deck gathering keys and starting bikes. Unfortunately Vincent grabbed Dum Dum's keys first and nearly broke his ankle trying to get his Harley started.

"Jap bikes first!" yelled Chaos. "They'll start quicker!"

He glanced out to sea, the little ferry crashing through the waves to face the Kraken, a salty spray drenching them all. The Kraken lurked beneath the surface, the seas stained black by its inky blood.

"Fucker's going under!" growled Chaos, a couple of centuries of pirating pulsing through his veins. "Fight crew! Spread out! It's going to come at us from below!"

The ferry plunged on, drawn further and further into deep, dark waters that were still lapping over the sides and now leaking in through the hull. Grim faces eyed the surface. Mr White's jaw was clenched so tight that he snapped his pipe. In a wide arc around the rocks and cliff-face, he piloted the stricken vessel towards their destination. A slow tension crept over them, just the breaking of waves and the thunder of motorcycles engines.

"We need to be louder," said Chaos. "Much louder! Mrs um...."

"Doris, dear," said the old lady.

"What I need you to do, Doris, is to hold the throttles open on these two bikes like this. Yes, that's right," he yelled above the sudden booming of Doris almost blowing both bikes up at the same time. "Just ease off a little so they don't go bang. We need to sound as big as possible to scare it away. And if I could borrow that grenade..."

No more than twenty minutes passed before the Kraken returned, a long dark cloud in their wake, gaining fast on the crippled ferry.

"I don't want to worry you," shouted Joker. "But I don't think it's very scared."

"More noise! We must have more noise!"

More hands were taken away from defence and from bailing duties and more of the bikes were revved and thrashed, but the cloud beneath the surface kept on coming. A first tentative tentacle reached out and received a quick jab from Scarecrow's fast blade for its troubles, the Kraken's black blood staining his hand.

"Are you sure this is going to work?" hollered Smiler. "I really could do with today not getting any worse!"

"Ah, about that," said Chaos. But there was no time to explain as another tentacle lashed across the bow, catching Zig Zag square in the chest and almost knocking him overboard.

"STATIONS!" roared Chaos, doing his best to turn a knackered old ferry into a seafaring battleship. It lacked the cannons he was used to under Teach's command, but they'd been mostly for show anyway, the man's reputation usually doing most of his fighting for him. But it was under Teach that Chaos had first encountered a Kraken and, with motorcycles substituting for cannons, he hoped to employ the same tactics that Teach had used in his attempt to beat it back in 1717.

Unfortunately they didn't seem to be working. Another exploratory tentacle got within inches of Andy One-Leg's one leg before he spotted it and gave it a wallop with a claw hammer, sending it slithering back over the side. The ferry pitched in the waves, the sea beginning to froth about it, great bubbles rushing to the surface.

"STAND READY!"

The attack was sudden and violent, the boat shaking so much that a couple of the bikes tipped over, Joker's bike leaking fuel onto the deck and trapping Smiler, whose day really wasn't improving at all. Vicious black tentacles slapped and flapped against every surface, grabbing and pulling at anyone and everything, each sucker a maze of nasty little teeth.

"WE NEED MORE NOISE!"

The club screamed and hollered and fought for all they were worth, beating back the attack, but they were keeping the beast at bay and not much more. Even Doris managed quite a war-cry, a throttle in each hand and Dum Dum's Harley spitting flames from the exhaust as she revved. But whatever Chaos was planning he was running out of time. Mr White's ferry was sinking.

CHAPTER THIRTY

Tyre tracks. That meant there was a road out of here, though there was no sign of any vehicles. The General had searched the building from top to bottom and found no signs of life, but many signs of death. It had seemed a tad suspicious that the bad guys just happened to have a secret hideaway out here in the middle of nowhere, and The General's suspicions were confirmed when he found the previous occupants nailed to the kitchen table. He stood and looked at the bodies, a middle aged couple, both long dead, both with translucent green skin and pointy ears. Whatever the hell they were they definitely weren't human. And they were definitely dead.

The General's Luger lay on the table beside them, unused even to put the couple out of their misery. In the kitchen a tap was running into an overflowing sink, clearly the cause of the hastily improvised water torture that The General had suffered in the cellar, and the cause of his involuntary twitch as he turned off the faucet with bloodied hands. He found no food and no clothing, aside from the remains of his own clothes which had been burned in an open fireplace. He managed to salvage his shit stained underpants, but even after they had been washed they were still far from Sunday best and had some unfortunately placed holes.

The General had no idea how long he had been bound to the chair when the bird had come - two days, three days, a week? Drifting out of consciousness, but never finding true relief due to the constant plop, plop, plopping, he'd heard a tap, tap, tapping and a scrape, scrape, scraping at the heavy wooden door.

He raised his head.

Plop. Plop. Thunk. Plop.

"Aaark!"

The tapping continued, accompanied by a flapping of wings, and then a metallic clink as a key hit the stone floor on the other side of the door.

"Aaark!" The bird tried again, clearly attempting to get the key into the lock.

Through blurred and teary eyes The General watched in fascination. Eventually there was a click and the door inched open as the bird pushed from the other side. It hopped into the room, a big black crow, looking, it had to be said, utterly exhausted and not at all happy.

"Aaark!"

The crow's black beady eyes looked up at The General.

"Aaark! Aaarkarant! Akkerrant!"

The General tried to focus, fear and fatigue and pain clouding his mind.

Plop. Plop. Thunk. Plop.

He had long passed the point where he had any idea what was real and what was still perhaps the unfortunate result of doing a couple of tabs of Stone's acid. He'd seen dogs turn into people, he'd seen angry and wounded wargs, and he'd seen under Zig Zag's crash helmet. A talking bird was positively normal.

"Akkerrant!"

The crow cocked its head to one side in a small jerky movement, apparently waiting for a response.

"Akkerrant!"

It couldn't have said that. And yet...

"Aberrant?" The General managed a whisper. "Help. Help me. Please."

"Aaark! Akkerrant!"

The big bird lolloped over to The General's chair and appeared to examine the business card at his feet. It was now soaked in The General's piss due to him being unable to hold it in any longer. Some of the letters on the card had become blurred. Rest In P e e.

"Aaark!" said the bird, and began pecking at the ropes that bound The General to the chair.

The bird was gone now, but The General had been left in no doubt that it had been trying to communicate with him. It had even managed a little Morse code, tapping with its beak the letters F E R O, though The General had no idea what it meant until he found a map alongside the gun and the corpses in the kitchen. His face twitched as he studied the map. Many of the place names seemed familiar and yet there were none that he could ever claim having been to. Where the fuck was London? Wales even? It would also have helped if there was a little red arrow with 'you are here' written on it. Thanks to the crow's Morse code, however, there was one name on the map that stood out from the rest. Fero City.

The General scoured the map for further clues. Mordor sounded familiar, although he couldn't remember why, but it appeared to be a county rather than a town or city. And much of the map was just empty space. Mountains, deserts, forests. In tiny, tiny letters The General spotted The Circle Of Seven, the map showing it as a single road leading to a roundabout with eight exits, all of which ended abruptly giving the look of a badly drawn flower. Fero City looked to be some distance away, but since there was no scale on the map it was impossible to tell. The General's face twitched again, but there was no more fear, no more pain. The General was still alive and he intended to stay that way. He checked again that the Luger was loaded.

Around the back of what turned out to be a modest cottage he found a small wooden shed containing, among other things, a bicycle. A ladies' bicycle, with a basket on the front. It was pink and had bells on it. The General stuffed the map into the basket along with a small length of rope and a hand scythe, and wheeled the bike outside. It jingled quite happily as if pleased to be out of that stuffy shed and going for a nice long ride in the countryside. The General took a hammer to the jingly bits, which did rather seem to dampen the bike's enthusiasm, but now it squeaked instead, a grating 'scree, scree, reeeek', on every other turn of the pedals.

Scree, scree, reeeek. Scree, scree, reeeek.

And so it was that The General set out into the big unknown on a pink bicycle, with a Luger tucked into his shit stained underpants and an involuntary twitch on his face, his upper lip pulsing while his left eyebrow quivered.

Scree, scree, reeeek, twitch.

It was unfortunate that he had forgotten about having I LOVE COCK written on his face, especially as his pulsing upper lip caused the word COCK to appear as it was throbbing.

Scree, scree, reeeek, twitch.

The nearest proper road was three miles away.

CHAPTER THIRTY-ONE

It was growing dark when White's Ferry finally sailed towards its destination, a cliff-top lighthouse blinking to lead the way to the harbour, where a small crowd had gathered to await their arrival. There were worried faces in the crowd. White's Ferry was never more than an hour or so late even in bad weather and was always back by sundown. No boats ventured out after dark and this was as close as they'd get to a search party until daybreak.

The crowd were somewhat surprised, then, when Mr White and his trusty ferry puttered into the small harbour blasting punk rock from a speaker that was lashed to its bow, and roaring with the thunder of motorcycle engines. Splattered and stained black with the Kraken's blood, and still trailing severed tentacles, White's Ferry now looked like something Dennis Hopper might have felt compelled to blow up in Waterworld. The image was no less strengthened by the sight of Aberrant MC on the deck, outlaw bikers and pirates alike. A few of them happened to be both. One of them even had a wooden leg!

"I think we might be close enough now to turn some of that off, if that's all right, Skipper," Mr White yelled at Chaos above the aural sodomizing of Extreme Noise Terror and a dozen bikes.

"Aye, aye, Captain," said Chaos, causing Mr White to turn crimson with pride.

In truth it was Chaos who had captained the stricken vessel, Chaos who had got them all through it in one piece. He'd even managed to patch the holes in the hull by dragging tarpaulin under the boat and then pulling it tight, a trick he claimed to have taught to "that idiot Cook on his way to Australia". Having spent much of his life creeping up and down the coastline, Mr White had what could be called modest seafaring ambitions, but that didn't stop him from being utterly in awe. Chaos had saved them all, and what was more, White's Ferry would no longer have to creep up and down clinging to the coastline. From now on it was plain sailing for Mr White. Captain White.

"The trick," revealed Chaos, "is to make yourself as big and loud and scary as possible. It's territorial, I think, like how crocodiles think an outboard motor is another crocodile. That's the theory anyway. No one's ever really done any proper studies what with no one believing in them."

"You mean I've got to listen to that bloody, er, music every time I go out?" said Mr White, quickly substituting 'racket' as it was Dum Dum's I-Pod so presumably he liked said racket. The speaker had been a stroke of luck since the fisherman looking fella's son just happened to have a guitar amp and speaker as part of his luggage. It hadn't taken long to hook it up to the I-Pod, Dum Dum's collection of uneasy listening nearly rivalling the noise of the bikes. He came up short on Ride Of The Valkyries, but five blokes from Norwich shouting a lot seemed to work just as well.

Chaos laughed. "No, don't worry about that. We had to make so much noise because it was all above water, that's why they don't go for the big engined ships. All you need is a bigger engine or..."

"Hang on," interrupted Joker. "I thought crocodiles attacked boats with outboard motors *because* they thought they were other crocodiles?"

"Well, like I said, it's a theory," grinned Chaos.

"But you said you'd done this before!"

"Well, yes," shrugged Chaos. "Once. And we had cannons and a lot more people then. And it didn't actually work. But either way I doubt it'll be bothering Mr White again."

This was probably true. Kraken's were known, by those who knew anything about them at all, to be highly intelligent creatures, and, if this one had any sense, it would be in no hurry to tackle something again, that had caused it so much damage the first time. Its tentacles would grow back after time, but it would still bear some heavy scars, and it would be a long time before it came near Mr White's ferry or Eyeball Bay again. Plankton didn't try to dismember you. Thus, when Mr White drew his ferry alongside the jetty it was to something of a hero's welcome, the Kraken having been defeated if not killed. Few had ever come back from such an attack and none could claim to have won.

216

It might take a day or so to repair the boat, maybe even a week, but the town wouldn't run short of calamari for a while.

"The ferry's not going anywhere tonight so if you'd like to leave the bikes overnight and unload them in the morning, that's fine with me," said Mr White, with as much hope as generosity. It had been a terribly long day and his ferry was no longer in any danger of sinking. "There's a very fine inn," he added cheekily. "Very good pies."

"That's most kind of you," said Mad John, casting an eye over the harbour, "but I'd rather the bikes were on dry land tonight. I'm sure you understand."

"Oh there's nothing to worry about," insisted Mr White. "This harbour's quite safe. Even before today's battle the Kraken had never attacked here because the water's too shallow... But, yes, yes," he added, not forgetting that the last time he had argued Numb Tongue had casually strangled him. "I can see that you would feel more at ease..."

"Makes them harder to steal if they're on a boat," interrupted Loud-As, the club's last meal in Eyeball Bay seeming a long, long time ago, especially since it had been mostly liquid.

Mad John glanced at him and then back to the ferry. "Indeed. And what if someone wasn't interested in stealing the bikes but in stopping them? What easier way than sinking Mr White's ferry?"

"Ah yes, now..." Mr White shuffled uneasily, suddenly viewing the bikes as particularly hot potatoes. "I'm sure it wouldn't take long to get them all on dry land, work up an appetite and such."

"Fucking appetite? I'm fucking starvin'," moaned Loud-As.

"As, I'm sure, is everyone else," said Mad John. "Nevertheless."

There were no further arguments and, once the deck had been hosed down of goo and blood and tentacles, it took less than an hour to unload the bikes, all of the club pitching in much to the surprise of the three prospects. Some of the crowd started to drift away, satisfied that there was no more excitement to be had, but just as many remained to watch these strange and dangerous looking men unload their machines. The wife and mother of the father and son had been waiting at the harbour and now clung to them for dear life while their luggage was unloaded. They left as quickly as possible, the woman keen to distance them from a day that could have cost her her family.

"Well, I'd best be off, too," said Doris, who, apparently unruffled by the experience of being attacked by a gigantic sea monster, had been deep in a one-sided conversation with Numb Tongue's knees. There was something about Numb Tongue and old ladies. Maybe they just thought he was a good listener because he never spoke.

"Still, I shall feel a lot safer on the ferry now that thing's been taught a lesson," Doris continued. "Bloody thing's always been a nuisance. Did you see what it did to all those windows in Eyeball Bay? Bloody menace it was!"

"But it's never attacked the ferry before?" said Mad John, with a curious look.

"Well, you'd have to ask Captain Pugwash," Doris nodded towards Mr White, "but not that I can remember."

"I almost forgot," said Chaos, offering Doris back her grenade. "I'm afraid Kraken tend to throw these back with unerring accuracy, as we discovered with cannon balls, so I thought it best if I kept this safe for you. Although, if I'm not mistaken this is the US Mk.1 which means it might not be safe at all."

"What? You mean it might go off?"

"Well, yes, possibly," pondered Chaos, carelessly waving the rusty little hand bomb about. "It's a fragmentation grenade. Except they didn't fragment very well because of the cast iron body, you see here? From around 1917, I think."

"So it's worth something then?" Doris brightened, perhaps considering passing it on to her grandchildren as an heirloom or popping it down to the Antiques Roadshow and sticking it under an expert's nose. Everybody else was backing away slowly.

"Well, it would be I suppose, it if wasn't live," considered Chaos, apparently blissfully unaware of any danger to himself or anyone else around him. Admittedly given that he was over three hundred years old his cavalier attitude wasn't entirely unwarranted, but, still, he had a tendency to strut around like Bill Kilgore when surf was up, which made lesser mortals very nervous. He turned the grenade over in his hands, looking for markings, and rubbed quite vigorously with his sleeve on what might have been a serial number. "Yeah, I'm pretty sure this is the Mk.1. Nasty little thing it is."

That had pretty much cleared the harbour of bystanders.

While it was being decided how best to dispose of Doris's hand grenade, Vincent took a moment to absorb his surroundings now that they were back on dry land. The place reminded him of the Isle Of Wight, no more dangerous than tea and scones on a Wednesday afternoon, and yet here was a little old dear with a fucking hand grenade in her handbag! And, let's be fair, that wasn't even the weird part. Old ladies did things like that sometimes. You'd see them on the news having their entire street evacuated because of something that had sat on their mantelpiece for the past fifty years. The weird part was, well, *everything else!* And not the least of it was all these seemingly perfectly normal people treating this as if it were perfectly fucking normal.

"Scarecrow's talking to his saddlebags again," said Dum Dum casually. "You think he's got a spider in there?"

See, there you are, case in point, talking fucking spiders!

Vincent took a deep breath. It had just been a long day, that was all. Ever since he was a kid, that day when he'd snuck into Mad John's study and poked his nose where it didn't belong, he'd known there was something very unusual about Aberrant MC, and he had always wanted to know the truth. Now he was finding out, and, all at once, it was little short of mind-blowing, a complete headfuck if the truth be known. It was like growing up spending every Saturday dinnertime watching TV from behind the sofa only to find out that Dr Who was real and so were the fucking Daleks. Except that if Vincent's suspicions were correct then Mad John was about twice as old as Dr Who and a lot more well known than the bloody Daleks!

He'd never forgotten that day, creeping down the clubhouse stairs, knowing he was doing wrong, but unable to stop himself. And although he was never caught he had always wondered if somehow his trespassing in the study had been anything to do with why his mother had moved them far away to the countryside. Certainly she had looked nervous when he started asking questions. Even though he'd been young, he remembered something in her eyes, perhaps not fear, but an uneasiness that was impossible to hide. If Vincent was even remotely close to being right then...

"I say, Scarecrow's talking to 'is luggage again," repeated Dum Dum, breaking the spell. "I reckon he might have one of them talking spiders in there."

"What? Oh no, no," blurted Vincent hurriedly, realising that Scarecrow was actually checking on his new girlfriend who was still hidden in his saddlebags.

Vincent had no idea what the implications of the couple getting caught were, but they probably wouldn't be good. Numb Tongue had agreed not to tell anyone until after his fight, but still the news wouldn't be any better coming from anyone else.

"Just talking to himself," said Vincent, as casually as possible. "We all do, sometimes. It's been a long day."

"S'pose," shrugged Dum Dum. "But it looks like he's talking to his bags."

It was then that Vincent saw Smiler striding straight towards Scarecrow. Scarecrow had his back turned to them, still muttering into his luggage. There was no time to warn him. He jumped when Smiler tapped him on the shoulder.

"Jesus, you made me jump!" said Scarecrow.

"No, it's me," said Smiler, with a broad grin. His face and teeth, stained entirely black, gave the smile a distinctly unnerving quality, his mouth an ugly sinkhole with just one tooth remaining white. His day hadn't exactly gone to plan so far - blacker than a miner, his nostril hair down past his elbows, and one soggy, and rather stubborn, cigarette butt still glued to his eyebrow. But, still, they were all in one piece, a little bloodied, but definitely unbowed. Most of it was the Kraken's blood anyway, although a couple of the club -Smiler included- could probably have done with a stitch or two.

During the battle Smiler had taken the backlash of a large tentacle full in the face. It had knocked him to the ground and hadn't done his much-abused nose any favours at all. He'd been lucky that it was the back of the tentacle and not the front, all covered in barbed teeth and horrible sucky things, but it had packed a punch that rattled him long enough to get him into trouble. A second tentacle had become entangled in his hair, dragging him, again, towards the edge of the boat.

"I just wanted to say, er, thanks, man," said Smiler, somewhat tentatively. "That was some fight! I nearly got pulled overboard a couple of times. It got a bit..."

"Hairy?" Scarecrow couldn't help himself.

"Yeah, very funny," said Smiler. "Fucking stuff won't stop growing and Joker didn't bother asking for the antidote. I'm thinking about wearing a back-pack on the front just to keep it in! But I'm serious, I wanted to say thank you."

"No problem," shrugged Scarecrow. He had fought as hard as anyone else. Maybe Smiler was thanking everyone.

"No, I mean, I wanted to say thanks," Smiler persisted. He seemed to be trying to look over Scarecrow's shoulder...at his luggage. "Thanks to your, er...." He nodded conspiratorially at Scarecrow's saddlebags. "Look, I won't tell anyone she's here, but she saved my arse back there. I was getting dragged over the edge and she came flying out of there, quick as a flash and cut me loose. I just wanted to say thanks."

Scarecrow stood dumbfounded, a deer in headlights.

"You're welcome," said a little voice from somewhere in his luggage.

CHAPTER THIRTY-TWO

With the rest of the club firmly established in the local inn - drinks on the house while they related tales of the Kraken - Scarecrow made his excuses and headed for the bikes, which were lined up outside. He found Dum Dum on guard duty and feared that he'd be cornered for company, but Dum Dum was in a reflective mood. The big half-troll sat on his bike, looking out at the sea and taking in the starlit night. Something was on that mind of his, but he chose not to share.

Now Scarecrow and Rain were sitting on the other side of the harbour wall, on what, when the tide was out, could very modestly be described as a beach. They finally had some time alone and were discussing the events of this particularly eventful day.

It felt good to be near the coast again, the sea air reminding Scarecrow of home, but at the same time reminding him how far away from it he was. It had been a long time since he'd even considered calling the Isle Of Man home, but for a moment he craved its safety, and missed the sanctuary of his parents and the sister he should probably know better.

"Would you rather I had stayed hidden?" asked Rain, a glimmer of sadness in her eyes.

"Christ, *no!* Of course not," said Scarecrow quickly. "From what I heard, half the club would be at the bottom of the sea if it wasn't for you. Joker said to say thanks, and Stone, and Smiler, well, you were there when he came over. Numb Tongue and Vincent already knew about you, and Loud's been acting weird. Well, weirder than usual. I mean, it's hardly a secret anymore, is it? It wouldn't surprise me if all of them knew and they're just winding us up. I wouldn't put it past them."

"It might be better if they did know."

"Well, of course, they'll all find out sooner or later, but..."

"I mean sooner rather than later," said Rain. Her face carried an expression of concern. "There's something I need to tell you."

There was a roar from the inn, another cheer as yet another toast was followed by yet another shot of something foul from behind the bar. Jagermiester's retarded bastard cousin. This last particular toast had been to "toasting", so it was a fairly safe bet that the club were staying here for the night. Loud-As and Smiler had already taken their boots off, though it would have been hard, even for Joker, to think of anything else unpleasant to do to Smiler. The innkeeper had politely asked, even after he'd been hosed down on the dockside, if he would sit on newspaper so he didn't stain the furniture.

But, still, it was a good night, a time for well earned celebration. The fishing community, always fearful of attacks from the Kraken, would be a little more brave from now on, some of them were already inquiring about sound systems for their boats. Vincent chuckled to himself, imagining that in a year from now it would be like the Asian car scene, all sub woofers and tricked out fishing boats. Then he realised, with a start, why the thought had popped into his head. Over in the corner above the bar, there was a TV. The signal was bad and the picture flickered, but it was definitely showing the BBC news.

"That's the last one of those you'll see for a while, man, and good riddance," said Stone, passing Vincent a dangerous looking joint. "Yeah, go ahead," he added, nodding at the joint. "You're on watch after Dum Dum, but this'll help you think."

Vincent smiled a wry smile. "I'm not sure I need any help with that. It's answers I need."

"Merely a matter of asking the right questions," said Stone. "Ask the right question and you will find that you already know the answer."

"Yeah, that's the sort of thing Mad John's been saying since I was a kid," replied Vincent. "But then when you ask him a question he never gives you a straight answer, it's all riddles and parables."

Beneath his Afro, Stone's lips pursed in a way that suggested he might find this amusing. It also suggested that he might be very, very high, and unable to move his face. His eyes, hidden behind overhanging hair, were almost closed. This was slightly worrying to Vincent because Stone had a tolerance for drugs, any drugs from aspirin to ketamine, that would baffle scientists and terrify pharmacists. If whatever was in this joint had got him that fucked up then Vincent wasn't sure he should have any of it, raging paranoia not being conducive to guard duty in a strange and foreign land.

Except that it wasn't foreign. Not at all. Foreign he felt he could deal with. Foreign was the same as everywhere else, just with a funny accent, dodgy food, and petrol pumps that were overly complicated. Vincent had been to foreign. It was in France. And, to be fair, Wales. This place was about as foreign as a drunk in a kebab shop. Until you saw the most normal of things, a TV set, and then it suddenly sank in just how far this place was from what Vincent knew as normal.

"You know," said Stone, his eyes now completely closed.

Vincent waited for the rest of the sentence, but nothing was forthcoming. Stone just stood there, to all intents and purposes, asleep. Vincent waited some more, but there was only the rise and fall of his chest and a vague smile on his face to suggest that Stone was actually still alive. He appeared to have passed out standing in his boots. Joker was on the other side of the bar, but he could smell drunken unconsciousness like a shark smells blood, and he wasted no time with his victims.

"Stone," hissed Vincent. "Stone, man, you've nodded off with your boots on there."

Stone opened one eye, very wide. It looked this way and that, up and down, and then it closed again.

"They haven't caught me in thirty years," he grinned. "And the last one that tried it has a tendency to wet the bed and bark like a dog for no reason. Woof woof!" Stone grinned again. "But I shall remember your concern. It is noted."

Vincent hoped this was a good thing. From the stories he'd heard about Stone's drug terrorism it sounded as if barking like a dog for no reason would be lucky escape. The man had an aura of kindness about him, and with it a sense of enormous patience, but there was no getting away from the fact that getting on the wrong side of him would lead to extremely dire consequences. One of Vincent's favourite tales involved Stone dosing a corporate meeting with large amounts of Viagra because he'd seen it in one of his favourite movies, but that was just Stone having a bit of fun. He had also been known to reduce grown men to quivering jellies.

Then again, every time Vincent had been gifted pharmaceuticals by Stone he had had nothing but a good time, always dosed with just the right amount of whatever they were partying with, just the right buzz for the right place. The man was a drug wizard!

"That's it, hit it again," said Stone, his eyes still shut, as Vincent puffed on the joint. There was a vague but welcome aftertaste of coffee.

"Stone," said Vincent, cautiously. "Can I ask you a question?"

"Boy doesn't listen," Stone tutted. "I already told you, if you ask the right question then you'll know the right answer."

"All right then. Can I check to see if my answer is right?"

"That's better," Stone smiled, though his eyes remained closed.

Vincent thought for a moment about his next words, his answer. And what if he was wrong? He'd be a laughing stock, better off invisible to the world again, possibly stripped of his prospect patch. Certainly he would never live it down. But, then again, he'd had a long time to think about what he'd seen, and, added to what he now knew for sure, it did seem at least plausible.

"Mad John's really old isn't he?" he blurted. "I mean, *really* fucking old, way older than anyone else in the club, and I know Chaos is at least three hundred years old." It wasn't what he had meant to say, but it would do for now.

"Don't you know that it's rude to ask an immortal his age?"

"But I'm not asking him," said Vincent. "I'm checking with you to see if I'm right."

"Is that was you're doing?" Stone smirked. He opened his eyes as if to make sure, and then closed them again. "Then I suspect you know the answer."

And Mad John's not his real name, although it does possibly begin with a J. Without just coming out and saying it Vincent suspected he'd get the same run-around if he asked that, too. After all, Andy and Billy were the only two club members who actually used their real names, and, even then, Vincent was pretty sure their surnames weren't One-Leg and Toothless. Joker claimed that his real name was Joe King, but that was almost certainly a lie. Joker had also tried to persuade Vincent that Dum Dum's real name was Stanley Dupp because every time he went to court the judge would say, "Will the defendant please Stan Dupp." This was definitely a lie. But then, when you considered that Dum Dum's real name was in fact Dum Dum, and he was part bridge troll, then the truth was no less outlandish than anything Joker might make up for his own warped entertainment.

The truth about Mad John, Vincent suspected, was far more strange than Joker's fictions. It was nothing less than world changing. And it would certainly explain why Bertha had kept calling him "your 'ighness."

"A word to the wise," Stone opened his big brown, kindly eyes. Like most of the club Stone had been a surrogate father to Vincent when he was growing up and he knew he could trust him with his life. Obviously, up until very recently he'd thought that Stone, like the rest of the club, had just aged exceptionally well in the years that he'd been away from them, the decade between, say, thirty and forty, being a lot different to the decade between ten and twenty. But, while it was still difficult to pin an age on Stone, he seemed to sometimes exude the wisdom of a great many years. Vincent could only guess: A hundred years? Two hundred years? Five hundred years or more?

"You will understand more in time," Stone continued, "but you must understand now, that knowledge is power, and power, in the wrong hands, is a very dangerous thing. I take it you've spoken to John and Dennis about the ring you wear and you know that it marks you? But you are not the only marked man among us. In our own way we are all marked, all of us targets."

"You mean those fucking shapeshifter things that are following us?"

"Them?" Stone scoffed. "Oh don't worry about them. Complete amateurs. It's a miracle they even found us and I'm sure Bertha's sent them on some fantastic wild goose chase, if they even managed to track us that far."

"But they can change into dogs!"

"Yes," Stone conceded. "Very big dogs. But I guarantee if you threw a stick for one of them they'd chase it. Trust me, they're idiots. Nasty idiots, but idiots nonetheless. Three blokes who have mastered licking their own balls are nothing to worry about."

"But Mad John's worried about something, isn't he?"

"John has good reason to be more paranoid than most," allowed Stone, his eyelids gradually lowering as if he was considering another quick nap. "We're dealing with a few issues at the moment, but, believe me, entire armies have tried to take this club down and failed. I wasn't trying to scare you, though fear can be a good instinct. You just need to know and understand that, more so than any other, whatever you learn of this club must stay within the club. Like I said, you will understand more in time. And now, if you'll excuse me, I promised I'd visit Flashback. I believe you are on guard duty."

And with that Stone closed his eyes once again and they remained closed.

"Guard duty. Right," said Vincent, and headed outside.

Dum Dum was looming. He didn't actually have to do anything in order to loom, it was a natural gift and something he could do sitting down. Right now he was looming against a lamp post.

"All right, Turtle," he grinned at Vincent, the Turtle moniker doing its best to stick to Vincent whether he liked it or not. He tried to ignore it in the hope that it would go away.

"Yeah," he said. "I just smoked one of Stone's joints though, so I don't know how long "all right" will last. I left him in the bar "visiting Flashback"."

"But Flashback's in Pentonville nick."

"Yeah, I know," said Vincent. "It does tend to make me a bit nervous about what I've been smoking, but it all looks peaceful enough out here."

"Oh yeah. Bloke came by about an hour ago walking his dog, some little yappy thing, and that's been it apart from a few of the club popping out for a bit of air or whatever."

Dum Dum was rarely bored, but even he was starting to think that guard duty in a place like this might be a bit of a waste of time. He'd spent that past half an hour counting the spokes on the front wheel of Mad John's bike and had been contemplating starting on the back wheel when Vincent had shown up. Aside from Aberrant themselves, the most dangerous thing in town was probably Doris, and she'd gone home to bed hours ago. Dum Dum's generous spirit was about to offer to stay outside and keep Vincent company, when his more than generous stomach rumbled to remind him that it was running on empty and wasn't entirely happy about it. He made his excuses and headed in search of pies.

Vincent made himself comfortable on his bike seat. At least it was a warm night and the view was nice, the harbour twinkling on the other side of a broad promenade. Admittedly in better light he'd probably be able to see Mr White's ferry from here, all battered and liberally coated in Kraken's blood, but the gentle town was unworried and at peace. Well, at least as at peace as it's possible to be with a bunch of lunatics loudly drinking the inn dry. Even then, the place looked like it had been there for centuries, one of those solid stone buildings with walls about four feet thick, so only the occasional cheer escaped.

Stone's weed was starting to kick in hard, but, true to form, it was a contemplative high, nothing too vicious, more like it was allowing his mind to tidy up a bit. The last few days had flown at such a furious pace that Vincent felt like it had all just been jammed into his head, all wargs and bridge trolls and magic rings, always moving, always charging. It was actually quite nice to be out here alone for a while with some peace and quiet to reflect upon everything they'd been through, and what might still come.

It was a given that wherever the club were headed was dangerous and Vincent also understood that in some way the three remaining prospects were passing, not only an initiation into the club, but a point of no return. If, indeed, they hadn't passed that already. There was no going back to everyday life with what they had learned here. And who the fuck would believe them anyway? Apparently that method hadn't gone too well for Dum Dum's mum, in and out of nut houses until they finally convinced her that she really was crazy.

Vincent was fairly sure he wasn't crazy, at least no more crazy than anybody else. The only logical conclusion, then, was that this was all really happening. They'd fought a bridge troll, and a Kraken sea beastie thing, in one day, and all in some weird and secret country that completely failed to show up on Google maps. Vincent's internal cogs began to click further into place. The joint was helping.

So.... If all this is real.

Vincent's wargskin jacket was making him sweat, but he still hadn't taken it off since he'd got it. He patted its thick leather, unlike any jacket he'd ever owned. He was definitely wearing it. He chuckled to himself about the thought of him sitting there patting his clothes to see if they were real or not. Of course your clothes are real numbnuts, or you'd be sitting out here with numbnuts. So, how about we practice this whole turning invisible thing? Wait a minute, you just said "we". You're not turning into Smeagol, are you? Vincent giggled to himself, trying to make himself disappear with no idea whether it was working or not. Stone's weed was really strong.

Down at the harbour the tide was coming in, water as dark as night creeping ever nearer to Scarecrow and Rain's feet, on what little remained of their beach. They held each other tight and gazed out to sea, to the sky, to the stars, their hands clasped.

Scarecrow's face announced that he'd made a decision before he did, a hint of surprise suggesting that it wasn't entirely the decision he'd been expecting. "I've got to tell them," he said. "I've got to tell someone." He didn't look at all happy about it.

"I love you," said Rain.

"I love you, too."

CHAPTER THIRTY-THREE

Vincent took some amusement from the fact that Zig Zag couldn't see him. The fierce looking little man... orc had been standing outside the inn for five minutes, poking around in his saddlebags and muttering to himself, completely unaware that Vincent was there. Not that Vincent had meant to hide. He just hadn't known how to approach the little fella without startling him and possibly getting half his face bitten off. And then, Stone's weed being what it was, Vincent had got a little confused about how long Zig Zag had been there and he felt like too much time might have passed for him to comfortably announce his presence without looking like he was spying. Which he was really, kind of, sort of.

Vincent hadn't meant to do that either, it was just that Zig Zag was so fascinating. With Dum Dum, now that he knew about him being related to a bridge troll, you could kind of see it if you looked at him right; the lumbering gait, the knuckles that nearly touched the ground when he was standing up straight, the slightly furry ears, his overall hugeness. And yeah, okay, Scarecrow's an elf. That would explain the good looks and lightning reflexes, though his ears were disappointingly normal looking. But Zig Zag was a totally different proposition. Dum Dum and Scarecrow looked human, so you wouldn't know unless you knew, but there was no fucking way Zig Zag was human! Two arms, two legs, and a head, that was pretty much where the similarities ended. There were a lot of teeth.

As Vincent watched, hoping now that no one else came out and saw him, a big black crow came flapping down and landed near Zig Zag. The poor thing looked exhausted, its feathers all askew, its spindly legs barely able to stand. It was the same crow that belonged to the wizard, Dennis.

"Aaaarrk!" said the crow.

Zig Zag made a horrible growling noise. He was talking to the bird.

Vincent listened carefully and at first he could make out nothing but squawking and growling, the bird and the orc deep in discussion. But then at last, very slowly, Vincent began to pick out a word here and there. They were speaking what, for want of a better word, had to be called English. It wasn't exactly what you'd call a pleasant noise, the bird like Janet Street Porter reading the works of Garry Bushell, while the orc sounded like more like Lemmy gargling concrete and wasps, but still, if you listened really hard...

"Gargle, gargle, growl, prosspectsss...."

"Squawk, croak, screech, aaarrrk, torture..."

Vincent was pretty sure there were birds who could speak better English than this scabby looking thing "aaarrrking" and flapping about all over the place. Thinking about it, there had been one at the clubhouse when Vincent was a kid, a foul tempered old parrot with a vocabulary that would make a whore blush. Vincent had learned most of his favourite swear words from it, including a word ending in unt and rhyming with punt. His mum had gone stamping up to the clubhouse and given Joker, the first club member she ran into, a considerable piece of her mind about that. And Joker had just stood there with his mouth opening and shutting, trying to get a word in edgeways. Unable to stop himself, Vincent let out a snigger at the memory. Both the bird and the orc stopped talking, suddenly alert. With the right ear you might have heard the orc say, "What was that?"

Vincent froze. Could the bird see him? It was looking straight at him!

"Aaarrk!"

The crow turned its head to one side. It appeared to see nothing.

And with that the bird and the orc went inside the inn, the bird hopping wearily and leaving a couple of feathers in its wake. Vincent walked over and picked up a feather, so black that it shone silver, and he was examining it when Scarecrow arrived.

"All right, Turtle," he said, but there was no humour in it, more habit. Scarecrow looked worried.

"What's the matter, mate? You don't look so good."

"It's Rain."

"Nah, not tonight," said Vincent, glancing up at the sky. "Oh, you mean, her, your missus, Rain."

Scarecrow nodded.

"She's not up the duff is she?"

Scarecrow looked at Vincent, confused for a moment.

"What? Oh no, nothing like that. You think I'd look like this if she was pregnant, you muppet?"

"I dunno," shrugged Vincent. "You've only known her five minutes."

"Yes, and we're getting married as soon as possible. Don't start."

Vincent shrugged again. He wasn't entirely sure this whole wedding thing was a good idea in the first place and he certainly wasn't going to point out that, since they seemed to be in a completely different country, with its own rules, the couple could probably get married now.

"So what is it then?"

Scarecrow shook his head lightly. "Rain thinks she heard...."

"I know what I bloody heard!" said a tiny voice from somewhere about Scarecrow's person.

"Rain heard..." Scarecrow corrected himself, "...Loud-As talking on his mobile."

"So?" said Vincent. "Zig Zag was out here talking to a big fucking crow a minute ago. Loud-As said it was okay to bring mobiles, remember? Be lucky to get a signal out here anyway."

"He was telling someone where we are," said Scarecrow urgently. "Rain heard him because he didn't know she was in my bags, but she's heard him a few times now. He's letting someone know where we are."

"So? Maybe he wants someone to know where we are. I wouldn't actually mind knowing myself."

Suddenly there was a flash of colour before Vincent's eyes as something exploded from Scarecrow's inside jacket pocket. It was about three inches high and moved like a hummingbird on speed, so fast that all you really saw was the colour, which was mostly pink.

"You don't understand," said Rain's tiny voice, the blur of her wings actually causing a breeze on Vincent's face. "He was sneaking off to call someone. He's been doing it every day when he thinks no one's watching. I followed him when we were in Eyeball Bay..."

"You followed him?" exclaimed Vincent.

"Shh... keep it down," hissed Scarecrow. "Yes, she followed him. But only because he was acting suspicious. And then, today, she heard him down by the harbour, like, going, "Yes, the Kraken slowed them down, we'll be here overnight," and stuff. He was giving our position away."

"That does sound a bit dodgy," Vincent conceded. "Why would he say slowed "them" down? You're sure it was Loud-As?"

"He's the grumpy one with the funny ear," said the blur of colour that was Rain. "Always poking at his back."

"Yeah, that's definitely Loud-As. And you're sure that's what he said?"

"I know what I heard," said Rain.

"But if you tell John or anyone, then they'll want to know how you know, which means telling them about Rain."

"Exactly," Scarecrow nodded grimly. "They're gonna think she was spying, which she wasn't, and..."

"You have to tell Mad John," Vincent interrupted. "If the club's at war and he's telling people where we are..." Vincent left the sentence unfinished, the implications being obvious.

"And what if we're wrong?" said Scarecrow.

Just then, the door of the inn opened and there was a flash of nothingness where Rain had been hovering. In an instant she had vanished back into Scarecrow's jacket or his luggage, it was impossible to know as it happened so fast. Clearly anyone's chances of seeing a faerie unless they wanted to be seen were very remote indeed.

Loud-As nodded to Scarecrow.

"Give us a fag."

Scarecrow rummaged in his jacket and handed Loud-As a cigarette.

"Light me," said Loud-As. Clearly he was in one of his huffy moods again.

Scarecrow lit the cigarette, all the time glancing at where Vincent had been standing.

"So, what's going on out here?" Loud-As exhaled smoke.

"Er, nothing," said Scarecrow cautiously, "Just doing guard duty. It's all quiet."

Loud-As shrugged and looked up and down the street as if confirming for himself that all was indeed quiet. He nodded to himself, perhaps unaware that he had done so.

"Well, I'll take guard for a few if you want to go and grab a bite to eat or something."

"Really?" said Scarecrow, surprised, Loud-As being the kind of person who saw kindness as weakness. He was not known for making charitable donations.

"Yeah, I could do with some peace and quiet for a bit, a bit of fresh air."

Scarecrow glanced again at where Vincent had been standing, guessing that Vincent had vanished. "Well, if you're sure," he told Loud-As. "I mean, I've only just started guard duty..."

"Go away," said Loud-As. He was not joking.

"Oh," said Scarecrow, a little taken aback. "Oh, okay. When do you want me to come back?"

"Just fuck off for five minutes," Loud-As grunted. "And get me a pack of cigarettes."

Loud-As waited a few moments after Scarecrow had left, and, sure enough, as Vincent watched unseen, he got his mobile out and started dialling, all the time with one eye on the door in case anyone came out.

"'Ello? Yeah, it's me, I haven't got long. The General's been found and..."

Clearly words were spoken on the other end of the phone.

"What? How the fuck should I know?" hissed Loud-As. "It was a big fucking bird. Why didn't you just kill him?"

More words on the other end.

"Well, that's just sick! You didn't need to torture him! That wasn't part of the deal."

Trying to catch what was being said by the other party, Vincent edged a little closer to Loud-As. He was close enough now that if Loud-As moved suddenly the two would bump into each other.

"...wanted to experiment with the pineal gland," said a man's voice on the other end of the phone.

"Couldn't you have just cut his head off?"

"And we still may" said the voice. "Though, given his chances of survival, we may have to do it posthumously. What's done is done. He won't get far."

"Yeah, well I don't like loose ends."

"Your likes and dislikes are none of my concern," said the man, impatience flickering in his voice. "And your only concern should be fulfilling your part of the deal...."

Loud-As began pacing back and forth, almost knocking into Vincent and making it impossible for him to hear the rest of what the man was saying.

"Yes, yes, I understand that," Loud-As retorted angrily. "But you'd be wise not to underestimate them. It's taken you this long to get anywhere near them and that's only because of me."

"...."

"Yeah, of course they're all still here," replied Loud-As. He stopped pacing and started poking at his back again, allowing Vincent to move closer. "Half of them are too pissed to stand up. We probably won't be leaving 'til about midday, but I don't see how you're gonna catch..."

"...."

Vincent still couldn't hear what was being said on the other end of the phone. He edged nearer, so close now that he could feel Loud's body heat, the stale smell of sweat and cigarettes, and beneath it something foul, rotten, like decaying meat.

"I can only slow them down so much without drawing attention," Loud-As continued, his fingers now scratching at his back from a new angle and still not seeming to hit the right spot. "I've already given you a whole night with the breakdown and if you hadn't been fucking about torturing people then you might have caught up."

"How we conduct business is also none of your concern." Vincent could hear the man again. There was irritation and condescension in his voice. Loud-As was his bitch. "The boy," he continued dismissively, "the one who wears the ring. He's still with you?"

"Well, of course he is," said Loud-As, pulling a 'duh' face at the phone. "He ain't fucking going anywhere is he? John's little golden boy, sun shines out his arse. He's probably in the bar with his nose up John's arse..."

"What do you mean probably?"

"What?"

"You said probably, he's *probably* in the bar."

"Yeah," said Loud-As, pulling another 'duh' face at the phone. "So?"

"He has an invisibility ring and you don't know where he is," said the man on the phone, his voice as cold as winter.

"Fuck."

Loud-As stopped scratching at his back. He froze and then, fast as lightning, spun on his heels to face Vincent. Vincent let out a gasp.

CHAPTER THIRTY-FOUR

"I think it might be a good idea if you went and got some clothes, Dum Dum."

Dum Dum stood transfixed, his jaw to the floor, an astonished look on his face, eyes unblinking.

"Dum Dum."

"Huh?"

"I said, I think it might be a good idea if you went and got some clothes.... for the ladies."

"Oh right, yeah, sorry," flustered Dum Dum, still struggling to tear his eyes away from the scene in front on him.

It was a rare day that Mad John ever had to repeat himself, but even he would concede that today was turning out to be a very rare day indeed. Alerted, like the rest of the club, to the sound of screaming from outside the inn, they had gone outside to find Loud-As being physically restrained by Vincent and two full sized, and exceptionally naked, faeries. Scarecrow, meanwhile, was lying in a large and rapidly growing pool of blood, with another equally naked faerie screaming for help whilst trying to stem the bleeding from a stab wound in his stomach. That particular faerie had calmed down a bit now that she had been assured that Scarecrow would be perfectly okay, but there was still no escaping the fact that she was completely naked, her allure being somewhat diminished by the fact that she resembled a scene from Carrie. Against such odds it had been understandably difficult to get everyone's undivided attention.

"Clothes," repeated Mad John, and Dum Dum lumbered off. "Right, would somebody mind telling me what's going on? One at a time, if you would," he added, as they all started talking at once. "Vincent?"

"I think he's broken my fucking jaw," said Vincent.

"Yes, I can see that," said Mad John. "I was rather hoping we could establish why."

"He was fucking spying," Loud-As snarled, having been disarmed and allowed to his feet. "Sneaking around with that fucking ring, spying on me, he was."

"No I bloody wasn't!'" protested Vincent.

"Fucking was!" spat Loud-As. "He was out here fucking sneaking about and he startled me so I took a swing at him."

"And then you stabbed Scarecrow because?"

It had taken some time to get the full picture and, even then, only after Loud-As had been tied to a lamp post and gagged to shut him up. He cursed and swore and spat behind the gag, but it at least quietened him enough for Vincent to tell his part. He told them about Scarecrow and Rain, how they told him they'd heard Loud-As on the phone. And then, when Loud-As came outside and couldn't see him, he'd stayed to find out the truth, which was that it was all true.

In the instant that Loud-As had turned, he swung his fist, the phone still in his hand, and connected with Vincent's jaw with a punch that was like being hit in the face with a tree trunk. The phone had shattered in Loud's hand and Vincent sprawled backwards into Zig Zag's bike, toppling it sideways as he fell. Loud-As pounced immediately, thrashing wildly at empty space before finding Vincent's thigh with another heavy punch, making Vincent yell out in pain.

Loud-As was upon him with incredible strength, knife in one hand while he grasped for Vincent's throat. Vincent managed to land some punches of his own, but they were futile blows, like punching an oak table, and his hands were bleeding before Loud-As even seemed to notice. The blade drew nearer, serrated and dirty, blunted but sharp enough. It was a hair's breadth from his throat...

And then suddenly there was a flash of pink and Loud-As screamed.

"My ear! My ear! Aaagh! Fucking get it off me!"

Loud-As dropped the knife and swiped at the faerie that was biting his ear, but in that moment Rain transformed to full size and head-butted him square in the face. It would have been a brilliant move if Loud-As had then done what most would do in the circumstances and fallen backwards clutching a broken nose. Loud-As had blinked. His eyes had narrowed. And then he kicked Rain as hard as he could in the knee. She folded like a pack of cards.

From then on it was complete mayhem. As Loud-As dived at Rain, Vincent remembered kicking him in the face a couple of times to little effect. And then, out of nowhere, there were two more naked faeries piling in, all four of them basically trying to stop Loud-As beating the others up. He was just so unfeasibly strong, like putting Brock Lesnar up against a bunch of school kids, and he'd been winning the fight until that little pink hummingbird appeared again, Rain transforming once more and attacking like an angry hornet.

Somewhere in the middle of all this, Scarecrow had emerged from the inn and dived in to lend a hand in restraining Loud-As. Unfortunately he dived in just when Loud's hand found the knife again and he'd taken a blade that was intended for Vincent.

"Well, that's fortunate at least," said Mad John calmly.

"Fortunate?" screamed Rain. "He got stabbed!"

"Yes, young lady," said Mad John. "And as you well know, he is an immortal so he'll be absolutely fine. Enough of the hysterics if you would, it really doesn't help. As you know, elves can only die in battle or," he added pointedly, "from a broken heart. Scarecrow just saved Vincent's life."

"But," protested Rain, somewhat more meekly, "that was a battle. He could have died."

"That?" snorted Mad John. "That doesn't sound like much of a battle to me. More of a squabble."

"Yeah, sounds like a bit of a barney," Apples chipped in.

"Five on to one and three of 'em's naked," added Joker. "That sounds more like an orgy than a battle."

The laughter broke the tension, turned it down a notch so the air wasn't static, and Dum Dum reappeared with a selection of moth-eaten frocks that the landlord had found in a box under the stairs. They had belonged to his deceased wife and, judging by the fashion of the frocks, she had passed on some considerable time ago. Perhaps in the Victorian era. Thankfully Rain had packed a few spare items and quickly dressed herself in jeans and t-shirt, while the dark-haired faerie - Vincent recognised her from The Dragon's Head - seemed grateful for any clothing at all. The third faerie, however, was having a little more trouble.

"I'm not bloody wearing that!" she swore, as Dum Dum handed her a particularly foul purple dress, his face a glowing crimson of embarrassment as he tried not to look at anything naked. His task was made virtually impossible by the fact that the third faerie, the one that insisted on staying naked, had so much more nakedness to cover than the other two. In faerie form she flew like a bumble bee, an impossibility that not so much defied Newton's laws as it took almost criminal glee in breaking them. Human sized she wasn't much smaller than Dum Dum.

"Well, I'm really going to have to insist that you wear something," said Mad John.

"You can't tell me what to do!" snarled the rotund faerie. "Stupid human clothes! This is horrible!"

"Perhaps so," conceded Mad John, "but nonetheless I will have to insist."

"Yeah? And what are you gonna do about it?"

In an instant there was a hand around the faerie's throat, her pudgy bare feet dangling above the pavement.

"Put," said Numb Tongue, slowly and deliberately, "some clothes on."

There was a popping sound, like a cork from a bottle, and suddenly the faerie was gone. Numb Tongue's closed hand was still raised aloft where the faerie had been.

"That's not fucking funny! Let me go!" screamed a small voice from Numb Tongue's clasped hand.

Numb Tongue's face flickered with annoyance and he tightened his grip. "Don't," he said into his hand, "bite me."

For a moment Vincent thought that Numb Tongue was going to squish the fat faerie and throw her to the ground like a crushed beer can, but instead he held his hand towards Mad John. Perhaps there was a flinch as the faerie bit him again. Mad John let out a resigned sigh.

"Listen, young lady," he said to Numb Tongue's hand.

"Chastity," said the hand.

"Excuse me?"

"My name's Chastity."

"Is it?" said Mad John, his eyes betraying a smile that the rest of his face wasn't supposed to know about. "Well, listen Chastity, I am a very patient man, known for it in fact, but I am not having a very good day. And Mr Tongue, here, doesn't do good days, so what I'd suggest is that you do as he says and put some clothes on. When we are all suitably attired we will go inside. And then," he added, his eyes casting over all of them, "I want some answers!"

With the party atmosphere and the other customers now long gone, the landlord of the inn shuffled around behind the bar pretending to clean glasses until Numb Tongue shot him a warning glance. This was club business, private, and the look on Numb Tongue's face told him, in no uncertain terms, that prying ears were likely to be cut off and fed to Zig Zag. The landlord made his excuses to be somewhere else and left them in peace.

And so the truth had slowly emerged.

It was, by any measure, a bizarre meeting, Mad John at the head of a long table made up of several shorter tables pushed together, quizzing each of them in turn and constantly prompting for as much detail as possible. And when they got to the end they had to tell it again.

Vincent had just got to the bit where Zig Zag was talking to the crow, which was now perched on a bar stool, when the damn thing went nuts and started squawking madly and angrily flapping its wings. Zig Zag snarled something at the bird and the bird screeched back.

"My apologies," said Mad John, and turned to Vincent. "It's probably best if you don't use the C word again. This is Raven...he's a raven, not a er, well... please continue."

Vincent continued, though he knew little more than he had already told, and then it was Scarecrow's turn, each answer checked and rechecked.

Dum Dum poked at something under his fingernail. He'd been trying to keep up, but it was all getting a bit confusing and suspiciously like politics. Dum Dum didn't like politics. From what he could understand, Scarecrow had met the naked lady with the pink hair at The Dragon's Head, except, obviously, she wasn't naked until a few hours after he'd met her. After that they'd decided that they liked being naked together a lot, so the naked lady had come with Scarecrow in his saddlebags. That bit was easy. Dum Dum had been naked with a lady before and he'd liked it quite a lot, too.

"But you had no idea that Snow and er, Chastity had come along for the ride as well?" said Mad John, gesturing to the two faeries. Snow, her long dark hair hanging over that pale and beautiful face, had her head cast down, ashamed and in trouble. The one named Chastity, against all possible odds, was more defiant and upright, a task made more difficult by the revolting frock she'd been forced into wearing.

"No," said Scarecrow solemnly. "The first I knew about them was when I came out of this place and everything was kicking off outside. I'd met them in that other pub, The Dragon's Head, but, I swear to God, I had no idea they were here."

"That won't be necessary," Mad John said sharply. "Might I ask you why you're here ladies?" There was a politeness to his voice, a civility, but the underlying tone was, "What the fuck are you doing here?" He looked both of them in the eyes. Snow lowered her gaze further. Chastity attempted, and failed, to out-stare him.

"Dunno," Chastity shrugged like a blancmange, making it difficult for Dum Dum to concentrate. "Thought it might be a bit of a laugh. I thought *he* was quite a good shag until I found out what a wanker he is." She pointed at Loud-As further down the table, his eyes glaring. "Didn't know you had all this fucking drama or I'd have stayed at home."

Surprisingly Mad John seemed satisfied with this answer. "And you, Snow? Why are you here?"

Snow's face remained cast down and she raised her voice no more than her eyes. "I didn't want to miss the wedding," she whispered, and only a keen eye would notice that she glanced, not at Scarecrow or Rain, but at Numb Tongue. Scarecrow's eye was keen enough to notice that Mad John had a very keen eye indeed.

Finally Mad John had heard enough, and only one story remained untold. He turned to face Loud-As, who glowered back. There was a menace about him, a cornered rat ready to make a last stand. Knuckles clenched.

"Well, well, I've known you for a long time Loudas..." said Mad John, pronouncing Loud-As weird, like Lewd-Us.

Loud-As stared back so intently that there was no peripheral vision, his blinkered eyes locked onto Mad John's. When he spoke, it was matter of fact.

"We are going to kill each and every one of you."

CHAPTER THIRTY-FIVE

Giant booms of thunder shook the earth, audible even above the noise of the bikes, and forked lightning lit up the horizon for miles around, its jagged white fingers clawing at tree tops and distant mountain peaks. The boom would come first, then a low rumble like far off artillery...one, one thousand, two, one thousand, three, one thousand... and then the sky would be split in two or three or four, as the vast electrical charges touched down. As storms go, this one wasn't fucking about. And Aberrant MC were heading straight for it.

They had been riding now for sixteen hours, the only respite being short and very infrequent stops to refuel the bikes. But even at this unrelenting pace, throttles wide open, Vincent noticed he was needing much less fuel, his bike doing four hundred miles or more to a tank, way more than its usual range. He wished it wouldn't. He wished they could stop somewhere and that he never had to ride a motorbike ever again.

For mile after mile after mile they had kept up this insane pace, ninety miles per hour or more, Vincent clinging on to his handlebars with a deathlike grip, grim determination written on his face. Everything hurt. His arms, his legs, his neck, his arse...especially his arse. Oh how his arse hurt! No matter how he shifted in his seat, and that wasn't much at these speeds, the pain came back in an instant, each buttock feeling like it had been tenderised with a sledgehammer.

"I hate this, I hate this, I hate this, I hate this..."

It started to rain. Aberrant MC had reached the edge of the storm, and still they rode on. No one was smiling.

The worst thing was not knowing how much further they had to go. For once, Mad John had told them where they were going, a place called Vernon Wells, a safe haven of some sort, but since Vincent had no idea where Vernon Wells was, or where he was, or even, for that matter, where he'd been, it wasn't really a lot of use.

After hours of questioning pretty much everyone, Mad John had called the club and its various uninvited guests back together in the inn. Loud's cut was on the table, Loud-As himself, shirtless, bound and gagged, his face all puffy and bruised down one side and blood leaking from his nose. Mad John looked terribly angry.

"We have underestimated our foes and overestimated our friends," he said, after a long and uncomfortable silence. "Loud-As has been poisoned."

Eyes cast around the room and then back to Loud-As. Loud-As saw none of them.

"When we..." Mad John began. "When we relieved Loud-As of his cut we found his back, his tattoo was done with poisoned ink. We found..."

All eyes went back to Loud-As. He was facing most of them at an angle, his back to the wall, but Vincent could see enough. Loud's entire back was alive with maggots, his skin literally rotting off.

"Because it was done over several sittings," continued Mad John, "the poison has had a long time to get into his system. Our only hope is an antidote and time is not on our side. We leave immediately, gentlemen." And then he added, "ladies."

"Fuck that!" Chastity cursed loudly. "I'm goin' fuckin' home, I am. You lot are about as much fun as a..."

Once again the fat faerie was dangling in the air, but this time she made no attempt to transform. This time Numb Tongue really would squish her.

"Unfortunately," Mad John said patiently, "that wasn't a request. I'm going to have to insist that you all come along until we have dealt with certain situations. If we remain here then we bring great danger to this town and to innocent people. And if our enemies catch you, then make no mistake, they will use the harshest means to get what they want. They tortured Ian, The General," it was rare that Mad John used his nickname. "If they think any of you know anything at all that might benefit them, then they will not hesitate to make your lives very painful and not nearly as short as you'll wish. You will thank them when they kill you."

Vincent remembered glancing over at Stone. What happened to "idiots who'd chase after a stick" and "three blokes who'd mastered licking their own balls"? The ball-lickers seemed to be picking the club off one by one, and Stone looked as worried as the rest of them. They understood the implications. Their enemies had made them turn upon themselves, made them weaker and made them suspicious. Mad John let his words sink in.

"Thanks to my dear friend Raven," he continued, his tone changed to business, "we now at least know who we are up against. They are not nice people. Yes, Dum Dum?"

Dum Dum had his hand raised like a school kid asking to go to the toilet.

"I thought we knew who they were. I thought they were shirtshifter thing-a-ma-jigs."

"Shapeshifters, Dum Dum," said Mad John. "And, yes, that's what they wanted us to think. A clever ruse."

For as long as some of them could remember the club had had three shapeshifters on their tails, complete buffoons who they'd taken much joy in sending on increasingly wild goose chases. For which a incredibly foolish old man was paying them enormous amounts of money, most of which came back to Aberrant for the anonymous tips that sent them in the wrong direction in the first place. It was rather complicated, but enormous fun until their hopeless bounty hunter friends had gone and got themselves killed. And, unbeknownst to Aberrant, three rather nasty wizards had taken their place.

"We don't know how long ago this happened," said Mad John. "But it was far enough back that the poison in Loud's tattoo has had him under their control for some time. As the poison spread, so he lost more control. We have managed to take the pain away, but there is little more we can do without the right medicines. We must make all haste. And, as if I need add, no one is to get tattooed until further notice. As from now the only approved artist is at Holy Cow. In Eastbourne. And we won't be going there any time soon."

"You heard the man," boomed Andy One-Leg, clapping his hands together. "Shit together! We're leaving!"

And so, with no further explanation, they left a town that Vincent had never even got to know the name of. Loud-As was too sick to ride his own bike - it seemed the fight outside the inn had taken the last of his strength - and so he was strapped upright to the back of Joker's bike. They were going to lock Loud's bike up and leave it behind until Snow offered to ride it.

"You're sure?" said Mad John, more concerned that condescending. "We won't be hanging about!"

"I can keep up," nodded Snow, the first time she'd looked anyone in the eyes since the faeries had been discovered. She was loaned some over-sized leathers and, true to her word, she rode Loud's 1100 Streetfighter like Valentino Rossi on a good day, her dainty frame hunched over the bike, eyes intent on the endless road.

And endless it was. They passed another one of those weird underground shops, but didn't stop, and then, some twenty or thirty miles later, a man on horseback. Mad John slowed the bikes to pass him, the only time he had slowed all day, and Vincent saw that the man was armed, a rifle across his lap and at least two shotguns attached to the saddle. He didn't look at the club as they went by, but his hands were on the rifle.

Hours later there had been no other signs of life, no other traffic, just endless, endless miles of the same unending road. It was dark and Vincent hadn't thought it was possible to fall asleep on a motorbike, but his eyes were beginning to lose focus, and even at these great speeds he found himself shaking his head to stay awake. Next time they stopped he'd see if Joker had any great speed, although crappy meth would do the trick.

As the club rode further into the storm, so the rain grew heavier and heavier, until at last visibility was down to no more than a few yards. Finally Mad John had no choice but to pull into the side of the road, the rest of the club lining up behind him. Mad John wasn't even wet, not a drop of rain on him or his bike, but whatever trick he was using wasn't something employed by the whole club. Admittedly Stone, Numb Tongue, and a couple of the others only looked a bit damp, but Apples, Zig Zag, Billy Toothless, and the rest were soaked to the skin.

"This is fackin' stupid!" announced Apples, his once white leathers clinging to him, cold and uncomfortable. "Fuckin' minces keep closing I'm so knackered, an' I might as well be driving with 'em closed anyway for all I can see."

"He's right," said Stone. "We can't keep going in this storm."

Mad John agreed. "If the storm is their doing then we may be playing into their hands, but they'll pick us off without even trying if we carry on in this."

"There's some caves nearby that should be safe enough if we don't go too far in," suggested Chaos. "You can't see them from the road, so we'll be able to have a fire and some food, at least wait out the worst of the storm. Should be safe enough," he repeated, as if to convince himself.

"Deadman's Maze? Are you sure?" Mad John raised an eyebrow, apparently aware of the caves and not entirely convinced that this wasn't some new interpretation of the word 'safe'.

"It's better than here," shrugged Chaos, a sudden boom of thunder emphasising his point. Lightning flashed across the night sky in an instant. One, one thousand, the storm was directly overhead. "There's enough of us to deal with any bother."

Vincent didn't like the sound of that at all. He didn't want any more bother. Failing his own bed, what he wanted was to curl up in his hopefully dry sleeping bag, inside his hopefully leak-free tent and not be bothered at all until it was time for breakfast, or preferably lunch. Though waterproof, his warg-skin jacket was so wet that it had started to weigh him down, and his boots were probably giving him trench-foot. Anything was better than standing out here in the pissing rain waiting to get struck by lightning, but he had quickly learned that 'bother' in Aberrant's world could mean anything from a flat tyre to pack of wargs armed with Uzi's. He didn't like the sound of bother at all. Then again, it really was pissing down!

Mad John took one last glance at the sky. "Take us there," he said.

It took almost an hour to reach the caves and whatever Vincent had considered to be the most miserably depressing ride of his life didn't even come close to the last ten miles or so. Chaos turned off the road onto what was little more than a muddy path between overgrown thorny hedges, and, while their pace was steady and careful, Vincent was not alone in dropping his bike a couple of times. Tempers frayed and it took a warm fire and beans on toast to calm them. Chaos, of course, had the means for such things among his supplies.

The caves themselves were hidden in a cliff-face that was itself hidden by trees and moss, and, from most angles, it was impossible to see the entrance. Only when you got closer could you see what looked like a crack in the cliff-face, jagged at the top and opening out as it reached the ground. The club set up camp in the entrance and made no attempt to go further inside. From this one entrance the caves went back many miles into the cliff, but no one was keen on venturing too far. At least it was dry, and, once they were all warmed around the crackling fire, Vincent couldn't help but ask.

"So, these, uh, caves... when you said mostly safe, I'm guessing you meant there's probably something large and hairy in there that wants to eat us?"

"I don't know about large and hairy," said Chaos, spooning baked beans into his mouth from a tin with no label. "Last I heard, they were all a bit skinny and pasty looking, they might even have died out, but yeah, if there's any of 'em left then they'll have a good go at eating you, given half a chance."

"They?"

"Bean Clan," said Chaos, still shovelling Heinz finest into his face.

"Bean can?"

"No, not bean can, Bean Clan. The Sawney Bean Clan. Bunch of fucking inbred lunatics, real Hills Have Eyes shit. They've been up here since they were run out of Scotland about four or five hundred years ago. Can't remember the name of the place now, but the Bean's used to live in a cave and eat passers by. The cops caught most of them and executed them, but a few of them got away and moved here. Nobody bothered chasing them this far. Well, a few did," Chaos added with a chuckle. "But they found far worse than the Bean Clan and usually decided to fuck off home again pretty sharpish."

"You're making this up?" Vincent said hopefully.

"I shit you not!" grinned Chaos. "Cannibals, the lot of them! Of course, if you don't believe me, you can always go and have a look for yourself."

Vincent looked back towards the caves, dark inside but for the occasional flicker reflected from the fire. It looked fairly small in there, but there was no telling how far the caves went back, and the name of the place, Deadman's Maze, didn't exactly inspire confidence.

"Nah, that's all right," smiled Vincent, his wargskin jacket steaming as it dried by the fire. "I'll take your word for it. I've seen quite enough weird shit for one day."

"Not gonna sneak around with your ring?" sneered Loud-As. He sat, hunched forward and unfettered, by the fire, seemingly too weak to escape even if he were so inclined, and with nowhere to go anyway. Stone and Chaos had done their best to tend to his back, but the infection was spreading.

"Not gonna sneak around like Smeagol?" spat Loud-As. "Fucking sneaky McSneak, with your magic ring."

"Ignore him," said Mad John sharply. "He doesn't mean it."

"Ignore him," Loud-As mimicked cruelly. "Jesus, is that best you can do? Ignore him! Ignore him! Wouldn't want your special little bum boy getting hurt."

There was a thump and Loud-As was out cold.

"Sorry, Loud-As," said Numb Tongue. He looked down at his still clenched fist as if half expecting it to hit someone else.

"Thank you." Mad John shook his head sadly. "I wish there were something more we could do."

"Other than punching him in the face?" muttered Joker, who'd had to bear Loud's dead weight on the back of his bike for most of the journey, Loud-As drifting in and out of consciousness and constantly slumping to one side or the other.

"At least he doesn't appear to be in any pain when he's unconscious," noted Stone. "But the fever is getting worse by the hour. We've done all we can, but he's simply rotting away. If I didn't know better I'd think..."

"Think what?" said Mad John urgently. "Any clue may help. We know they've used powerful spells mixed with poisons, but....well, you've seen. Nothing seems to work. He's dying."

"But why would they kill him?" asked Vincent. "I mean, if he's their man on the inside or whatever, it wouldn't make sense to kill him before they got what they wanted."

"No, it wouldn't," agreed Mad John. "Unless they already have what they need, but I'm afraid I sincerely doubt that. Perhaps the poison wasn't supposed to work so fast, though judging by the state of his back he's been fighting it for some time. Stone, if you know anything that might be helpful then now is not a time for secrets."

"I have seen a wound like his before," conceded Stone. He, too, looked tired, the warmth gone from his eyes and replaced with sadness and resignation. "A friend of mine in Texas was bitten by a spider, a Brown Recluse. Rather like the Brown Extrovert."

"Except they're bigger and not quite so shy," said Dum Dum glumly.

"Boris," whispered Mad John. "No, it can't be."

CHAPTER THIRTY-SIX

Vincent awoke with a start, from wild and vivid dreams, and looked about him, unsure for a moment where he was. He was still in a cave and still the rain came down outside. It wasn't worth the trouble of pitching tents so instead the club had curled up around the fire in their sleeping bags in the entrance of the cave. It was a miserable night and most opted to try to sleep as soon as possible. Dum Dum and Scarecrow were posted on guard, with the aptly named Rain joining them, but even they were silent, a dark cloud hanging over the club, literally and metaphorically.

Vincent had laid awake in his sleeping bag for a long time, listening first to the rain and thunder, and then, as the storm moved on, to the rain and the sound of snoring and occasional farting from other club members. When sleep came, at first Vincent dreamed of the bridge troll, his mind reliving the moment when he'd lobbed the stone at its head and it had swung around with that big wooden club. It had missed him by inches, a rush of air passing his face, but then, in the dream, he had turned to see Mad John being dragged away, his face bloodied and beaten. Vincent couldn't see who or what was taking Mad John, but he knew that it was bad, not just for Mad John, but for everyone, every man, woman, and child on earth. If Mad John was taken away then all of mankind would suffer for his death.

Rubbing his eyes, Vincent glanced around. The light from the fire was fading and it was still dark outside, but he could see Mad John sleeping on the far side of the cave, his own sleeping bag rolled and serving as a pillow. The rain had eased up to a steady downpour and the snoring to a reassuring rhythmic pattern. Just a bad dream, although the waking reality wasn't much better at the moment, holed up in some cave in the middle of who knows where with a bunch of Scottish lunatics. Although technically, after five hundred years, they weren't really Scottish anymore, just lunatics.

Chaos hadn't seemed that bothered about them, claiming that the last he heard they had all died out, but Vincent had quickly learned that Chaos was not a good gauge for danger, as he didn't seem to consider anything at all to be dangerous.

Vincent lay for a while longer, listening to the rain and the snoring, and willing himself back to sleep, but it was no good, he was awake now. He sat up and stretched, his body a little more rested, if not entirely at its best. Coffee would sort that out and Chaos usually had some that they could brew up over the fire. The fire was low now though, just embers and the occasional muted crackle, and as Vincent looked about him, he realised that everyone was asleep.

He got up and tiptoed to the fire, nudging Andy One-Leg's smouldering boot out of the ashes. The sole spat and bubbled, a thin smoke rising from where it had been about to catch fire, Andy oblivious as usual. One of these days he'd fall asleep with his real leg in the fire and then he'd bloody feel it, but at least he had successfully argued the case for sleeping with one boot on without waking up with a bright orange face and poo that glowed in the dark. Joker was sleeping, too, his boots, as usual, very much not on his feet.

"You're awake," said Dum Dum quietly. He was sitting a little further into the cave, somehow unseen until now despite his bulk, just another big rock until he spoke.

"Oh, hey, Dum Dum. How's it going?"

"I let you sleep a bit longer, but you're on watch," said Dum Dum, yawning. "The thunder's stopped, but it's still pissing down."

"Anything going on?"

"Nah. There was a fox outside earlier and a couple of mice, but unless they're going to change into shirt-lifters I think we're safe enough."

Vincent smiled. "Shapeshifters, Dum Dum, not shirt-lifters. That means something completely different."

"Well, whatever they are, there's no sign of them. There's coffee in that flask if you want some. I'm gonna get some kip."

Dum Dum was snoring within minutes, a baritone to Billy's occasional farting and the rest of the club's assorted wind instruments. Vincent helped himself to lukewarm, sugarless, black coffee, and, against his better judgement, lit a cigarette, without the cave exploding. He found a few damp twigs and put them on the remains of the fire, which went out, so he propped his flash light against some rocks to better light the cave. His wargskin jacket had dried out and was more than warm enough, so Vincent settled down for what he hoped would be a very dull and quiet guard duty. It was about five minutes before Loud-As woke up.

"Smeeeagol."

Vincent ignored him. It was funny when Dum Dum did it, because there was no ill intent, but Loud-As was just being a wanker. He looked awful, his face a concrete grey, his eyes sunk far back into his head, weak like the last days or hours of a cancer patient.

"Smeeagol," he croaked. "I know you're awake, Smeagol. There's no one else on watch and they wouldn't leave me unguarded."

Vincent ignored him some more.

"Oh come on, Smeagol, I know you're there. I'm only fucking with you."

"Well don't," said Vincent bluntly. "They said I didn't have to listen to you anymore."

It was unclear if Loud-As had been officially stripped of his colours and thrown out of the club, but certainly there was no reason to take any shit from him, especially since he couldn't see Vincent.

"Did they?" Loud-As sneered. He struggled to shift himself into a more comfortable position, but it was clear that the infection was spreading, rotting him to the bone. The club would be leaving just as soon as dawn broke but with who-knew-how-far in front of them, and driving conditions that would slow them to a crawl, it looked like Loud-As wasn't going to make it. At this rate he'd be lucky if he lasted until dawn, just a few hours away. He let out a death rattle, dry as the desert, his voice a rasping wheeze. "Can't say I blame them. Nasty business," he added, as if talking about someone else.

"Can I get you anything?" asked Vincent.

No matter what he had done, it was hard not to feel sorry for Loud-As. Vincent had never really liked him much, aside from the increasingly rare moments when he managed to be civil, funny sometimes. But no one deserved to die like this, slowly turning into some sort of fucking zombie, in this damp and godforsaken cave.

"You could get me a drink." Loud-As managed a chuckle. "There's a bottle of Southern Comfort in my saddlebags, just for emergencies and rainy days, like. I think this probably counts for both."

Vincent rummaged in Loud's luggage. There were no spare clothes, no spare anything really unless you counted on running out of weapons, explosives, or alcohol. He seemed to have that part covered though, with not just one, but four bottles of Southern Comfort, several sticks of dynamite, some sort of hand held machine gun, a couple of small black hand guns, two machetes, and a police baton. There was one spare boot.

Cautiously, Vincent placed a bottle near Loud-As. Loud-As struggled to open it. He took a long swig, his eyes closed. In this light it appeared to Vincent that the liquid was leaking straight out of him, soaking through the bandages that seemed to be the only thing still holding him together. Loud-As noticed him staring and looked down at himself. He let out a pained chuckle.

"You don't have to worry about me no more. I don't know if they're asleep or just left me, but even if they was here I wouldn't be much use to them."

"What do you mean?"

"Voices," said Loud-As, his own voice a little stronger thanks to the booze. "The three of them fucking talk to me day and night, and the more I fight them, the more I fall apart. There's no fucking way I'll make it to Vernon Wells in this state."

Vincent said nothing. What was there to say? Sorry? Loud-As had never been particularly nice. Not that he wished this on him, but sorry seemed wrong, inappropriate. He offered Loud-As a smoke, warily lighting it for him, still remembering his enormous strength in the fight outside the tavern. Vincent's jaw wasn't broken but it was badly bruised, and he had a black eye that covered half the right side of his face.

"John always said I had trouble knowing the difference between being a bad ass and being a bad person," said Loud-As. He exhaled and smoke came from his neck and chest, places smoke shouldn't come from. "He was right, too. And the worst thing is I have no idea why. I just charge at things without thinking and..." Loud-As took another long swig. "I never meant harm. I never meant bad things."

"So why did you do it?"

Loud's head slumped forward a little through weakness or shame. "Because I can't tell the difference," he sighed. "Because I can't tell the difference. I thought, what the fuck? It doesn't matter if they're dead. It's not like there's much we can do about it so the club might as well still get the money. I thought I could deal with them on my own."

All of the club had known about the three inept bounty hunters that were completely failing to track them. They took bets on just how far in the wrong direction they could send them, and, on the whole, generally treated it as a bit of sport. The idiot trackers were extremely well paid by a nasty, but generally fairly harmless man, who never had a hope of finding them, and sooner or later he would run out of money and he'd be forced to give up.

In the meantime he paid these idiots large sums of money and the idiots gave most of it to Aberrant for misinformation about where they were. The idiots then spent vast amounts on travel expenses trying to get to wherever the next useless lead was sending them. Admittedly their expenses were paid, but somehow there always contrived to be some sort of mishap, some unforeseen expense, so they ended up in the worst hotels, in the worst towns, often in the wrong country. To the keen observer it might appear that they were simply spreading wealth around very poor neighbourhoods, while having an utterly miserable time. It was a sport that Joker played particularly well.

But then these three other jokers got themselves killed.

"They must have seen it in me, a weakness, I suppose," Loud-As said heavily, his eyes downcast. He took another swig from the bottle. Some of the liquid leaked out of his neck.

"The three that were chasing us, Mastin and his cronies, they weren't any harm to anyone really. They fancied themselves as Satanists, magicians, but most of it was bollocks, they were barely more than illusionists with some head games thrown in. But then something a bit more powerful came along and took their place, the real fucking deal." Loud-As tried to catch his breath. There was a wheeze that wasn't there before. He was growing weaker. Vincent realised that he was hearing a deathbed confession, the last words of dying man.

"I thought they just wanted the money, so I cut them a deal. The old man kept on paying them and they pretended to keep looking for us, except now they'd be looking in all the top holiday destinations and we'd still get a cut." Loud-As let out a hollow laugh that turned into an uncomfortable cough. "Bad people, see?" He turned his head, trying to look Vincent in the eyes, but missing by a couple of inches. "By the time I found out what they were capable of, it was too late."

"And the rest of the club never knew?"

Loud-As shook his head. "It was easy enough to keep it quiet. We used to send Mastin and his mates all over the world. I thought they'd just fuck off and spend their share of the money on hookers or something, but they wanted the real prize."

"The invisibility ring, you mean?" Vincent nodded attentively.

"That fucking thing?" gasped Loud-As. "Don't make me laugh. *I* gave you that! Well, I didn't so much give it to you as I couldn't get the fucking thing back. I stole it years ago from this right couple of nutters, and they came looking for it, so I stuck it on your finger just before your mum took you off to the countryside. Did a couple of spells to make you forget about it. I took a fucking beating for that, I can tell you, but I never told them where it was. See, I never meant harm. If I'd told them where it was, then they'd have come after you to get it."

"But they told me it was unlucky on this finger! Why did you do that?"

"I was in a hurry, I charged in." Loud-As took another swig from the bottle, another drag from the cigarette. Both leaked out most disconcertingly. "I suppose I hoped it might protect you in some way. It works when you're in danger."

"It makes me invisible when I'm on my bike!" protested Vincent.

"Yeah, well, technically you are in danger," said Loud-As. "Dangerous things, motorbikes. Especially if you're invisible." He managed something that could only pass for a laugh on a dying man, he chest rising and falling to a soft wheeze. He was clearly in a lot of pain.

"Shall I wake Stone or someone, get you some painkillers?"

Loud-As shook his head. "I want them to leave me here," he croaked dryly. He took another swig to wet his throat but it just came out the sides of his face and neck, soaking through his rotting skin. "Tell John I said to take me further into the caves and set a trap. Tell him to leave my phone, too, the GPS should still work. He'll know what to do. The Bean Clan ain't quite as dead as Chaos seems to think. There's still a few dozen of them living here that will make a nice welcoming committee for anyone that's following us."

"But they're cannibals! They'll eat you!"

Loud-As looked down at his withered and putrid body. Once he had been as strong as an ox, built like a stone wall.

"Not much left." Somehow Loud-As managed a laugh. Once he had been another person, a person who hadn't fucked it all up so badly. "Besides they won't eat rotten meat, that's all I am now."

"Look, I'm sorry kid, I never meant for any of this..." Loud-As let out another horrible wheeze. He was beginning to smell. Well, he was beginning to smell more than usual, and it wasn't a smell that would wash off, or a smell that Vincent would ever forget. "At least this way I might not die a traitor, I might be able to slow them down a bit, keep them from their prize."

"But what *is* the prize?" said Vincent urgently. "What are they chasing us for? What's so valuable that they would do this?"

Loud-As managed to raise his head, but it was a struggle. He looked at Vincent, at him this time, not off to one side but at him and into his eyes. Maybe Loud-As could see him now.

"The prize is John," he said. "Your father."

CHAPTER THIRTY-SEVEN

When morning came the rain was still falling and tempers were growing ugly. The club were supposed to leave at first light for another hellish ride, another race through this fucking monsoon, to try to save Loud-As. But Loud-As was hardly breathing, barely more than a collection of bones held together with leather and bandages. His collar bone was visible in ways that shouldn't be possible from the outside. The smell was intolerable. But still, Loud-As was alive.

"We can't just fuckin' leave him here," Smiler shook his head, his long, flowing nostril hair swaying sadly as he did so. "It's just wrong. We need to get him medicine, an antidote, something..."

"There's nothing more I can do," Stone said. "Nothing more *we* can do. The poisons are laced with spells and we don't have an antidote for either. Chaos said he'd seen something similar in voodoo many years ago, from where the idea of zombies comes from, but when we tried the cure for that, it just made him worse. It's another four hundred miles to Vernon Wells. He'll never make it, not on the back of a bike. He's dying, Smiler."

"Then we give him a proper send off! We take him to Vernon Wells and we give him a proper burial. We don't fuckin' leave him here to rot!"

"It's what he wanted," Vincent interrupted. "He told me it's what he wanted. He told me a lot of things," he added, glaring at Mad John. "I don't care what you say, that's what he told me. He wanted to be taken into the caves, he wanted to set a trap, make up for letting everyone down." There was another daggered look at Mad John. "I don't give a fuck what you say, I'll carry him there myself if I have to. He was fighting them, trying to protect you, *all* of you and your fucking secrets!"

"You watch your north'n'south, son," spat Apples. "This is club business. The less people know," he glanced at the three faeries, "the less they can get in Barney."

"Oh yeah, that seems to be working out just fine, doesn't it?" Vincent brimmed with angry sarcasm. "Fucking half of us will be dead by the time we get there! Wherever the fuck *there* is!"

Scarecrow expected Mad John to say something, to stand on his bike seat like he always did and say, "Gentlemen, if I might have your attention". That quiet, calm voice, that cut through any argument and lead them towards reason. Instead he looked pensive, worried. He kept looking at Vincent like he needed to say something urgent, something that couldn't be said here. It was Numb Tongue's voice that finally cut through them.

"Enough! We set the trap! You all know the rules!"

He stood in silence, meeting them stare for stare, daring a response. Numb Tongue understood death better than anyone else, right now. He goaded it, taunted its cowardice for taking someone else all those years ago, instead of him. His entire being screamed in the face of death. Well, screaming might be a bit on the wordy side for Numb Tongue, unnecessarily verbose. Instead he glared at death, faced it down. Come and have a go if you think you're hard enough! He understood the right to die. It had taken love to make Scarecrow understand that, but now that he did understand it there were no other alternatives. It was how Loud-As wanted to die. It was his right. Scarecrow now suspected there was club rule on the matter.

There were no further arguments, nor were there any when Smiler insisted they return to give him a proper burial. By the time they'd finished Loud-As looked like some sort of zombie suicide bomber, sticks of dynamite strapped to the remains of his chest, a rusty hand grenade clasped in his hand. He had woken briefly, regaining consciousness long enough to take the grenade from Chaos. "Thank you," he whispered. But now he was unconscious again. There was no place for long or tearful goodbyes. Smiler and Vincent elected themselves to carry him. He weighed nothing.

With heavy hearts the rest of the club packed up their belongings, waterproofing everything as best they could. At least the rain disguised their silence. Smiler and Vincent returned half an hour later, their faces grim. Inevitably they had found tunnels at the back of the cave and they chose a path at random, a flashlight guiding the way, a spray can marking their route. There were bones here and there in the tunnels, rabbits maybe, sometimes something bigger, but no other signs of life. They left Loud-As in one of the maze of tunnels and carefully followed the paint trail back. Loud-As was still alive when they left him, a drunken, festering, time bomb, with a grenade in one hand and a bottle in the other. He was smiling.

The club rode off into the rain. Thankfully, for once, Mad John set a sensible pace, a steady sixty that rapidly became monotonous. The road was dull, endless miles of flatness, the mountains long behind them. Dum Dum's bike ran out of petrol at one point, Chaos refuelling him and those who were running low, but they only stopped long enough for fuel. There was no cover from the rain here, no respite, and Scarecrow was not alone in mentally counting the miles away now that they finally had a number to count down.

Four hundred miles, Stone had told them, back at the caves. Four hundred miles at sixty miles per hour, let's say fifty to be on the safe side... that's eight hours, assuming they didn't stop for fuel again, and Christ knows the bikes seemed to be running on air. So that's eight hours minus... Scarecrow worked it out in his head: still a fucking long way in this weather. He hoped this Vernon Wells place was worth it, that it was the Utopia that Rain had described as they sat in the cave last night, so far from Utopia at that point that it wasn't even funny.

"I've heard rumours about the place for years," Rain said, her namesake bucketing down outside. "I've never been there, of course, but I've heard it's astonishing, though I must admit I wasn't sure it was a real place until now. I heard the mountain is carved into a cathedral. There's forests and waterfalls and magical parties... It would be a beautiful place to get married."

But the talk of marriage seemed a long time ago, before they'd left Loud-As to die alone in the caves. Now the only thought was of getting to the place in once piece. Scarecrow shifted in his seat, trying to mentally readjust as much as to change his riding position. Rain had finally agreed to return to his saddlebags and was at least safe and warm, though she looked none too happy about travelling with the fat faerie, Chastity. It was one less thing to worry about, one less thing to get in the way of counting miles. And it wasn't as if Scarecrow didn't like riding, he lived for it, but this was just an endurance test even for him. There was nothing fun or remotely enjoyable about it.

"My bollocks are wet," he muttered to himself. Then, "Four hundred miles, piece of piss. You can do this.... Wish I had a wargskin jacket. Why haven't I got a wargskin jacket?" You haven't got a wargskin jacket because you were sneaking off to see Rain when Bertha was handing them out, he thought, and then went back to counting miles. He had counted two hundred and seventy five before the rain stopped and the sun came out.

At a guess it was early afternoon, not long past noon, and the sun beamed happily at them from high in the sky, the rain and dark clouds disappearing in their mirrors. Instantly it made riding a pleasure and warmed the soul, as only sunshine can so far from home. Maybe this Vernon Wells place had hotels and took credit cards instead of talking into a hatch with a flame-thrower aimed at it. Fucking hell, a bath would be nice...

And then, quite out of nowhere, there was a man on a bicycle. His progress was painfully slow and he weaved back and forth across the road, bumping along on the dirt for a while before righting himself onto the tarmac. The club pulled in beside him.

"All right!" the man beamed, as if unexpectedly running into friends in the town centre and not, as they were, in the middle of sodding nowhere, literally hundreds of miles from the nearest town. He had a crusty punk rocker look to him, jeans held together with patches, and a black leather jacket that had seen, not just better days, but entire decades that must have been rather more fortuitous. An old fashioned ghetto blaster was bungji strapped to his handlebars, playing Mungo Jerry's greatest hits through its one remaining speaker.

"Anyone want any acid? It's nice shit, man," the crusty smiled a toothless smile from behind tangled dreadlocks. "Mellow, like. Not too many monsters in the parasol, y' know?" He chuckled to himself at some private joke, unsteady on his feet. Clearly he had sampled his own wares.

It probably shouldn't have been a surprise that both Stone and Chaos said "Yes", but in some ways Scarecrow was glad that he could still be surprised by anything at all. Wargs? No problem. Elves and faeries? Got that covered. But those two dropping acid on a ride like this, with another hundred odd miles to go... Acid that had just been given to them by a crusty punk rocker on a push-bike, listening to Mungo Jerry's In The fucking Summertime? Now *that* was something else!

"You need anything?" asked Stone. "You need a ride? Food?"

"Oh no, man, I'm good," the punk smiled, apparently oblivious to the fact that, despite the company's best efforts, he was about as far as it's possible to get from his local Tesco. "Got a bit of Mungo to see me through the day," he patted the ghetto blaster and joined in the song: "Have a drink, have a drive, go out and see what you can find." He did indeed seem quite hap-happy.

"If you're sure. You've still got quite a ride on that thing."

"Oh yeah, yeah, thanks man. No, I'm all right. Just chillin', innit." He seemed to find this very funny and then was lost in song again: "We love everybody, but we do as we please! Life's for living, yeah, that's our philosophy!" It was difficult not to be cheered. At least someone was having a good day.

"You know it's another hundred and twenty miles to Vernon Wells from here?

"Yes, yes, quite fine, thank you," said the man. "Unless," he reconsidered for a moment, "unless you've got any cake?"

Stone shook his head. "No, no cake, I'm afraid."

"No, I suppose you wouldn't have really," grinned the man. "Hundred and miles and twenty from anywhere. Although you would have had cake if I'd really wanted cake, so save me some when you find it, if you would. I'll probably want some cake later."

"Of course," said Stone, as if he'd made perfect sense. "Chocolate cake, I'd imagine," he added, and dropped some more acid.

CHAPTER THIRTY-EIGHT

The thunder of engines drowned out Mungo Jerry as the tripping punk waved them a cheery goodbye. He looked happy enough, if occasionally baffled by the workings of his push-bike, but Scarecrow couldn't help wondering how he got out here in the first place, and, more importantly, how he was going to survive.

With the clouds gone there was nothing but sunshine and sky, proper big sky that went on forever. It reminded Scarecrow of the ride from LA to Vegas, that long blast through the desert, that he'd once done with Numb Tongue, Mental, and Chaos. That had been years ago, before he was even prospecting for Aberrant, before he had any idea of what he was getting himself into. He'd put most of what he'd seen on that oh-so-long weekend down to drugs, although, in hindsight, the Absinthe faeries may well have been real.

But it was the same feeling, the big open skies and endless horizon, the same feeling that the bright lights are just over the next hill. Maybe he and Rain really could get married in this Vernon Wells place, maybe the club's fortunes would change for the better. Maybe he was just feeling more cheerful now that it had finally stopped raining. And maybe they should go back and make sure tripping bloke realizes he could die out here if he's not careful.

Aberrant had gone no more than thirty miles further when they encountered a car coming in the opposite direction, matte black with the roof sawn off, Motörhead blasting from the stereo. A couple of thirty-something punks were in the front and there was a large orc taking up most of the back seat. The club pulled over again and the car pulled up beside them. Clearly its occupants were known to Aberrant.

"Good day to you! Fancy meeting you here!" the driver grinned at Mad John before his tone changed and he added, "Are you okay?"

Mad John looked tired, a fire still burning, but without any warmth. "We lost Loud-As today. He was poisoned."

"Poisoned? Who'd poison him?"

There was a growling noise from the orc on the back seat. It wasn't an orc like Zig Zag, who, by some remote stretch of the imagination, could, despite all the teeth, in a dark room, be considered vaguely cute: it was his size and his slightly furry ears. This orc wasn't in the least bit cute at all. And you'd know if it was in a dark room with you, because, unless it was a very big room, there wouldn't be a lot of space. Either way you would want to vacate the room at your earliest convenience, especially since this particular orc had a crossbow across his lap. The orc growled some more, a sentence that possibly included the word 'funeral'.

"I'll let you know just as soon as we have word," replied Mad John, possibly a little relieved that he could talk to somebody who hadn't seen the living bones they left behind. "There are some...complications." The main one being that Loud-As wasn't entirely dead yet. "I know you were friends though, so you'll be more than welcome. I'll keep you informed."

"Please be sure you do," said the driver. "I'm sure we'll see you tonight if we're back in time. Hopefully we won't be too long. Got to go and look for Billy Hoffman. He was supposed to be here yesterday morning with a new batch of acid, but he never showed up."

"This Billy," Stone grinned a wide grin. "Scruffy looking fella with dread-locks, and his arse hanging out of his trousers?"

"Yeah, that's Billy. I take it you've seen him?"

"We passed him about thirty miles back. He was having some trouble negotiating a push-bike."

"Fucking push-bike?" exclaimed the driver. "It'll take him weeks! What the fuck's he doing on a push-bike?"

"Listening to Mungo Jerry, mostly," said Stone. "We did offer him a ride, but he seemed more than happy, very much at one with his omm, if you know what I mean."

The driver and his passengers were relieved to know that their friend was okay, if not entirely surprised to learn that he was tripping his nuts off.

"I suppose we should go and get him," said the driver. "I know he likes to commune with nature and all that, but it's not exactly the best idea at the moment unless you want to commune with a cave troll. Big one by all accounts. He hasn't hurt anyone yet, but it's best to keep out of his way. I mean, he can't get into the city or nothing, but it's still better to be safe," he gestured to the back seat and the large orc with the loaded crossbow. "Don't want to hurt him, but there's not much else we can do until he fucks off. We think he's probably lost."

"Well, if you know which way he went then we can probably help," said Mad John. "Our dear friend and prospect, Dum Dum, here, has a way with trolls."

Dum Dum waved sheepishly at the occupants of the car. His Harley had started leaking horrible black goo some miles back and he was trying to ignore it burning through his jeans where it had blown onto him.

"Why don't we wait here until you've retrieved your friend," Mad John continued. "And then we can all head to Vernon together. I'm sure some of us could do with a break."

"Don't suppose you've got any cake?" added Stone.

"Cake?"

"Yes, chocolate cake."

The driver looked puzzled for a moment and then remembered, "Got some chocolate cake vodka, if that helps."

"Yes," Stone smiled a knowing smile. "I expect that's it. Your friend Billy said to save him some, if you'd be so kind."

It felt good to be able to stretch their legs for a while and there was much stamping of feet and pacing back and forth. Vincent's legs had never ached so much. Ever. Everything ached, arms, legs, brain...especially brain. He'd had time, on this long ride, to be angry, and then to stop being angry. And then to be angry again. And then sad for a while. He was ashamed, but he'd even had a bit of a blub for a few miles.

And then the sun came out. And he thought...

These lunatics that were chasing Mad John, his dad. Clearly they were not nice people. And if they were capable of torture and of murder then kidnapping a child would be, well, child's-play. Vincent thought back to his own childhood, back to when his mother had moved them to the countryside. He'd thought about it many times and the memory always seemed hurried, not running away exactly, but certainly rushed.

If it was around the same time that Loud-As gave him the ring, then maybe there was a connection. And perhaps it was more than a coincidence that this was the same time that Vincent had been snooping around in Mad John's study, poking his nose where it didn't belong, and finding out things he shouldn't be knowing. Vincent hadn't figured it all out yet, but he knew there had been a very good reason for them suddenly moving away, and an equally good reason for not knowing who his father was, until now. They had been trying to keep him safe from the kind of people, possibly the very same people, who poisoned Loud-As and tortured The General.

He heard Stone's voice in his head: "Ask the right questions and you will find that you already know the answers." When he had come back to the clubhouse on his twenty-first birthday, less than a year ago, they had been expecting him. They even had his prospect patch waiting for him.

Stone ambled over as the bikes ticked and cooled in the afternoon sun. "Well," he said, and took a deep, deep breath, his eyes closed, his face turned to the sun.

Vincent waited for him to say something else and when he didn't Vincent tried to think of something. But it was all too complicated, too emotional to put into words. Buried somewhere underneath all that emotional baggage was an epiphany. He had always longed for adventure, for the motorcycle club, the prodigal father... Perhaps the father most of all. And now, here it all was, ready or not.

"It rarely comes when you expect it, but you always get what you wish for," Stone said finally, his eyes still closed.

"Can you read minds?"

"Auras and poker tells, mostly," Stone dismissed. "What lies in people's eyes. We really should go to Vegas sometime."

"That's a no, then."

"Well, if you meant can I have a good poke around inside that half empty noggin of yours, and wonder at its inactivity, then, no, and I've yet to meet anyone who could. Some people are easier to read than others."

"What about Flashback? You talk to him."

Stone opened one eye, its pupil the size of a dinner plate, and peered at Vincent.

"Perhaps that noggin of yours isn't so empty after all. I shall have to keep an eye on you." He closed his eye again. "Yes," he said. "I can converse with Flashback through what people refer to as telepathy, but I can no more poke around inside his noggin than I can yours. I can tell if he's awake and we can converse, but I can't see inside his mind."

"But they can, can't they? The people, wizards, or whatever the fuck they are that's following us, they can get inside minds, can't they?"

"So many questions on such a fine day," Stone shushed. "All in good time. Right now you should enjoy and appreciate the right now. They will... regret," Stone savoured the word as if tasting it, "yes, sorely regret their actions. But all in good time. Right now I suggest you take this."

With his eyes still closed, Stone handed Vincent a pill.

"What is it?"

"Again with the questions," sighed Stone. "It's pure MDMA with a few little ingredients of my own to further enhance your journey. I take full responsibility." Stone winked, which is quite difficult to do with your eyes closed. "Consider it a gift."

By the time the car returned, now with an extra passenger and a push-bike strapped to the back, Vincent was in absolutely no doubt that he was feeling the effects of the drug. There could be no other possible explanation for why he felt the need to introduce himself to the large and terrifying orc in the back seat. Not that the orc could see him, which caused some confusion, but Vincent felt he'd very much like to talk to him about orc stuff and what it's like to be an orc. He had an overwhelming desire to learn some orcish swear words. Maybe he could get someone to translate for him later, as the club were preparing to move on again now.

"How's the noggin?" his best friend, Stone, slapped him on the back. "You ready to ride some more?"

"Fuck yes!" beamed Vincent. His face was starting to hurt from smiling so much. Thanks to Stone's pharmaceutical prowess, he now felt ready for pretty much anything.

"Good, good," said Stone. "Not far now, and then we will celebrate the life of our fallen brother and welcome a new club member. Perhaps even a wedding, I suspect," he nodded over at Scarecrow and Rain, still stuck together like Joker was playing another prank.

Vincent grinned a big cheery grin, but couldn't think of anything to say that wasn't a question. And if he knew the question, then the chances were that he already knew the answer. At least, that was what Stone would tell him, so he closed his eyes and took a deep breath. The sun felt good on his face and he was aware of the weight of his wargskin jacket. It was making him sweat, but he didn't want to take it off.

At first there were too many questions in Vincent's head for him to focus on any one of them, all of them shouting at once, until his mind came back to the weight of his jacket. But this time not just its literal weight. He had always thought that the 13 patch all the club members wore was the same as all other outlaw clubs, they all wore 1% patches and 13 patches as part of their colours. But now that he thought about it, as the sun beat down upon his face... It was one *of* thirteen. Disciples.

"Very well done," said Stone.

Vincent opened one eye, its pupil the size of a dinner plate. "Stop looking at my aura!"

CHAPTER THIRTY-NINE

Vernon Wells loomed in the distance. There was no mistaking it and no question that they could be headed anywhere else. There *was* nowhere else. But, still, there was no mistaking it, a mountain carved into a cathedral, its great snow capped spires seeming to touch the sky like fingers reaching for the heavens. The mountain rose out of nowhere, blanketed with forest until about halfway up where the trees thinned and the cathedral began. And as they drew nearer the sun began to dip behind the mountain, too early to set, but eclipsed by the mountain itself in just such a way that it shone from behind the cathedral like some vast and fantastic halo. Vegas this was not.

Not that it didn't have many pleasing parallels as Vincent, Rain, and Scarecrow were now discovering as they wandered what was presumably the red light district of an entire city built into the mountain and its forests. They were underground now, though it was impossible to tell how far, and music boomed from neon lit clubs with suggestive pictures in their windows.

"We've been this way already," said Rain, as they turned down another narrow alley. "I remember seeing that picture and thinking we should try that later."

"But there's three girls in that picture!" said Scarecrow.

"Yes, I can see that," giggled Rain, giving him a friendly pinch.

"Will you two get a room for fuck's sake!"

In fact, they had rooms, the entire club being housed in a plush hotel, the bill for which Vincent very much hoped was being covered by someone else.

He had spent a few minutes exploring his room and found that the bedroom had a tree growing through the middle of it, and then discovered the balcony which he guessed must be on the east side of the mountain, affording a fantastic view of nothing much but growing darkness and desert. He could just make out part of the road they had arrived by, apparently the only one in or out of the city on this side of the mountain. It disappeared into the forest, eventually arriving, as Vincent had found out, in a huge underground car park. An hour later, having taken much needed showers and a complimentary bite to eat, they were exploring the city. And an hour after that they were completely lost.

"Apples said a few of them were meeting at a place called Auntie Bert's All Night Drinkery," suggested Vincent. "Maybe we should try to find that."

That was the last thing Vincent could remember.

Actually, no. He remembered now that Auntie Bert, the proprietor of Auntie Bert's All Night Drinkery, was a large and extremely unconvincing transvestite with a handlebar moustache and phenomenally hairy arms. It was difficult to forget Auntie Bert, although he seemed to be trying his best to make them forget everything by pouring endless shots from curious looking bottles.

All the hell-raisers of the club had been out partying last night, Chaos, Smiler, Andy One-leg, Apples, Joker... It was understood in some way that they were saying goodbye to Loud-As, although no one said as much until just after midnight when he died. They all felt it at once, as if a dark cloud had passed over the room, but Smiler spoke first: "A toast to our dear friend," he said simply, and raised his glass.

They each drank a shot of something utterly foul and sat in silence for a moment. Vincent couldn't help feeling a little guilty that he didn't miss Loud-As. Apparently he'd been okay before the poison set in, but all Vincent had ever known of him was a cantankerous wanker. Either way, Aberrant MC's idea of the grieving process was well under way and had showed no signs of slowing down several hours later when Vincent had apparently left them to it.

His memory was coming back, but it was still a little hazy. There were vague recollections of a techno club where semi-naked faeries flitted back and forth above the crowd, their sparkling wings reflecting colours in the most erotic light show Vincent could ever imagine. That had been late into the night, so late in fact, that Vincent remembered stepping out of one club into bright daylight. A gay dwarf had helped him to find his room.

Vincent sat bolt upright up in bed, worried for a moment, but no, he wasn't still wearing his boots. There was no sign of the dwarf, either. Reluctantly he got out of a bed fit for a king and searched for his clothes. The evidence suggested that they'd put up quite a struggle when he'd tried to take them off last night. At least finding his t-shirt, with the logo for the punk band the Dwarves on the front, helped to fill in a few blanks about how he had ended up being escorted to his room by a small, heavily bearded man wearing little more than a studded codpiece. He remembered now. Oh Christ did he remember!

They had been in another nightclub - though Vincent couldn't imagine why they'd left the last one - and he had wandered off to find the toilet, only to find himself opening the wrong door and walking straight into the gay dwarf disco.

"Ah," he said, turning to go back and finding a mirrored wall with no sign of a door handle. Reflected in the mirror was a small army, since they didn't have much choice, of similarly bearded, mostly leather clad dwarfs, all staring in his direction. There was no question that they could see him, head, shoulders, and indeed torso, above the crowd, wearing a Dwarves t-shirt emblazoned with a skull and crossed penis emblem. And for some time Vincent was extremely popular as he made his way across the dance-floor, trying to find the exit. There was a lot of "Excuse me", and "Sorry, was that your foot", and Vincent was probably fortunate that he didn't speak any dwarfish. That's when Thurk had showed up to his rescue.

"Eeenglish, you speak Eeenglish?" Thurk beamed up at him, all snowy white teeth behind the regulation dwarf beard. "I ler-ned many of Eeenglish and such, yes. You lost, I help. I thinking you are in this place in accident, yes?" Thurk gestured towards the dance-floor, a sea of beards pulsating like some huge living carpet.

"Yes, mate, definitely the wrong place," nodded Vincent. "I was in another club and I went for a piss and ended up in here. To be honest I just want to go back to my hotel."

Whatever the hell time it was, it was way past late, and the newness of this fantastic city, not to mention Stone's drugs, was starting to wear off, quickly revealing the many aches and pains of a long, long journey. Vincent needed to sleep at some point and finding the Aberrant crew again at this time of the day and/or night could be a really stupid idea. Tomorrow was a day off, so best to make the most of it.

"What name is hotel? I take you. I take you, yes, hotel, what name?" Thurk enthused.

"Um." Vincent didn't know. They had gone into the place through the underground car park, and in all the excitement he hadn't thought to check what it was called before they all went out. He was with people, after all. They were staying at the same hotel. He wasn't going to get lost...

"Fuck! I um, I remember it was in a place called Vernon Wells."

"Yes, Vernon, yes. Name after actor man, Mad Max, yes, in his-story writings."

"No, no," Vincent tried again. "A place. A place called Vernon Wells."

"Yes, this place Vernon Wells, name after actor man, hair like yours hair, yes."

"You mean the whole city's called Vernon Wells?"

"Yes, yes!"

Thurk was only too eager to be of assistance. He was a funny little man... dwarf, as camp as Christmas, with an accent somewhere between Italian and very posh English. Unfortunately he wasn't much help at first, even with a map.

"Here see, Vernon," Thurk pointed to said map, which was conveniently posted at knee height outside the nightclub, or day club as the case may be. "Here we in Heyra, yes, see Heyra." Vincent looked to where Thurk was pointing, but none of it looked even remotely familiar. Actually, a lot of it looked hugely familiar, just not as place names.

"There's a place called Frank Zappa?"

"Yes, here, see, Frank Zappa," Thurk beamed helpfully. "Name after singer man, many fine moustache!"

"Yeah, I know who Frank Zappa is," said Vincent, peering closer at the map.

"Yes, yes," smiled Thurk, obviously under the mistaken impression that he was making progress. "And here Bukowski, name after writing man and drinking, and here..."

"Wait, what's this?" said Vincent suddenly, his finger stabbing at the map somewhere on the other side of the city, a couple of inches which could be miles away, somewhere between Bill Hicksville and Gandhi Gardens. "Aberrant. I'm with Aberrant," Vincent pointed hopefully at his prospect patch. "This place here is called Aberrant, too. Do you know what this is?"

Thurk's jaw dropped, a hairy little hand covering his mouth.

"Oh my!" he gasped. "Oh my!"

He turned excitedly and said something in dwarfish to the nearest passer by, who in turn was so overcome with emotion that he had to sit down.

"Oh my! Oh my!" he repeated. "Excuse and pardon, please. Many, many honour in meetings you."

Thurk bowed awkwardly, and, given what he was wearing, quite unnecessarily.

Vincent brushed his teeth and washed his face. So, Aberrant Hotel eh? At least now he could be fairly sure that there wasn't going to be a horrendous bill at the end of all this. They owned the damn place! And most of the city, too, if what he understood from Thurk was correct, though the concept of ownership seemed confused. It had been difficult to get much sense out of the little fella after he'd found out that Vincent was with Aberrant.

"Oh my! Oh my! You here with the..." Vincent hadn't understood what the dwarf was saying, but it sounded like the Encesti man and the mighty Grom, whatever that was. "Oh my! Such honour! Oh my! Such dorzanda! Many dorzanda! You with the Encesti man!"

"No, mate, Aberrant." Vincent tried miming the actions of riding a motorbike. "Aberrant Motorcycle Club."

"Yes, yes!" gushed Thurk. "Much dorzanda!"

"I don't know anyone called Dorzanda or Grom."

"No, no, Grom," said Thurk. "Sorry my Eeenglish. I ler-ned many from a book, yes. Grom mean many brave man, the man who not speak but fight, yes? Dorzanda is dwarf word, mean much love and adore, much worship, yes?"

Vincent thought about it. Man who not speak but fight could only be Numb Tongue.

"This Grom fella," he said. "He wouldn't be about three times your size, with a face full of scars, would he?"

"Yes, yes! Mighty giant!" said Thurk, with an expression of awe. "He fight orc champion, bring peace to Gurn Mar, yes, yes! Much dorzanda!"

Had to be Numb Tongue.

"Yes, I'm with Grom," nodded Vincent, finally feeling that they were getting somewhere. "Big man, come to fight, yes?" he added, picking up Thurk's bad English. "I'm not sure who Encesti man is though. Is there another word?"

Thurk paused, hopelessly overcome with emotion and having trouble finding the right words in English. There were tears running down his cheeks, which didn't get far before his beard mopped them up.

"Sorry, sorry, my Eeenglish," he repeated. "Oh such dorzanda! Encesti mean...the Farthen...the holiest. Encesti man build cathedral. Encesti man is, how you say Jesus."

CHAPTER FORTY

It was just after midday when Scarecrow spotted them, just a vague hint of something on the horizon at first, dust devils or heat vapours or something. He and Rain had been exploring the city with a view to finding a location for their wedding and, on their way to visit the cathedral, had stumbled across the East Watchtower, a solid wooden structure that rose above the trees. At the top of a long flight of stairs they discovered, to much embarrassment, a teenage couple playing strip poker, but once the pair had hurriedly put their clothes back on they gave Scarecrow and Rain the best they could offer by way of a guided tour. Not that there was much to see beyond some old photos of the tower being built and some newer, rather less interesting photos of people installing solar panelling.

The teenage boy worked in the tower as a lookout, but, as he repeatedly explained, there was very rarely anything to look out for. Because they were so high up you only had to do any actual looking every hour or so. If you spotted anything then there was one of those old seaside telescopes to check it out with, and, given that this was the only road in or out of the city, you still had plenty of time to alert someone if it was anything more threatening than a hippy on a push-bike or party of dwarf tourists. Apparently they got a fair amount of both. Aberrant had been the last to use the road and that had been four days ago.

"Well there's something coming now," said Scarecrow. "And it's moving pretty fast!"

It had taken the boy a few seconds to locate what Scarecrow was pointing at, elf eyesight being rather better than something that had been rusting
away on Brighton pier for many years and, according to the slot, still took old
pennies. The telescope squeaked like a very sorry mouse as the kid panned it
around and then his jaw dropped. "Holy shit!"

Thundering across the desert, with a huge dust cloud in their wake, Mental
and Flashback were making time. The fact that they weren't using the road and
were heading diagonally towards the city didn't appear to be slowing them
down at all, but then technically, as Scarecrow soon found out, they weren't
riding motorcycles anymore. He and Rain looked at them now having rushed
down to meet the arriving club members in the underground car park. They
definitely weren't cars either. One of them snarled at Scarecrow as he drew
closer.

"Wouldn't get too close to him right now," said Flashback, casually patting road dirt from his leathers. "He's been overheating a bit and tends to get
a bit tetchy."

"But what *is* it?" asked Scarecrow, taking a hasty step back. Flashback's
idea of "a bit tetchy" meant it would probably take his arm off!

"That's Boomer," said Flashback proudly. "Started off as a Harley Bad
Boy, but I did a few mods here and there."

"A few mods?" stuttered Scarecrow. "But it's a..."

Frankly, Scarecrow had no idea what it was. There was, he had to admit,
a vague motorbike shape to it, like if you squinted really hard it could be
Flashback's jet black Harley parked there beside Mental's Z1000 chop. But on
the whole, all things considered and everything, it looked more like a fucking
lion. It was currently cleaning its teeth with a long and worryingly sharp claw,
which extended from its paw like a switch-blade. It looked at Scarecrow with
some disdain.

"Boomer, this is Scarecrow," said Flashback, slapping the beast on the
rump. "Don't bite the prospects!" He laughed and slapped the beast again and
it nuzzled against him affectionately, almost knocking him off his feet. The
lights in the underground car park highlighted a set of teeth that wouldn't look
out of place in a shark. Beside Boomer was another equally ferocious looking creature, roughly the same size but wider in girth and with a bright red
mane and hindquarters. Mental's bike had a bright red petrol tank and rear
mudguard.

"But it's..." said Scarecrow, his flabber utterly ghasted.

"Yes, magic, quite," said Flashback, with a hint of annoyance. "Haven't they been showing you anything on this run?"

"Well, I er..." said Scarecrow, feeling not a little put out.

Not for the first time he thought he'd been doing rather well keeping up with this wild new world, what with finding out he was an elf, getting engaged to a faerie, and generally riding through hell and high water to get here. He'd met orcs, wargs, dwarfs, trolls, and all manner of interesting species, *and* his best friend from childhood had turned out to be a famous ogre. It wasn't exactly his fault if he didn't know that one could magic a motorbike into a living breathing beast that bore uncanny hints of its former self.

"Well, I'm sure there's plenty of time for that," dismissed Flashback. "Where the hell is everybody? What sort of welcome is this?"

"I, er..." Scarecrow began, having had no idea that the pair of them were even out of jail. He hadn't been given any club duties since they'd arrived here and, aside from a day-long meeting with Mad John two days ago, had been given the freedom to do as he pleased. But a prospect was never off duty, and the truth was that he hadn't seen any of the club since last night and had no idea where any of them were right now. Thankfully he was saved from further questioning when Dum Dum showed up, slightly out of breath.

"Everyone's waiting upstairs," he huffed, exchanging hugs with Mental and Flashback, before doing a double-take at the motor beasts. "John said to say there's food and beer and to take you straight there," he added, his eyes still on the creatures.

"Of course," said Flashback, lifting his luggage from Boomer's back and giving it to Dum Dum to carry. "Scarecrow, I want you to feed the bikes while we're gone. Boomer likes raw steak dipped in petrol."

"Rare for Dave," added Mental, nodding at his own monster motorcycle. "And he likes it marinated in WD40 if they have any."

"Dave?"

"What?" said Mental, slightly affronted. "Dave's a perfectly good name."

Yes, for a person, thought Scarecrow, not for a Z1000 Kawasaki beast that is currently licking its own testicles. He couldn't help noticing that amongst the luggage on Dave's back was a small cage containing a large spider, almost too big for the cage like it was wearing a restraint. Boris.

Dum Dum led the way back through the hotel, although the two club members seemed to know exactly where they were going. Even Dum Dum knew the way, up through the lobby and into the special lift on the left that only went to one floor. At the top there was a short corridor with a big wooden door at the end, the door itself caged off like a drug dealer on a council estate. Dum Dum had to wait outside.

He'd done a lot of that in the last few days, but he had never been inside the room. Like the other prospects, he'd had a day-long meeting with Mad John, but that had been in John's hotel room, on its balcony, overlooking some heavy fortifications, to be precise. A stiff breeze had buffeted them as they'd smoked endless joints and polished off the best part of two bottles of vintage whiskey. Dum Dum had been on duty ever since, on call twenty-four hours a day running endless errands, but he couldn't have been happier. Finally he was getting his colours.

Well, okay, it wasn't a done deal yet, but Mad John had pretty much told him. The vote had to be unanimous and he would have to complete one final task for the club, but the odds were very much in his favour. Of course, it was a bitter/sweet feeling. Dum Dum now understood that the only way into Aberrant MC was by filling a dead man's shoes, and if not for Loud's death then he might still be prospecting for decades. But with that came an even greater pride. Dum Dum would finally be one of the thirteen.

"How long have you known who I am?"

It was one of those random questions that Mad John threw at you and, for once, he hadn't needed to explain it.

"Not long," shrugged Dum Dum. They were well on their way to finishing the second bottle. "Since we got here I suppose and I saw the cathedral."

"And you worked it out for yourself," said Mad John. It wasn't a question.

"I suppose so," said Dum Dum. "You *are* in a lot of songs."

Mad John chuckled. "Yes, I suppose I am, although I must confess I find most of the hymns very depressing."

"And you have got a halo," added Dum Dum, as if everyone else was a bit stupid for not noticing it.

"It's actually my aura and we all have them, but, yes, if more people looked at what they were actually seeing then they might find the answers they were seeking. A lot of people think you are stupid, Dum Dum, that you are a fool, but you are not stupid and you are nobody's fool."

"I am a bit slow sometimes," admitted Dum Dum.

"You are painfully slow sometimes," Mad John laughed. "But slow and stupid are not one and the same, and a quick thinker is just as quick to make mistakes. If you were to drive past a street sign too fast then you would be unable to read it. You are painfully slow and yet you arrived at the correct answer before anyone else and without anyone's help."

Dum Dum had been free to ask any questions he might have at this late stage before joining the club, so he had asked if dragons were real, but, on reflection, it probably wasn't the sort of question Mad John had meant. His final task for the club, he now knew, was to track down the cave troll that had been wandering these parts of late and persuade it to wander elsewhere. That hadn't sounded too bad until Mad John had explained to him the key differences between cave trolls and bridge trolls, namely that cave trolls were much bigger and generally a lot less friendly than bridge trolls. Dum Dum had only met one bridge troll so far, and he hadn't been very friendly at all.

Outside the big, wooden, caged-off door Dum Dum paced a small hole in the carpet as he nervously waited to be called. Today was the day he would leave and so, as the meeting drew to an end, his task grew ever nearer. And the more he thought about it, the more he worried.

The thing that worried him was not the cave troll. His hand was feeling much better and he still had his brass knuckles. The thing that worried Dum Dum the most, the more he thought about it, was getting lost. He would be alone in his task, and he knew beyond a doubt that he could and would complete it, but whether he could find his way back again was a totally different question. Now that they were out of the city, out of London, he could figure out east and west easily enough, but tracking a cave troll across the desert and then finding his way back again sounded rather more advanced to someone who was used to following bus routes to find his way home. His only hope lay in his bike. That worried Dum Dum, too.

Finally the big wooden door swung slowly open and Joker stuck his head out, nodding at Dum Dum. It was time.

As instructed, Dum Dum headed down to the car park to wait for the club. He was already packed and ready to go, and found Scarecrow doing a few last-minute adjustments to his Harley for him. Whatever he did to it, however, it just never seemed to run right.

"I appreciate the help," said Dum Dum. "But it might not make much difference now. Flashback's gonna do a spell on it and turn it into one of them things." He nodded at the motor-beasts currently tucking into slabs of steak.

"Really? Fucking hell!" said Scarecrow. And then he looked again at Dum Dum's bike and the small puddle of unknown fluids it was leaking. When you started the thing up it frequently spat flames from the exhaust and the carbs, and you had to lean to the left to get it to go in a straight line.

"Oh," said Scarecrow.

CHAPTER FORTY-ONE

The East Watchtower swayed disconcertingly in the wind, but you got used to it after a while, like standing on the deck of Mr White's ferry. Apparently it was part of some ecosystem design but Vincent couldn't be bothered to read all the notes in their display cases, the gist of it being that the watchtower was a part of the forest, growing with the trees around it. Elf technology. Not that it felt particularly safe when the wind picked up, but Vincent had been assured that that was perfectly normal. He'd been assured that quite a lot of other things were perfectly normal, too, everything from wargs to faeries, yet he still had the occasional urge to bang his head on the table like Basil Fawlty: "Is it a dream? No! That means we're stuck with it!"

He panned the telescope across the darkening horizon, but again there was no sign of Dum Dum. The big man was running late. Very late. What if he didn't make it back?

Vincent wasn't ready for his full patch, he knew that now. Mad John, his father, had been right about that. Not that he didn't still want it, perhaps more so than ever, but it came with a weight of responsibility that he wasn't strong enough to carry, certainly not right now, when he could barely carry the baggage of his own emotions. At the moment, Vincent wasn't sure that he was capable of anything more complicated than making the tea, let alone full membership to an outlaw motorcycle club that pre-dated motorcycles by a couple of millennia, and whose president, his father, was known to every man, woman, and child on earth as the fucking messiah! Well, there were other names, too, over seven hundred of them apparently, including Nazarene, Shiloh, and Morningstar. But it all amounted to much the same thing. When Loud-As had told him that Mad John got himself "banged up", he had meant it literally. He still had the nail marks on his hands for Chri...sake! Which made Vincent the son of the Son of... Well, talk about a headfuck! It certainly made swearing more difficult.

Unlike Dum Dum, Vincent had had a lot of questions for Mad John and they had talked long into the night, although Vincent often found that he was simply confirming what he already knew. His father gave him straight answers, no riddles and no subject off limits, even though some were obviously painful.

But how do you fill in the gaps of two thousand years? When his father's first wife, Mary, died he had gone into mourning for a thousand years and built the cathedral in her honour. Admittedly, that took up quite a bit of the slack, filled in a few years, but, still, they skipped entire centuries, world wars, revolutions, the rise and fall of empires.

Remarkably, during that entire time, the dwarfs who were mining the mountain for iron completely failed to notice that Mad John, nee Jesus Of sodding Nazareth, was carving a gigantic cathedral into the top of it. In fact he had almost finished the damn thing before someone thought to stick their head above ground and find out what all the noise was about. It was an interesting meeting by all accounts, but if there's one thing dwarfs appreciate it's good masonry, and so they had coexisted for a blur of centuries, the dwarfs mining their iron, Mad John like some demented professor in his cathedral attic. He became friends with the dwarfs, healing their sick when he could, and when he outlived even the oldest of them they began to realise who he was.

"I had to draw the line at them putting crosses everywhere," he told Vincent. "Do you think I *ever* want to see a crucifix again?"

Anyway, they had all been getting along quite happily, with Mad John continuing his role as reluctant messiah, when the orcs that traded for iron with the dwarfs suddenly decided that they weren't paying for it anymore and kicked off a huge and bloody war. Not wanting his dwarf friends to be mindlessly slaughtered, or indeed to have pot-shots taken at a cathedral that had taken a thousand years to build, Mad John had got some of the old crew back together to lend a hand. And that old crew included none other than Thomas Didymus, aka Doubting Thomas, aka Stone, a man called Reprobus, aka Saint Christopher, better known these days as Numb Tongue, and one

Judas Iscariot. Apparently Loud's recent betrayal wasn't his first. And it was pronounced *Loudas* not Loud-As.

"I guess I should have seen that coming," said Mad John ruefully.

Fast forward to twenty one years ago, if that's possible without getting a nosebleed, and you'll find what is now Aberrant MC generally kicking the bad guy's arses and messing with authority at every available opportunity. Unfortunately Mad John's resurrection, so to speak, hasn't gone entirely unnoticed, so when his second wife, Tess, Vincent's mother, gave birth to their son, it was imperative that they kept him safe from the armies of nutters who'd quite like to nail his father up again - everyone from the Catholic church to Nestlé, by the sound of it.

"Moving you away was one of the hardest decisions of my life," Mad John told Vincent. "I wanted nothing more than to be as much of a father as I could be to you, but when you stumbled too close to the truth, we had no choice. We were already taking too many risks."

Ironically, it was probably Loud's ring that had saved Vincent's life, making him invisible when he was in danger, or even when he *thought* he was in danger. During that time there really had been bad guys looking for him, which was part of the reason that his father had disappeared, trying to put them off the trail. They wanted to kill off the bloodline once and for all and Vincent's parents had already decided that they needed to move him away. He had simply forced their hand with his snooping.

They knew nothing of Loud's ring, however, and as a result Tess had appeared uncaring, virtually ignoring her own son until the two drifted apart. It was for the best that she genuinely had no idea where Vincent was until he'd turned up at the Aberrant clubhouse on his twenty-first birthday, but, still, it had made for a lonely childhood. Vincent knew this too, now, because he had also been reunited with his mother in the last few days. She lived here in Vernon Wells and had been keenly awaiting his arrival.

So no, Vincent wasn't ready for his full patch just yet, what with one thing and another, but if Dum Dum didn't come back then the club's options were pretty limited unless there were more prospects somewhere that Vincent didn't know about. Scarecrow was obviously next in line but Mad John had already told him flat out that he wasn't ready for his patch yet either.

He was training long hours with Numb Tongue, helping him to prepare for his fight, but his remaining time and energy was focused on Rain and their forthcoming marriage. Not that that was a bad thing, and Mad John wished them both well, it was just a question of priorities. A full patch member needed to be fully committed to the club, willing to lay down his life for them without a second thought. Scarecrow wasn't in that place right now, and perhaps never would be. Love had thrown a spanner in the works.

It was clear that Mad John had chosen their meeting places with some care. Dum Dum was as good as in so they met in a comfortable, well stocked hotel room, but his meeting with Scarecrow took place in a quiet part of the city, in a small café affording the most fantastic views of waterfalls and mountain peaks. The offer went unspoken but was nonetheless clear. This is a nice place to settle down, you can have this if you want it, no taxes, clean air, fresh mountain water, solar power, a community living in harmony...

And Scarecrow was thinking about it. All that training with Numb Tongue was making him painfully aware of the alternative. Basically he could settle down with the woman of his dreams and, assuming she never broke his heart and he never went near any battles, live an enormously long and happy life. Or he could join Aberrant MC and become some sort of ninja wizard whose job description included protecting bloody Jesus from just about everyone on the planet. Two thousand years and everyone still wanted to nail him up for doing a few magic tricks and suggesting that we all try to get the fuck along.

Vincent's meeting had taken place high in the battlements built into the mountain on the west side of the city. There were no comforts here, no frothy coffee or vintage whiskey, just a stone seat beside a rope up to an enormous iron bell. They had alarm systems and all manner of complicated booby traps these days, the bell being a relic of a long gone age, but the intent was the same. Bad things came from the west and if you saw anything coming then you rang the bell to let everyone know about it. Aberrant MC were heading west.

Vincent remembered looking out at the nothingness of the desert, perhaps imagining a faint red glow on the horizon. You couldn't actually see Fero City from the West Watchtower, but it was close enough, less than two hundred miles, and only a couple of hours by bike if there were any decent roads. Vincent was glad there were no decent roads, just a dirt path that apparently ran through a minefield, but road or no road they were going there all the same. By meeting here his father was letting him know of the dangers that lay ahead, giving him the option of an easy out, even though he knew that Vincent would never take it. Looking out from the battlements, he would, however, admit to being quietly fucking terrified.

"You have good reason to be scared," said Mad John gravely, a hand resting on his son's shoulder as they looked out at the night. "If there is a place on earth more like hell then I have yet to hear about it, and certainly have no desire whatsoever to visit it. If you decide to come with us then you do so, like all of us, at great risk. And don't think that ring of yours will help, it won't. No magic works within the walls of Fero City. They will see you."

Having been conned so many times by wizards that it was almost embarrassing, orcs, Mad John told Vincent, had a big problem with magic. So much so that Fero City was built almost entirely of iron, the only metal known to effectively block magic, and that faint red glow at night was indeed a reflection of the city. Most crimes in Fero City - and there were very few because there weren't that many laws - resulted in the death penalty. It just took a lot longer to die if you'd committed a serious crime. Anyone caught trying to perform magic, even down to the simplest card trick, would take weeks to die. Murder was the only comparably serious crime.

"Orcs are an extremely violent race," explained Mad John. "So violent that they have lost battles, lost wars, because they've slaughtered half their own side before the enemy even shows up. After the wars they were hunted down and executed like vermin whether they had any part in it or not, and finally they realised that they were facing extinction if they couldn't unite and fight back without killing each other."

And so, thanks to Aberrant, every five years the orcs held the Orc Olympics, a gladiatorial bloodbath where scores were settled once and for all. And every five years Numb Tongue fought their champion in order to stop the orcs from attacking Vernon Wells, the irony being that they didn't need him to fight anymore, the city being well enough protected. But if he didn't fight then the orcs ran the danger of becoming an endangered species again. In ways that would horrify Greenpeace Numb Tongue was now saving them from themselves. By killing one of them every five years he saved the lives of thousands.

"Unfortunately," said Mad John, "this year the fight falls on the anniversary of the night his wife and unborn child died. No one knows how he's going to take it. Just so you know where you stand, we will be heading into an extremely volatile situation. No one will think any the worse of you if you decide not to come. But if you wish to continue prospecting for the club then we all go together and we can't take up any slack, it's all or nothing. I won't lie, I'm a little afraid myself, but Zig Zag reports that it's relatively calm at the moment. Thirty-nine reported murders, two riots, and the Fero City court-house is on fire, but nothing too crazy so far."

Zig Zag and the orc from the car had apparently gone on ahead to do some scouting, although, being part dwarf, Zig Zag had to disguise himself as a child so he didn't get lynched. Until the games were officially started the laws pertaining to murder did not apply to non-orcs. At all. If you didn't move quick enough you were food.

"You should avoid eye contact with them whenever possible, but never look away first, it's a sign of weakness," said Mad John.

Vincent had long ago made his choice and needed hints for survival rather than discouragement. He needed to know how to stay alive.

"It's probably best to avoid speaking to them if you can," his father continued. "Stick close to the rest of the club, especially the fight crew. You'll need your wits about you at all times. And remember, they are terrified of magic, and a frightened orc is a very dangerous thing."

Vincent couldn't help recollecting what Mad John had said about coming 'tooled up', and, in light of what they'd found in Loud's saddlebags, thought that now might not be a bad time to start dishing out the hardware.

"A lot of orcs are still of the opinion that guns work by magic, and it might be a good idea if we kept it that way," replied Mad John. "The last thing any-one needs is for them to learn to shoot at people. We never had any intention of taking guns into Fero City. That's how we were finally sure that Loud-As was no longer in control of himself."

Or maybe just selling them out. Again.

"If there is trouble and we have to fight, then fight dirty," Mad John con-tinued. "Go for the eyes! Blind them if you have to, there's no law against that. Just for dad's sake don't kill anyone."

"For dad's sake?"

"It was a joke," said Mad John. "You'll find a sense of humour will also be useful."

CHAPTER FORTY-TWO

Dum Dum clung to the back of his motor-beast for dear life as it approached speeds that he dare not even think about. All he knew was that if he fell off at this speed then it would hurt. A lot. But still he urged the beast to go faster and, against all odds, it roaringly obliged. Vernon Wells was in sight now - or would be if Dum Dum didn't have his eyes closed - and he had to get back as fast as possible to warn Mad John, warn the club. The shapeshifting shirt-lifters were on their way, and they weren't happy bunnies.

Actually completing his final task as a prospect for Aberrant MC had been remarkably easy for Dum Dum, but he was acutely aware that if not for Numb Tongue's generosity then he would probably be hopelessly lost, and up poo creak without a boat, let alone a paddle. Thanks to Numb Tongue, Dum Dum was currently doing just over one hundred miles per hour across the open desert. He opened his eyes a fraction just as the beast launched itself across a ravine some thirty feet or so wide, and decided that, all things considered, he really didn't want to see where he was going. Mr Shiny seemed to know the way.

It had been obvious, rather faster than immediately, that Dum Dum wasn't going anywhere on his own bike. For all Flashback's bluster and showman-ship - and it was, with all credit due, a pretty impressive magic trick, turning a Harley Davidson Shovelhead into flesh and blood - there was still no dis-guising the fact that the results were worse than dismal. It had taken about an hour of Flashback prancing around and waving his arms about and speaking in tongues, which sounded suspiciously like he was making it up as he went along. Then, finally, after another quick burst of gibberish for good measure, there was a flash of bright blue light from the end of Flashback's silver tipped cane, just the way Dum Dum had seen wands on TV, and Dum Dum's motorbike became his motor-beast.

"Oh," said Flashback as he stepped back, his magic complete. "Oh dear."

"You can change it back again, right?" said Dum Dum.

"Uh, normally yes," said Flashback. "But I'm not sure it would survive."

It was indeed a truly wretched and pathetic sight, Dum Dum's former bike having clearly been thrown together from any old odds and sods that would fit. As a bike it was never much to look at, but as a beast it was a walking disaster.

"No wonder it won't go in a straight line," said Scarecrow, aghast like the rest of the club. "The legs don't match up, they're all different sizes!"

Nothing matched up. Even the beast's ears were different sizes, its milky eyes both different shades of rust. The beast coughed and farted at the same time, yelping in pain as it scorched its already hairless and burned anus with a lick of blue flame. The last of its whiskers faintly smoked. Dum Dum was ashamed to see that the creature had several misplaced vertebrae in its back from where he had once punched the petrol tank in anger and put a dent in it. He leaned forward to pet the beast and it backed away, cowering like a dog that's been beaten too much. He kept his hand outstretched and slowly the beast edged towards him, sniffing at his hand before eventually nuzzling against his ample stomach. He patted its head and it coughed again, setting his boot on fire. It was leaving a rather nasty puddle on the floor.

It was then that Numb Tongue had stepped forward and, with unprecedented generosity, not only lent Dum Dum his own bike, but actually *gave* it to him. Club rules clearly stated that each member should have a working motorcycle of 900cc or higher and what with Dum Dum's XS1100 being smashed to bits by a wild warg and his Harley farting flames, he suddenly found that, technically, he no longer qualified for membership. Without Numb Tongue's offer there was a good chance that he'd have to wait for his colours, and he now understood that the waiting list could take decades.

But as much as Dum Dum was overwhelmed with gratitude, he was also deeply concerned. Mr Shiny was not something that would be given away casually. Sure, Numb Tongue had other bikes, but Mr Shiny was special, a hand built, twin-engined Harley, custom designed to accommodate his height.

At six feet eight inches Dum Dum was on tiptoes when he sat on it, which he had done with some caution.

Mr Shiny was more than Numb Tongue's pride and joy, it was his *bike*, an extension of him, a reflection of him. Not that it reflected anything at all, but even that spoke volumes about the man. Flashback's bike, Boomer, was black because black looked cool, all polished and gleaming and sexy, and "hey, baby, you know these engines vibrate in such a way that if you were to sit on the back..." Numb Tongue's bike was black like his soul. There was no chrome, no fancy silver skulls on the handlebar grips, no dashes of colour or go-faster stripes, it was just black like midnight, black like emptiness. Only Numb Tongue knew why it was called Mr Shiny and his giving it away not a week before his big fight wasn't a good sign.

Dum Dum risked opening his eyes again and not for the first time wished that he hadn't lost his goggles. Vernon Wells was coming up fast, the mountain and its cathedral growing ever more vast as it grew nearer. Dum Dum only hoped he could get Mr Shiny to stop. In truth he'd had very little control over the damn thing since Numb Tongue gave it to him, but at least it had stopped leaving him in a heap on the ground every time it pulled away, Mr Shiny in flesh and bone being no less a monster than the bike had been.

After Flashback performed his magic for a second time, it had taken Dum Dum about eight hours to track down the cave troll. Actually, Mr Shiny had done all the tracking while Dum Dum held on tight and hoped for the best. He'd expected a fight and had his brass knuckles ready, approaching the cave troll with caution, confident that he was only one swing away from a one punch knock out. Instead, it transpired that the cave troll, having shared his cave for many years with some mad hermit type, spoke perfectly passable English, and had no intention of eating anyone.

"Stric'ly rabbits for me these days," the big cave troll told Dum Dum. "Goats sometimes, when I can find them. Humans have guns and orcs don't taste very nice."

Dum Dum resisted the urge to say, "No, they doesn't, does they precious."

Orcs, the cave troll explained to Dum Dum, were the reason he was looking for a new cave to live in. Since the truce was called in the war, Fero City had been expanding to the point where the outer parts of the city now sat perilously close to his old cave, and the orcs were becoming a nuisance. They weren't particularly a threat, at least not yet, the cave troll being about the size you'd expect a cave troll to be and therefore more than able to look after himself. But the more the city grew, the more the orcs would be a problem and, rather than wait for the inevitable, the cave troll was moving. Harry the hermit had moved long ago.

"Well, I suppose if you promise not to eat anyone you might be able to live in Vernon Wells," offered Dum Dum. "I could have a word with the bloke that's in charge if you like. I'm sure they could use someone of your size around the place, bit of muscle and that."

"That's most kind, but no," said the cave troll. "If it's all the same to you I'd just like to find another cave somewhere."

Dum Dum shared some of his provisions, rabbits being a bit thin on the ground, and the two had talked for a few hours before Dum Dum decided to get some rest in preparation for the ride back to the city, his task completed. The cave troll, apparently nameless because you don't need a name if you're the only one of your kind for about two hundred miles and you live in a cave, left him in peace.

It was about five or six o'clock, the grey blue of very early dawn, when Mr Shiny nudged Dum Dum awake.

"Gerroff! I'm sleeping!"

Mr Shiny nudged him again.

"Go'way, I'm sleeping."

But Mr Shiny wouldn't let Dum Dum sleep so eventually, after much cursing, he clambered to his feet and dusted himself down.

"This better be good," he muttered. "What, is Timmy stuck down the well again or something?"

Timmy wasn't stuck down the well. Instead, not more that a hundred yards from where Dum Dum had been sleeping, someone else had set up camp during the night. Their camp had been hidden by boulders and such, in fact they were directly on the other side of a giant rock, but as Dum Dum got closer he saw three men sitting by a small fire.

One of them, blond and perhaps recently handsome, was in a bad way, an arm missing, severed at the elbow, his face tattered and torn. A creepy looking little man was tending his wounds, while the third man looked on with an air of vague disinterest. Dum Dum was in absolutely no doubt who they were. The blond man was shaking and moaning, his body in considerable shock, a sickness spreading through him that Dum Dum had seen only too recently.

"I've got all the bits of skull and bone out, but the infection's taken hold," Creepy told the third man. "There's nothing more I can do. He's dying."

"Well, put him out of our misery then. Anything to stop that awful moaning."

"Not yet," said Creepy, carefully placing bone fragments into a clear plastic bag and then into a black doctors bag. "If we let it spread some more then I might be able to extract enough to use it again, jab a few of those disciples with it." He made a motion like injecting someone with a needle. "No need to waste perfectly good poison."

"Well, can you at least shut him up then?"

"Oh yes, I can shut him up," smiled Creepy. He withdrew a large silver syringe from the black bag. "I like shutting people up."

Evidently Loud's booby trap had worked. Dum Dum learned, as he listened, that the blond bloke had been sent into Deadman's Maze to spy on the club, only to return on his hands and knees with his face torn to pieces. Hand and knees to be more precise, since he had just solved an ancient Zen koan. Loud-As had literally blown up in his face.

For a moment it crossed Dum Dum's mind to go charging in and knock the crap out of the other two, but he had seen enough powerful magic in recent days to make him cautious. After all, if Flashback could turn motorbikes into flesh and blood then these two might easily turn him into a toad, and Dum Dum really didn't want to be a toad. He still wasn't entirely sure about being half troll. Instead he watched and listened, trying to gather any information that might be useful to Aberrant.

Finally Mr Shiny slowed to a less terrifying pace as they rejoined the road into Vernon Wells, and the winding path into the city and the underground car park. Having spotted them from the watchtower, Vincent was waiting as Mr Shiny skidded to a halt, almost spitting Dum Dum off the highside.

"Welcome back! We were starting to worry ab..."

"No time!" puffed Dum Dum. "Where's your dad?"

"Er," flustered Vincent, not yet used to having a dad. "I think him and Mental are over in the West Watchtower."

Dum Dum took off at a run. "Got to warn them!" he called over his shoulder. "Can you feed the bike please?"

Inevitably Dum Dum had to wait for the lift, but it gave him a moment to collect his thoughts, it being rather difficult to concentrate whilst off-roading at a hundred miles per hour. Slow not stupid, Mad John had told him, slow not stupid, and Dum Dum may have been slow, Mr Shiny's velocitas ride notwithstanding, but he certainly wasn't stupid. He knew what he'd seen and he knew what he'd heard. A man named Mr Shockos, Greek of origin, and now the mayor of Vernon Wells and owner of the ubiquitous black Moto Guzzi, was planning on selling Aberrant out. The specifics of it sounded suspiciously like politics to Dum Dum and he didn't completely understand it all, but the result would be the same. Aware that the club were virtually untouchable within the walls of Vernon Wells, Mr Shokos was giving the bad guys free passage through the city and planned on sneaking them out of the west gate so they could set a trap in Fero City. With Aberrant out of the way Shokos could rule the world or some such nonsense. Dum Dum wasn't going to let that happen.

Already out of breath as he reached the West Watchtower, Dum Dum launched himself up the stones steps two at a time, his legs almost jelly when he got to the top and panted his story to Mad John and Mental.

"...and this Shokos bloke's gonna get them through the city without anyone knowing," Dum Dum gasped. "And.."

"Dum Dum."

"..then he's gonna give them powerful spells, more powerful than what they've already got..."

"Dum Dum."

"..and that's really bad cos it was them that made the big storm that got us stuck in the caves and..."

"Dum Dum," repeated Mad John.

"Yes, John?" said Dum Dum finally pausing for breath.

"We know."

"You know?"

"Yes," Mad John nodded. "We know. We know all about it. Mr Shockos is taking a great personal risk, but he is doing so for us. He is on our side."

"But they said.." began Dum Dum, somewhat deflated.

"I'm sure they said a lot of things," Mad John smiled. "And I shall be only too happy to hear them, but first there's something I need you to do. I have one final task for you."

"Yes John," said Dum Dum, who rather thought he was finished with tasks for now. "What do you need?"

"I need you to sew these on before your big patch party tonight. Welcome to Aberrant MC."

Dum Dum finally had his colours.

CHAPTER FORTY-THREE

"**A**re we there yet?"

"Oh, you'll know when we're there," Andy One-Leg told Scarecrow. "And, believe me, you won't be wishing you'd got there any quicker."

The club were all crammed into a heavily modified, matte black school bus, and, while the suspension had been seriously upgraded to the point where it wasn't far from a monster truck, it still bounced around in such a way as to dislodge internal organs every time they hit a big bump.

Scarecrow looked out of the wire mesh windows at yet more desert, his kidneys doing battle with his liver as the bus hit another gigantic pothole. His hangover from Dum Dum's patch party two days ago wasn't completely gone and not for the first time he wished that he'd stayed in Vernon Wells. The offer was still there, and he knew deep down that he and Rain would probably take it, especially now. But there was also no way he could miss Numb Tongue's fight, particularly since the sullen old bugger had agreed to be his best man if he won.

He and Numb Tongue had grown a lot closer during their long hours of training in Vernon Wells, the big man opening up more than ever before and even instigating a few conversations. Maybe it was because he expected to die, for his long battle with life to finally be over. If anything he seemed relieved. It hadn't been a life that many would envy.

Heartbroken after his beloved first wife died of old age, Numb Tongue had moved to Rome where he fought as a gladiator for many years until people started to get suspicious about why he wasn't dead yet. Forced into exile he fought his way around the world, eventually ending up in China where he studied and trained with Shaolin monks.

"Nearly joined them, too," said Numb Tongue. "Until I met Ai."

Ai was Numb Tongue's second wife. Her name was Chinese for 'love' and he had loved her with all his broken heart, until time had taken her away, too. Numb Tongue returned to fighting and vowed never to love again, never again to watch someone he loved grow old and die. Then he met Sunshine, the faerie, and it was love at first sight.

"Before I agree to be your best man, I need you to understand that," said Numb Tongue. "I need you to understand that you don't have any choice. Once you give your heart to a faerie you can never get it back. It's a curse, not their fault, but a curse nonetheless. You will love her no matter what."

Sunshine, it transpired, had not been kind to Numb Tongue. He didn't go into details, and it was astounding that he'd said this much, but it was clear that she had done him more damage than any of his fights, slowly wearing away at him, gradually destroying him. She had stopped loving him, stopped treating him right, not long after they were married, but Numb Tongue had no choice but to love her always, even though it made him hate himself. The only thing that would break the curse was the love of another faerie, but love was a closed and heavily fortified door, locked and bolted, with the keys thrown down a very deep well. Besides, who would love that scarred, bitter, old bastard? Death was the other option.

"I'm not saying they're all like that," conceded Numb Tongue. "If you find the love of a good faerie then they will love you and no other, and they will love you beyond measure. Find a bad one and, in your case, if will be fatal. I don't want your death on my hands."

"But catch twenty-two is I have no choice anyway?"

"I wasn't trying to talk you out of it, just warn you," said Numb Tongue. "In my case it was a life sentence, in your case it would be a death sentence."

"Excellent!" grinned Scarecrow. "So you'll be my best man then?"

"I'm not wearing a suit."

In light of what they'd learned just moments before setting off for Fero City it had all got a little embarrassing, like saying goodbye to someone at a bus stop only to have them get on the same bus. Mad John had done his usual pep talk before they left, warning them all once again about the dangers that lay ahead, and when he was done he pulled Scarecrow to one side.

"There's no delicate way to ask this," he said. "Did you impregnate Rain this morning?"

"You mean, did we..." said Scarecrow, completely taken off guard.

"Yes."

"Er, yes."

"More than once?"

"Well, yes, as a matter of..."

Mad John grinned. "Ah, well, in that case, congratulations. She's pregnant. Triplets."

"Triplets?"

"Yes, three of them. I would get a move on with that wedding of yours if I were you."

"But how?"

"Well, as I understand it, a man puts his..."

"No, not how like that! I mean..."

"Well, I'm afraid it's Joker's wife, Lilith, you see," began Mad John. "Her predictions have been a bit off of late."

A bit off was putting it mildly! Once a well respected witch and soothsayer, Lilith, now in her third century, was apparently growing senile and, as a result, increasingly less accurate in her predictions. She tended not to do much in the way of soothsaying these days, choosing instead to potter around the garden thinking she was her own next door neighbour, but whenever she did sooth or say, she still commanded enough respect for people to take her seriously. Quite how she had mistaken Rain getting pregnant for Numb Tongue's death was anyone's guess. Or maybe she had predicted Loud's death and the pregnancy had nothing to do with it, but then, she frequently confused herself with her own great granddaughter, also called Lilith, who was staying there to keep an eye on her while Joker was away.

The irony was that Lilith senior had possibly caused the pregnancy by failing to predict it! The only reason Scarecrow had been awake so early was because he was listening for a rooster to crow three times, and, since Rain was also awake, one thing lead to another. Zig Zag, meanwhile, had eaten the only rooster in the city just to be on the safe side. And because he was hungry. Mad John had just found this out.

"So Numb Tongue's not going to die?"

"Well, I certainly hope not," Mad John smiled. "We got a second opinion and I'd say he has a fair chance now, the same as always."

Numb Tongue sat at the front of the increasingly bouncy bus, his face an unreadable mask as he stared out of the window. Whatever he was going through he was choosing to go through it alone.

"We are all Numb Tongue's prospects today," Mad John had told them. "We are here to get him through this for better or worse. Whatever he needs, he gets."

Right now Numb Tongue needed to stare out of the window and be left alone. Not that there was anything to see yet. They'd set off just before dawn under the shadow of the mountain, the darkness following them for many miles. No one had spoken much and when they did it was somehow muted, like they were at a funeral, with the same kind of nervous jokes and nervous laughter. Vincent felt sick with terror. Daylight didn't help much. The lighter it got, the more you could see, and sometimes ignorance really was bliss.

At Rain's behest Scarecrow had learned all he could about Fero City in the last few days, much of the information coming from Numb Tongue. What he learned had been, like most history, rather unpleasant. Fero City had once been the capital of the Abomi Nation, matched in size only by Atro City with a population of thirty-six thousand orcs. After the 'great culling' the remaining orcs had been given the land on the understanding that they left everyone else alone, which they had managed to do for many years, turning instead on each other. Atro City was all but wiped off the map, which was around the same time that the orcs of Fero City decided they weren't paying their bills any more and started a war with the dwarfs.

In the end it had been up to Aberrant to sort it all out, and so, after many years of negotiations, the Orc Olympics were devised as a way of everyone settling their differences. And it had worked. Kind of. The orcs had made murder a crime, or at least made murdering other orcs a crime, and now they generally only killed each other every five years, which not only kept the population under control, but also stopped the orcs from having a go at anyone else. Unfortunately the orcs hadn't thought to make any other forms of violence illegal so they had a habit of maiming each other, the victim then waiting until the next Olympics and, since they usually had an arm missing, hiring someone else to kill the orc that had maimed them. It sounded horrific.

"I can't help feeling sorry for them," Numb Tongue told Scarecrow during one of his more talkative moments. "They're like pitbulls, bred for fighting, and now everyone wants them gone, but it's not really their fault and they're not all like that. I mean, you've met Zig Zag and he's a nice enough fella."

Calling Zig Zag a "nice enough fella" was stretching it a bit as far as Scarecrow was concerned, but he got the message all the same. There were a handful of orcs living in Vernon Wells these days, all born long after the truce, and blaming them for the sins of their great-great-grandparents was like blaming German teenagers for Hitler. Scarecrow had even managed to learn a little orcish and found that Zig Zag was something of a comedian behind all those teeth. He'd needed a sense of humour being part dwarf. On the other hand, Scarecrow could see why you wouldn't want to sit in a room with something that was known for its hostility, just because someone had told you it wouldn't bite.

"So what would happen if you didn't fight?" he asked Numb Tongue.

"It would be about a week before they raised an army and attacked Vernon Wells."

Scarecrow had done a bit of research on that, too, and the fact was that the orcs would be slaughtered if they attempted such an attack. Sure, they'd have been a terrifying prospect a few hundred years ago, and you probably wouldn't win a fist fight with one of them now, but most of the orcs were still running around with axes and spears. A handful of well placed snipers on the walls of Fort Wenty could pick them off before they even got close, their heavy siege weapons equally useless up against RPGs. In his own strange way, Numb Tongue was being compassionate, a conservationist.

Vernon Wells was long behind them now and Scarecrow longed to be back there. It wasn't just Rain, though he missed her dreadfully already and they'd only been gone a few hours. It was the city itself, a paradise of waifs and strays, of artists and anarchists, all living side by side and working for a common good. It was the kind of place that only worked without politicians, a small heaven on earth. And now they were going to hell.

The bus lurched to one side as it hit another sink-hole that was moonlighting as a pothole, causing Scarecrow to bang his head on the mesh window. They were on a road now, of sorts, though it wasn't much better than just driving across the desert.

"Sorry," yelled Smiler from the driving seat. "Had to go around a dead horse."

An hour later they passed a road sign, all rusted and torn and covered in blood. The letters, in orcish, were unlikely to be warning visitors to 'please drive carefully'.

"What does that say?" asked Vincent.

"Roughly translated," said Chaos, "Welcome to the Abomi Nation: Go Away. Death Is Here. The graffiti at the bottom says 'Grunyag was here', but he's misspelled was and here."

CHAPTER FORTY-FOUR

The first thing that hit them was the smell, an all pervading stench of excrement and death that seemed to bypass the nostrils and go straight for the gag reflex. Of course, dead horses, and orcs shitting in the street didn't help, but that wasn't even the worst of it. You had to really try to get a place to smell this bad, maybe set fire to some plastic bags filled with kim chi and raw sewage and then rub the remains in fresh dog shit. Even then, you wouldn't get the full effect, the full ambiance, of a place that used heads on iron spikes as decorations and had toilet facilities like Reading festival in 1972.

Already the bus was starting to attract unwanted attention, such as the occasional rock hurled by what was presumably the orc equivalent of delinquent teenagers. Already Fero City was living up to its name. Vincent's hands were shaking. For once he wished that his invisibility ring would work, but, just as Mad John had told him, pretty much everything in the city was made of iron, which neutralised any magic. Anywhere else the ring seemed to work just fine on orcs, mostly, Vincent realised, because he was scared shitless of them. But as soon as they reached the outskirts of the city, where they stopped to pick up Zig Zag, its power began to fade. Zig Zag could see him now for the first time. He growled something at Vincent as he got on the bus.

"He says not to worry," Joker translated. "They'll probably eat you last because there's not much meat on you."

"Very funny."

"I don't think he was joking."

Zig Zag sat down with Mad John and Flashback, quickly imparting what he had had learned from his recon trip. Evidently he had learned a great deal, though Vincent only caught a few words. Apparently it was something to do with the vocal chords, but even when Zig Zag was speaking English it sounded like a junkyard dog gargling gravel. He appeared quite calm and pleased with himself, so hopefully it was good news.

"Gentlemen, if I might have your attention," said Mad John finally, his voice hushing the world. Even the bus stopped bouncing around for a moment. "Good news. Our two remaining wizard friends are here and, as you would imagine, they're having trouble hiring any guides or bodyguards, so we've provided a few for them. Numb Tongue's fight is sometime tonight: it starts to get dark around eight thirty, so he could be fighting any time from then, although we're guessing it will be more like midnight. Hopefully our friends won't try to use any magic before then."

"But I thought you said magic doesn't work here?" Vincent heard himself asking.

"It doesn't," Mad John replied. "But we're rather counting on them not knowing that, yet."

As the bus drew further into the city, so the smell grew more and more intolerable, and flies buzzed in huge swarms around the remains of various dead things that were too far gone to eat - mostly dogs, but occasionally the body of something that had walked on two legs. Every once in a while there was the clatter and crash of a rock hitting the outside of the bus.

"Despite all the iron, some of them still aren't entirely sure that the internal combustion engine doesn't run on magic," Mad John explained as Vincent involuntarily flinched at another hurled rock. "Don't worry, we'll be ditching the bus soon."

"And then what?"

"Then we walk."

"Oh good. That sounds much safer."

It was only five minutes later that Aberrant abandoned their bus, somewhere in the suburbs of Fero City, and continued on foot. So long as no one set it on fire while they were gone the bus would still be there when they got back, though its resale value would probably not have been enhanced. Vincent felt the stares as soon as they got off the bus, angrily inquisitive orc eyes in every direction as the club stepped down onto the road. Almost immediately a stone was thrown, narrowly missing Joker's ear. It felt like a scene from The

Warriors and Vincent hoped it wasn't going to be a long walk. He most certainly was not, in any way, digging it. He tried to see without looking, never stopping his gaze in any one place in case he made eye contact, but everywhere he saw orcs. Aberrant were outnumbered on every street corner.

And still they walked on, parting crowds even here. Another rock came their way and Mental caught it and threw it back. Way off in the distance was the sound of pounding drums, the sound that marked the opening fight in the Orc Olympics - the Olympics where there was only one sport. It was going to be a long night.

The streets were open and wide, the buildings like warehouse blocks, well built but rusting and dilapidated, the iron of the structures giving off a deep red glow in the sun. As Scarecrow had learned, most of Fero City had been built by slaves in the early years, but the buildings had a nasty habit of falling down, and so, since discovering vast quantities of diamonds on their land, the orcs occasionally offered exceptionally good wages to anyone with even the most rudimentary architectural knowledge. If a particularly important structure was being built then they would even employ bodyguards to ensure that no one was robbed or murdered before they finished the job.

The arena was by far the biggest structure in the city, its curved iron walls dominating the landscape like some giant spaceship had touched down and been left to rust. From as far as two miles away you could hear the chanting and the drums, the shape of the arena serving to amplify what already sounded like the football terraces in hell. If nothing else, the orcs had got their war chanting down to a fine art. Vincent was reminded of Manchester on a Saturday night. Within a few blocks of the place the noise was deafening.

"I wish I'd listened to what my dad said when I was a kid," said Joker.

"About what?" said Vincent.

"Dunno, I wasn't listening, but I bet it was something about not coming here. Watch your step there, son, you nearly stepped in shit."

Closer still, the crowds grew thicker, thousands of orcs all heading in the same direction. Most of them were drunk and very aggressive, the rest just very aggressive. Though there were surprisingly few fights there was still no doubt that it could all kick off at any moment if not for a heavy security presence that made the NYPD look like boy scouts. Those fights that did break out were hurriedly broken up by black clad, baton-wielding, orcs. They behaved much the same way as any baton-wielding authority figure did when met with little resistance, lashing out at anything that moved. Anyone who resisted was hauled off and given exciting opportunities to fight in the Orc Olympics, participation in death matches not always being voluntary.

Aberrant followed the orc cops. Everyone who was fighting had to register first, and the quickest way to get there was to follow whoever was being dragged there, kicking and screaming, against their will. Well, they kicked for a bit and then it was mostly screaming.

Hundreds more orc cops lurked around the registration centre - another iron warehouse on the far side of the arena - making it absolutely clear that no one was going to kill anyone until they had signed the appropriate documentation. Assistance would be given if necessary. Aside from the unlucky few who would sober up to find that their drunken brawl had got rather more out of hand than they remembered, only serious fighters went anywhere near the place. Numb Tongue stopped and gestured to the rest of the club to wait for him a safe distance from the main doors. Safe being a relative word.

"I'm sweating like Gary Glitter in PC World," muttered Apples, tugging uncomfortably at the collar of his jacket. "Fuckin' runnin' all down me Gregory."

It wasn't just the heat that was making them sweat. Standing still, the club were a small island in a great sea of orcs, and it caused them to attract far too much attention. Not that they weren't getting a lot of attention anyway, but at least when they moved with the flow of the crowds they didn't have orcs suddenly running into them and tripping over them. One of them flared up briefly in Smiler's face and Smiler quickly butted him to the ground, where another orc tripped on him. The two orcs got to their feet and thought about fighting, either each other or taking on Aberrant, but by now the cops were watching and they thought better of it.

"We should move from here," said Chaos. "Numb Tongue will know where to find us."

Moving across the flow of the crowds was almost as troublesome as standing still, but the club made progress to another rusty, warehouse-shaped building, identical to all the others except for a sign outside written in orcish, and possibly blood. In case some of its clientèle couldn't read, there was also a badly painted mural depicting some orcs drinking. There could be no mistake that Aberrant MC were going to an orc pub. It was unlikely to be happy hour.

CHAPTER FORTY-FIVE

Vincent and Scarecrow had been on guard duty outside the pub for about ten minutes before things started to turn ugly. And they'd just got a great deal uglier in the shape of a large and smelly orc who was clearly getting in both their faces in the hopes of provoking a fight. Vincent could feel his legs shaking, but he stood his ground as the orc belched insults into his face, his breath so bad that it was starting to attract flies. Vincent was fairly sure his eyes were watering, though he dare not blink. If he was going to have to fight someone then this fella was definitely at the top of the list, and he'd be going straight for the eyes. But he wasn't going to do it with a bunch of cops watching.

Orc law seemed vague and unfair at best, and in the short time they'd been on guard duty the two prospects had seen arrests made seemingly at random, each one with a complimentary kicking. And yet here was a large orc very conspicuously picking a fight with them right in front of the cops. Vincent wasn't taking the bait. Unfortunately a small crowd was forming.

"We're going to have to do something," said Scarecrow.

"Like what?" said Vincent.

Scarecrow shrugged. Then he blew the orc a kiss, which seemed to have the desired effect. The orc threw a wild punch at the space where Scarecrow had been standing, his great fist connecting with the wall. Angered further, the orc then attempted to head-butt another space where Scarecrow had recently been standing and, again, connected with the wall before falling into a crumpled heap on the ground, completely out cold. It was over in seconds, which was roughly how long it took for a second orc to rob the first one of any valuables. Scarecrow never even took his hands out of his pockets and could in no way be accused of fighting anyone. He had broken none of Fero City's nine laws, or either of its two by-laws.

"Like that," he said.

For a foolish moment, as the orc police thwacked their way through the crowds towards them, clearing a path in traditional police fashion, Scarecrow assumed that they were coming to arrest the orc thief. He quickly changed his mind when he and Vincent came under a hail storm of batons that rapidly cleared a wide circle around them. Vincent faired the worst, though Scarecrow was eventually overwhelmed and fell to the ground beside him, where orc boots and batons had an easier target. The two prospects were vigorously pinned to the filthy ground, faces pressed into the dirt as more blows came down, their arms bound behind them.

And then, suddenly, one of the orc cops let out a hideous shriek and leapt away from them, pointing his finger at the backs of their jackets. More cops backed away and, in the confusion, the prospects got to their feet. Something about their patches was making the orcs very uncomfortable. They began shouting at one another in orcish, the leader getting particularly irate about something called 'dush'. Vincent had no idea what it meant, but he said it a lot. Having discovered that orcish is a fairly basic language with many of its words having more than one meaning depending on how they're used, Scarecrow tried to keep up with what was happening, but the big orc was talking too fast.

"What's going on?" Vincent said, struggling to get loose from his bonds.

"Fucked if I know," said Scarecrow. "The big one's in charge, but the rest of them won't do what they're told, which, I think, is kick the shit out of us. I think they've seen Aberrant patches before."

The orc in charge was a huge brute, maybe eight feet tall, with a heavy skull and cauliflower ears, his mono-brow so low that it could serve as a moustache. Without formal introduction it was clear that he was not a nice individual by the way he struck out at anything within range, including his own officers. But, still, he was having trouble persuading them to go anywhere near the prospects, and the argument grew increasingly heated until he cracked one of his officers in the teeth with his baton, knocking him to the dirt.

Suddenly the orc strode up to Vincent, his baton raised again. Vincent was defenceless, his hands still bound behind his back. And then there was a roar in orcish that wouldn't have sounded out of place on a Slipknot album, a challenge from somewhere in the crowd, and Numb Tongue stepped forward.

The strange thing was that, here in Fero City, Numb Tongue wasn't even that big or scary looking. In what had formally been the real world his appearance had stopped traffic and caused all in his path to back away, but here he was of no more than average build, and comparatively handsome, all things considered. Despite the scars, most of his face was still roughly where nature had put it, and certainly his breath didn't attract flies. And yet the huge orc lowered his baton and seemed uncertain of himself for the first time. He lowered his voice, too, and while it was clear that he was unhappy about the situation, it was also clear that the orc was grudgingly backing down. Numb Tongue roared again, getting right up in the orc's face despite being the shorter of the two by several inches. He beat his fist against his chest, snarling at the orc: "I Grom Kuzum!"

The orc wanted none of it and wouldn't look him in the eyes.

Vincent suspected that he would never fully understand what happened next, but Numb Tongue took a knife from the orc and cut the orc's right arm with it, a deep gash across the forearm. Then he spat in the wound and gave the knife back. "Go," he said in English, and the orc left, his arm bleeding badly from the wound. Numb Tongue severed the prospects' bonds with his own blade, and then, all of a sudden, there was a line of orcs all offering Numb Tongue knives, all with their right arms outstretched. Numb Tongue took each knife and cut its owner across the forearm, spitting into each wound.

"Autographs," explained Scarecrow, seeing Vincent's bewildered face. "Well, sort of. I was reading up on it and it's something to do with being challenged to fight in the orc games, and sort of an autograph at the same time. They only do it for the elite fighters, otherwise it's worn as a mark of shame."

"So I'm guessing the first one wasn't getting an autograph?

"Doubt it," said Scarecrow. "It looked more like he was getting the mark of shame. Don't ask me how they know the difference."

It was a good half an hour before Numb Tongue finished signing autographs, his hands and feet now covered in blood. During that time another small gang of orcs had formed, this one standing further away and not looking at all like a fan club. Scarecrow noticed the shamed orc loitering somewhere near the back, doing his best to keep out of sight, but evidently ready to jump in if the odds should change in his favour. Numb Tongue had spotted them too.

"The cop was accusing you of using magic on him." Numb Tongue nodded down at the still unconscious orc who had started all this in the first place.

"But I never touched him!" protested Scarecrow.

"*Because* you never touched him."

The orcs were still keeping their distance, for now, and numbered less than a dozen, but it would only take the smallest of sparks to ignite the powderkeg and for all hell to break loose. Scarecrow had learned enough about orc law to know that all accusations of using magic were always taken extremely seriously. Indeed, most of the city's nine laws, and one of the two by-laws, pertained to magic and to the horrible ways in which one would die for attempting to use it in any way at all. It probably didn't help that orc methods of detecting such crimes were almost Python-esque in their cruel absurdity.

A stone clattered off the iron roof, way off target, though the intent remained. More curious onlookers stopped to see what would happen next.

Numb Tongue nodded at Vincent. "Get John and Dum Dum."

The moment Vincent went inside the bar, so the gang of orcs edged closer to Numb Tongue and Scarecrow, sizing them up but not yet ready to attack, or at least not ready to make the first move. Another stone came but fell short of its target, landing near Numb Tongue's feet. Tension filled the air. Admittedly Vincent hadn't been much of a deterrent, but orcs can count - up to a point - and now they would be up against two instead of three. Numb Tongue's fearsome reputation as a warrior was the only thing holding them at bay.

And then there were five, as Vincent returned with Mad John and Dum Dum, and the orcs backed off a step or two.

Mad John assessed the situation. "How many?" he said.

"Fourteen, fifteen," Numb Tongue shrugged. "Couple more lurking. We could take them easy, but not without causing a stir. One of them accused Scarecrow of using magic, so I marked him."

"I see," said Mad John, considering the options.

It was widely thought that orcs were dreadful tacticians, but in truth they were not tacticians at all. Their only tactic was outnumbering the enemy and charging at them. As such, they were not difficult to outwit and very easy to ambush, but nonetheless extremely dangerous. True, Aberrant could simply leave by the back door and the orcs might wait a few hours before there were enough of them to venture inside. Or just as easily they might burn the bar down, or get inside to find the club gone and think they disappeared by magic. Either way, Aberrant would be dealing with an angry mob long before nightfall.

"You know more of orcs than I," said Mad John, as another anonymously thrown stone missed its target. "How do you want to play this?"

Numb Tongue stared out at the pack of orcs. Some of the orc cops had come back in line on the side of their commander, and the group was growing in number and courage.

"Check with Zig Zag first, but I think a show of strength. We walk straight through them to the arena."

Mad John nodded. "Vincent, go and get the others. And get a pint of ale for Numb Tongue. I would imagine he's thirsty after all that spitting."

"Right," said Vincent. "And shall I get some crisps?"

CHAPTER FORTY-SIX

If it was loud outside the arena then it was positively deafening inside. Great booming chants seemed to shake the very foundations of the place. And in the long, ill-lit maze of iron corridors that wormed below, Aberrant MC made their way to Numb Tongue's backstage dressing room. It was only thanks to Zig Zag that they didn't get lost several times, all arena corridors throughout the universe apparently being designed by Escher when he was in a bad mood, and possibly drunk. Zig Zag was navigating by familiar blood stains on the floor, walls, and occasionally the ceiling. They didn't expect Numb Tongue's dressing room to have a star on the door, but when they found it there was no door at all.

Still, at least it was a safe haven of sorts, safe, again, being relative. They were deep in the bowels of the arena, the stench and heat being as one would expect from bowels, and they were literally surrounded by thousands of orcs, all baying for blood, and some of them baying for theirs. But, like all arenas, nobody got backstage without a pass. Indeed, arena security being what it is, it was difficult to get backstage with a pass, so Aberrant's little fan club outside had no chance of getting to them.

Just as Numb Tongue suggested, they had walked straight through them to the arena, meeting no resistance, and for now they were safe in the belly of the beast. Or perhaps, given the smell, somewhere near the anus. There was no telling how long they would have to wait, so Zig Zag slipped away to see what he could learn while the rest of the club tried to make themselves as comfortable as possible in a room that clearly wasn't designed for the task. The room wasn't big enough for all of them to pace at the same time without looking like the world's smallest circle pit so some of them waited outside. Every now and again there was a roar from the arena as another fight began or ended, some ending quicker than others. And all the time there was chanting. Numb Tongue sat in the corner, alone in his thoughts.

It was over an hour before Zig Zag returned to bring them news and, again, he seemed pleased, his body language filling in some of what Vincent couldn't understand. Which, despite his best efforts at learning a bit of orcish, was most of it. Evidently the two wizards were in the arena's visitors enclosure, a heavily guarded cage from which non-orcs could watch the fights without getting raped, stabbed, eaten, or otherwise violated. Getting to and from the cage was your own problem, but the wizards had employed more guards, blissful in their ignorance that their guards had already been employed by Aberrant MC.

As a precautionary measure all the needles in Creepy's doctor bag had been confiscated during a random search that wasn't entirely random. No weapons were allowed in the arena, but in truth no one really bothered to look for them and stabbings were common. So far the wizards had attempted no magic, but that was to be expected if they were saving it up for something big. Not that anyone knew exactly what they were planning, but it had taken Flashback two days to recover from performing his motor-beast spell, and no one in their right mind would want to stay in Fero City for two days. For now it was stalemate, a waiting game, both sides unable to make a move.

"Plan B, then," Mad John grinned happily. "Good, I always preferred plan B."

Plan A had been extraordinarily simple. Wait for the bad guys to show up at the arena, confiscate their weapons, and then, knowing that their magic wouldn't work, go and get them and bring them back to the dressing room from whence they would never be seen again. The club even had a couple of spare backstage passes.

The problem was that, with a little posse out looking for Aberrant, it was almost impossible to get to the visitors enclosure without someone spotting them and the situation quickly getting out of hand. Aberrant may have employed some security of their own, but that didn't mean that they could be trusted to stay on their side if accusations of magic use were being thrown around. And it was one thing to be outside a bar when that happened, but quite another if it occurred in the middle of a packed arena. Plan B relied on Numb Tongue winning his fight.

Zig Zag slipped away again. An hour later he returned to inform them that it was raining.

"I like fighting in the rain," said Numb Tongue, and everybody looked at him, taken aback by his careless chatter. They waited for more but, of course, there was none.

"I suppose it washes the blood away and water's a bit less slippy than blood?" offered Smiler.

But Numb Tongue was back in his own world, busily chopping himself out a big line of coke, which Vincent took to mean that drug testing was not an issue for the athletes here. It wasn't hard to imagine an orc on steroids and, despite his mind's best efforts, Vincent tried not to. But with nothing much else to do, his imagination was beginning to wander. He didn't like where it was wandering, and it didn't help that the orcs had started a new and particularly unpleasant sounding chant.

"Do I even want to know what they're saying?"

"Doubt it," said Smiler.

"Let me guess: 'you're going home in a fucking ambulance'?"

"Have you seen a hospital since we've been here?"

Vincent thought about it and, no, he hadn't seen a hospital. Then again, he hadn't seen a toilet either, which was almost certainly a blessing. He tried not to think about orc toilets now, but again his mind had other ideas and filled in the blanks for him by reflecting upon the orcs he'd seen shitting in the street. Orcs didn't have toilets. Not for the first time Vincent wished he was back in Vernon Wells.

And then, finally, the message came, five fights to go before Numb Tongue fought the orc champion.

"Gentlemen," said Mad John quietly. And Vincent would swear until the end of his days that the chanting stopped. "If I might have your attention..."

And now they were walking the final corridor to the centre of the roofless arena and to the cage that awaited, Numb Tongue at the head of the pack, the undefeated champion. And the noise and the heat became incredible, like walking into the path of some gigantic jet engine. It was both terrifying and exhilarating, thousands of oil lamps lighting the vast arena through the warm rain, thousands upon thousands of orcs all yelling and screaming, and the stench of blood hanging heavy in the air.

As they got closer Vincent glanced up at the iron cage, about fifty feet across and fifteen feet high. Then he looked up at the crowds, and for the first time thought that maybe they weren't going to make it out of this alive - fifteen of them against fifteen thousand or more if things went wrong. Just then, a streak of forked lightning lit up the night sky, illuminating all those faces just for a split second. And now Vincent was certain they were going to die.

Moments later a giant orc clambered into the cage and began shouting and hollering, pointlessly trying to be heard above the cacophony. The orc seemed furiously angry, but, to be fair, most of them seemed like that, and even at ringside Vincent could barely hear him and had no idea what was being said.

Scarecrow grinned at him: "Would you like a translation?"

"Not if it's going to upset me," Vincent managed to joke. "I'm just glad it's Numb Tongue fighting him and not me!"

"Numb Tongue's not fighting him, you muppet! That's the announcer! He's saying what a great and mighty warrior Numb Tongue is. He's saying that he's undefeated in a hundred fights...no wait, I think it's a hundred years... It's a hundred something, anyway, and orcs don't usually like counting that high."

"Well, who's he fighting then?"

"Dunno," said Scarecrow. "They announce the champion first."

When the orc Bruce Buffer had finished his ranting, Numb Tongue stepped up into the cage, his fist raised above his head. He paced the cage, a truly fearsome sight, and then with his head back, he howled in orcish, "Lok'tar Ogar!"

"That means..." began Scarecrow, but his voice was lost in the roar of the crowd as a fresh chant began.

"Grom Kazum! Grom Kazum!"

Numb Tongue beat his fists against his chest and returned their cry. "Grom Kuzum!"

"And that means 'giant human'," yelled Scarecrow. "I think it might be his name here."

The announcer began ranting again, spittle flying from his mouth as he got increasingly excited, but until the day that someone thought to give him a microphone there was no chance of him being heard. Given that orcs didn't have electricity, that day was a long way off, but, just to remind them of its presence, lightning forked across the arena once more. And in that split second they saw Numb Tongue's opponent for the first time. The orc champion.

"Holy mother of fuck!" gasped Vincent. "What the fuck is that?"

"Orc berserker," said Scarecrow. "I hope to God Numb Tongue knows what he's doing."

Vincent looked out at the arena, a hell-hole of violence and filth, all building to its inevitable and bloody climax. "I don't think God knows about this place," he said.

CHAPTER FORTY-SEVEN

There were no formalities when the cage door closed, no shows of respect or testing of waters. The orc berserker simply charged like he'd been let off a leash. He was gigantic even by orc standards, nine feet tall or more, the size of a troll, and built like the outside lavatories that the city was so sadly lacking. But it wasn't just his size that was formidable, it was his blood-lust and unharnessed rage, his sheer ferocity. As the orc launched at him across the cage, so Numb Tongue dodged left and managed to land a heavy punch. But the orc berserker was on him again in an instant, a whirlwind of teeth and fists. Once more Numb Tongue dodged left, but a glancing blow to the temple sent him sprawling to the floor. Although he rolled and sprang back to his feet, he looked dazed and unsteady, legs like Elvis, and almost a surprised look on his face.

For a few dreadful moments it looked as if plan B was already going horribly wrong, but then, out of nowhere, Numb Tongue landed a roundhouse kick that caught the berserker square on the jaw. Anything else on two legs would have been knocked out cold, but instead the orc merely faltered for a second and then kept on coming. It was long enough for Numb Tongue to deliver a second kick that caused a groan from the crowd and a very surprised look on the orc's face. The big orc crumpled to his knees, clutching his balls, and Numb Tongue went in for the kill.

It would be said later that the orc berserker had brought shame to the event and to his race by cheating, but it wouldn't be said much by orcs, who rather expected that sort of thing and were shamed only by losing. Either way, there was no denying that a knife had been pulled and that Numb Tongue was slashed across the forehead, a great flap of skin hanging down to reveal the bone below as blood poured down his face and into his eyes. Blinded for a moment, Numb Tongue stepped back, and sensing weakness the orc advanced.

It was also said later that the orc champion took a full five minutes to die because Numb Tongue refused to use the knife and beat the orc to death with his bare fists. And this was also true, although it's possible that the orc bled to death. And, in fairness, it does take longer than you'd think to beat an orc to death. The two fighters rolled around in the rain and blood for a while, gouging and punching and scratching and biting, but the orc was no Royce Gracie and was soon fighting on a broken ankle. After that Numb Tongue simply picked him apart, broken nose, broken wrist, another kick to that broken ankle, until the orc could take no more. They fought for thirty-five minutes.

When the fight was finally over Numb Tongue climbed wearily to his feet, bloodied and almost broken, but still undefeated. His raised his fist in the air and threw back his head: "Grom Kuzum! Lok'tar Ogar!" And, as lightning filled the night sky, the orcs took up his chant: "Grom Kuzum! Lok'tar Ogar! Grom Kuzum! Lok'tar Ogar!"

But while Aberrant were jumping up and down, cheering and shouting in celebration, Mad John had a worried expression on his face. Vincent followed his gaze up to the visitors enclosure to see the wizards looking back and smiling.

"You think they're up to something?" said Vincent.

Mad John nodded. "I'm certain of it. The question is, what are they up to? I have a feeling this storm is no accident."

Somewhat redundantly, Vincent was about to point out that magic doesn't work in Fero City because of all the iron. But then he realised that, technically, the storm wasn't in Fero City but several thousand feet above it, and perhaps had been summoned from many miles away. But what use would a thunderstorm be?

Up in the cage Numb Tongue lowered his fist and made a gesture for silence, then he called for the announcer to join him. There was a murmur around the arena that, because the brain is a very strange thing, reminded Vincent rather inappropriately of South Park. With blood still pouring from his head Numb Tongue spoke to the announcer. There seemed to be some confusion at first, but then the announcer stepped forward and began ranting in orcish.

"What is it? What's going on?" said Vincent.

"Plan B," said Mad John.

As Scarecrow explained it, under the rules of the orc games any champion who won a death match was entitled to request another fight with pretty much whoever the hell they wanted so long as they were in the arena. Often the fights were desperately one sided, though not always quick, little more than legalised murder. It was also part of the rules that if the champion chose not to use that privilege then it carried over to the next games, and Numb Tongue, aka the mighty Grom Kuzum, had been saving them up. Suddenly there were a few very worried faces in the crowd.

"How many has he got?" asked Vincent.

"Seventy-nine."

"Oh," said Vincent.

The weird thing was that Creepy and his friend of many names and trick business cards didn't appear shocked or even surprised when they were called for. Indeed a paranoid man might think that they looked suspiciously smug as they were lead towards the cage. But then, Vincent couldn't help thinking that it pays to be paranoid when you're dealing with men who can summon thunderstorms. He knew next to nothing about magic, but he now understood that Aberrant had lured the wizards here in order to disarm them. And if Aberrant were wary of their magic, then it sure as hell wasn't just card tricks and pulling coins out of unsuspecting toddlers' ears.

So far as Vincent could tell, there were at least three wizards in Aberrant MC, although Numb Tongue wasn't among them. But here was Aberrant avoiding magic completely and opting instead for brute force. Flashback could change motorbikes into flesh and blood and only needed a bit of a lie down for a couple of days, most of that, Vincent suspected, being due to a hangover. But apparently that was nothing to the two men who were currently walking down the aisle towards the cage. The taller of the two men, the Nick Cave, Withnail wannabe, casually pulled out an umbrella and, right on cue, lightning flashed across the sky. To give them their credit the wizards had style.

And yet, as battered as he was, it was impossible to see how either of them could possibly win a fight against Numb Tongue. Even if they fought him together, which was probably against the rules, Numb Tongue would fucking dismantle them!

Unless...

"He's saying it's an honour to have the mighty Grom Kazum find revenge in their arena," shouted Scarecrow, as the announcer continued ranting. "May he taste the blood of his enemies and shit... I think that was shit, on their souls and into their eyeless skulls. The tall bloke's up first and they want to know his name."

"That's something we'd all like to know," frowned Mad John.

After their release from prison, Flashback and Mental had done all they could to trace the three wizards, now down to two, but all they found was a trail of dead bodies and dead ends. They left very few witnesses. The tall one never had the same name twice, though he seemed to be the leader, and there were whispers, hushed rumours, that the one everybody instinctively called Creepy was a former SS officer, Dr Oskar Dirlewanger. But Dirlewanger's trail went cold, as did his body, in June 1945 when he was beaten to death by Polish guards. Not that dead necessarily meant dead, but that was where the trail ended. They found no information at all about the third wizard, but he was definitely dead. Dum Dum had watched him die, and then watched Creepy feed bits of the body to a dog, which had also died.

Across the other side of the cage the tall wizard flourished another expensive business card to one of the orc officials, but the orc looked at it in puzzlement and then tried to eat it. The wizard shook his head and gave a look that one would imagine on the face of Alan Rickman just after he'd stepped in dog shit. Then he stepped up into the cage and gave a little bow. Lightning crackled across the sky and the wizard smiled at Numb Tongue.

"It's the storm!" burst Vincent. "He's going to use the lightning!"

And the cage door closed.

CHAPTER FORTY-EIGHT

It was said that the flash was visible in the night sky for hundreds of miles around, like some mini Hiroshima turning night into day, but then people say a lot of things that aren't strictly true. Certainly all the lights in Vernon Wells flickered for an instant sending a ripple of unease throughout the lower regions of the city, deep inside the mountain where the population was still mostly dwarfish. The orc wars were long forgotten by most these days, a few pages in the history books, but some of the older dwarfs remembered the time from their childhoods. They remembered the terror of finding packs of blood-thirsty orcs roaming the long tunnels, they remembered the blood, and the loss of life. Some of them had lost entire families.

Admittedly things were different now. When the war started, all those hundreds of years ago, there was no Vernon Wells. The dwarfs had lived underground, their home known only as Gurn Mar, or Green Mountain, until Vernon Wells sort of sprouted up above it. Despite its sprouting over the course of a thousand or more years the place didn't even have a name until the mid-1980s when there was a sudden influx of refugees from Thatcher's England, all trying to get away from an Orwellian future. Which is why there were now so many odd place names.

But it wasn't just punks and hippies that fled Thatcher's vision, everyone from teachers and doctors to military experts, thinkers and visionaries, all of them came to begin a new way of life. And just recently there had been another influx as the Occupy movement floundered or became too violent, and more pioneers headed west, this time without actually stealing the land they were bound for. Most people made an effort to learn Dwarfish. They just wanted a new start, a shot at a new life that didn't revolve around paying taxes to bomb people they'd never met.

In theory there were two entirely different cities, though these days the only way to tell where one ended and the other began was by the architecture and the fact that the lower city didn't get any sunlight. Well, that and all the beards everywhere. Despite what Thurk had said, Vernon Wells itself had turned out to be a borough of the city, like Camden is to London, the city itself still unnamed. It was, however, incredibly well defended, particularly by the heavily fortified and oh-so-amusingly named Fort Wenty.

The trouble with orcs, though, is they're just stupid enough to have a go anyway, and one lone orc getting through the defences could cause carnage and spread panic throughout the city. The week of the Orc Olympics, as they were so innocently known, was always a tense time for the elders of the city, knowing what was at stake if Numb Tongue lost and that it would take just the slightest spark to ignite another war.

But there was no war coming, no armies of orcs from the west. It had been three weeks now, and the only orcs to come anywhere near the city were the ones who already lived there, no more than a dozen of them, all on best behaviour in case suddenly they weren't welcome anymore. The watchtowers were still manned around the clock, but every day the tension eased a little, until finally Zig Zag came back with news.

When the cage door closed on Numb Tongue and the wizard, all hell broke loose. The wizard was struck by lightning, but, just as Vincent suspected, he had somehow harnessed its power and suddenly the cage was alight with magic. There was a blinding flash and Vincent saw the wizard fire a spell at Numb Tongue, saw Numb Tongue dodge and roll, the spell melting a hole in the cage behind him. A second spell caught Numb Tongue in the back, knocking him to the ground. Screams and curses flew up from around the arena, the orcs both terrified and enraged by the sight of magic being used, not just in their city but in the middle of their arena. After that it was sheer pandemonium, orcs and bikers and wizards all fighting at once, all trying to get at or away from each other.

Aside from melting the iron cage, the surge in magic caused Vincent to vanish in an instant. In the chaos that followed he was knocked to the ground and quite badly trampled, until Smiler managed to pull him free from the pile of orcs that had fallen over him. Vincent thanked him by poking one of the orcs in the eye as he came at Smiler from behind, narrowly missing him with a metal chair. The stunned orc let out a horrific scream and clutched at his eye, distracted just long enough for Smiler to grab the chair and smash it over the orc's head. Another orc charged forwards and Dum Dum knocked him out cold with a single punch, while up in the cage Vincent saw Numb Tongue stamping on the wizard's face.

Vincent looked back on that night now and was convinced that it was a miracle that they all got out of Fero City alive. Not the sort of miracle his dad was famous for - walking on water being a damn good party trick, but little use in a fight on dry land - but a statistical miracle, so many against so few. And yet, not only did they escape, but according to Zig Zag they were pretty much in the clear.

There were still rumblings of discontent, particularly about Vincent's sudden disappearance, but these were overshadowed by the fact that they had all witnessed Numb Tongue kill the man, a wizard no less, who was responsible for using magic in their city. And, yes, there was still a small posse baying for Aberrant's blood, especially those who'd received a poke in the eye and a swift kick to the wedding vegetables. But more than anything there was outrage that a wizard had used magic inside Fero City arena, and there could be no doubt that Numb Tongue had killed the wizard. Numb Tongue was already a hero, but now he was a legend.

In all the confusion Creepy had slipped away, but it hadn't taken long for the orcs to find him. They approached him cautiously at first, wary of his magic, but the surge in power had passed and he was defenceless against them. The only problem with the rumour that he'd been beaten to death by orc guards was the fact that no one could find the body, but the orcs seemed satisfied that he was gone and no longer their problem. In all it had been a relatively quiet opening night for the Orc Olympics, with actually fewer deaths than normal reported.

And, if the truth be known, there was politics even in a place like Fero City. And like politics everywhere it all came down to who had the biggest army. It was a worrying development that some of the orc tribes in Fero City were starting to take an interest in guns and gunpowder, the younger orcs less afraid of magic because they had never encountered any. But even the most stupid orcs knew that they didn't have nearly enough guns to start another war, and in Fero City you got into power by being slightly less stupid than the rest.

The Orc Olympics gave them the opportunity to retain their proud heritage of violence without getting wiped out, and those in power wanted to keep it that way. There were seventy-seven unsanctioned deaths in the arena that night - unsanctioned meaning orc deaths that occurred outside the hastily repaired cage - but by happy coincidence Numb Tongue was allowed seventy-nine, so he still had two left over in case anyone felt like arguing. The rest was just semantics and paperwork, smoke and mirrors, the orc authorities doing a little magic of their own to smooth things over. Sure, Numb Tongue was supposed to call the fights after each win and not take them all on at once, but this was a minor rule infraction, certainly not murder.

Not that Numb Tongue had actually killed seventy-seven orcs, most of that being down to other orcs, but it was easier that way and definitely didn't do his reputation any harm. The mighty Grom Kazum was still undefeated.

In reality the club had to drag Numb Tongue from the cage and fight their way out of the arena, carrying his dead weight as he drifted in and out of consciousness. He had lost an enormous amount of blood and was suffering the effects of the spell that hit him in the back. If not for the protective spells woven into Aberrant's colours he would have a big hole in him, but instead, by strange luck, the spell deflected and cauterised the wound on Numb Tongue's forehead, probably saving his life. It was going to leave a nasty scar, if there was room, but after spending a couple of weeks in Vernon Wells hospital he was going to be just fine. Better than fine. Snow was tending to him night and day, changing his bandages and soothing his freshly scarred brow.

When Numb Tongue was well enough to receive visitors Scarecrow rushed to his side to return the wedding ring he'd been entrusted in looking after for the duration of the cage fights. The rules forbade jewellery and Numb Tongue stuck to the rules, but it was the only time he ever took it off. The odd thing was that it didn't fit anymore, too tight to go back on his wedding finger and too loose to go on the rest. Which didn't make any sense. Unless...

Scarecrow and Numb Tongue exchanged glances, reading each other like books, and Scarecrow simply smiled and nodded. Okay, we'll talk about it when you're ready to talk. There was only one possible reason why the ring didn't fit. Numb Tongue had found love, he was cured of his curse.

"I'm still not wearing a suit," he said.

And so, when Numb Tongue was up and about again, they buried Loud's remains in a quiet ceremony on the edge of Green Mountain. There wasn't much left of him, but they buried what Dum Dum, Smiler, and Chaos brought back from Deadman's Maze and listened to a few of Loud's favourite songs in the grey mountainside drizzle. Most of them weren't at all suitable for a funeral, but somehow Turbonegro's Shake Your Shit Machine lightened the mood. There were no tears.

A week later Scarecrow and Rain were married. They had planned on getting married as soon as Scarecrow got back from Fero City, but decided to wait until Numb Tongue was out of hospital and Loud-As was buried. Scarecrow had given up his prospect patch, but the club held him no ill will. And good to his word Numb Tongue was the best man, even managing a speech of sorts, if fourteen words counts as a speech. Mad John was an inspired choice of minister, too, utterly hilarious throughout the ceremony, and you couldn't really get much more official.

"Deeply bewildered, we are gathered here today in the sight of my father..."

It turned out that Mad John didn't always take this whole son of God thing too seriously and, despite being misinterpreted for two thousand years, he still had a sense of humour. And turning water into wine was still a neat trick, even if it did leave them all with a stinking hangover. It was a wonderful ceremony, topped only by Joker passing out with his boots on. He would look like Cousin It for many months to come and now talked as if he'd been huffing helium.

Two days later Mad John announced that Aberrant MC were moving on. The clubhouse in London was protected by all manner of spells and booby traps, but its location as a safe house, hiding in plain sight, had been compromised, and they wouldn't be returning. Not for a long, long, time. Same with Numb's gym. When Vincent brought up the question of getting his stuff back he was told that he should have thought about that before.

"I did warn you that if you'd forgotten anything then it was best that it remained forgotten," said Mad John.

And the truth was that Vincent didn't really miss his stuff. He'd never had much to begin with. And he certainly didn't miss London. Well, maybe a bit. But London would still be there, cold and grey and damp, when he got back. And there would still be nowhere to park.

He'd miss Vernon Wells though, miss this brilliant, vibrant, city, and miss the mother he was only just now getting to know. He had a strong feeling that they wouldn't be coming back here any time soon either, maybe not for five years until Numb Tongue had to fight again. Vincent's mother was mortal and already looked much older than he remembered, perhaps in her early fifties. How many more times would he see her? It felt like on the one hand he had gained a father who would live forever and on the other he was saying good-bye to his mother, having only just said hello. It was with a heavy heart that Vincent packed his few belongings into his saddle bags. The club were leaving at noon tomorrow and he was on prospect duty for most of the night, now the only prospect for Aberrant MC.

Over on the other side of town the drinks were already flowing in Auntie Bert's, many of the club wanting to enjoy their last night in Vernon Wells. After what happened with the tranny in London, Vincent was amazed to find out that Auntie Bert's was Mental's favourite bar. But then, as usual, there were a lot of things that Vincent was amazed to find out. Like how the tranny had actually been an undercover cop, and that Mental and Flashback had wanted to go to jail for a while to "See a man about three dogs".

All of the club had known that something was amiss when the protective spells woven into their colours started to fade, not least the one that kept cops away. And, as Mental put it, "what better place to find out stuff about criminals?" Thankfully the spells were getting their power back having had a good charge from the electrified cage.

Vincent's first club duty, when he arrived at Bert's, was to go to the bar and get the drinks, and he'd been waiting quite a while. Which was strange because it wasn't like the place was busy, and Bert seemed to love Aberrant, always keen to serve any of them first, drinks on the house. The music was as loud as ever though, so Vincent waved at Bert again, down the other end of the bar. The only other customer was a long-haired, long-bearded man who appeared to be wearing only his underpants, or what was left of them. You got all types in this bar. The man twitched and muttered to himself - "Scree! Scree! Reeeek!" - and was apparently the cause of some rather unpleasant smells, but, despite nursing an empty glass, he didn't appear to be trying to buy another drink.

Vincent waved again. "Oi Bert! Club's got some dusty tongues over here, mate!"

Bert looked up from his chores and straight through Vincent like he wasn't there. He looked at bearded underpant man, then back to where Vincent was standing. Then he shrugged and went back to his chores.

"Well, that's fucking weird," said Vincent to himself. "He's always been able to see me before."

Which means...

In the split second it took for Vincent to realise he was in danger, Underpant Man let out a horrible screech - "Scree! Scree! Reeeek!" - and pulled out a gun. With his hair out of his face it was clear to see that it was The General, a little thinner and covered in shit, but The General all the same. God only knew what he had been through on his journey to Vernon Wells, but clearly the endless screech of his pink pushbike had driven him completely insane. The water torture had been bad enough, and then, after his escape, the diet of rats and bugs that really hadn't done his underpants any favours. But it was the bicycle that sent him over the egde. Scree! Scree! Reeeek!

Unable to see Vincent, he aimed the gun directly at the back of Mad John's head.

Vincent held up his hands and managed "Wait!" before The General fired.

"Ah, I didn't see you there Mr Vincent, sir. What can I get you?" beamed Auntie Bert from behind the bar.

Vincent looked at him blankly, then looked down at his own hand. Then he looked at The General, dead at the other end of the bar, a bullet through the middle of his forehead.

"Sir?"

Somehow, miraculously, the bullet had ricocheted off Vincent's ring and hit The General right between the W and the A in TWAT, the word now faded but still clearly legible. Vincent looked, again, at his hand, and then at Bert, resplendent in a violet wedding dress, his handlebar moustache just so. Bert grinned expectantly.

"Er, thirteen pints of lager please, Bert."

Vincent was still in a trance. He had just killed a man and no one even noticed! More to the point, he had just saved a man, his own father, and, unless you counted Gordon Bennett, the only bloke in the world whose name was a swear word. Jesus Christ!

They sat, now, around a long table on the far side of the bar, Aberrant MC, Mad John and his twelve disciples.

The song on the jukebox ended. Killing me softly.

"Gentlemen," said Vincent. "If I might have your attention..."